Kathini

A story of love,
loss and a little boat building

Written by

Ana Paula Pinto Damasceno

Acknowledgements

It's such a daunting endeavor for me to commit to anything. Don't get me wrong, I finish what I start - well, at least most of the time, but there have been things that I haven't found the wherewithal to finish and so it seems urgent to thank the people who directly or indirectly supported me along the way so that I could complete the herculean task of managing the multiple international trips and then tucking myself away into corners of the planet to write this book. My friends and family provided me with a lifeline of support in various forms even if just their company late night in São Paulo, having a glass of wine in pajamas, listening to my yapping (that's you I'm referring to Paula Martinez), but the first person to mention here would be Mr. Charles Graham, my beloved 'favorite brother in law' as I've often referred to him. Charles had a million excuses to pull the plug on this project from beginning to end, but he refused to go without seeing his vision through - and _that_ is inspiring.

Building Kathini was complex in so many ways and the time following the dramatic events that occurred along the endeavor were daunting enough to leave me reeling in the frenzy - but I'd come home to the sweetest reception always - my beloved Kleou laying on the sofa - processing her day - offering tea, wanting to know what interactions had occurred between myself and the boat designer. My sister Analida who would not end a conversation without checking if I needed anything - and by anything she meant _anything_ - think of a person you know with a heart the size of a traffic jam in Los Angeles on the Friday before a holiday - that's her - a specimen of generosity and thoughtfulness. Along the way I thrived every time I got to visit with my sons - Carlos already lived on his own in Brazil and I missed him dearly, Marco was... well, you've gotta read the book to answer that question, and the time I had living alone with Danny was exactly the prize I needed to find at the bottom of the cereal box. And then there is Kevin, who like Kleou - is this mix of family member with best friend and warm molten chocolate melting over your ice cream - but Kevin was there guiding me once the book was written and put together funds with my family for my birthday so I could afford the book formatting and other publishing costs and then gifted me with his own rendition of the book cover design which is the one tenderly wrapping the text you now read.

I need to mention Mike - who married me in the thick of all this and has hung in there with me despite all my stunts and emotional decision-making - and I'll just leave that there. Thank you darling for being my safe harbor. I often remember the villagers of Cajaíba - faithfully occupying their posts at their windows as Ed and I marched in and out of town, waving happily as we passed; but especially that time I arrived without him - the compassion in their eyes is brand-ed in my memories. I'd like all the suppliers and representatives I mention along the narrative, to feel my virtual hug of gratitude as I treasure the special relationships I developed with them through the countless calls, interactions and emails it took to get our gargantuan orders organized. I am petrified of the people I've failed to mention but am committed to keep an ongoing list and publish each edition with an updated list because YOU were a pixel in this picture and I don't want your love to go unnoticed. Eternal gratitude. Already as I say this I remember I did not mention my trusted friend and editor David Helsten who made this book so much more readable - but please know, if you are reading this you are in my heart.

Thank You Universe ♥

to my sons Carlos, Daniel and Marco
and to my soul family – you know who you are

Contents

Los Angeles, CA - August 28th, 2015
Excerpt from personal diary:

"Last night I dreamt I was walking down our pier. I could see the day meaning to break as it faintly illuminated the sky in the distance. I took in the horizon confidently as I paced forward, but when I looked down at my feet, I noticed they looked frail and bony and I found there was no pier below me. I felt powerless as my heart beat fast with the anticipation of the inevitable plunge into the waters below - but I couldn't fall. I couldn't walk. I couldn't turn back. The absence of the pier under my feet held me hostage. As I write this, I recognize the feeling I've learned to navigate daily, since life brought your fate to my door and left it there for me to unwrap. A parcel I have been unpacking daily along with memories of your eyes betraying your repressed heart and their unfathomable darkness signaling the tempest in which we were about to lose ourselves. Your anguish is mine when my happy-natured spirit stirs turbulently with the memory of yours."

***

Bahia, Brazil 2013

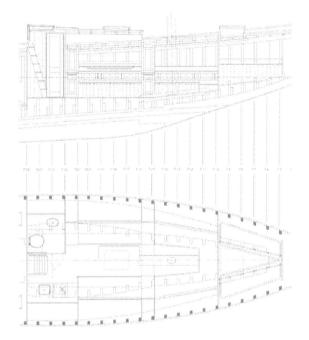

Kathini

A story of love, loss and a little boat building

The speedometer of the rib boat marked 45 knots as we whisked across choppy waters. I was no expert, but I could tell we were moving at an ungodly speed, slamming fiercely across the waves. My curls twisted wildly behind my head signaling the frenetic vortex created by our vessel as it sped furiously across the Camamú Bay. Above us, an electric blue sky and an ominous mood looming over us as Jorge, our boatman, ramped the boat off the crests of the waves inclemently, his face remaining vacant even as our vessel repeatedly spanked the water on its way down. I glanced at our other passenger, the seasoned Mr. Burnett, to check for any sign of distress but his eyes were dark and fury instead of fear, seemed to occupy them.

**

Moments earlier Mr. Burnett and I had been at the boatyard where we were building *Kathini* - a 56' classic wooden ketch sailboat in the north eastern coast of Brazil for our client Mr. Charles Graham.

Edward Burnett had been commissioned to build Kathini in Brazil over a meeting planned in London where Charles resided with my sister Analida, his wife of 20 years. Since we were building in Brazil and Ed was not familiar with Portuguese, I had committed to translating instructions between him and our small team with lead builder Zezinho (zeh-zee-niu) in a fourth generation boat building village of less than 1,000 inhabitants. Building in the tropics, one faces many particularities due to the humidity and heat which lulls life to a minimum pace where most anything takes priority over productivity. This in particular, triggered Mr. Burnett's ill-tempered mood that day.

"Could you ask him what has been the cause of the delay in cutting the planking stock and setting it out to dry as I requested six weeks ago?" Ed sparked, especially hot and bothered one afternoon. We had not stopped for lunch and were still running on the fuel provided by our frugal breakfast of fruit and tapioca.

I pitched my voice to an especially compassionate tone before I posed the engineer's question to our builder, as to soften the accusatory tone of the inquiry.

"Have you been having trouble cutting the planking timber and setting it out to dry?" I enquired soothingly.

"No," came Zezinho's simple reply, worded in his usual fashion and accompanied by a lengthy discourse of excuses. "The thing is we were meant to start cutting earlier and my cousin was supposed to help, but then he didn't, because his nephew was born and also when he finally *did* come, it was raining, so we cut a few bits but it's just been slow because it's been so wet and you know - we try to stay out of the workshop when it's raining at a slant - cuz the wiring there..."

"For God's sake..." Zezinho's soliloquy was abruptly interrupted. Ed's face flushed with irritation. "Do we have a reason yet? Why is it that every question needs to be answered with a complete declaration of how the weather was and how everyone was feeling? I just..."

Ed stopped short before completely losing his composure. Zezinho looked at me with an understanding of our engineer's tone, yet still searching for its content.

"He's just wondering why we're chatting so cheerfully while he's getting old waiting for an answer..."

I said with a chuckle, keeping upbeat meaning to infuse Zezinho with assurance. Our lackadaisical attitude definitely did not help temper Ed's uncharacteristic outburst.

Mr. Burnett glared up at me, eyes manic with indignation as he shot back.

"Ok, well can we just get an answer now? For fuck's sake, we're not here for tea and biscuits!"

I had seen many sides of Ed so far, and while it was completely understandable that it was unbearably hot under that zinc covering and we were hungry, there was an underlying murmur that spoke to my inner ear. I gazed so deeply into Ed's eyes in my astonishment that it seemed to disarm his rage.

"Ok! Right. I'm... I'm sorry." he muttered. "Let's just call it a day shall we?" He declared as he tossed the tape measure he was grasping and stood up decidedly. He directed a nod at Zezinho, attempting a grin, as he motioned for the entryway.

"Where's Jorge?" he asked after our boatman, the native who had been taking us back and forth between the Graham family vacation home in Barra Grande and Cajaíba, where Kathini had been under construction for nearly three years.

"That's odd..." I remarked, not seeing Jorge's head pop up from between the seats of the Lillybelle, the family rib boat named after Analida and Charles' daughter Lilly, where he was known to steal a nap after lunch on especially hot days as this.

Ed opened his mouth as if to speak, reconsidered, then filled his lungs to proffer yet another thought, but instead just gesticulated with his arms, as he turned back round on the pier so we could look for Jorge in the village.

In Jorge's defense, we had never left work before 5 pm and it was barely 3:30. So I offered an excuse for our boatman, knowing he could very well be napping elsewhere.

Nearly 60 minutes later, Jorge emerged carefree, in his usual nonchalance. He started toward the pier unhurriedly passing over the emanating vibe of discontent that Mr. Burnett exuded. Ed issued a snide remark about his disappearance under his breath and settled in the seat beside me in the Lillybelle. One needn't speak a lick of English to understand that Ed was cross and that it would be prudent to stay out of his way.

We arrived back at the house before 5:00 pm, just as the sultry day was beginning to cool. The ocean breeze was inviting and I craved a little alone time in nature to replenish my energies.

"You wanna hit the beach for a little cool down?" I asked tentatively.

I understood Ed was under a lot of pressure to finish construction and thus deliver to his client a finished product in a timely manner, but his objective did not seem to be on anyone else's mind, in this parallel universe of the tropics where no one was in a rush to accomplish anything.

Edward had been lost in thought the whole way back to the house, visibly unhappy with the day's events. His reply to that fact came as confirmation that he was not ready to snap out of his discontent just yet.

"I'll be in my room checking emails..." he said, appending dryly with a flat: "see you at dinner", before swiftly disappearing into the sanctity of his room. His body language reinforced the notion that there was no chance of a change of heart to his demeanor in the near future.

"K..." came my reticent reply, as I shrugged and walked towards the serenity of my own quarters.

Our trusted groundskeeper Olivan, and other members of staff, were nowhere to be seen, as they were not expecting to find us back so early, and were more than likely tending to the affairs of their own homes located adjacent to the Graham property.

I sauntered to my room to freshen up and slip into a clean bikini. I usually worked in a bikini, an indecently short pair of cut offs and a t-shirt - always prepared for the possibility of a pleasurable dip in the ocean. I grabbed a colorful striped towel from the rack and headed out to a convenient spot, located at the end of the garden lawn. For a split second, I considered a walk and then a dip further down the beach, as the water straight in front of the house seemed especially unruly - but the allure was too great to entice me to tread the hot sand between my toes any longer than necessary. I glanced over the ocean and noticed a smoother spot in the middle of the bustle, and decided to make my way in. I knew better than to go in much deeper without having anyone with me, so I went in waist-deep and crouched down to cover my shoulders in the refreshing water. I closed my eyes and leaned my head back to saturate my curls in the detoxifying water. I began breathing deeply, releasing the day's pressures whilst humming a chant I could not remember the words to. When I thought to stand up again, I noticed I was in deeper than I'd intended to be, so I began treading towards the shore. A swell coming in lifted me softly, sweeping my feet up slightly and then dropping me in again with the water level above my bosom. Before I knew it, my feet no longer made contact with the sandy bottom.

"*It's ok*", I comforted myself. "*All I need to do is make it in a foot further*".

Even I, notoriously *not* a strong swimmer, could swim that small distance - I reasoned. I tried a few strokes over water and then tried swimming underwater, but every time I looked up to assess how I was doing, I was horrified to see how far out I was being swept from the beach. The realization that there was absolutely no one in sight and that I was at a terrible disadvantage to this current seemed to immediately suck all the air out of my lungs as panic set in. I began desperately flailing in the water all the while coaching myself - '*it's ok, just swim out of the current - to the side Paula, to the side!*' I said to myself, encouragingly. I began taking a few strokes out to the side but seeing the shore farther and farther away made the panic seize what strength and breath I had. The thought of potential death actually calmed me into the thought that I was no longer in control, and I cried out a meek and barely audible "help!", as I turned to float on my back, trying desperately to think through the blinding fog of fear impairing my better judgment.

'*Think Paula, think...Just let yourself be carried out. Once you're out of the current you can swim back in...*' I reached for optimism rather than despair.

I knew truly that I did not have the stamina to swim that far; even on a good day, I certainly would not have the stamina to do that on this one. I felt tears daring to surge out of the corners of my eyes. I quickly floated into an upright position again in an attempt to keep the tears from streaming and obscuring my already tainted view. I scanned the beach again exhausted - no one. I looked around again, floating on my back once more. My breath was erratic and I felt the crippling effects of hyperventilating.

'I'm not going to make it...' I thought - and then immediately - *'I wonder how I'm going to make it?'* surfaced in my mind, replacing the negative thought pronouncement with hope. I looked out towards the ocean, away from the shore... *'maybe a passing boat?'* I mused. I turned back around to face the shore, my eyes wildly scouring the space around me. I became frantically aroused, spotting a long thin torso wading in to the right of where I had entered into this nightmare.

"Help! Help!" I whimpered, slowly taking focus on the lean silhouette and realizing it was Ed.

I considered waving my arms but my legs were getting weaker and I was now feeling that with every wave a little water was getting into my nose and mouth. I closed my eyes and tried to gather strength for one last loud cry, when suddenly I spotted Edward's face, wrestling as it was between bewilderment and concern. He was closer to me now but still far off to the side, nevertheless focused and determined as ever.

"Paula!" he shouted, "are you in trouble?"

I gathered all my strength to respond to his query, but the little air I had in my lungs was now just enough to keep me afloat. Ed hesitantly moved closer to assess the situation, when suddenly his features changed radically, as the reality of my plight engaged his swift and affirmative action.

"Ok listen to me, you can do this. You're going to swim toward me," he commanded firmly, while reassuringly waving me towards him with the stroke of one calm hand - leaving no room for my weakness to overwhelm my efforts.

His tone and confidence made my breathing become more paced, and a sense of calm began eradicating my fears. It was reminiscent of the times I had recently relied on him for encouragement when I was drowning in tasks that were so far over my head in the managing of our boat project. Yet through his unbridled conviction he'd reassured my efforts, edifying my fortitude. His eyes, now fiercely focused, locked-in on me with profound intensity, displaying the sort of divine assertion that instills hope.

"That's it, just keep coming, we're getting you out of there," he coaxed assuredly. He held out his arm as a beacon for me to swim towards, although he was still a good six meters from me, he continued talking, encouraging me by asking questions.

"Can you see my hand?" It seemed he was edging back toward the shore at the same pace I was... treading water backward until he felt confident that he could let me grasp his hand without pulling him under.

Gasping for air I reached for Ed's hand, as he lunged eagerly forward, pulling me toward the safety of him decidedly by the right arm. I released my weary body into his care completely, as he floated me dutifully onto shore. He seemed to be relieving himself of built up adrenaline along the way, asking incessant, rhetorical questions under his breath: "How did you get yourself into that?" "Why were you swimming alone?" "What if I hadn't come out..." he cooed. Being familiar with the ocean as he was, he couldn't wrap his head around the stupidity of my innocently wading straight into a rip current.

He walked me up to the oceanfront kiosk on the edge of the lawn, steading me along. Taking my towel from its hook, he placed it round my shoulders like an offering. I was alarmingly quiet and disoriented, as his questions swam buoyantly in the depths of my daze. Within moments, I found myself rolled up in the towel, sitting with my knees propped up under my chin, arms hugging my legs to keep the towel in place. I sat staring out at the ocean for what seemed a timeless moment. I was incredibly aware, but my thoughts seemed dream-like in nature, wildly skipping from one track to another. At some level I realized that what had taken place had surely happened within a 10 - 15 minute span, if that, but it seemed like time had stopped. It was incredible to me that I was presently on this side of the ocean looking out at what had almost been my fate. I kept going back to wondering what had prompted Ed to come out to the beach, and what would have happened had he not emerged from his quarters at the very moment he did. My children would have been receiving news of my demise that evening, I imagined and grieved for their near loss and of what might have been if it weren't for Ed's miraculous intervention.

Delving further into this parallel world, I thought back on how this project had come into my life when I most needed a lifeline. I wondered if they'd carry on with the project without me. I recalled how Ed and I had met and how this whole endeavor had changed our lives. I had been through so much since then. In my reverie, I knew that time was progressing because the skyline was growing more mysterious in color. Darker shades of indigo were beginning to appear in dramatic strokes across the horizon. Ed himself seemed to be recovering, and as dusk settled silently all around us, so too the expression of concern melted quietly from his features, giving way to one of contemplation.

***

April 2010:
The decision to build

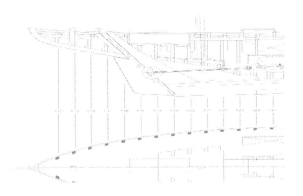

Kathini

A story of love, loss and a little boat building

Charles and Analida had found their ideal vacation home in Barra Grande, just a few years after having discovered the charming region of Camamú Bay in Bahia while on holiday. Alluring, with its expanse of wild shoreline off the beaten path on the northern shores of Brazil, they came back year after year, captivated by the natural, unkempt beauty of the place, with its long stretches of wide, unexplored, postcard-like beaches. Their family comprised my sister Analida, her British Kenyan-born husband Charles, and their four children, began enjoying their holidays in Barra Grande every year thereafter. Over time, the house began to resemble the ideal that Analida had in her mind as the perfect holiday home. The houses, which were now attached as one conglomerate, had originally been built in 2004 by an attorney and his architect business partner. At the time, the individual structures were created for each to enjoy separately with his family, until the Graham's purchased one of the homes from the architect who decided to sell after settling a divorce. Both houses were rustic and charming but far from their current state of polish and infrastructure. Since then, the Graham's had acquired the second house, putting in a glorious emerald-green lawn, solar heating, an infinity pool facing the ocean, and upgrading all the rooms and bathrooms reflecting a sophisticated simplicity and cleanliness. A wall was knocked down here and there to produce the open plan that suited our noisy, Brazilian, music-loving family, particularly on our favorite family holiday for which we all piled together at the house: New Year's Eve.

I first traveled out to Barra Grande in 2009, during a hiatus in my career in the real estate and mortgage industry, partially caused by the notorious meltdown that occurred a year earlier, though also due to a co-occurring personal meltdown. I had an intense pull in my spirit to dedicate myself to a new occupation, more suitable to my natural interests and calling. I confess, I had no idea what that calling might have been at the time. My need to discover it had become essential in sustaining my wellbeing, direction and purpose. I'd moved from Brazil to California back in 2002 and lived on the outskirts of Los Angeles where I practiced real estate in the then booming Santa Clarita Valley. Our area was hit hard by the mortgage crisis, so when Analida asked if I would fly out and give her a hand with organizing the vacation house, taking some linens and kitchen items out to her from the US, my rational mind initially protested against such indulgence, but my heart whispered "a shopping spree followed by a week on the beach and a little organizing? What's not to like?"

***

My first trip out brought seven days of non-stop rain. I initially accomplished a lot of organizing during that time, as well as having had the opportunity not only to get generally acquainted with the 'lay of the land' in these parts, but also to the rhythm and rhyme of working in pace with the locals. The electrician we hired to rewire the precarious existing wiring of the house, was also the town priest, infamous as well for his strong inclination to imbibe the local spirit called 'cachaça'. The sparse economic structure of the community made it common for workers to accumulate varying trades and capacities in their working skills to make ends meet, which generally meant they were proficient in none of them. They all shared one vibe in their work ethic however, the *'Bahian'* ethos of: 'live first – work if time allows'.

Around the bucolic little town of Barra Grande, time is slow and abundant and there is plenty of space for contemplation. Certain things are never left for later - like a nap, or a friendly invite to kick a soccer ball back and forth. People are loyal to all calls of nature here and a cocktail or beverage in good company is seldom refused. There is always time for a 'cervejinha' (little beer), a 'caipirinha' (little cocktail), or a 'cafezinho' (little coffee). We Brazilians use the diminutive "-inha' or "-inho" to refer to all things cherished, and beer - chilled to glacial temperatures, or the local spirit crushed with limes, ice, and a ton of sugar are the preference, second only to our celebrated coffee.

Upon arriving to the region of Camamú Bay, where Barra Grande is nestled, the air is lush with a soothing humidity and one feels welcomed and favored, like being admitted into a secret society, initiated warmly into this little-known enclave. Most access is via the small town of Camamú crossing the Camamú Bay by boat, as the roads leading in are unpaved and greatly impacted by the torrential rains that pour down in a tropical vengeance, between the months of June and August. These torrents also make spontaneous appearances throughout other months of the year, though almost always giving in to the relentless rays of sunshine that quite often form double rainbows in the pale blue-gray of the post-shower sky.

The community's roots date back to 1561, a time of colonial expansion when the Portuguese were settling their royal family in Brazil and taking over several indigenous regions. Camamú, specifically, was inhabited by the Tupi people called *tupiniquins* and was transformed by the settlers into a Jesuit mission, effectively making the local roots Catholic. At that time, Bahia was rich in gold and diamonds and many other resources, making it a much-coveted land. Over time, historical events such as the invasion by the Dutch and the advent of slavery, left obvious sociological marks on the region. Including the predominantly African traces bred into the indigenous substratum of the local people, ensuring their herculean body types and effusive cheer, as well as their notorious ability in all things musical. Here, a unique belief system that is a hybrid of Catholicism and mysticism expresses the rich, colorful and mystical faith of the region. The little town of Cajaíba lays quietly in this fountainhead of rich, colorful, and diverse experience.

***

One afternoon after lunch, Charles wandered over to the cozy oceanfront veranda, where all the family and guests were having 'cafezinho' – espresso shots, which we Brazilians hold dear.

"Would anyone care to venture out on an expedition of the Camamú Bay this afternoon?" he asked enthusiastically - his grayish-blonde hair now matted into the shape of the cap he'd worn on an earlier beach run. His hopeful grin suggested that we should all be delighted to go on such an escapade.

A silence fell over the group, who clearly had post-lunch plans of their own, ranging from napping to connecting to what feeble internet connection there was to check their social media updates. Eyes veered in different directions, looking to avoid contact with the man suggesting such an outing. Charles added spiritedly: "there are only *seven* spots, plus myself..." he emphasized, accentuating the point that though the opportunity was up for grabs, there was limited space, making the occasion a more desirable undertaking for the lucky initiates. As it turned out, the exploratory party consisted of the boatman Jorge, Charles and an old mate of his who had accepted an invite to visit from the UK, and, last but not least - myself. Together we four putted around the bay, taking in all the cozy and inviting little beach coves as well as the darkly lush and mysterious mangroves. It was that afternoon that we came across the sleepy little village of Cajaíba, with its smiley, colorfully dressed children, noisily playing by the pier - half-shyly, half boisterously waving at us as we pulled in.

***

The people of Bahia are known for their slow, long-drawn speech that takes its time coming forth, in a way letting one know that they've got plenty of it to linger. Family life is a priority and the children belong to the village. Everyone is related somehow, regardless of any evident blood ties. When you're a close friend of the family, you'll either go by 'Tio' or 'Tia' enjoying uncle or aunt status in multiple families. Homes are built to last generations, with the help of family and friends, and often families will contribute an old sink or a door that's been lying around, maybe a few dozen bricks, or pool-in with some beers, a chicken and some potato salad for the 'roofing day' bash. All in making do with what little resources exist in the little village, where much is achieved through the harmony of togetherness. There are no mortgages to be paid and as parents age, the children move in with their spouses and raise their own children while tending to their elders. Those children will eventually marry and have children of their own, taking over the front of the house, while the elder parents settle into the side or back quarters, and life will cycle through in its incessant, bucolic manner, leaving no one to hunger, no one in need. There is no poverty, in that life is simple for all, and everyone's requirements are met. There are no Jones' to keep up with, no need for competition. There are no street dwellers, other than the occasional town drunk who will nap in any slither of shade that the colorful architecture can afford. The community celebrates and mourns together and if there is one thing there is little time for here, it is worry.

***

Our party arrived to Cajaíba in classic white-man fashion - sunscreen slathered on pale complexions, bearing hats, sunglasses and cameras, with the telling expression of excitement blended with the curious expression that one displays when visiting a place for the first time. Our saving grace was to be accompanied by Jorge, the Graham boat man, a local who was known and trusted to the little village and who could give us both a quick tour and a condensed history of the place. Jorge, a strong, sinewy black man of few words – seemed remarkably placid, bordering on impassive-- but had been known to stop his four boisterous young boys in their tracks with one silent and piercingly, disapproving glance.

Jorge was a local of Campinho, a village adjacent to Cajaíba, where he was born and raised on the land, helping his family by working in one of the local economies: red palm oil extraction. At the time in his early thirties, he was married in local fashion - sharing two of four children with his wife with whom he currently lived, but hadn't been formally wed to, that is until the massive wave of Protestantism swept over the region in the 90's, converting most all of the locals to what are currently known as evangelical religions. Being a member, Jorge had no choice but to wed in the church so as not to live his life in sin, and as such, he dutifully toted the family to Wednesday and Sunday services and ensured that they heeded other appropriate decorum as deemed by the local church.

Having been brought up bayside as well, Jorge's experience darting in and out of the keys in the region of Camamú Bay came in handy when Analida and Charles were looking for someone to tend to and pilot their boat - particularly when they began visiting the region more intensely, after having purchased their vacation home.

Charles de-boarded our vessel, climbing onto the artless little concrete pier. Placing his hands on his hips, he arched his broad shoulders back and inflated his chest with a long breath and a grimace; his stretch signaling a ceremonious preparation for the adventure ahead. I followed behind taking pictures, smiling and waving, greeting the locals with a hearty 'boa tarde!' which bid them 'good afternoon' in Portuguese. Jorge walked us down the long, somewhat precarious pier - roughly 100 yards to the landing, at the end of which, we encountered the lazy, unpreoccupied pace of a typical Cajaíba Sunday. We were soon to find out that the weekday 'bustle' was not more than a notch or two up from the Sunday pace. The locals typically do not work on Mondays, as to recoup from the weekend, nor on Fridays, as to prepare for the weekend. Time was abundant in this unique place and was certainly not a commodity like we were accustomed to back home.

We walked past the town bar where stacks of beer crates exposed what the past few hours' activity had been, as did the prolific eruptions into laughter and rowdy voices. As we walked past the bars and towards the residential area, the voices and music grew fainter. We walked towards the boatyards which were seemingly abandoned, housing quite an array of unfinished boats parked one after the next. The boats were made of impressive bits of timber and could have easily been dated anywhere in the past century as far as style. We were told that business was slow because the demand for this style of boat was in decline and that many of these boats either had been sitting or could potentially sit for years to come without an owner.

We were led onto the deck of a boat that looked like it hadn't been worked on for quite a while and made our way onto the deck via the makeshift scaffolding. Jorge had lurked away, reemerging by the time we were safely on board with its proud builder Zezinho in tow. We were introduced and shook hands, diving straight to the point, our objective having been foretold in our introduction.

"This is Charles, and this is Paula.... they're interested in your boat." Jorge was a man of few words.

We were hardly interested in purchasing a boat, but Charles had recognized these boats to be the ones he had marveled at over frequent holiday visits, and other occasions. These were the very style of boat that trolled about the bay during carnival, their decks laden with skimpily-clad women, provocatively displaying their samba skills. Meanwhile, on the passing men-only boats, massive amounts of liquor were consumed and the rowdy occupants demonstrated what they'd like to do to the women by shouting out the explicit lyrics to the lascivious songs that erupted from the boom boxes on deck and thrusting their hips.

"How long 'til this one is completed?" Charles asked.

"No...", replied Zezinho, who we soon found had the habit of starting his sentences in negation. "We'd only complete this once we actually *had* a buyer. That way we could finish it to their liking." He replied, hoping to have satisfied Charles with the reply, punctuating his statement with a slight grin of deference.

Charles poked around the structure, which had clearly not undergone any work in recent months, if not years, with a curious expression on his face.

"And how much would something like this cost to complete?" he queried.

"At least 350..." Zezinho replied, referring to the value of $350,000 Brazilian Reais. "It really depends on how the owner wants it finished..." he added, signaling that that figure was an absolute guess.

Charles took the number in, likely considering the Brazilian Real to Pound Sterling exchange, which was at just over four to one at the time.

We finished our tour, bid our goodbyes and headed back to the Lillibelle. We rode back over the rolling waves with the sun setting, and made our way to the pier at Barra Grande, where we had left our vehicle to take us back to the house.

***

Life in LA had begun for me with the end of a 17 year long marriage to the father of my three boys. We married young and were a classic case of lovers that grew apart as we grew up. It would have been amicable, except for a series of unfortunate events that pointed towards my possible infidelity, topped off by the detail that I married soon after our divorce to a man whom I met the very day I moved out of our home.

Marcelo was Brazilian born, but had been living in the United States for about ten years when we met. He was cousin to a fellow teacher of mine at the English school where I had been teaching English as a second language for the past 10 years in São Carlos, where my first husband and I had settled and raised our children. Marcelo was visiting family that year and was stuck for a while longer than anticipated in Brazil after losing his passport during the visit. I arrived late on what was my moving day, to the celebratory luncheon which marked the beginning of a semester at the school and took a seat at a table all the way in the back so as not to disrupt the event with my late arrival. By chance Marcelo, who knew no one, sat alone at that table. Thus, our friendship began with a lot of laughter and by the end of lunch the sensation was that my thirst for affection and fun camaraderie was soon to be quenched after having been starved as a working mother and full-time student caught playing house way too seriously from the age of 20.

10 years later, I was just recovering from the upheaval that moving to another country after a divorce can bring, and facing my second divorce - this time in the amicable fashion I wished the first had been - just lovers who came to terms with the fact that they were great individuals on their own but not compatible to each other - kind of like hot dogs and mango. It was in this aura

of looking for a lifeline that would pull me out of the sameness of the loan processor job that I had been stuck in after leaving real estate, that Charles presented me with his idea, while visiting Brazil for Christmas of 2010.

**

"Do you think it would be possible for us to build a boat in Cajaíba?" Charles threw out casually in conversation, over coffee on the oceanfront veranda of the house in Barra Grande after a meal.

"I mean, wouldn't it be nice to have our own boat to party on at New Year's or for the day and whatnot?" he continued taking a minute to bask in his own proposition before looking over to elicit my response.

"Wait...are you thinking of..." for a minute I thought Charles might be considering the boat we climbed onto.

"No, no, not buying that unfinished boat. I've gone to visit with a reputable boat designer back home in Devon and I'm thinking of commissioning a project from him. It would be a simple, bespoke, elegant gentleman's day-sailer." He said, the idea clearly materializing in his mind with every word.

"Hmmmm", I pondered with the mind of the optimist I am known to be. "Do you mean he'd design the boat and Zezinho would build it?"

"Yes, and the architect would come, say every so often - six months or so, just to oversee the process and make sure everything is going accordingly," he continued. "I think not only could Zezinho use the business but this could eventually generate some jobs for the locals too, could it not?" He pursed his lips, aspirating what seemed like a cubic meter of air holding onto a long breath, as if to further savor the case for his vision and then added "...and that might be desirable...." the last syllable of that utterance hung in the air in an attempt to convince its interlocutor.

"Ya... that seems... interesting," I said, lips smiling with the comic aspect of his proposition. I believed, as did Charles, but knowing the community reputation for slow work and fast paced avoidance of commitments, that it was a great idea with an undeniable chance of failure. For the sake of keeping the perspective alive, I topped that reply off with a dreamy: "That would be wonderful ...", as I flared my eyes widely.

"What do you think darling?" Charles ran the idea past Analida, who was at the table on the adjacent deck preparing for a meeting with a realtor regarding the house next door.

"What about, my love?" she answered, being pulled into our fantasy momentarily.

She listened as Charles explained his vision to her with growing enthusiasm and confidence, only to be shot down by her categorical response.

"Whatever for my love? So they can deliver a cross between what you wanted and what they're used to building that won't float and will sink to the bottom of the bay, along with the hard-earned money we invested in it?" She was a no-nonsense businesswoman who prided herself on being savvy, punctuating her views with terms of endearment to keep them more palatable, but sparing no truth.

We both shifted a little in our seats - I felt uncomfortable by her shooting him down although I completely understood her point. I cleared my throat and focused on a beetle that was battling to climb the leg of the center table but kept a channel open whilst waiting for Charles as he strategized his rebuttal.

"I don't see the issue at hand at all - with proper coordination and planning they can build a boat, it's not a new concept to them," he defended. "In fact, they've been building them for generations."

"Darling, these are simple people who live their lives peacefully by building their boats at their own pace and time... They'll never understand your sophisticated boat, designed by your sophisticated designer - Oh God, how much *was* this design? I hope you haven't committed to anything yet - I've only just recouped our deposit for the Pilatus you wanted..." she retorted with a sigh.

Analida had a loving way of tearing you to shreds from the bottom of her heart, though I had learned, from 46 years of being her younger sister, that she truly came from a place of care and concern while doing it. Charles was now engaged in a discussion he was eager to win.

"I don't see a problem - we'd be helping them to update their construction techniques and stimulating the economy in that little village at the same time." He knew her heart for social enterprise all too well, and milked it for all it was worth.

"All the while flushing thousands of our hard-earned pounds down the toilet while we're at it," she interjected. "Why don't we just donate to a local school or nonprofit? I don't know, Charles, if you think it's wise to dump all this money into some crazy venture then be my guest - just know I warned you!" And with that, she wandered off to find a pen - a prized commodity in these parts of the tropics.

Charles turned to me for reassurance - "Don't you think that this could work?" Before I could answer he concluded "I think it'd be an interesting project."

"Well, how would we go about it? I mean, what would the next steps be?" I asked, shining my didactic skills upon the problem.

"I'm going to schedule a visit with the designer and see if he's willing to come down on occasion to supervise our project. Maybe when he comes you can come too and translate? Is that something you'd like to do?"

I took in the possibility of coming down another time to Brazil on my thin divorcee budget, always tainted nonetheless, by my relentless can-do attitude before replying - "It is...depending on when we'd come it should work..." I said, tentatively, trying to feel the statement in my spirit to see if it was agreeable or causing pangs of anxiety.

"Well then, we'll try to schedule something for Easter. I'll visit with the designer and let you know. Do you think you'll be able to take time off by then?" he asked matter of factly.

"Mmmhmmm..." came my reply, uncertain what the near future held for me.

***

2011 started-out with a bang - not only with the fireworks on the beach that year, but I was extremely dissatisfied at my job and my heart felt cheated at the gnawing truth that I was not dedicating myself to something meaningful - something I had a passion for. As connected to my spiritual side as I was, I had been unemployed in the US before, the last time being when the small brokerage I'd hung my real estate license with closed. Two of my sons had recently moved in with me to my cushy apartment home with resort amenities, only to witness the next few months of my desperation; receiving threats of eviction, incessant phone calls and mail demanding payment of our bills. I did whatever I could to keep up with our expenses by taking the odd job babysitting, driving or selling any valuable items I could to put food on the table. Luckily, one job led to another and I was able to climb my way back into a somewhat comfortable salary again. I wasn't a loan processor by training, but having worked at a small company I got to wear many hats and had learned the basics of loan processing. I was able to land a position through an acquaintance who was in the business of title insurance and thought I'd suit the position at a broker's office.

Though the ravages of poor credit and moving to a smaller apartment kept our lifestyle quite frugal, we were able to adorn our lives with the simplest of joys and we got through the phase with dignity and joy and were closer than ever as a family. It was in this scenario that we received the news that my youngest son Marco, who had immigrated with his older brother Daniel to live with me months earlier, would have his visa interview this coming month in Rio de Janeiro. I scraped together funds for his ticket and off he went. I was excited to finally be wrapping up this long process and with the perspective of his finally becoming a legal resident. The day of his interview however, was a nightmare we would never forget. He called sobbing asking us to please send him $600 immediately because he had been denied and needed to file for an appeal if he was ever to come back home. They took his passport and told him he would not be able to return to the US for the next 10 years.

This caldron of events hurled me into an imbalanced state of mind which drove me further into the urgency of living a more purposeful life. At this point, life felt like it had been a constant uphill battle and like I was always having to overcome something. I felt like I couldn't get a leg up. I decided I was going to get out of this mess no matter what it took. I lifted my chin and challenged life with the defiance of a fierce woman and mother. That of course, punctuated by the messy snot-bathed breakdowns I'd have every so often, when I would throw myself down on the floor and pray to anything that would hear me, in supplicating sobs of despair. Life progressed in that disheveled state until one day in March I heard from Charles.

The news actually came by way of Analida in an email one morning. She inquired whether or not I could join for the Easter holiday, explaining that Charles would be bringing the boat designer and that he was still set on the crazy idea of building a boat in Brazil. I hadn't shared the full extent of how my year had gone thus far with her because I dreaded causing worry - for no reason other than I believe in trying to figure things out gracefully - like the runway model that twists her ankle from atop her stiletto heels and smiles broadly through the pain as she completes her walk.

"I'd love to," I said. "I'm just not sure I can. Marco's immigration case is becoming more complicated than I anticipated and I thought it could be solved with a letter of explanation, but as it turns out I might need an attorney." I explained, substantiating my hesitance.

Her reply concluded that since it was to Charles' benefit that I come, he was offering me the ticket.

"It'll be a nice little reprieve from all the tension Paula - come on...live a little!". "Live a little" was her little trademark way of suggesting that it was a good opportunity to indulge.

"Besides, you'll get to see Marco when you layover in São Paulo..."

Emotions of joy swirled in my sinking heart. The very thought that Marco's situation might not yet be solved by then clouded the joy of her suggestion, but I agreed to the arrangement and remained in expectation.

Marco had been caught in a conundrum of immigration law regarding studying in the US. I had brought the boys into the US on tourist visas, with the intention of filing an adjustment of status upon their arrival - which I did - but since the law stated that no child may be left out of school due to immigration status - I was able to enroll both Danny (my middle son) and Marco (my youngest) into high school - but they were enrolled before I filed the adjustment of status because the school year was beginning and I didn't want them to miss school. A tired and cranky officer at the US Consulate, in Rio de Janeiro, where Marco was called to perform his immigration interview, denied Marco's visa but we weren't provided a reason - perhaps because the officer was acting on a hunch, making it so he could no longer come back into the country. On Marco's birthday, March 30, 2011 he received his passport stamped: 'CANCELLED' all over what had previously been his entry visa. It quickly became clear that this was not going to be a quick fix and the feeling of having majorly fucked up my son's life in general weighed heavily on my pillow at night.

***

April came around and I prepared to go to Brazil for the Easter holiday. While I was looking forward to some time in paradise and to meeting with family and friends, my spirit was bruised and tender from the latest happenings and I felt like I needed miracles...lots of miracles. I needed Marco's situation to be cleared up. I needed Danny's upcoming immigration interview to *not* go the same way as Marco's had, and I needed to find a life activity that would put my qualities to use and sustain my family. I needed to settle down whether single or married but find some goddamn stability. My oldest son Carlos had never been interested in moving to the US or to Montreal where his father took up residence after our divorce. He was dating an older girl at the time and was in love - and who was I to stand in the way of love - though puppy in its quality? Soon Carlos began university and was swept away by the affairs of his own adult life. As close as we had always been - our phone conversations extending into well over 60 minutes at a time, we were living in parallel planes though always there for each other. I missed him dearly and it hurt that my life decisions had led me away from him though that had never been my intention. Seeing my mother remain in an unhappy marriage for 50+ years of her life in the name of what she claimed was *'for our sake'* if nothing else, drove home the lesson that one should never compromise one's happiness for anyone else's sake because it causes unhappiness to the ones who most love you when you're not happy. I decided early on that my priority in life would be happiness and after my first divorce - the word of the day was 'authenticity'. Being authentic regarding who I was, who I wanted to be and conveying that to my partner took precedence over anything else. I had strayed from my true self in the past, to not make waves, at the cost of becoming someone far removed from the person I had meant to be. All that said, when I moved to the US in 2002, I moved for no one's sake nor to anyone's harm - I just moved because that's what life presented and I weighed it in my heart and took the plunge. I left everything behind and arrived with two suitcases to begin my new life.

***

I arrived a day earlier than the folks coming from the UK and flew straight through São Paulo, planning to stop for a few days on the way back to visit with Marco and see if I could look into legal solutions for his case.

Olivan, the groundskeeper, was there to greet me. Once a barman, Olivan could serve up an epic caipirinha when guests arrived and that was his claim to fame - aside from his reputation with the local girls. Olivan was a charming, dark-complected native in his mid-twenties, who was always wearing a big smile. He handed me the icy, lime green cocktail, asked how my journey had been and then took my bags up to the *parrot suite* - a suite we had named such, in jest of its location directly over the parrot dwelling that housed Ike and Tina, the house parrots. Ike and Tina squawked excruciatingly loud as early as the sun announced itself, even before staff arrived to serve breakfast and make preparations for the day. I walked my cocktail over to a hammock and sipped on it gratefully enjoying the quiet laze of the afternoon.

***

The next day began at sunrise as I floated out of the room and onto the lawn, my soul imbibed with bliss under the influence of lush nature all around. I moseyed over the lawn to find a friendly patch on which to practice some yoga. The recent turn of events had inspired me to revisit the practice that had saved me when I had small children and was overwhelmed by the lack of sleep and those long busy days with work and school in my twenties. It was a relaxing and wonderful morning nevertheless, as I walked the beach, still virgin of footsteps in that early hour of the morn. I explored, taking in the beauty of a meandering path that returned me to the house to welcome the newly arriving guests with a smile on my face. They were flying into a nearby landing strip in a light plane freighted especially for the occasion and being collected by one of the staff who doubled up as pool man and driver. I heard the Range Rover rambling up the bare stone drive, bringing-up the Graham's and their guests.

I walked out to the front of the house with Olivan who steered a delectable tray-full of lime green cocktails around for the welcome. A wide smile plastered on my face as they began piling out of the Rover - first Analida, then Charles, a few other guests but I stopped counting when I saw the most relieving sight in the world! Marco and Carlos had been invited and flown up by Analida and Charles as a surprise to cheer me up with their presence. I was tear-eyed and ecstatic, wearing the glow of absolute happiness when I was introduced to Mr. Edward Burnett - B. Eng. Hons.

***

Brazil notoriously houses the largest catholic community in the world despite its extremely diverse religious potpourri, making Easter a major holiday - comparable to Thanksgiving in the US. Most begin celebrating at noon on Thursday or on Good Friday, making it a wonderful long weekend opportunity for travel. That year there were maybe 16 of us, between family and friends, and we were a noisy bunch at meals - 7 teenagers between mine and Analida's children, a few of the kids' friends, a cousin or two and some of Analida and Charles' friends. All the meals were served at the long wooden table made of a solid native timber that comfortably sat 12 - but we squeezed in Brazilian style, loud and intimate in our interactions. Subjects of all sorts were introduced at the dinner table - from work, to investments, to mocking each other, and Charles' all-time favorite subject - history trivia.

Our first meal together that trip was a late beach-style lunch, with plenty of salads, little chicken filets, rice and beans - our favorite staple in Brazil. Lunch was usually a lot more casual than dinner as it interrupted crucial beach activities like paddle ball, or lounging by the pool posting selfies. It was acceptable therefore to present ourselves in light beach attire and eat buffet-style, as opposed to dinner when everyone was showered and preened for the occasion.

I was beside myself and in a euphoria for having my babies with me, who at the time were a bit beyond babies really, at the ripe ages of 19 and 22. We served ourselves and sat at what is usually used as the breakfast table - on the corner opposing the ocean veranda and nearest the kitchen.

"How are things my love?" I asked Marco.

"Okay", he replied soulfully, "but we've got to get this situation solved Mom - I'm already missing a semester at school as it is and... I just miss being home," he said, with pleading eyes that broke my heart.

"I know baby...I'm looking into finding an attorney and I'm looking for the best immigration attorney out there - I don't care what it takes, we're getting this figured out, okay?"

Marco nodded, expressing a dry swallow as he looked out towards the ocean in quiet agreement, his eyes glazed over by the strain of withheld tears. We both knew my current financial situation.

"Mom! Didn't you teach your son to not leave his socks around the house?" Carlos erupted in clamorous fashion with his freshly served plate and a teasing grin on his handsome face.

"Shut up! I never leave my socks around the house - you're the psycho who needs everything in place all the time!" Marco shot back - half annoyed, half partaking in their brotherly ritual of banter.

The next words were a jumble of Marco speaking over Carlos' accusations, punctuated by the exchange of a few sharp insults which I was skilled at diplomatically bringing to a fizzle with a few words of agreement and order followed by a sonorous *I love you*... It worked every time, though sometimes the last words heard were mine being mocked by the more offended of the two, in a high-pitched tone to mimic my own. The three boys - Carlos, Danny and Marco had always been extremely close and were not shy at all about delivering insults or criticism to each other when called for, so Carlos had taken to picking on Marco for being messy.

Carlos had decided to live instead with his grandparents until he began college, so shortly after his grandmother's death, just as he moved into his father's childhood home - alone, Marco moved in with him.

It was divine timing that Marco came to live with Carlos in São Paulo. Carlos was living a pretty intense lifestyle, punctuated by late nights, booze and partying that led to a few risky situations with driving home in the wee hours and needing to be up and ready for work the following day. Marco was quick to get on his case and began hounding him about his lifestyle. Not that any of us had anything against a few wild nights here and there but it was truly starting to affect Carlos' decision-making and wellbeing.

***

Coffee was served customarily on the oceanfront veranda, now populated by my boys as well as all the Graham's', their guests, the boat designer (still recuperating from the noise level at lunch amidst the array of parallel conversations) and lethargic teens who were laying across the furniture, feet dangling, commenting on social media while others made plans for the afternoon. Mr. Burnett managed to follow Charles' conversation intently, despite the music blaring from a Bluetooth speaker - that, judging from the selection, was clearly coming from one of the teens' iPhones and not the usual collection of classic rock or Brahms that would be blaring from Charles' own. Our boat designer nodded his head in agreement, making carefully assembled remarks that displayed his level of education and upbringing.

"So, do all of you enjoy sailing or is one of you a more avid sailor?" Ed had risked posing a question to the Graham children during lunch.

There was an awkward moment while thoughts raced to find a polite way to reply that none of them took an interest in sailing - at all. A few mumbles and giggles conveyed the gist of the response while Will, the second born, answered in full unmistakable fashion.

"None of us sail, know anything of sailing nor enjoy any kind of boating for that matter." Will returned politely as the expression on the engineer's visage dulled.

"Would you like to head out for a little reconnaissance shortly or shall we rest today and head out early tomorrow?" Charles amended in a tone that attempted to return some levity to the conversation.

"Out today would be ideal if that's not an inconvenience" Ed responded courteously.

The three of us set out to Cajaíba in the rib boat along with Jorge who steered us out of the bay like a bat out of hell. Being a local, he had not been brought up with power boats and was newly fascinated by the speed and exhilaration of power - fast had become his style.

***

August 2011:
The First Trip

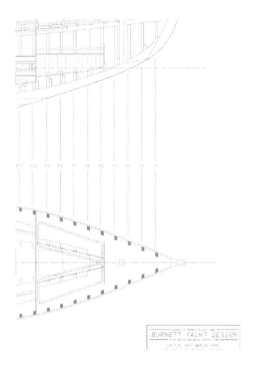

Kathini

A story of love, loss and a little boat building

Summer progressed in sunny California with normal precision. I returned from the April outing to Bahia well rested and determined to balance life out with whatever fortitude I could find. I revisited many of the tools I had learned in previous years of navigating life - yoga, meditation, chanting or whatever grounding practices I could muster contributing to my much needed hold of sanity. What is called "June gloom," regarding the weather in these parts, was behind us now and the heavy weight of not solving Marco's immigration issues by that point caused the oncoming swelter of heat to be ever more difficult to bear some days. It helped that I was seeing a baby boomer surfer with a pad in Costa Rica - he kept me company and we both enjoyed Led Zeppelin and long days on the beach - aside from both being Sagittarian thrill seekers. One thing I had learned about myself over the years was that being outdoors in contact with nature made life a pleasant endeavor no matter what I was going through. That summer of heavy loan processing punctuated by long action-packed weekends and a quick getaway to Costa Rica had definitely made our impending trip to Brazil that August come around more quickly than expected.

We flew into Guarulhos airport where we convened, taking a flight to Ilhéus in Bahia where a driver was readily waiting to drive us the 3 hours to the beach house for what was to be the first stage of our boat building endeavors. Analida, Charles, Ed and I weren't particularly chatty, yet the trip was pleasant, the splendor of natural beauty along the way making easy distractions. Ed and I had not had much interaction during our April trip together. He had used his time to absorb the scope of the project, considering Charles' aspirations and expectations as well. I had enjoyed my time with the boys and concentrated on replenishing myself in nature.

Every morning would start with hopping out of bed at sunrise, assessing the day from my patio and then finding a kosher spot on the lawn for some yoga. In all fairness, I didn't have many reasons to look forward to building a boat. For one, I was looking for a new direction in life away from sales, finances and real estate, and boat building was definitely not one of the life purposes I had envisioned for my mothering, nurturing, tree hugging self. Aside from that, I had recently been in careers that involved competitive, type A, masculine-oriented energy and working with what I anticipated would be a snobbish, hairy-nosed Brit with unattainable standards and a craving for disappointment did not have me looking forward to very much about this project. Hot afternoons in Cajaíba translating building instructions that I little understood to locals who didn't really want a woman in their workplace, much less giving them instructions - aided my resolve.

My half-brother and his newly wed wife, who had asked to use the house for a private holiday that week, were at the house when we arrived and departed the next day. We had arrived in time to partake in a late lunch, then coffee, all sat comfortably on the oceanfront veranda when Charles chimed in.

"So, tomorrow bright and early we begin to build?" Charles queried, half-jokingly half hinged to hope.

"I've brought some material which I believe shall facilitate the process and allow for Zezinho and his team to organize their stages of construction." Ed replied, bringing the expectations to a realistic, more sobering, state of affairs.

Charles looked impressed, as I raised a doubting eyebrow in his direction.

"I'd like to begin by calling a meeting here at the house if that's possible..." the boat architect continued, establishing the tone of how he expected things to run their course.

"Surely", Charles enthused, affirming the motion.

"...so that I may discuss the process with them,' Ed marched-on, "and then share some materials that I've prepared for their use," he stated pointedly."

"Agreed," Charles sustained, rolling the possibility over in his mind and perhaps the likelihood of a meeting with Zezinho and crew, wherein reading architectural plans.

"If we could schedule that to everyone's earliest convenience then we could move forward, " Ed concluded.

Zezinho and Raimundo arrived early the next afternoon, freshly bathed and laundered in their very best t-shirt and shorts and displaying clean feet, slipped into their "dress' flip flops. Ed had instructed us to clear the large living room of its furniture, hauling it to one side so that he could open a few plans on the floor. We welcomed our visitors, walking them over to the oceanfront veranda where coffee and refreshments were waiting to fuel our afternoon, all of us deep in wonder of how our meeting was going to turn out.

"I'd like to thank them for coming please" Ed began speaking, intently.

"Ele gostaria de lhes agradecer por terem vindo até aqui" I paraphrased.

Zezinho and his buddy Raimundo, who was to be his partner in this endeavor, sat gingerly poised on one of the teakwood benches.

"O prazer é nosso..." they replied, stating that it was their pleasure as we ceremoniously exchanged smiles and courteous body language.

Ed made brief statements, as far as expectations and project structure were concerned, following it up with requests for suggestions from our guests and in this way the afternoon progressed. Ed proved to be extremely mindful of local customs and ways, being that he premised every proposition with prompt follow-ups of an unassuming nature like: "Could you ask them if that sounds right," or, "how would they usually go about this in their experience?" The initial timidity of our guests eased-up somewhat and they became more relaxed and forthcoming.

Financial arrangements as to how payments would be made and at what pace were discussed and then which items would be sourced locally and which we'd import and supply. It was a long and tedious translation process but I was closely tuned in and taking notes. Roughly three hours later our guests were departing with the promise of returning the next day for a presentation of the project itself.

After dinner, over coffee on the veranda, we came to the agreement that our meeting had met its objectives.

"What did you think of the day Ed? Did you find communication flowed to your satisfaction?" Charles inquired.

"Very much so," Ed replied, in his polished manner. "I think it was brilliant. I very much enjoyed meeting Raimundo as well - he seems like a bright chap". And then added courteously nodding towards me "Thank you for translating this afternoon Paula".

"You're welcome," I replied, happy with his acknowledgement - "I'm wondering how I'll get on tomorrow with more specific terminology," I added. "but I'll do my best."

We reviewed plans for the next day while sipping on port and a few formalities later, we were all off to bed and in one accord - that our day would begin with breakfast, 8:00 am.

***

It was likely just past 7 a.m. as I was heading back from my beach walk, when I spotted a tall, quirky figure on the horizon standing on the beach, right out in front of the lawn where I habitually practiced yoga.

"Good morning" Ed chirped as I approached.

The human aspect of Ed was much more visible now, his tousled brown hair and plain white T-shirt denoted he was not on a mission currently, but was just a chap taking in the morning breeze on the beach. He seemed much more relaxed in stark contrast to the polished image that he had been bandying before, when we had first met back in April. We hadn't really had a chance to talk on our own and I was aware that all he knew of me was my social-face as well. From the general context of conversation at mealtimes and around the Graham's, he had surely gathered that I had 3 near-adult boys, was divorced and lived with two of my sons in

California. He had likely also surmised that I was not afraid of making a fool of myself, as one night from our previous trip had proven so vividly. After dinner, Analida and I had put on loud music and were dancing and singing unsynchronized lyrics at the top of our lungs, along with Lilly and her friends in the lounge. Charles later censured Analida, stating that we should be more mindful of our behavior around guests, as he had caught a vibe of discomfort coming from the engineer. I was quite aware that the world Ed belonged to was different than the one I lived in. He seemed to follow a ceremony for everything and his demeanor emanated the incense of private boarding school, whereas I was just coming into my own and proving to be as free-spirited as they come.

"Good morning" I replied… "you're late," I added teasingly.

An expression of perplexity came across his pronounced features, just before I elucidated.

"Well, you missed yoga practice, and more importantly a delicious exploratory walk along the beach." I grinned a salty smile.

Confusion melted into what would be the first non-work affiliated laugh I witnessed come across his face, refreshingly boyish and authentic.

"Oh … well my apologies, I'm not sure I was advised of that part of the program." he proclaimed in kind.

"Well you have quite a feat ahead of you - how could you get through the day without a little dose of beauty and deliciousness to start the day?" I speculated, lightheartedly.

"*Deliciousness*?" Echoing my words, he repressed a brief chuckle and regaining his wit added, "Well I apologize, but I'm afraid the 24-hour journey halfway around the globe might have blunted my ability to awaken with the birds and express my appreciation for umm… *deliciousness*," he offered, allowing his snarky British tone to come through enough to keep the humor going.

"That's fine," I conceded. "I'll expect you tomorrow at 6:00 am for yoga and we'll go from there."

"Ooooo no, no.... no yoga for me. I can't even touch my toes and I'm hopeless at that kind of stuff." Ed volleyed back, seemingly reaching the limit of his spontaneity.

Just as I was filling my lungs, to offer him my spiel about how yoga is not just about touching one's toes, he pressed on unabated "...but if I'm awake, perhaps I could join you for the walk bit."

"Fine," I said - quickly succumbing to his yoga aversion. "A walk it is then..." I added for closure, shifting my feet toward the direction of the breakfast table now.

"But that's if I'm awake by the time you go..." he added his admonition as if it were small print in an advert.

"I'll give you a courtesy wakeup call if you're not..." I called over my shoulder - now thoroughly enjoying our matinal exchange turned into virtual arm wrestle.

After breakfast, Ed took a place at the dinner table to examine his drawings while Charles paced the deck and took calls from his office in the UK which was 4 hours ahead. Our designer calculated and made notes and wore an expression that clearly indicated a warning to not interrupt his thought process, so I made myself scarce but available. Close to noon, Charles resurfaced to announce that lunch would be served within the next hour. I wandered in joyfully, refreshed from my morning routine on the beach and having caught up on some mortgage files while listening to Tibetan mantras in my room as the curtains billowed under the warm breeze.

***

Our crew of two arrived just before 2 pm and were quickly enrapt, taking in the giant plans being unraveled on the floor, where we had previously cleared the furniture as instructed, the white cement floor now serving as the perfect platform. The first large drawing read: "Structural Arrangement - Project 145". The years of claimed boat building experience seemed to vanish before Zezinho's eyes. Eyes now dazzled by the perplexing amount of small numbers and minutiae notated throughout the drawing. Ed was undisturbed providing a calm and reassuring explanation to each detail, requesting they relate what their understanding of the drawing was in Portuguese to me. He was patient and allowed for long periods of silent assessment, encouraging Raimundo when he pointed at something and explained what he understood of the plans. As the presentation progressed, Ed became ever more literate of the expressions on their faces, discerning when the lights were on and when there was a complete lapse of understanding. Ed was acutely aware of these telltale signs and paced his presentation accordingly.

When it seemed we all had taken in the drawing at hand, it was neatly rolled up and we were introduced to a second drawing marked: "Frame Lofting - Project 145". The scale was 1:1 so the sheets of tracing paper fit into one another like a large puzzle. In this instance, it was clear the lights had come fully-on, the men's features illuminating with understanding whilst Raimundo and Zezinho busily exchanged in agreeace of each other's comments in enthusiasm, in an exchange that required no translation. The afternoon went by in an exercise of communication and individual perceptions that left us all pleasantly fatigued. Tired yet utterly inspired by the perspectives we had viewed and the tasks that lay ahead. The consensus was that we were off to a good start, realizing at a deeper level it would be no easy venture ahead. By late afternoon we were all ready to disassemble and reconvene the following day. We agreed to come by Cajaíba to check out the spot the following morning where Zezinho proposed the boat be built and concluded that from there we would discuss the next steps of the process before parting ways for the evening. Charles was exhausted and all of us were quick to bid each other goodnight and retire to our suites.

***

The house, as well as all the suites in the Barra Grande house face east and sunrise pours directly in through the double doors that give entrance to each. Depending on the time of year, the golden pink hue graced the rattan doors of these quarters shortly past 5 a.m. The lawn stretches majestically from the deck of the rooms to the romantic thatched-roof kiosk on the sand, punctuated by tall palm trees, meticulously manicured by a local who climbs up their tall core every so often, feet girdled in a thick rubber band wielding a stone-sharpened machete. The sinuous silhouettes of the trees against the backdrop of the sunrise truly instill a sense of marvel and of being in paradise. The house was built using mainly large wooden trunks, bearing the unique characteristics of their original form. The sliding rattan panels at each entrance allow in air and the sound of the ocean, making slumber in these quarters especially magical.

This morning specifically, the tide was receding, revealing treasures the ocean had left behind the night before. The head-on breeze graced each asana I performed that morning, adding an extra sense of liberation and release as I held onto them. That night, like many a night, fear had crept over me in my sleep and with a sinking sensation in my stomach I'd awakened from a nightmare where I had been inside a crumbling building. Following the fidgety meditation practice, the realization was that I was determined to find peace right where I was - no more waiting around for things to change - I was out to *make* them change from the inside out and be content along the way. The repercussions of the past few years, the stressors of fending for myself and my children, doing whatever it took to get by, were still being processed in my unconscious mind, but I was using every tool in my tool box to aid the process - thus the newly re-found habit of waking up and heading straight into yoga and meditation. I had discovered yoga when expecting my first child at age 22 and it had proven efficient in holding me together through navigating three raging little boys under the age of five through broken bones and stitches and trying to stay connected with who I aspired to be. Years later this practice once again became my guiding light and oasis.

I rolled my mat up and walked it back to the deck where I slipped on my flip flops, releasing my curls from their band on my head, as I glanced over to the third bedroom on the ground floor. I wasn't sure what time the clock showed but knew it was time for my walk. I made my way to the sliding door and hesitated for a second while I decided what to do. Should I knock or...? I cupped my hands around the side of my eyes to shade the glare and peeked in between the wooden reeds.

"Hello?" the enunciation had barely left my mouth as I was being mindful not to startle our British boat engineer.

I shifted the weight on my feet, looked over my shoulder as if to take inspiration from the palm trees and tried again with a little more enthusiasm.

"Wake up call...?" I shyly uttered as my eyes grappled to adjust to the darkness within the dormitory. Gradually, I began taking in the form of a sleeping bundle laid under sheets - one large foot heroically peeping out from underneath. No response.

"Edward!" I asserted boldly, just as he was rolling to one side, causing him to leap up from the bed, fighting the sheets off of him as if under siege - sheer alarm on his face. He squinted towards the door desperately seeking his interloper, until at last his eyes caught focus of my smiley face and waving hand through the wooden reeds.

"Hi!' I said enthusiastically now. "Time for a walk!" I blurted half regretting my attempt to awaken him.

His eyes rolled back into his head, as he plopped himself heavily back onto his pillow with a grunt, which spake a mixture of "fuck what a fright" with "fuck I forgot". He lifted his forearm across his face, sheltering his eyes from the sunlight streaming in through the reeds before mumbling a chastened, "I'll be right out".

***

The matter of having dogs at the house had been discussed scrupulously and Analida was vehemently opposed to the idea of stray dogs roaming around her property. She pouted when she explained that she felt sorry for them - but would have nothing to do with the ticks, fleas and other inconveniences that they could bring with them, such as - well, poop on her beautifully manicured lawn. Being the dog lovers that they were however, she eventually talked herself and Charles into ordering three Vizslas from a regional breeder. Snap, Crackle and Pop were siblings from the same litter - Pop being an afterthought as he would likely be put down as the leftover runt. They were a rarity in achieving what any dog owner could possibly wish for - well-trained, obedient, and neutered as they were, they knew better than to pee or poop on the lawn and were not too jumpy - or at least they knew to discern who was game to be jumped on and who was not. After the initial fierce wagging of tails and shifting of paws in their greeting ceremony, they would - if not otherwise engaged - retire to their business of looking flawless, strewn across the deck that matched their shiny red-brown coats perfectly. This particular morning, they were going about their usual business of restlessly waiting in their kennel for Roberto, their caretaker and trainer to come release them for their walk on the beach.

Ed approached the kiosk that perched over the boundary between the lawn and the sand in large strides - looking down attentively, placing attention on his every step, almost as if avoiding landmines that were invisible to the rest of us.

"So, is it a habit of yours to sneak up on innocent people in their slumber?" he queried, in a playful tone that revealed a trace of annoyance.

"No." I shot back plainly. "I choose the more slothful types" I mused.

A smile, clearly aborted mid-birth, almost positioned itself across his face, but he managed to catch it just in time lest his delight at my comment be revealed.

"Which way should we go?" Ed asked, starting toward the ocean.

"Let's go left!" I decided.

"No, I mean right" I corrected, watching as he started-off in the opposite direction.

"Left, left, left I mean!!!" I released a bubbly giggle, tickled that he was disoriented by my marching orders. I enjoyed the uptight awkwardness so naturally exuded by him.

We veered to the left, but early in our trek he warned he could not walk very far, stating that he had lots of planning to do for the day and was suffering from some freakish condition in his knee which he was elated to describe to me in gory detail, amused as he was by my shrieks of disgust.

"So, tell me about Ed Burnett" I began, having duly acknowledged his protests and ailments.

"There's nothing to know really..." he returned uninvolved, in a retort to suggest an end to such talk.

"Ok...where did you say you're from again?" I pressed on.

"Well, I was born in Ashford, a small town in Kent, and raised in Falmouth, where my parents owned a chandlery and live to date." he expressed without much interest ...all quite uneventful."

"Oh, right... and how was that?"

"It was alright, you know, I grew up..."

"I figured as much...thanks for that." I replied in earnest. I caught on to his discomfort and deftly shifted topics.

"Oh! Look at these slimy creatures!" I interjected, coming to a bright pink, slightly lilac, jellyfish-like organism that lay agonizing on the wet sand. "I wonder if they burn you like the big jellyfish do?"

"Hmmm...might do," Ed replied, now towering over the little colorful blob I was pointing to with interest.

"It's nice it's low tide huh? I love exploring all the pools and things that were under water just hours ago".

He looked out over the ocean with a slight squint, as if assessing my comment, then shrugged his shoulders. "Ya…" he droned, barely audible, maintaining his long-legged strides that left me consistently half a body length behind him.

I walked as fast as I could to try to decrease my disadvantage in relation to him. We carried on silently, my steps in double time to his own.

"So what does a day in Totnes look like? Do you get out much, what do you do with yourself?" I was hoping to bond with our boat builder as I was much more interested in making an acquaintance than keeping the formal work protocol going.

"Well, you know, it's a small town - I work and I keep few acquaintances." He said in short. I sensed that questioning any further would turn our conversation into an interview.

I nodded and we walked along silently for a while until I ventured "And what are you planning for today, are you thinking we might actually put two pieces together by the end of the day?"

"You know, " he offered, stopping short in his tracks. "I think I'll head back to the house and work on that. Will you be carrying on, or…?"

Having been met with standoffish and monosyllabic grunts thus far I surrendered: "I'll carry on" and quickly appended, "thanks for your company" restarting my steps in the original direction to maintain equanimity.

Ed averted his gaze and half nodded. His lips drew a fine line producing a smirk that could have easily been taken for pain or amusement, or both, as he started back in the direction from which we came.

***

We had planned 5 days for this trip which we deemed would be enough time to get the ball rolling with the project. When Edward, Charles and I arrived to Cajaíba that afternoon, Zezinho was alone.

"Where's Raimundo?" we asked in unison.

Zezinho pressed his lips together as if to repress a smile. "Oh, ya... he had to go home".

"Oh, right... but we'll see him again?" I asked, assumingly yet seeking confirmation of that assumption.

"Well, it depends on if you'll be here Monday afternoon," Zezinho stated hesitantly, knowing that we were in town for only two days more. "Raimundo lives in Valença which is about 2 hours from here by road" explained in his colloquial Portuguese. I translated the bits as we conversed, but still there was a waft of confusion in the air as to why Raimundo was absent. Seeing our expressions of perplexity Zezinho went on to elucidate the matter. "Well, you see, Raimundo is known to be quite the drinker given the opportunity" he stated plainly, "and he married a woman who is a church goer and won't let him out of the house on weekends, which is when everyone drinks - so he has a curfew - you know, to keep him from bad company...".

The three men erupted into laughter. Zezinho, having had the courtesy to hold his laughter til Charles and Ed were caught up through my translation. In between breaths he added - "so he has to be home Friday by 2 and can't come out again til Monday at 2." They shared a few seconds of cacophonous laughter.

Most women in this community do not enjoy the equality that women enjoy in America or Europe, as far as their social experience and freedom. Bahia however, is known for the occasional mama-type authoritarian, and those women reign absolutely supreme in their homes. They are wise, strong-willed, respected and for sure the only women who would ever get away with telling a man what to do in this part of the world. Early on, girls are trained to help with tasks at home, learning to cook, wash and clean amazingly well, often using these attributes to lure in a potential spouse. More recently however, despite a somewhat conservative upbringing, girls are being exposed to a more lewd culture, where women are objectified. This is dominantly disseminated via television, cable tv and the internet, and sexualization often occurs on the early end of their teen years, making teenage pregnancy a very common occurrence. It is true also that the bucolic rhythm of tropical living lends itself naturally to early parenthood - quite commonly before marriage. The confluence of conflicting values, along with the impact of the social change brought on by modern means of communication, create a pretty unique mix in a community generally known for being a melting pot like Bahia.

"Oh dear," Charles suddenly realized, "I hope we didn't cause trouble for him yesterday!"

"Nah," Zezinho said, still smirking. "She opened an exception, since she knew it was for work."

The amusement disolved into a quick tour of jackfruit trees that were flourishing on the peninsula. They are one of the many trees native to the region that bear a commonly used timber in the boatyards, due to their abundance, resilience and availability. We walked a good part of the way along the shoreline, where all the boatyards are set up. Most boats are built directly by the beach so as to facilitate launching, which is done by a few dozen grunting men, heaving and rocking the boat down wooden tracks that have been doused with soap and grease and launched onto a rising tide.

The little village breathed boatbuilding. There were piles of timber, many bits insinuating their future use, strewn into what initially seemed like random piles. As our tour progressed, Zezinho explained that each pile belonged to a different family and that many times bits or parts were passed down from father to son, or exchanged, but that everyone owned their own piles. Like most every other villager, Zezinho had never been to boat building school, but as the social structure of the village dictated, being the eldest son of a renowned boat builder, Zezinho would carry on the family heritage and continue the family business. Of course what we had not known at the time, is that Zezinho, even at his ripe age, had never built a boat in his own boatyard, or even established a boatyard of his own. Rather, much like the other locals who, even if not encumbered with building a boat for a client, had been summoned for other labor like heavy lifting or stepping a mast or to help in a launch. We later found this to be a great encumbrance and the cause for a year's delay in our endeavor.

"Where is *his* boatyard?" Charles inquired thoughtfully.

I began the translation.

"We can choose a spot to build along the waterline - somewhere around here." Zezinho continued hurriedly, making a general motion with his hands indicating a broad berth of flat unused land - "this is a good spot", he concluded, suggesting what appeared to be a spot with no signs of previous use.

"I'm not sure I'd like the boat to be built in the water." Ed confessed. He seemed to be pondering the case as well as the ramifications of Zezinho's suggestion at the same time. "Can we build back a few feet from the waterline?" came his suggestive query.

Zezinho started towards a plot of vacant land across the way that lay next to a small structure. Judging from the chipping layers of weathered paint, it had clearly been painted several different colors over the years - there was a faint inscription: '*Casa da Fe em Deus'- House of Faith in God,* the hand painted lettering read.

"This plot belongs to my father" said Zezinho enthusiastically shooing the chickens roosting in the sawdust that lined the floor of the adjacent lot which housed some vintage saws and woodworking tools.

Ed gave the plot an approving once over and emitted a nod of agreeance.

***

Plot chosen and plans discussed, we left our visit with the promise that we'd be back in a few months to check on progress, which entailed finding a proper keel piece, starting work on a few frames and perhaps lead-on to a mock sternpost assembly.

That evening we enjoyed dinner and all seemed in good spirits. The fact that the Grahams customarily kept an impeccable selection of wines seemed to aid in the release of any tensions the day may have evoked and there was enough energy still about for all of us to be engaged in an after-dinner game. It was something akin to a limbo broomstick game that Ed had uncharacteristically shared with us. I excused myself as early as good manners permitted, feeling somewhat worn out after the long day of interpreting stretches of conversation in Cajaíba, as well as negotiating a round of pretty stiff Caipirinhas before dinner, and retired to my quarters.

***

The day shone in with encouraging radiance. I glided through my *vinyasas* and spared no time in getting on with my walk. I had decided to stay an extra two days, but a group of people, including Mr. Burnett and my two sons, were leaving that morning. As I walked onto the beach to greet the sun, now glistening on the ocean with the golden hue of sunrise, I stopped to contemplate the day and take in a deep breath of silence. I felt burdened, not only by the reality that I didn't know the first thing about boat building, but that I was going to be flying home to a *job* in two days that was not of my heart's calling. Deep inside I knew I was in the midst of much needed change in my life. Some were major changes that I had been putting off and others that I simply didn't know how to go about making. The onset of fear, doused with a thick layer of doubt, made me feel a little sick, despite the glorious day before me. As I was deciding whether to hold back the tears or release them in a torrent of vulnerability, my knees buckled violently up from underneath me, as two of the dogs bolted me from behind full speed.

"Fuuuuck!!!!" I exclaimed, utilizing an expletive I rarely vocalized. As I spun around daunted in an attempt to avert another violent run in, I saw Ed arriving with dog number three.

He tightened his pace, hurrying his last steps in my direction as if coming to my rescue. His expression, part concern - part amusement for the scene he had just witnessed, including the crude interjection he'd just heard leaving my sweet little mantra-chanting mouth.

"Oh dear... I'm afraid we've disturbed your deep state of meditation - I'm so sorry," he apologized, half tickled as he approached - "Are you ok?" he appended in legitimate concern.

"I'm alright…" - I stated - still annoyed at being startled but enchanted with the mix of humor and concern that composed his expression. I didn't know what else to say really and stood there sort of guarding my legs from any further collision, as the dogs excitedly frolicked around us anxious for their walk.

"Have you been on your delicious walk already or…." he left the inquiry hanging as I replied in grunt-like fashion and then mumbled a nearly inaudible: "no… let's go".

Our walk included stopping at every jiggly, bobbly, wiggly thing that had been left on the beach by that morning's tide, punctuated by conversations about the horrendous growth under his kneecap. I shared my expert recommendations on how to flex and roll his feet, favoring the full range of movement in his step as opposed to slapping his feet down like a primate which restricted the natural movement of his hips. I modeled a few steps to encourage him, and he tried to imitate, but his attempt was so hopeless we ended up laughing and mocking each other. He told me about his black lab Susie, who was his family, his trusted wingman and sailing companion and ran through a few of the points he wanted to bring up and clarify with Charles before Charles had time to become confused by too many questions floating around his head. Eventually, we turned back to the house in order to get to the breakfast table at an acceptable time so as not to keep the Graham's, ever punctual, waiting.

***

First email exchange on Aug 16, 2011
Subject: *Absolutely no Business Content*
Ed!

I hope this finds you well at home and in the sweet company of your trusted companion Susie. I especially chose the title of this email so as not to be mistaken for the wretched business client who interrupted your much-needed rest at home.

Needless to say, I burst into laughter upon finding Charles' lengthy email to you filled with questions regarding our next steps just a day after you departed. You were indeed correct when you predicted that on our beach walk weren't you?

I, on the other hand, find myself perfectly entitled to bother you seeing as I'm neither a client nor business associate in any way. The special coaching on the catwalk and the uncanny wake up calls I provided you with were entirely gratuitous. Therefore, no business relationship at hand.

I didn't look you up on Facebook as in thinking it over better, I considered that reserved as you are, you might feel invaded. You are welcome, however, to look me up in case you agree with the conclusion reached in my earlier paragraph 3.

The weather has been quite pleasant since you left, but terribly boring without your stupid broomstick party games to amuse us after dinner. I'll be sure to introduce that to the next dull dinner party I attend and make sure to credit you for it.

Do enjoy your time at home and send news if you have a minute.

be well,
Paula :)

Reply:

Hello Paula,

Thanks for the note. I got back yesterday lunchtime and am now having a chilled-out morning in the office working through the various emails. Charles was indeed pretty quick off the mark with his! I now need to edit the summing up letter I wrote on the plane...

Susie is in a grump with me for abandoning her for so long over the past couple of months, she needs to go to the vet for an injection soon too so that won't help. Pic attached.

Quite happy to be Facebook friends. I don't put much on it, and won't feel in the least invaded.

Keep practising the broomstick thing, it's a good one for livening up a boring party. I for my part am pointing my toes and wiggling my hips - dog somewhat disturbed but she will get used to it!

All the best,
ED.

January 2012: The Purple Heart Keel

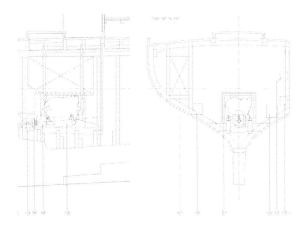

Kathini

A story of love, loss and a little boat building

The next few months were about looking into purchasing fastenings for the framework. We had decided that Zezinho would choose a prized bit of timber from which we would fashion the main keel. Ed provided me with a list of sizes and types of fastenings I was to provide for our next trip down. My days were filled with work on mortgage files and research on where to obtain these fastenings in the sizes and shapes as specified by our designer. I quickly learned that according to the standards held by Mr. Burnett every nut and bolt that would go into this project would be of the utmost quality. In my lay mind, buying an infinite array of shapes and sizes of bolts in quantities ranging from 500 - 2500 would have been complicated enough, but the main requirement was that they all be made of C655 or C651 which is a high silicon bronze, corrosion-resistant alloy used specifically in marine construction, not available however in Brazil, let alone in Bahia.

In the midst of preparing the logistics for our next trip down, I was tending to Charles' expectations standing in as project manager. He wanted a list of the timbers in stock, classified by element in which they were to be used - complete with date of felling, sawing and arrival. To be included in this spreadsheet were costs per job, unit costs, state of manufacture and forecast of time and cost, along with the cost of direct and indirect materials and labor, overhead and updated units completed - all conveniently expressed in a multi-colored, multi-currency Excel spreadsheet that I had zero experience in creating.

Meanwhile, a call a week to a small flip phone that was provided to Zezinho was in order - to check in on progress in real-time. There was no cell phone service or internet in Cajaíba per se, but I could often reach him if he was in the nearby and slightly more developed town - Camamú. If we were able to schedule a call in advance, he'd agree to be standing at the very end of the pier where there was a slither of service on most days. I had been home for almost a week now and had exchanged an email a day with Charles, in addition to two or three exchanges with Ed - including the friendly arrival email previously transcribed. It was time to call and see how the project was going back in Cajaíba with the collection of timbers for the big construction launch.

"Hello, Zezinho?" I was finally able to reach him one morning, after a few failed attempts.

"Hey Zezinho, it 's Paula."

"Miss Paula - how are you?" Came his reply with enthusiasm.

"I'm well thanks. I'm just calling to see how you're doing with finding the timber for the keel and other bits".

"Oh...no, no, ya, no, I haven't really gotten to do that yet." he said, amidst a chuckle that indicated: *Oh right, that thing I said I'd do and you believed I would, ha ha.*

"Ok... - I understand - has it been raining still or...?" I offered an excuse for his inertia.

"No, no, it's been beautiful since you left - ya, no it's been nice..." he said, entering quickly into a silence meant to separate him from blame.

"Oh right, well I know how things can get, um, busy...." came my second attempt to allow him to agree to a proper excuse and to make his silence less awkward - at least for me.

"Actually, my nephew has been sick and I had to take him to the doctor's office in Camamú one day..." came his lamentable rebuttal.

At least I'd discovered what he'd been up to one day out of the seven since we'd left. Going to Camamú, or pretty much anywhere from Cajaíba, entailed hopping on one of the painfully slow local boats as speed boats were a less economical option of transport in this region. Waiting for a local boat to stop by was a feat in and of itself and would entail calling the boat operator to request a pickup which could take a couple of hours, notwithstanding the dodgy mobile phone service as well if you were lucky enough to get a signal on either end.

"Oh, I'm sorry to hear that. Is it serious?" I empathized, still trying to validate an excuse for the non-work he'd completed.

"No, no. He ate some pizza and he's been throwing up since..." came the guiltless reply.

The next few months my calls went much the same way with Zezinho, until they began to become more and more spaced due to a loss of wind in my sails. I was at a loss for understanding the procrastination. I knew the reputation people in Bahia had for being slow to action, and I thought it was important to respect that fact, in lieu of blowing up with him and burning all the bridges right then and there. It was an exercise in patience and humility, trying to find the right formula that would keep him committed, without showing undue offense toward his lackadaisical ways and that would surely blow the top off the whole project. Instead of calling every week I figured maybe every 10 days would suffice.

"Hey Zezinho, any news?" I paused in hope after the inquiry one day.

"Oh, ya... it's just my nephew's in the hospital. They said it might be a liver problem." he replied assuming this was the news I was after. I expressed my concern briefly before moving on to inquire about the keel piece.

"Ya, I just haven't been able to do that, you know? This whole thing with my nephew has us up in arms." he stated flatly.

The email exchanges between Charles and I contained the flawless spreadsheet structure as envisioned by Charles - but we still had no data to populate it with. Ed was busy with his preparations to deliver a project and then go on its maiden sail with his client in Turkey in October and truth be said I had my marching instructions - all I had to do was follow through with procuring and purchasing the fastenings as specified. I was now prepared to move forward with the purchases as I had found most of what Ed had requested and was concentrating on finding a manufacturer to supply us with ¾' threaded six-foot silicon bronze rods to be used as keel bolts, in a process we supposed would be only a few months down the road.

My optimistic and cheerful, 'it's all good' attitude got me through October, thanks mostly to the sunny California days, which made my job at the mortgage office more palatable. While the office lighting and cubicle layout chipped away at my Sagittarian spirit, the fact I was single and my 'children' were off doing their own thing now, meant the weekends were exclusively dedicated to intense self-care and beach time. I usually left home early on Saturdays, only to return after enjoying a full day of whatever it was I felt like doing. Be it a trip to a museum, nature hike, beach day, or coastal drive, followed by either cocktails or an eventual pot brownie and movie. Along the way I would sometimes meet a fellow adventurer and enjoy his company for a while but dating was not on my chart. Between both marriages, I had been married for 25 years and had raised 3 boys - so this was strictly 'me' time now.

My calls to Zezinho were consistent, but not manic. I was extremely compassionate and even creative in helping him come up with excuses for not having found a keel piece, so we could get on with step one of our project, but he never used excuses - he would just naturally narrate whatever activities his day had consisted of without concern for reprimand.

"You know, I went to visit my godmother in Valença, and I got to playing ball with my cousins and then my godmother cooked my favorite dish for lunch, so I ate a lot and fell asleep on the couch - so yesterday was gone."

He then offered within the space of my utter lack for words - "And the day before, I had to go into town to visit my nephew who is still in hospital and very ill."

Quickly, it became clear that Zezinho was in no hurry to begin this project. When I asked of his interest in the project, he replied "oh, no... this project is a dream come true for me, because the whole town is betting that I can't build this boat... but I can."

My first call to Mr. Burnett came two months after we had all sat on the ocean veranda in Barra Grande to agree what the first phase of the project was to consist of. A conversation that ended up part business, part therapy.

"I'm sorry it took me a while to connect" he offered, upon finally answering my skype call.

"I don't use this contraption often and the cables were all tangled behind the desk..." he explained.

"That's fine..." I replied into a blank screen. I didn't dare ask him to turn on his camera at the risk it would take another 20 minutes to set that up and my plight was brief.

"Thank you for taking my call," I offered. "I just felt you might be able to shed some light on a situation I've come across and that I'm not quite sure how to deal with."

"Of course..." he said, sounding fully present and poised for my revelation.

"Well, I was calling Zezinho every week initially, to follow up on everything and in particular to see how he was doing looking for the keel piece but we're coming into November now and I've seen no progress."

The silence on the other end made me briefly glance at my screen, to check that our connection was still active before I continued on with my concerns. "It's hard enough just reaching him on his cell phone and when I do it's the same story - either it's been raining or it was a holy day, or there was a celebration or his nephew is ill..." I paused a little before I spewed "and it's just so frustrating that I keep following up and there is no progress and I'm expected to send in progress reports and keep moving forward on my end but there is nothing going on there - there is *nothing* going on there but weather! They have not stacked or cut a piece of wood and don't even get me started on searching for a keel piece...." I paused looking for a reaction.

There was an uncomfortable lapse which could have been due to connection or consideration, but his response came as a question.

"And what do you suppose *is* the real issue?" Ed asked, in a pondered, studious manner, as if still considering my every utterance. "I mean, do you think he's having second thoughts, or has he realized it's not worth his time, or is it just that the money's not enough?"

He trailed off his questions to make room for my own perspective to be voiced.

"'Well, I actually asked him outright. He told me that this project is a dream come true for him, but he has prioritized everything else in his life as a barrier to getting started." I surmised. "Charles is starting to lose his patience. I've deposited money to build the shed as requested, and to buy the chainsaws and fuel they need to go fetch the keel piece they need, but Zezinho has not made any effort ….and urgh…" I began feeling flustered again. "I'm really starting to wonder about all this…." I exasperated.

"Listen…" Ed said, in a calm and reassuring manner. "It's not a conventional project. This is a remote job in a community with different habits and these issues will crop up now and again and you'll be fine. Just keep in touch with him and try to get on his side. Be his ally and keep providing Mr. Graham with what it is that he's asking for…"

At this point I crumbled. "He's driving me mad with all the pointless spreadsheets! We have nothing to put on the goddamn spreadsheets! These people work in their own way, in their own little world, from their piles of inherited wood and it's not the way we're used to!" I vented.

"Yes, just... listen..." he cut in. "Keep calling Zezinho every week or 10 days and just make it clear you're on his side. You don't want him to feel like you're his boss supervising him, but someone he can count on to get what he needs to complete the project; meanwhile appease Charles' appetite for spreadsheets - keep producing them and it is what it is - just - listen, don't get yourself frazzled over this - how are you doing with purchasing the bolts?"

The conversation went on for another 10-15 minutes and it calmed my spirit. I came away with the realization for the first time that Ed understood the terrain I was treading like a ranger who leads the city-folk through the woods. He made sure that everything kept moving along and made it clear to me that he would lead whenever needed and also in releasing any stuck cogs in the wheels. He also made me feel that he trusted in my competence, which was as surprising as it was reassuring. My next conversation with Zezinho created a lasting bond between him and I.

"Hey Zezinho, how's it going?"

"Oh, hi Miss Paula..." his voice sounded grave.

"Psh, call me Paula - no need for formalities." I chuckled as I repeated the same words I uttered to him the first time we met. "How's it going with you there? Beautiful day?" I asked inquiringly, a proactive approach to keep the conversation light.

"No, we've had a very sad occurrence in our family..." There was a short, heavy pause. "...my nephew passed away just last night," he pronounced, through what resonated as whimpers meant to hold back the excruciating sobs. The pain of losing an eleven-year-old nephew oozed through his words and it broke my heart.

"I'm so sorry, oh my God, that's horrible. My sincerest condolences to you and your family. Did he belong to your brother, or...?"

"No, he's my cousin's son, but we're all very close here and he was like a son to me - we're all devastated."

In Brazil, we are all raised with the custom of calling all close friends of the family uncle or aunt and it is not uncommon for an adult to scold or protect a child like it's their own in the absence of their guardian. In a village like Cajaíba, families are knit even tighter and they are firm believers that it takes a village to raise a child. Being a community of just over 1,000, they share their sorrows and joys very closely - in essence, this community is truly a family and the familial bonds dictate the sociological landscape of this colorful little township.

Zezinho explained to me that his nephew had actually been diagnosed with a congenital liver dysfunction after having felt sick rather consistently over the past few months and once diagnosed his end was brief to the dismay of his young parents who were barely 20 years older than their oldest child. The village was mourning. My calls were now more personal in content and I let Zezinho know I was calling exclusively to see how he and his family were doing with the loss. Christmas was now only weeks away and all our first semester of boat building had produced was an awkwardly improvised zinc shed, on what was seemingly a random patch of land that the local chickens appropriated as roosting ground.

***

Keeping Charles at bay, while giving him the impression that the project was making progress, though at an extremely slow pace, became impossible. The annual family trip to Bahia was quickly approaching. Christmas and New Year's Eve were a Brazilian tradition that Analida made sure to perpetuate in the family and the Graham's customarily invited one or two families plus immediate family members and a few stray friends to partake in what was a luxuriously relaxing and beautiful holiday season. Packed with all things delicious, from gliding across the greenish blue waters of the Camamú Bay in water skis, or in the sexy little Italian Riviera-style boat Analida had gifted Charles one anniversary, to the long lineup of fresh salads and atypical local dishes that were served buffet-style for all 40 guests in the main dining room. Large beautifully decorated dishes were displayed upon the custom-made, solid wood table, that was crafted especially to accommodate such a crowd. In Brazil, January 1st often celebrates Iemanjá - an African deity, syncretized with a catholic saint Our Lady of Seafaring (Nossa Senhora dos Navegantes) with offerings and the celebrations by seaside are so beautiful and significant that participants have adopted the tradition of wearing all white on New Year's Eve and bringing candles and flowers to the beach, to light and make wishes for the New Year. With the nearing of the holiday season and guests to take around the bay in the Lillibelle, Charles was anxious to show his boat project off to his guests.

"This is preposterous!" he protested in his thick, British accent that exuded the polish of an aristocratic education one late November afternoon over a phone call. "I mean, what is his problem?" I had naively offered the nephew story to create room for some compassion but to no avail.

"I understand, and it's horribly lamentable - but didn't he die over a month ago? What did he do the months before and the month since?" he queried sensibly.

Charles is a sensible and cultured man. Far more compassionate and understanding than one would expect in the high-powered investment world, where he touted his extraordinary networking skills. Charles could hold a conversation with anyone, from the doorman to the prime minister in the same candid and involved manner. All invariably animated by his personal collection of precisely dated historical anecdotes, quotes and trivia which was his undeniable trademark. Such was his delight, as he would recite witty limericks in jest of notable historical characters, imitating their accents and other humorous mannerisms, or his penchant towards academic history, with questions like: 'Does anyone know which of the Dakotas first became a State after a squabble with Great Britain in the early 1800's?' A typical attempt of his to get the dinner conversation rolling with our collective children and friends, all in their mid-teens or early twenties and whom one might suspect were far more interested in Beyoncé and Backstreet Boys trivia than in the Dakota purchases. That being said, he would many times possess the only authentic chuckle of joy amongst the guests at the table - unless they were fellows from his boarding school days.

Charles was not having it today, it was time to play hardball. "Well, you can tell him that the project is off then. If he's not interested we'll find someone who is." His words came like rumbling thunder announcing a storm. "Or I can just purchase a yacht anywhere, Analida has rightly mentioned that more than once, I don't know why I insist..." he ranted in dismay.

I remained quiet on the other end of the line, knowing that he was more than entitled to be cross and frustrated with Zezinho and the whole exercise we had just been through, building the shed and procuring the bronze bolts. We ended this particular conversation with the understanding that we would all go for our usual year-end holiday and give Zezinho one last chance to get his horses underway or that would be the end of that.

**

Rainy season extended well into December in Bahia that year and heavy rains were now the main reason we were given for having no progress at the yard. Zezinho had been instructed to find a main keel piece measuring at least 12 meters in length and 40 cm across, in one of the noble timbers of the region, that would lend itself best for the task of being the backbone of the 56-foot yacht that Mr. Burnett had conceived. He was also to start with getting plank stock sawn, stacked and drying as well as finding proper pieces for the stern post assembly. In a nutshell, the keel is the backbone along which you mount the frames, the part that resembles a ribcage. After this 'rib cage' is assembled, the planks go over that to make the hull of the boat. One builds the deck up over that on which to walk upon and makes whatever use of the area under it he finds fruitful. There you have it - boat building 101, and way more than I ever knew about building boats at the time.

My next phone call with Zezinho was likely not the tone Charles expected his message to be conveyed in, but I followed my gut - "Hi Zezinho", I said, faltering a bit. "I hope you and your family have found some comfort after your nephew's passing." I uttered, fully knowing that there is no such thing.

"No", he answered in his usual fashion, "we have found comfort in knowing that he is in the company of the good Lord and his angels."

"He is...." I agreed, allowing a little silent space for acknowledgement, before I carried on with the business side of things. "I wanted to let you know that we - Charles, family and I - will be coming to Bahia for Christmas and New Year's and that Charles feels that if construction is not underway by then, that perhaps we'd better leave the project at that..." I ran out of words to complete that thought.

After a small lag, he replied a little confused, "you mean leave the project?"

My "Mhmmm..." to his question was filled with compassion as well as affirmation.

"You mean not build the boat anymore?" he reiterated.

I confirmed with a long but reticent 'ya....'

"Well, that would be a shame," he continued puzzled. "Does he not want the boat anymore?" he added, his native naiveté missing the threat contained in the action I'd proposed.

"He does," I answered, hesitantly "...but he's starting to think maybe you don't *want* to build it for some reason..." my words tumbled out.

"Oh..no, we've even found a piece for the keel - hopefully Mr. Ed will be happy with it." In Brazil, we use the title Mr. before a first or last name, the former being the more casual.

"Oh!!" I exclaimed, elated. "Why that's great news!" I said, wondering why he hadn't sent the good news ahead before. "Wow, well could you send me some pictures of it and the details and measurements?" I inquired. I had left him my old Toshiba laptop and a digital camera to help with communications.

"No, when my daughter comes for the weekend, we'll definitely do that then. Don't you even worry about that", Zezinho affirmed zestfully.

"Oh, is the laptop difficult to use?" I responded, assuming his intimidation to technology was the issue. "I can give you a few basics when I next come - I'm a great teacher!" I said, jokingly, noting here however, just for the record - that I actually am a good instructor.

"No, no", he said, chuckling at my concern. "My daughter's got the laptop, but also, I don't know how to use it but she does, so I gave it to her to use at school. She's studied you know." he added proudly.

By 'studied' he meant she'd received schooling around those parts and that she was commuting to a local college in Camamú for night school.

"You *gave* her the laptop?" I reacted. His frankness had disarmed me.

"I did! She loved it!" Zezinho sounded thrilled.

"Oh…That's great…." I eased in gently, "but I left the laptop there so *we* could communicate and you could send pictures… so it would be nice if *you* used it." I wasn't quite sure how to politely convey to him that it was definitely not okay for him to give away his work computer to his daughter.

Slightly annoyed, but also highly aware of the fact that I was having this conversation with someone not on Wall Street or in any type of office setting at all for that matter, but a simple fellow doing what had been passed down to him as organically as the color of his eyes, I caved into his manner of reasoning. "Nooo, I'll use it when she comes", he confirmed, "my daughter comes home, on most weekends. It'll be even better because she can communicate with you directly for me, so don't worry, we'll use it." he added enthusiastically. I finally agreed that the weekend was indeed a good time for him to send the pictures and updates.

"And do you have the camera, or...?"

"No, ya," Zezinho interjected, "I've got the camera here somewhere and my daughter - she'll work that too - she's a smart one." He assured me.

We were bidding our goodbyes when he fit in what seemed an important side note before completing the call.

"Miss Paula, I hope Mr. Charles doesn't think I'm dragging my feet or don't want to build his boat for him. This is a dream for me and I'm grateful for the opportunity God has sent me - by his grace, this boat is..." he trailed off, seemingly at a loss for words, but I understood where he was going.

"Of course, yes, please don't worry," I said assuredly. "You understand, Charles lives in a world where there's a timeline for everything and he needs a plan to go by and that's just the way it's done in the city you know?"

I was left with the feeling of mutual relief after that call. It was starting to become clear that it was a lot to pull together under one objective - different lives, distinct customs and quite diverse life perspectives - these were parallel universes converging and I held the maestro's baton in hand.

***

Kathini Graham had been at the helm of a thriving real estate career and had a no-nonsense perspective on life. It was cut and dry for her when it came to business, to her private affairs and to raising her children. Charles and his siblings, therefore, had been educated in the best private schools available and been brought up to not waste time conveying how they felt, or how they thought things ought to be, but to simply "get on with it", an ingrained part of the British cultural repertoire. She arrived in a small plane at the local airfield along with Ginny, Charles' younger sister. They were this year's guests of honor for Christmas and New Year. My boys and I would usually arrive closer to the New Year holiday after our family Christmas, but this year I arrived in time for Christmas and the boys flew to São Paulo to have theirs with their Dad and his side of the family. The holiday never truly began until all the cousins were united in Bahia. There was laughter and ease but every minute together had the flavor of the holidays and the excitement that young hearts feel when they are left unattended with others of the same age and plenty of food and liquor.

As customary, we had lunch and were then offered coffee on the veranda. Analida and Charles had just closed a deal on their neighbor's house which was built in mirror image to their own, thus forming a neat little compound shaped in a U. Charles' mother was rocking herself gently in one of the two heavy wooden rocking chairs that faced the ocean. It was her first visit to the property and to Brazil. From the veranda of the original home, she was contemplating the freshly remodeled twin property before hearing Charles' steps approaching.

"How do you like it all?" he asked his mother catching her off guard.

"I'm wondering why you put that fence in so high," she replied, clearly caught mid-thought. "It spoils the view" .... she retorted, sparing no space for a reply.

"Yes, well Analida thought it would be important to fence the property from the vacant land beside it, so people wouldn't come wandering through here inadvertently," Charles elucidated.

"Yes, well people can wander in from any direction here really, can't they? It's not exactly a gated community," she responded. Her stunning blue eyes were intense and testament to the beauty of her younger years. She reflected back to Charles' original query. "It is quite pleasant here … yes," she concluded.

***

Next day was glorious, as is customary to the region, and I was ecstatic to have the whole day to myself to lounge around the pool, walk along the beach or do whatever my little adventurous heart desired. I ducked into the kitchen early to find Leyla, the family's trusted property manager, stealthily having her morning cigarette while gazing out the window and waiting for her pot of water to reach boiling point. Leyla was a tall, lean and well-kept woman who in her earlier days had been married for a brief period but had lived independently since then. Now, just arriving at 50, she displayed the practicality of a drill sergeant, which came in handy running the house for the Graham's and in a setting where work and attention to detail took no priority.

"Well, well, well…. look who fell off their perch early…" Leyla taunted me fondly.

"Looks like I'm not alone either" I volleyed back.

"No room for slacking here," she said, in her military fashion while scrutinizing the breakfast fruit with trained eye. "Especially now that the queen has arrived," she added, referring to the

Graham matriarch's arrival a day earlier while blowing out her last puff of smoke and extinguishing her cigarette.

"Oh ya, good luck with that, and if you need any help, I'll be out on the beach meditating." I teased, rolling my eyes as I reached across her to fill my bottle from the clay water filter that sat on the sink.

Leyla's attention was now sharp on setting the perfect breakfast table, making sure to include orange and apricot marmalades which were Charles' favorite. She called out the morning's first orders to Girlene, who had just arrived for the day.

Girlene was a slender girl with lively eyes and fiery temperament. Barely in her 20's, she lived nearby, and rode her bike along the beach every day in a shortcut to the house from her neighboring village. "Gi", as we called her, was exceptionally bright and aware of everything that was going on around her. She had an acute ability of knowing everything that was going on in the house before anyone made mention of it. This was especially entertaining to the teens in the house, as it was not uncommon for there to be all sorts of 'hookups' and other mischief amongst them and the guests they'd bring along for the holidays, and Gi knew of all of it.

"Morning," she mumbled, nodding her head in salutation as she moved toward the pantry in preparation for breakfast. The typical Brazilian breakfast (coffee, fruit, cold cuts and fresh bread) was offered to all the guests and generally served from 7am to 10 or 11, or whenever Charles would walk by and notice the table still set and unoccupied and put his foot down. He'd express boldly his annoyance at the fact that the youngsters had stayed up too late and were not making good use of the day. Analida was a lot more understanding of this trait in the young and would intercede to curb his rampaged inclination to wake their children.

"Darling, the kids are on their holiday - let them be." She'd defend them sweetly. "They wake up early all year..."

Their oldest son, Alex, was Analida's son from her previous marriage. Alex was a witty and mild mannered young man, who, like his siblings, had been educated in renowned private boarding schools in the UK from an early age. He had a passion for fashion design, and was just starting his University studies in California, making him the first to flee the nest. William, Charles' first born, was particularly handsome and quiet at first glance. His bolder colors shone through however, when he and my eldest son Carlos would get together. Wandering back from the beach at dawn and exuding the scent of the hodgepodge of liquor they had ingested all night. They'd hobble towards their rooms under the first rays of daybreak for much needed sleep, until a bothered Mr. Graham would come in quoting Winston Churchill, or spouting a limerick in which mostly he took delight. Lilly, their 16-year-old daughter, was blossoming out of her awkward stage, growing fast into the head turning beauty she'd inherited from her proud Mum. Last but not least was their 14-year-old son Patrick, who was living with his uncle – mine and Analida's brother Frank, in the countryside of São Paulo, where he was being coached and developing into a young, world-class tennis player with a local trainer. They were a beautiful clan, each with their own dreams ahead to fulfill.

I headed out across the lawn while the house was still sleepy to find the beach untouched. A golden shimmer skimmed the ocean which was brimming with a full tide. The moon was still in the morning sky, and the air pleasantly warm, though undoubtedly announcing a hot day ahead. I walked to the right of the house, along the beach to find a smooth patch on which to practice some yoga. The lawn wouldn't suit this morning as the house was full and I would surely have to break concentration with morning greetings as the sojourners awoke. Having time early in the morning to center myself before each day had become more than a simple luxury and I knew that without it, small events could easily become triggers to my frail emotions. I glided through my practice and moved on to my walk - several subjects swirling about in my mind - I was happy to be there but things didn't feel settled in my heart yet - I felt like a caterpillar, dormant in its cocoon, struggling for its wings to break through - I didn't know if it was going to hurt, but the wait and the effort were challenging.

The afternoon brought with it our first trip out to Cajaíba, to assess the progress since our last visit in August with Mr. Burnett. This time, it was Kathini Graham, her cotton white hair neatly tucked under a tasteful blue bandana, Ginny (Charles' sister), Alex, Charles and I, whisked across the waters to visit the location where the classic yacht was to be built. Charles had forewarned our guests not to expect much, as he hadn't had significant news of progress thus far - but everyone knew that the boat had been designed by the renowned wooden boat designer Edward Burnett. Ed had recently received much acclaim for the design of the classic barge 'Gloriana" gifted to HRM Queen Elizabeth II on the occasion of her Diamond Jubilee.

"Here we are!" Charles proclaimed enthusiastically, springing tall to his feet. The pier in Cajaíba wasn't very sophisticated and there were only a few craggy concrete steps, dangerously covered in slime, to aid a person climbing onto it. From the rib boat, the pier could tower perilously over one's head, especially at low tide.

Charles and Jorge saw to it that his mother and sister de-boarded safely. Alex and I hopped out with some ease - the first due to his youth and myself due to the fact that I now had two trips experience.

We strolled down the pier that led into what could be considered "downtown" Cajaíba. Although it was a central place of assembly for the townspeople, it consisted mainly of a bright yellow enclosure to the right of the square, that seemed to be an inoperant bar with a tiled dance floor, and to the left what looked like two lemonade stands side by side but was actually a bar, where locals assembled for beer any time of day. Directly adjacent was the town church and a large fig tree, planted in the middle of a rounded curb as to give it a town square feeling, along with a map of the village and surrounding bay.

We walked down the long cobblestone boulevard, which could be considered a main street, running along the waterfront of the village. Seldom was a car seen on this thoroughfare however, as the auto fleet in Cajaíba could be counted on the fingers of two hands. Charles' six-foot two-inch build, coupled with the fair skinned lot of us speaking English, made us conspicuous as we paraded towards the south end of town, taking in the effervescence of this bucolic Saturday morning with marvel. The 10:00 am sun shone well into the high 80's, and was enough to keep us moving forward at a steady pace, as the temperature rose steadily.

"Here we go - watch your step now." Charles warned, as he veered right onto a small footpath through the tall grass and toward the faded structure that was once known as "The House of God", as the faded lettering indicated.

Charles was entertained while verbally transferring his newly gained knowledge concerning the history of this little edifice to his guests, as I continued-on a few steps ahead, now in awe of the large tin structure with zinc roofing erected before me where months before there had been merely a plot of land serving as a near tenantless chicken yard. It was quite an eyesore, despite being quite well constructed, it just didn't belong in that setting. The other 'boatyards' around the area were just incidental building spots on the waterfront, where one would assemble their project according to need. It was on the opposite end of Cajaíba that the boat yards had more established perimeters. Albeit that on our side of town, boat building might have been considered more of an informal affair, there were definitely no boatyards in the area with walls, let alone a roof and swinging gates mounted on either side. It was from the side of this shiny anomaly that Zezinho emerged smiling to greet us.

"Welcome!" he said cheerfully, immediately retreating into formality upon spotting our guests. Zezinho bowed his head ceremoniously, a universal show of respect and greeting irrespective of culture and language.

We exchanged greetings and introductions and then moved into the gleaming structure where we were met by a long piece of unfinished timber strewn across the plot as well as a few kids that had come to see the foreigners. A modestly robust red chicken hurried her chicks out of the way as we stepped closer to what we believed was our main keel piece.

"Here it is..." Zezinho said, displaying a candid stroke of his hand toward the piece, as if revealing the magic of his work over the last six months.

"Right... well yes, and this is the main keel piece I gather?" Charles uttered, taking his hand to his chin in an attempt to demonstrate some degree of involvement.

"Ya...." came my reticent and affirmative monosyllabic response, feeling a little foolish in translating the obvious.

Charles' mother was still enthralled, taking in all the colors and scents, the novelty of being in such a rustic setting. Her stark white and unblemished trainers tread carefully over the sawdust carpet lining the shed floor, as she took a few tentative steps towards the recently unveiled masterpiece, her mind seemingly searching for an articulate comment to express.

"This is purple heart timber" Charles prompted. "The designer seems to be quite impressed with the fact we found one straight piece sized to suit as our keel", he added, examining the bit.

Charles and I began the next question in unison: "And is it in fact...." my version in Portuguese and his in English but everyone understood and shared the query as well as the tension-releasing laughter that followed. Zezinho signaled for us to walk over toward one of the extremities, as he mumbled something that prompted one of the youngsters to hand him a hand saw that was camouflaged in sawdust. We all watched as he sawed off an end bit of the keel to expose its bright aubergine interior.

"Wow..." said Alex, he and Virginia had been on their personal reconnaissance tours but stopped to gasp at the radiant color of the fresh-cut purple heart wood. This, at last, prompted the Graham matriarch to speak.

"It's exquisite...." she proclaimed, and then amended her statement, having considered the role this bit of wood would have in the project, "but it won't be visible at all, will it?" she foretold.

"No," Charles agreed, "It'll be below the waterline. But it is apparently quite well-suited for its part." he concluded. I stepped in for a conversation with Zezinho while Charles and Kathini carried on their conversation and Alex and Virginia meandered around the perimeter of our shed exploring fruit trees.

"What do you think, Miss Paula?" Zezinho asked, picking up on my intention to have a little private interlude.

"Well, I think the complexity of the project is finally sinking in," I said, referring to the time and fray it had taken for just this one bit of timber to manifest.

"No, it's quite a big project and I'm not even sure I've ever built anything like it..." he confessed, letting the statement hang in the air as if considering the reality of it for the first time and feeling its weight.

"It is..." I echoed compassionately. "I realize you must be overwhelmed with the calls and the emails and the templates. I know it's all new to you..." I said, watching Zezinho shake his head in disagreement, yet interpreting the gesture to mean he was of the same accord.

"No, we're gonna get it done," he asserted. "People are saying we can't do it but I'm telling you we can and by God we will!" There was a pinch of resentment in his voice that gave me the impression he was defending himself from an accusation I was not privy to.

We chatted a little more as we meandered over to a tree in the lot behind our yard that was chocked full of cashew fruit - a local delight known as 'cajú'. He chose a few for us to take home for juice and caipirinhas while I translated a few fun facts about the cashew tree for the Grahams who had rejoined us, including the fact that what we call cashew nuts are actually not nuts at all but seeds that if not properly prepared and roasted can be extremely toxic.

As we made our way back through the village, over the same cobblestone drive that had led us in earlier that morning, the intention in my heart was to use the time to understand Zezinho and how things in the village worked. He told me about his daughter who 'had the smarts' and was being educated in the nearby Camamú. He told me about his son Sidney who was off working in a nearby town, a hard-working boy. He confided about his first wife - his children's mother, and described how they'd met and later divorced but how their relationship was basically amicable. We made a right onto the pier and made our way towards the Lillibelle. Jorge, who was known for his ability to arrive and leave without being noticed, had made his way past us and had already untied the boat and was skillfully positioning her for us to embark.

"So, now that we have the main keel piece," I began tactfully to Zezinho, "do you think we can start working towards the stern post assembly?" I asked, searching his demeanor for some inkling of affirmation.

"No, absolutely. Now we're gonna move right along," he assured me. Next time you and Mr. Ed come, we'll have made excellent progress!" His eyes shone with belief in his statement.

"Ok then," I conceded. "We're planning to come early this year," I offered as incentive.

Zezinho nodded his head in nearly wild agreement, adding an affirmative: "We'll be ready! And I'll start working on the planking wood too," he asserted with confidence.

We said our goodbyes, bidding our happy Christmas and New Year wishes and in shaking our enthusiastic builder's hand once more, I assured him there was no need to call me Miss Paula.

March 2012: The Sternpost Assembly

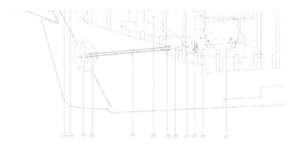

Kathini

A story of love, loss and a little boat building

I f you know anything about Brazilians, it's that we are a festive and happy people who love large family gatherings. Yes, we love large and *loud* family gatherings and there is inarguably an indecent amount of food no matter how poor one is deemed to be. Everyone brings a dish, or an ingredient to a dish, and where there is food - there is celebration. Schools let out for summer vacation just before Christmas, only to return after Carnival, a celebration which is world renowned for its scantily dressed twerking *mulatas* in beautiful street parades. The mulatas are a beautiful mixture of white and black blood. Carnival marks the state of affairs in which Moses found the village after he came down from receiving the commandments in the bible. What all this translates into is, that officially, the year in Brazil begins after Carnival which usually falls somewhere in late February to early March. It's a moving date since it needs to end 40 days before Easter Sunday which is always celebrated on the first full moon of the spring equinox when Catholics believe Jesus rose from the dead. Adding to the fact that in Cajaíba, work weeks were essentially 3 days long, it was already well into February when we finally received pictures of a mock sternpost assembly. Dozens of emails had been shot back and forth between Charles, Ed and I in the meantime, with calls placed to Zezinho twice a week. It became increasingly clear to me that it was of the utmost importance that everyone be kept 'warm' by being included in what was being discussed and planned on all sides.

What had begun as a side job, occupying 4 - 5 hours a week, was quickly starting to overflow into my mortgage file-filled days. With progress starting to show, it was decided that the upcoming visits would occur at determined trigger points within the project of which we had one likely coming up within the next 30 days. The sternpost assembly was soon to be complete, now that the pictures of the mock assembly had gained Ed's approval, and Zezinho and crew were now assembling the actual bits for inspection and working on making a few pairs of frames from the stencils Ed had sent, so that at least 3 of the 40 pairs could be ready for inspection when we arrived.

It was coming up to a year since Marco had been denied residency in the US and his entry visa revoked. I was starting to feel overwrought, juggling liaisons between the immigration attorney back east, whose costs were quickly racking up, with his $600 dollar per hour fees devouring any income I could produce. I felt I was flailing and this quickly tainted my days with anxiety and overwhelm. I found myself waking up at varied hours of the night, gasping for air as if submerged in a turbulent sea of unrest, feeling nauseous, heart racing with fear of how things were going to progress. I was now well into my forties and had not yet managed to get my act together. I felt my children had grown and all I had shown them was two divorces and a lot of struggle.

The question of how I was going to dismount this chaotic merry-go-round, that now stirred my life, made me seesaw between outbursts of anxiety and striving for balance. I prayed, I searched. I thought of my mother's sage advice and her fervent faith. My mother was a beautiful, dark-complected woman with a gentle spirit. She had been born out of wedlock to a native Panamanian woman, who'd been swept off her feet by a rich and powerful Spaniard. She was given up for raising to a modest couple in the small village of Ocú, in Panama. Her biological father saw to it that she had the best education available by picking up all the expenses for her education at the top Catholic boarding school in Panama City. The unique mix between being raised on a farm, connected to the rhythm of nature and agrarian lifestyle, with her studies in a more sophisticated environment where the children of well-traveled businessmen were educated in 3 languages, made my mother a quite well-rounded woman who taught me early on that suffering was an integral part of life and that it must be navigated with grace. She would often admonish me when I would have the typical hormone induced breakdowns that teen girls do.

"Sweetie, life comes with a little bit of everything and you can't just accept the good things and discard the challenging ones. You need to face them both - heroically and gracefully. You don't want to be the person who falls apart in adversity like a poorly made shoe and you don't want to overflow from happiness into crude indulgence when things are well ...you just need to find your balance."

The importance of balance was driven home by the fact my father had fought in the second World War and was severely imbalanced by the presence of what we know today as PTSD. Being raised by my father who left his parent's home at age 13 and then joined the air force displaying a tremendous dose of discipline and dedication, was hard on me. I felt like I was never living up to his standards because after all, who can compete with a man who left home at 13 and crossed the country to settle in the harsh domain of Rio de Janeiro – a cosmopolitan city since its inception, and then went off to war? There was nothing I could ever do to feel relevant – any first prize in running track or learning a new routine in gymnastics, it was all so small compared to packing your life up and going off to war. Like every well-meaning parent, my father would often parade that by saying things like "when I was your age I was working all day and holding two jobs – all I ask is that you bring me home an A."

***

Communications had improved greatly over the months with the regular calls I was making and getting through. Leaving the laptop and camera with Zezinho was proving a worthwhile investment, as all the involved received the encouraging pictures of progress over the weeks. Ed's thoroughness in examining all the pictures I forwarded him was impressive. He was quick to send them back to me with markups of where corrections were to be made. Soon it was decided that what we had established as a trigger point for an inspection had been reached and arrangements for a trip back out began to take shape. Both Ed and I were on a tight schedule as I had a full-time job and Ed was in the thick of his commission to complete the royal barge for delivery. We decided we'd meet at Guarulhos airport in São Paulo and head to Bahia from there.

We exchanged brief emails and set off for our third trip to Brazil.

Tue 2/28/2012, 2:01 AM
Good morning Paula,

I don't know what your travel plans are, but I understand we are on the same flight out of São Paulo at 9:15 on Thursday morning.

Where do you want to meet?

For info, my mobile no. is +44 7970 190759

Looking forward to the trip.

ED

***

I spotted a tall, well-groomed figure taking unusually long strides in my direction when I arrived at the airline check-in area at Guarulhos International.

"Good morning" he said, wearing a somewhat repressed smile while extending his right hand out for a greeting.

"Hi!" I interjected effusively, flinging my arms around him and landing two short and sonorous kisses on either side of his well sculpted face.

"Oh ... huh - hi!" he stuttered, seemingly flustered by my business protocol - then regaining his composure added: "we'd better get moving - we don't want to miss our flight," he said, spinning around and heading towards the check in line, as I galloped behind him trying to keep up with his stride.

"Did you have a nice flight?" he asked, once we were settled in the check-in line.

"I did - thank you. How did your knee behave on the trip?" I inquired, knowing that he had undergone surgery, to remove the 'gunk' that had accumulated under his kneecap, as he had described it.

"It was fine actually - you know, I was laying down most of the time."

"Oooooo.... a business class traveler we have here" I taunted. "Fancy.... meanwhile the translator travels with the bananas in cargo - I see where this is going..." I said, rolling my eyes now entering the front of the queue to check in our bags.

"I travel business class not because I am of any more importance than you, but because after my last job in India, I learned that these long-haul trips for 3 full days of work followed by another long-haul trip home just don't favor my productivity." He defended himself of such indulgence. "I can't afford to be so exhausted when I get back to the office, so I've included that bit in my service contract...." and then added humorously "along with a request for a life-long lasting supply of Hobnob tea biscuits."

"You ask for tea biscuits in your contract?" I burst out in laughter throwing my head back, tickled by the fact that such amenity was included in Mr. Burnett's service contract.

"Well, I don't actually *demand* the biscuits..." he reasoned. "I just throw them in to see if my clients actually read through the whole contract...and for personal amusement..." he added, restraining his smirk.

At that, the next attendant called out an impatient "próximo!" calling out for next in line.

I checked us into our flight and turned around to address an oblivious Mr. Burnett.

"I got us premium seats," I bragged, fanning myself with our boarding passes, once we'd completed our check in.

"Well done!" He replied - not knowing I had used his knee surgery to obtain the benefit.

"Oh noooo... thank *you*..." I replied mischievously.

Arriving to Barra Grande, where the Graham property is located, is not for the faint of heart. Between the 10 - 12 hours of international travel, plus the domestic flight with a layover in Brasilia, and then the trek from Salvador to Camamú, and finally a boat ride to the 'Barra,' (pronounced Ba-ha) made for nearly 24 hours of solid travel, especially for one originating in Totnes in Devon. Add a 4-hour train ride to London and you've got 2 days scratched from the 5 days we had scheduled. We arrived to find the staff with dinner prepared and Olivan waiting smiley-faced, toting a tray with two perfectly iced lime caipirinhas for us.

We sipped on our cocktails, tired but in good spirits, despite a delay in our layover that had set our arrival back 2 hours. Olivan set our bags in our rooms and returned to ask us what time dinner should be served.

"All I need is a shower and I'm ready," Ed disclosed, shooting an inquiring look my way.

"Ya, I just need a shower too... so an hour?" came my *guess-timation*.

"An *hour* ?!?..." he gasped, quickly amending his outcry with a nod of agreement and amending in gentlemanly fashion - "an *hour* it is".

Dinner was served punctually as requested, followed by a light passion fruit flan and coffee on the veranda. The house felt awkward and empty without the usual banter and ceremony that usually filled its spaces so we each headed to our separate rooms shortly before 9:00 pm to get a good head start in the morning.

***

Sunrise lured me out of bed early and I didn't feel it wise to disturb Mr. Burnett from his much needed and replenishing sleep. I wafted past his room as quietly as my bare feet allowed, resisting the temptation to throw even so much as a glance toward the direction of his resting chamber. As I passed the main house, towards the ocean-facing veranda, I slowed down to contemplate a glass of juice or a piece of fruit before my yoga practice when I was suddenly startled by an unexpected and sonorous greeting.

"Good morning!" the voice said, my shuddering body alarmed by the unexpected greeting scoured the space for my interlocutor. A tall slim figure emerged from the laundry area - cigarette in hand.

"Were you expecting a ghost?" Leyla the house manager said, a familiar smirk etched across her thin lips - she seemed entertained by my startled reaction. Leyla actually managed the house from afar, as she lived a few states away in São Paulo, flying out only on occasion, for some hands-on management or inspection when needed, I wasn't even aware she was to be with us that week.

"Oh!" I exclaimed, throwing my head back in laughter, as I walked towards her for a hug and the two customary kisses. "My, and what a beautiful ghost we have here!" I said, taunting her in truth, as she was always so smartly and stylishly dressed.

"Did you arrive last night?" she asked, knowing quite well the answer. My reply just offered her more time to elegantly puff on her long thin cigarette, white smoke filling the air.

"I did! Me and the engineer...yes," my reply now hanging there in awkward silence, as I watched her next statement taking form from her vibrant expression. She gave her head a quick slant, peering at me sideways and mischievously, added,

"You guys don't really think you're going to get this thing built, do you?" she queried doubtingly, looking highly amused while awaiting my reply.

"Well...." I hesitated, not quite sure how to formulate my response that was being blatantly interrupted by her intrusive laughter.

"The whole town is in an uproar about this project. It's been almost a year and Zezinho hasn't been able to put two sticks together! He's so useless!" she gasped, her laughter now becoming an ongoing chuckle. "These people here in Bahia, are you kidding me?" she continued, "they couldn't work on a timeline if their lives depended on it! Why just getting the electrician to come install a light bulb can take months in this place!".

The time it took for her to elicit another puff of her cigarette allowed me the time to get a comment in edgewise.

"Well it's moving slowly, but Zezinho said he really wants to build this boat..." I offered, now feeling a bit foolish.

"Psh, of course he wants to build *this* boat, because he's never built a boat and he calls himself a boat builder!" she was truly amused at the thought that I could for a minute believe that this boat would ever float and her hearty laughter was proof of it.

I wasn't as much offended by Leyla's mocking as I was sorry for everyone involved in the project - Charles' money, Ed's time, and what I was just starting to recognize as a sense of hope in me that this project was leading me somewhere new.

My expression must have displayed the contents of my mind, as a graver tone came over Leyla when she said, "don't worry, now that he built that ridiculous shed around the project, no one will know how badly he messed up!" she assured me, turning away towards the kitchen before calling back over her shoulder with a deflection from her doubts.

"...you gonna take coffee before or after your yoga?"

"After..." I replied, following her past the rattan doors and into the kitchen to continue our conversation.

Within a beat I had a sudden change of heart and decided to take the path towards the beach instead. I knew Leyla well - she was not really mocking me or anyone for that matter, she had simply become far too acquainted with the ways of the local people with whom she'd been working with the past few years and had lost her naivety toward their distinctive behaviors. I too had been in charge of setting up guest rooms and helping with the house in the past and knew exactly what she was alluding to. I guess my sense of reality had been eclipsed by Charles' ambitious enthusiasm and Ed's tenacious leadership. My mind was alternating between thoughts of '*so why do I feel let down*?' to a budding compassion for the real reasons behind Zezinho's building of the shed around his yard... he was the laughing stalk of his town.

I went about my morning ritual and returned with the expectation of finding Mr. Burnett about, tending busily to his notes. To my surprise, his room appeared quiet, the doors still sealed from the night. I glanced over to the breakfast table and noticed it was still mostly set, with the customary selection of fruit, cheese and breads. I made my way up to my newly inaugurated 'princess suite' as I had just anointed it. The recently purchased section of the house had a spacious suite, which took the full top floor, twin to the one Analida and Charles occupied in the original side of the house. Instructions were that I was to occupy this new suite whenever I was there.

"It's the least comfort you can have after a day in that grimy boatyard with sweaty men!" Analida insisted.

I gratefully accepted the oversized room which was light and invoked the ocean breeze through its large, folding wooden doors. It gave me a feeling of joy and comfort, possessing its own oceanfront veranda and hammock adjacent the Jacuzzi in the overtly spacious bathroom. I climbed the stairs and freshened my curls - which were now threatening much dreaded frizz from my having forgotten a hair tie on my way out for my morning ventures.

I walked back across the wooden deck passage that sectioned the two houses and stopped at the first room. I succumbed to my curiosity, bordering on concern regarding Mr. Burnett's whereabouts, and cupped my hands around my eyes to peer in, squinting to obtain focus between the rattan reeds. As I began making out the objects, flip flops, closet, bathroom door ajar... I came across Ed's silhouette in bed - still under the white sheets and looking up at the ceiling with a puzzled expression on his face, as if trying to solve an equation in his head. That very second his eyes happened to meander over to the door and our eyes crossed. I watched his expression turn from initial fright into a glare of disbelief and confusion as he quickly recognized me.

"Oh! Uh...breakfast is ready!" I cried out, turning away quickly and making a beeline towards the kitchen at twice my normal pace. I was embarrassed to think he might have suspected I'd been there spying on him, or something creepy like that. I struck up a conversation with Leyla again who was now in the company of Gi and calling out orders through the kitchen window to Olivan.

"Make sure you scrub the pool tiles today! That pool looks like a slimy pond!" She cursed under her breath, spinning around to find me standing there in front of her.

"You're back!" she squealed. "Where's the engineer? Breakfast is ready," she reeled off perfunctorily.

I told Leyla and Gi what had just happened and we all cracked up at the absurdity of it.

"He's gonna look at you funny all day, Gi cajoled, poking fun at my slapstick misery.

Leyla took the opportunity to remind me of our earlier talk. "That boat is never gonna sail," she began. "Might as well just have fun with the whole thing!" she continued, beaming a look towards Gi for backup and confirmation. "Isn't it true that Zezinho is the laughing stock of Cajaíba?" she asked.

Gi pursed her lips, side-glancing as she twisted her nose - readying us for her ultimatum. "They say even his Dad said he doubts Zezinho will ever build that boat!" and then as if to underscore the fact, repeated in a pitying voice "...his *own* father....".

I saw that Ed was just taking his place at the breakfast table so I made my way around the counter and through the doors to meet him. Before I had a chance to say anything he laid out one of his taunts.

"Should I expect to receive a personal wakeup call daily?" he mocked, a boyish smirk adorning his morning face.

"You're welcome," came my quick riposte, making light of the ridiculous situation and handing him my coffee mug, "sugar and cream but keep it dark please" I smiled.

***

We had been waiting for Jorge at the pier for about 20 minutes when we saw the Lillibelle darting out from the horizon at what seemed an unreasonable speed.

"There he is!" Ed pointed out "Are you sure you told him we were to meet at the pier at 8:30 am?"

"I'm pretty sure I did..." I said, being fully aware that I had mentioned our meeting time twice the night before, when Jorge had dropped us off at the Barra Grande pier.

"Maybe he didn't understand..." I offered - being the inveterate peacemaker. Ed looked at me a bit irritated but then satisfied that we were finally going to be on our way.

We found Cajaíba warm and sunny, the town silent, as we made our way down the pier and over the cobblestone path. Ed's long confident strides positioned him far ahead of me. I walked at my natural pace, unhurried, sensing an odd vibe in the air when we arrived. It was a work day but everything seemed strangely quiet. We veered off onto the little dirt path towards the newly built shed.

"Shed still standing - check." Ed said under his breath notingly, as if keeping score of progress. Zezinho came out to greet us.

"Hello!" he said, as he shook Ed's hand up and down an exaggerated number of times.

"Olá..." Ed replied, displaying a courteous effort to utter some Portuguese. "Could you tell him it's good to be here and I'm excited to see the progress so far?" he asked, turning to me. Zezinho, heeding his request, led us into the shed through the double leafed gate, and waved us over to the keel piece and a few of the frames he had assembled.

"This here is Wilson," he said, gesturing toward a kind-faced man enthralled with his hand chisel and mallet, chipping away at a frame.

"Ohp!" came Wilson's brief reply, his eyes shining up at us brightly from his tanned, leathered complexion. He didn't make eye contact for long before averting his attention back to the task at hand. If he noticed our intent for further engagement he kept it to himself, leaving us to the brief one syllable greeting that is common to the local folk and returning to his work.

"That's Wilson's dog Tutti," Zezinho added, as a white furry bundle grumbled heroically, forewarning us that there would be trouble if we came any closer.

"Oh! Why hello Wilson's helper!" Ed said to the canine, after hearing my translation.

The day's order of business began by moving about the yard with Zezinho, visiting each bit of work that he presented. Ed seemed to be interviewing Zezinho rather than inspecting his work. He was interested in why each bit was chosen and why they chose the tools they did for each task. He examined the frames, acknowledging their good choices, making suggestions where he saw room for improvement and always inquiring how they came to conclude each choice. One aspect that was questioned for example was how they chose to append the bits of timber as they had. Zezinho candidly replied to the questions and Ed stated his concerns, followed by how he might have executed the same task in his own way and the pros and cons of each approach from his own experience.

"I'm a little concerned that the overlay in these joints is so short. I'd like to see them overlap at least 50 cm and also be fastened by 3 bolts - staggered as such." He pointed to where he'd like to see each bolt placed.

I conveyed the ideas in translation the best I could, mimicking Ed's hand and arm gestures that illustrated why and how a longer overlay would provide extra leverage. The day moved along in like-manner, constant and without a break. I did my best to navigate the hunger pangs my protesting stomach punished me with from lack of sustenance.

"What time should we break for lunch?" I gently suggested.

"I think I'd rather work through lunch and we'll just grab something on the way home," Ed submitted, as if we'd be dashing past a few drive-thrus on our way through Camamú Bay in the Lillibelle.

He ignored, or didn't notice my discomfort, moving along with his queries and instructions. "How are they getting along with finding the plank stock? We need to lay those out for drying asap," he instructed cursorily. I did my best, keeping up with his pace throughout the afternoon as expected. All the while allowing plenty of time for Zezinho to reply elaborately in his own tongue to Mr. Burnett's requests - Zezinho's replies invariably starting in the negative. We continued working up until the point when I could tell Ed noticing that the light was beginning to fade from Zezinho's ordinarily bright and encompassing eyes, after I had translated a final directive to him and he drew a blank. It was only then that Ed acquiesced to ending the workday with a simple,

"Ok, no problem - we'll pick up from there, bright and early tomorrow morning."

We crossed town and made our way back to the Lillibelle. On our way, I made small talk with Zezinho who insisted on walking us to the pier.

"So how do you feel after this first day of hands on work with Ed?" I asked.

"Oh, this is important," Zezinho exclaimed enthusiastically. "This is just what I needed to experience, because, you know, those drawings and all - I can't even look at them without my head hurting." We both laughed, poking fun at all of the little numbers and keys and bits that were on the plans.

"Trust me - I know," I spoke in confidence. "I wonder how all this is going to come together as well." I sighed.

The expression on Zezinho's face suddenly displayed sorrow. "People here doubt that this boat will ever float - but it will. I don't know how it's going to get done but by God's grace He will help me to build it". His words seemed to have a layer of hurt and self-encouragement at the same time and gave me the impression that they were in fact the very words he was in need of hearing.

"You will Zezinho," I replied encouragingly. "We will," I added for assurance. "Ed is a good man and he's investing a lot of time and effort into this project because he believes it is possible." I was happy to ride the wave of motivation with him.

We carried on walking a good 4 - 5 steps behind Ed who purposefully forged ahead of us in long strides, clearly enthralled in the mental annotations he had accumulated throughout the day. Jorge's head poked up from between the seats of the Lillibelle instinctively, just as we stepped into range of view. It seemed we had interrupted a nap.

We skimmed the waters as the sun made way toward its closing spectacle for the day. Strokes of pink, with charming hues of baby blue amidst the gray streaks of decorative clouds, were announcing sunset as we disembarked on the Barra Grande pier.

Ed now towered above me reaching back to offer his hand. He cautioned me to climb out in one committed stroke.

"You've got to commit to it! One big committed step - go!" He coached me confidently.

The water was tousling and hesitating could lead to scraping my knees harshly against the raw concrete steps. I followed his instructions and cleared the huge gap in one step.

"It worked!" I said effusively, standing safe and sound at the top of the stairs.

Ed acknowledged my comment with a quick head nod that was also meant as a motion for me to walk ahead.

Our arrival at the house triggered Olivan to bring out the customary cocktails and then lead us to the ocean front veranda for a little spread of freshly roasted peanuts and chips. Olivan loved wowing the guests with excellent service, so he enjoyed hearing us ooh and aah over his timing and perfection.

"Oooh" I said delightedly. "These peanuts are still warm!! And they smell like heaven!" I proclaimed, unaware of the fact that it might not be so much that the peanuts were perfectly roasted as the fact that our last meal had consisted of a cup of coffee, a slice of papaya and a bit of pineapple 14 hours earlier. Ed shifted a bit on his feet, seemingly uncomfortable with the prospect of being treated to cocktails and appetizers while on business, but he quickly succumbed, under the influential odors, the effusiveness of my comments and also having himself adhered to the sparseness of the nutritional timeline aforementioned.

"Por favor, fique à vontade" Olivan urged us enthusiastically, a prompting to enjoy the alluring set up and the final golden-pink hues that now paled in the horizon before excusing himself.

Ed sipped on his cocktail and looked over the horizon stiffly.

"Oh my God, you have to try these..." I urged, as I held out a small hand-carved wooden bowl filled with the salted little treasures.

"Psh...You sound so American," he shot back mockingly, "Oh my God..." he repeated, mimicking me in an exaggerated American accent.

"I'm not American!" I declared in my defense, deflecting any offense that might have been intended by his snide comment.

He looked back at the ocean, squinting as if trying to make something out in the horizon that might distract him from our conversation, and then, still unable to contain himself, he said under his breath, "you sure sound like one" just before taking another uptight sip of his lime cocktail.

"What*everrr*..." I said self-deprecatingly, keenly aware that I sounded like an Angeleno valley girl. After a brief pause from the reoccur I appended, "How are you feeling after our first day?" I was still unsure if Mr. Burnett was moody due to lack of food, or if he had seen signs that this project was a waste of his precious and heralded experience.

Shifting the subject to work made him put on a contemplative face and lift his generously sized nose a bit, as if taking a whiff in the air before he replied, "I'm not sure yet. I mean Zezinho seems ok, but why did Raimundo disappear?"

I reminded him that Raimundo lived in a neighboring town and that he wasn't always available to come to Cajaíba when we were. "Remember Zezinho said he's working on another job in his town?" I suggested.

"Yes, but *why* is he working on another job? Not like there isn't enough work to do around our boatyard..."

I allowed his statement to hang in the air a bit while I contemplated it myself and then emitted a reticent "mmhmm....". Zezinho's comments about everyone saying he would fail at building this boat and Leyla and Gi's comments earlier in the kitchen came to mind.

***

The next day I made sure to make arrangements for food before we left the house. I asked Gi to make sandwiches and pack the breakfast leftovers and joked with her saying -

"The last thing I need is a crabby engineer!" rolling my eyes and enjoying a shared chuckle.

As I turned to head towards my room to freshen-up Gi's eyes followed me with that signature facial expression of hers that said, "I see what's going on around here..." She had this way of reading people that is quite common to the locals - they don't need as many words as we city folk do.

We had a productive day marking the keel out for the 40 frames. Initially, Zezinho had turned about as white as a ghost when he saw Ed rolling out his oversized, crisp, white mylar plans on his dusty vise table. The silence was deafening as our engineer meticulously examined his drawings, furling his wide brow as if to mentally rehearse how he should go about explaining the task for the day. Zezinho and I were holding our breaths in baited anticipation when suddenly Ed popped out of his trance proposing an earnest deduction, "OK! Let's get started?" he said, clasping his hands together and rubbing them as if to express that he had at last reached a plan he believed in.

Zezinho's eyes seemed to glaze over as Ed began to unhurriedly explain the scale of the drawings. He produced a ruler and a mechanical pencil from his briefcase. He pulled out a few pre-selected drawings and introduced them each in a logical manner, stating what they each were showing and pointing out how each led to a more detailed aspect of the previous one and then to a cross section-view that contained the dimensions in more detail.

I saw terror looming on Zezinho's face, so I was especially frugal in choosing my words and explaining to him that which I too was just learning, in the most elementary way I could, so as to instill a sense of calm rather than overwhelm. Ed proceeded heedfully, making sure to keep his words and props straightforward. He kept on at this pace, pausing to allow the concepts to register and just when Zezinho released his brow in an indication that he had finally processed the information - or had at least given into what amount he had processed - Ed said,

"Great! Now let's move over to the keel. Can you ask him to bring a sheet of paper, a marking pencil and his measuring stick?"

He left us exchanging glances as he excitedly pranced over to the long piece of timber lain across the sawdust floor. I transmitted our instructions and watched Zezinho make his way over to a large old wooden wardrobe that served as an all-purpose tool box. As he opened one door, he wrestled some items that were disheveled while he tore a piece of pink wrapping paper that looked like it had previously lodged a sandwich along with a blunt pencil. He pulled his pocket knife out and adroitly carved a point on his newly found writing instrument. He tucked the prop behind his left ear and took a deep breath as we walked over to Ed, who was crouched at the extremity of the keel piece, eyeballing it with one eye closed and the other one squinting.

"Could you ask him which orientation he believes this piece would best serve?" Ed asked.

Zezinho's expression morphed into one of contemplation, after having absorbed my translation.

"In other words, would this be the bow and that the stern or...?" Ed prompted the contemplation further.

Ed took a step aside as Zezinho now positioned himself in a crouch, one eye closed, assessing the question at hand.

"This should be the bow," Zezinho declared at last, confident to be sharing the same perspective as Ed.

I wasn't sure what difference it made at all, but apparently, they were considering where the widest bit of the piece was, according to the shape the frames were ordered in and where the masts were going to be positioned.

The two exchanged a glance of agreement and made a few gestures over the bit of timber, suggesting that they were communicating in a realm only the two of them could understand.

"Ok, well..." Ed said, as he stood up tall to face the next challenge. "So how would he move a bit of timber this big? We need to turn it around because the bow needs to be built that way," he said, continuing, pointing to the front of the shed that faced the ocean.

I looked at him incredulously. "You want them to pick this up and turn it around? It must weigh a ton!" I had pointed out the obvious to which Ed grinned and said, "I'd say it weighs more, but they got it in here from the forest - they should be able to turn it around somehow...".

I looked at Zezinho somewhat reticent about the absurd request I was about to make of him, but when I hit him up with the task, he took no longer than a second or two to consider, then smiled and replied, "of course".

Zezinho had been gone for about 10 minutes when the first of three men arrived. Ed had expressed some curiosity that Zezinho had walked off without much explanation and I taunted him saying he had scared him off the project. Another two men arrived thereafter and soon there were about 12 men jesting and jeering - some shirtless, all in shorts, most in the local rubber flip flops called Havaianas. They were soon joined by others and finally Zezinho showed up about 20 minutes later to give us an update.

"I need two more but most of the men are already buzzed..." and then added, "you know, it's Thursday..."

Ed and I exchanged a silent look, both privy to the fact that it was only about 10 a.m. as well as both holding back a smirk. Zezinho called back, "Oh! Lemme fetch Jorge and his brother in law!" as if intuiting our thoughts.

Minutes later Zezinho came back with the two others, the informal banter now turned to shouts of encouragement and displays of strength.

"Come on! Let's do this you sissies!" one of them shouted.

They exchanged grunts and gestures as they agreed on which way the task would best be performed and then like ants they congregated around the piece. After one throaty command the massive timber was lifted in grunts and yelps. Like cowboys rustling cattle around it went, revolving around its middle, the men taking short synchronized steps in unison on the sawdust floor - turning the bit completely around in its orientation. Before letting the weight down there was a lot of yelping and hissing about the exact timing when suddenly a loud thump announced the end of the operation. The men erupted in boisterous expletives and insults - but they were clearly satisfied with their success. One of them examined his flip flop, now covered in blood because the keel piece had nicked the outer edge of his pinky toe when it tumbled down. Blood gushed from the small but deep gash and he smiled proudly as the others taunted him. Each examined the marks and scuffs the extreme weight had left on their calloused hands and some picked away any skinned bits causing them to bleed and callous up nicely for future use. One older worker was proud to announce he had done the job three beers into the day and then they all went off, pushing each other in their vociferous brawling - back to their normal routines. Ed and I had been standing back in the midst of all the banter, as it was clear they needed no help or guidance in the endeavor whatsoever.

When the noise level went down again to a mere din, Ed looked at me in amazement and said, "Right...." in that way Brits do when they are bereft of words, and then he added - "let's get to marking." We spent the rest of the day marking the frames.

Ed and Zezinho shifted into a flow of their own, which called for little to no translation so I wandered off to find some chilled coconuts to serve with our sandwiches. The men ate sat on the keel and I did the same. I asked Zezinho how he was doing and he seemed content, so when we finished our sandwiches within 10 minutes, I asked Ed if he would be okay with my going off to do some reconnaissance.

"Ok..." he said, reservedly, "Will you be long?" he asked.

"Noooooo... I just want to see what's around in case we need anything," I assured him.

With that, I wandered outside the shed and into the sunlight. My eyes squinted with the burst of hot light. The zinc roof sheltered us from direct rays and a few degrees of heat, and I could already feel the top of my head searing under the hot sun. I made a mental note to bring a hat the next time and made my way down the grassy cut to the main path and then ventured to the right - away from where we normally arrived. The cobblestone road picked up again about 20 steps to the right, where there was a small merchant on the corner. The homes were mostly hand built by the families' ancestors and construction was simple and functional - two or three rooms, a kitchen, a bathroom, a living area, which these days invariably donned a TV and most every house had a veranda from which you could nod to the passers-by and call out from, as a means to stay connected. Simple greetings like, 'It's a scorcher!' or, "How's your Mom doing?' or, 'Come by later - I'm baking!' In this way the little village was indeed like one large family.

As I walked by, I too was granted some form of recognition, either with a nod or a simple monosyllabic greeting. Everyone knew who we were, but we were still strangers, and, more importantly, foreigners - *gringos* as they locally refer to anyone not from Brazil. I walked about 200 feet and saw a bar coming up on my left. The bar was lined with men wearing the glazed expression of inebriation and engaging in loud conversation over the samba-style music that blared graphic lyrics, enticing female dancers to dance lower and lower and twerk their hips wildly. I was wearing short jean cut off shorts, a bikini top and a skimpy tee over that, so considering how men tend to lose their filters under all those conditions, I decided to turn around and head back towards the safety of the boat shed before suffering any embarrassment. I walked quickly, until I cleared being within earshot of the music - falling back into my normal pace thereafter, now savoring the waterline to my right - lazy and bucolic. Each little structure unique, some seemingly abandoned, while others were freshly painted in bright colors.

"How was that?" Ed inquired, as I approached them coming in from the outside. "Did you find anything of interest?" he added, reminding me of why I had gone out in the first place.

"Oh, ya, you know… more bars than commerce really," I said, raising my eyebrows in an attempt to convey a bigger picture through my tone and expression.

"Oh, right…" Ed said in return, his expression now conveying the fact that he had picked up on my communication pronto. "Well, we're just wrapping up here," he sighed - "you want to translate our plans for tomorrow and we'll be on our way?

We deliberated for a while longer and spoke about the plans for what would be our third and final day in Cajaíba on this particular trip.

"Tomorrow I want to get that keel on the planer," Ed declared, as we were packing up to go. "You might want to tell him that so we can get a few sober men in here tomorrow to do that."

"You think they have one here somewhere?" I asked, not quite sure what a planer even looked like.

"What? Sober men or a planer?" he smirked, rolling his eyes as I giggled. Walking out of the shed Ed nodded towards an old rusty piece of equipment in the adjacent lot and said, "There's your planer…now tell him so he's prepared to put that thing to use".

Zezinho and I fell back a step or two as we discussed the day. He seemed to be loosening up a bit, getting the hang of working with Ed.

"It's funny," Zezinho marveled. "They measure everything huh?" he said inquiringly.

"They dooooo...." I replied, finding it amusing that the locals didn't. "Ed says tomorrow we need to plane and shape the keel and leave it ready for you to begin the sternpost assembly?" I probed to see if that in fact was a possibility on Zezinho's horizon.

"Oh ya, does he wanna do that tomorrow? Because if he does I gotta round the men up bright and early before they start drinking - it's Friday..." Zezinho left this notion hanging in the air as it required no explanation and I confirmed the intention.

***

That evening over dinner, we discussed what building a boat like this in a location such as Cajaíba would entail.

"Well, judging from your report today - there won't be much we can source in the village except the timber." Ed explained, replying to my question about how I might prepare in supporting the project through its consecutive phases. "Do you think we could source any fastenings in Brazil?" Ed inquired, his expression reminding me of a quizzing teacher.

And, like a fifth grader, I answered - as if I was being quizzed on a topic that I clearly had no comprehension of, "Well ... Umm... what is it that we're looking for exactly?"

He proceeded to explain that he didn't have an exact count yet but that we should start with about 500 ½ inch threaded silicon bronze bolts in varied lengths and about 500 ¾ inch of the same bolt in varied lengths as well. My attention drifted as he explained that amongst these, 300 of them would be *hex tap bolts* and another amount was to be *slotted flat head* and then proceeded to describe something about thread count and keel bolts. I wondered how surreal it was that I was slowly becoming more and more involved in this project, and wondered if this was going to be a blessing or a curse. I felt it was time for me to step out of the life of having a job just for having a job's sake and explore my natural talents. Truth be told, I wasn't quite sure what those talents were, being that type of person who can be made to enjoy most anything, if I was out of doors and meeting people. Mr. Burnett was explaining how it was imperative that the bronze be of a specific grade and another slew of specifications, as I reached for a sip of wine and tried to hone back in on the conversation. Ed returned to his original question regarding the fastenings.

"Do you think we could find those in São Paulo maybe, or perhaps another large metropolitan center? If we can, do you think you could coordinate transportation to Cajaíba?"

Before I could swallow my sip of wine he amended, " If we can't, would we then source those in the US?" As I took in a breath to say God knows what, having no intelligent comment to add, he incorporated, "I have a much better idea of where to source these in the US, but that means you'd have to organize a container and the clearing of customs since we need those arriving in Cajaíba in a matter of months," Ed spewed forth, his brow now furrowed from the storm of thoughts raging through his head. Looking back, I'm glad I was under the influence of being at ocean level, fatigued from the day in the heat, along with my second glass of wine after our pre-dinner cocktail. I stared blankly back at him and then abruptly slapped the side of my thigh which startled him.

"Got him!" I announced proudly, loudly smacking the mosquito that was flagrantly feasting on my tanned limb. We discussed matters a bit more, until I began to nod off and Olivan came in to ask if we needed anything else.

"Oh! Heavens, no." Ed replied. "I'm so sorry we didn't dismiss them earlier!" and then, turning to Olivan, he risked saying in a heavy accent, "Boa noite. Obrigado." with a courteous nod of his head. We bid each other a good night and agreed to meet the next day at the breakfast table.

***

The next morning, as I was coming back from my walk, I saw Ed with the dogs on the beach, just in front of the house. It was already quite hot at this early hour and I had been for a walk and a swim. My hair was still streaming salt water as I approached and unexpectedly smacked two wet kisses on Ed's cheeks. I seized the opportunity and added a hug, leaving two large wet boob marks on his clean work t-shirt.

"Good morning!" I said cheerfully - clearly refreshed from the night.

Ed also appeared rejuvenated and fresh, but clearly disconcerted by my brazen greeting.

"What? Don't...Oh stop it now," he protested, trying to avert my affection to no avail.

I giggled with delight. "Hey, when in Brazil.... you know, do as the Romans and all that!" I blurted elated.

A smile made its way past his customarily ceremonious expression, as he lifted his hands in an outward display, as if figuring what to do about the wet prints I'd left on his T.

"Didn't you wear that one yesterday anyway?" I taunted, alluding to the fact that he dressed like a cartoon character - always in khaki bermudas and a plain white or dark blue tee.

He shook his head, giving in to my incurable bouts of silliness. As I spun back towards the house and walked away from him, I had the impression that his eyes were judging me in what surely was the tiniest bikini he had ever laid eyes on.

"I'm just gonna rinse and I'll be at breakfast shortly!" I called over my shoulder - now deliberately swaying my behind like the girl from Ipanema.

It was a glorious morning, as I crossed the emerald green lawn of the house over to my "princess" quarters. I blasted some chick tunes from my little Bluetooth speakers in the bathroom and left the doors to the oceanfront veranda open wide, so I could enjoy the view and the breeze from the shower. I was still humming "Love on Top" when I arrived at the breakfast table.

"I don't mean to rush you but we do have to get moving - we have a big day ahead of us" Mr. Burnett began urgingly.

"Alright, alright...." I replied, serving myself some fruit no more hurriedly than I would have before his plea.

"Coffee?" he offered.

"Yes please. Dark and sweet like your women..." I teased, venturing.

He shrugged off my comment as he poured my coffee - highlighting its irrelevance.

"On our way back to São Paulo, I'd like to stop in Camamú to see what sort of chandleries they have there, '' he continued nonplussed. Can you see to it that we get picked up with ample time for that please?" He asked, sliding into his business tone as easily as into a comfy pair of slippers.

"Yes sir," I sighed under my breath, a little frustrated, firstly for not knowing what a chandlery was but mainly because I had hoped to enjoy the beach a little longer the next morning before heading to the airport, but sobeit.

***

We arrived in Cajaíba just after 9:00 a.m. Zezinho had the sternpost assembly mounted, with a few bits of timber held in place by chains, as Ed had requested. Ed analyzed the structure, staying mindful by framing his comments and corrections as questions rather than criticism.

'Could you ask him how he plans to join these bits of timber for that role?' or, "Could you ask him if he believes he can find a more suitable bit of timber for the deadwood? This one seems to overshoot our objective."

We didn't see Raimundo this time around. When asked, Zezinho replied nonchalantly, "He's off working at another job in his town." After translating this fact, Ed asked me to inquire as to *why* Raimundo was seeking work elsewhere.

"Oh... well, this isn't his part of the job you know? He's gonna be involved in the more refined bits like the deck and cabin. Wilson here is going to be putting the frames together and then planking - that's *his* job."

"Can he have more than one person performing a job at a time?" Ed inquired, bewildered. He could not understand why we had barely seen anyone working at the yard the whole of the days we were there.

"It's all under control," Zezinho explained, averting our curiosity. "Each person has their role. It's how we work here." he added for clarity.

Once inspection of the assembly had exhausted all comments, Ed requested it be disassembled and the keel piece taken to the planer in the lot across the way. This time Zezinho came back with the army of men within minutes and the task was performed in quite an orderly fashion - although the grunting and cussing still composed most of the language the men proffered. It was extraordinary that these men could carry that cumbersome bit of timber nearly 150 feet across ankle deep grass in their rubber flip flops and then run it through the planer, a planer that - in Ed's neck of the woods - would have been long retired and cursed as unsafe 10 years earlier. At the moment however, the antiquated machine was securely or at least satisfactorily functioning, and ground down our keel piece suitably. The roofed lot housed about five different pieces of machinery, including the planer, and most possessed no hand guard or safe electrical wiring, being connected by a striped cord to the dumbfounding amount of wires that stuck into a strip of outlets that was connected to a wooden post. I wandered around the workshop marveling at the vintage pieces of machinery and feared even glancing at the wincing men, in the likelihood of witnessing a finger flying off, and settling in with the sawdust. The workshop floor was deep with the evidence of years of work and the purple shavings looked like purple tulip petals landing on the pale floor. They were vivid, and filled our nostrils with the sweet aroma of fresh cut timber.

"Alright then." Ed resolved satisfied. He appeared impressed finally, the whole ordeal at last completed and the bit back in its resting place. He made sure to thank everyone with a nod and a grimace and then made it a point to sit down - just him, Zezinho and I - so that we could review Zezinho's list of tasks for the upcoming weeks. It was agreed that Zezinho would complete a few main projects, amongst which were to finish the sternpost assembly, clamping it onto the keel - according to the instructions I had translated earlier, finish cutting and assembling the frames, (or at least 20 of them) and finalize the stem and forefoot and find and cut planking stock, laying it out to dry.

"How soon does he think he could commit to having these tasks completed?" Ed inquired, expressing a new understanding of the limitations posed by the local set up.

"Oh...well, no... I think we could get that done in a couple of weeks..." Zezinho proposed cavalierly, his tone seeming void of any commitment. One thing I had learned about Zezinho, was that he was uncomfortable making any kind of estimate, whether of time or finance.

"Ok," Ed replied. "Let's do it this way - how long to cut and assemble one frame? A day and a half say? So maybe we can count 3-4 frames a week with two people working on this task?" We revisited each task group, looking to isolate each one into smaller tasks in order to better appraise their consumption of time and labor. We narrowed everything down and rounded the time up to three months. This would mean returning around April/May as it was still early February.

On our walk back to the pier at the end of the day, Ed made sure to reiterate his previous point of having plentiful labor. "Please tell him I'd like to see the agreed work completed within the timeframe he proposed, and that we are happy to step in and cover any labor that he is not prepared to. We just need to get the project going..."

Zezinho's face waxed somber with commitment, "Don't you worry now," he assured us, "we'll have it all done within 3 months' time... tops," he added, displaying an encouraging thumbs up to back up his promise.

As was the custom, we were whisked off by Jorge in the Lillibelle shortly before sunset and dropped off at the Barra Grande pier. The sky displayed radiant hues of violet, kissing the amber clouds that were reflecting the dimming sun, as it made its way to its resting place for the night. The breeze seemed to match my skin temperature to the exact degree and I felt a floating sensation, as I breathed deeply, relieved for having completed this first trip. This feeling however, was short - tainted by the realization that back home I had mortgage files to deal with upon my return to the US. I was also off to São Paulo for a short stop over to see Marco and was no closer to solving his immigration case than I had been six months and thousands of dollars ago. I felt the weight of despair trying to wrestle its way through each of my sanguine breaths.

"What's that over there?" Ed asked, as we got to the end of the pier pointing towards lights beaming under a thatched roof.

"Hmmm... I'm pretty sure it's a bar," I replied, happy to be pulled out of my self-defeating thoughts.

As we stepped off the pier, Ed swung to the right and straight towards the alluring little spot, while throwing me a side-glance seeking my approval. I expressed silent approval displaying curiosity by joining him, as he led our way onto the sand path, still damp from the recent tide. The languid lull of bossa nova reached our ears, echoing smoothly from the small speakers that were carefully balanced on the ceiling beams.

"Welcome!" a bright voice exclaimed, interrupting our initial circumspect inspection of the surroundings.

"Por favor..." a tanned muscular attendant who seemed to belong in the 80's musical group Village People, said as he motioned us forward toward one of the empty tables.

"Portuguese? English?" he asked, looking to confirm which language to speak as he toyed between Ed's European features and my Brazilian bio-type.

"Boa noite," Ed ventured gingerly in Portuguese.

"Table for the couple?" our host proclaimed with a wide smile catching on to Ed's heavy accent and eager to practice his English on us. His eyes suddenly turned bright with excitement "honeymoon?" he inquired.

"Business..." Ed mumbled flatly, as we were led to a cozy little wooden table under a tree. Two rustic, wooden Adirondack-type chairs, donned with colorful pillows fashioned in flowery patterns faced the beach side by side.

"Please," our host said, indicating the two idyllic seats as he brushed off any leaves that might have landed on the roost under the persuasion of the warm tropical breeze. He returned swiftly with menus.

"I'll just have a beer thanks," Ed said, having given up on displaying any more skills in the Portuguese language.

"Uma cerveja por favor," I said, ordering up one of our national brand beers before settling back into the cute hand sewn cushions and emitting a sonorous sigh. I backed my sandy feet out of my flip flops and propped them up on the edge of my spacious seat.

"Ok, that's it. I'm officially off duty" I declared jokingly, though absolutely meaning it. "I'm not translating another word of anything today - you sort it out," I shrugged, emitting a friendly smirk.

Mr. Burnett, white feet still lodged in his damp, saw-dusty docksides, was stiffly perched on the edge of his chair in his best effort not to look too comfortable while *on business*. Our server returned with what seemed an abnormally iced cold beer. He served two small glasses on his tray and offered us each one, as he nestled the ice-cold bottle inside a styrofoam sleeve on the table, adding a delicate little candle and flower arrangement as well. Ed made a quick wave away motion with his hand, as if to restrict our table from receiving such trivial accessories, but my effusive expression of gratitude overrode his attempt.

"Oh! Those are perfect! Thank you so much!" I exclaimed in local accent. Ed plopped defeatedly deeper into his chair.

We sat quietly sipping on our beers. Mr. Burnett was already two glasses ahead of me when our host returned with a suggestion. "Would you like another beer or would you perhaps like to try our house cocktail?"

"Oh? What's the house cocktail?" I spoke, muffling Mr. Burnett's immediate response for more beer.

"It's fresh lemongrass and mint leaves, crushed with lime, rum, agave and ice - it's highly refreshing and detoxing - we call it our anti-stress cocktail" our host explained effusively.

"We'll take two!" I replied enthusiastically, seeking complicity from Mr. Burnett. "Right?" I confirmed, as he returned a blank stare, not too sure what he was agreeing to.

Night had fallen gracefully around the quiet little cove, finding us tired, relieved and pensive. I remained silent after ooh-ing and aah-ing over how beautiful the garnish to our cocktail was, delighted by the brilliant jade-green hue of fresh mint and lemongrass. Mr. Burnett equally expressed his approval of our choice and then returned to the mental confabulations that his taciturn facial expressions revealed. The warm breeze and pensive sipping lulled us into our separate worlds and we were in quietude for quite some time before remembering that the staff were likely waiting for us back at the compound, surely wanting to serve our dinner and get on with their evening.

When we finally arrived back at the house, Olivan came out all smiley faced with two cocktails in his hands asking what time he should serve dinner.

"I suggest they leave dinner on the range and we serve ourselves from the pans in the kitchen," Ed reasoned. "We'll just eat after we shower.

There's no sense in their serving us - we're not guests - we're just here for work." And then graciously seeking my approval with a slight bow of his head he added - "if that's acceptable to you of course".

"Oh my goodness, that's the most sensible thing I've heard you say today - I don't want to feel rushed. I need to scrub in dark places today..." I taunted.

I then translated our plans to Olivan, who looked at us both wide-eyed as if he had seen the ghost of his long lost great grandfather behind us.

"Nooooooo...." Olivan groaned aghast, he could not even consider such travesty taking place in the Graham compound.

"Yes... Olivan..." I said soothingly, giving him the most convincing look I could muster under the influence of the gelid beers and cocktail I had just guzzled a few moments before feet in sand, currently coddling the second cocktail safely in my hands. "Don't even..." I slurred. "We truly will feel more comfortable if we just help ourselves - you've done so much by cooking such a wonderful meal already."

After much coaxing, we were off to our showers - Olivan reluctantly having agreed to our discomfiting request.

"Please do not hesitate to call me if you need *anything*..." came his final utterance, as he left us on the deck by the hammocks.

***

Subject: Bahia visit
Date: Fri, 16 Mar 2012 14:35:39 +0000

Dear Charles,

Firstly, please accept my apologies for taking so long to report back on our visit to the yard. Going away for a week tends to result in quite a pile of things to deal with on my return!

Anyway, I do think this was a very constructive trip. I was able to pick up on a few things that would have been a problem if not dealt with and went away pretty confident that the basic construction is on the right track. It was also, as ever, enjoyable to spend time there. The keel timber Zezinho found is indeed an impressive piece of wood. Being a natural thing however, no piece of timber is perfect and a lot of what we do is focused on making the best of a bit of wood. In this case, there is one knot in the keel and I was a little concerned with where this was going to end up relative to the mast step which is the highest loaded area in the boat. So, we ended up flipping the timber over and turning it around so the knot is now aft where it doesn't matter and we have the best bit of the timber where we want it. In the course of doing this, we worked together in re-marking the shape of the top of the keel and I was able to demonstrate the accuracy which he should really be working to - this perhaps is the single most important thing we did. Otherwise, the timbers Zezinho has sourced look good and we discussed the various components of the backbone in general.

One of the main reasons for my wanting to go out there was centered on the spacing and general arrangements of the joints in the frames. I was able to explain the concern to Zezinho and he has agreed to rectify the problem. With the precedent set I am hopeful that the remainder of the frames will be made with joints suitably staggered.

We also discussed a few other details and it seems he is thinking further down the road which is of course a good thing. Overall, I think the main point to bear in mind is that Zezinho is not accustomed to working from drawings and doesn't immediately recognise how much information they contain. He is confident and accustomed to making judgments himself, and tends to default to this rather than really looking at the drawings. We talked through it all again, but it is apparent that in the time that has passed since August he rather forgot a few of the niceties and was therefore inclined to follow his own solution. In small items this is not a bad thing, but we need to be careful that he does not build himself into a corner, or make a departure from the plans that forces us to change something more fundamental further into the project.

We agreed that the best time for the next visit would be when he is ready to start planking. He estimated three months for this, but I expect it will be rather longer....

Otherwise, it seems that cash flow is one of the main reasons for a lack of progress to date. I understand that Zezinho originally declined a payment upfront, saying that he didn't need it and probably thinking that he didn't want the responsibility either. Now however, it is clear that he did rather mis-judge what he would need and that has delayed the work. Most importantly, any interruption due to a lack of ready cash results in the other chaps pushing off to do other work and all involved forget what we had agreed in terms of techniques etc.

Again, my understanding is that you were having difficulty agreeing with Zezinho how money might be allocated or kept track of. I would suggest that it will always be the case that builders like Zezinho cannot count financial management as their greatest skill and he will always find it hard to predict and manage the need for funds. Discussing this with Paula, we were wondering if it might be possible to set up an account from which she can make small (accountable) disbursements as needed, either to Zezinho or for materials etc. This would enable you to make larger lump sum transfers to the project without having to rely on Zezinho's cash management.

In the name of getting some figures together, I did a bit of a stock take of the timber that is now on site. Attached to this is a spreadsheet that we can enlarge and maintain as necessary. Within the sheet, the volume of timber is calculated and related to Zezinho's stated value in two cases. He wasn't keen to give the values of the other pieces without a bit of thought, but perhaps we can encourage him to do so. Either way, if we take his valuation of the pile of planking stock at 4000 BRL, it works out at around 2475BRL per cubic metre. This is semi-finished timber, in other words, we can assume 25% of the original bulk has been wasted in getting it to where it is. We can expect an additional 25% wastage before this timber is in the boat. On that basis, I have entered suggested costs per cube for the other pieces as measured and depending on their state of finish. The keel is obviously a special case given the difficulties of locating and extracting it. The very provisional result is that there is perhaps around 19000 BRL in the timber currently on site.

As a matter of interest, big bits of Iroko (an equivalent tropical hardwood) currently cost about £1200 per cube in this part of the world in a semi-finished state. So, at today's exchange rate we are looking at 3400 BRL per cube for Iroko here, versus 2475 BRL per cube for the equivalent timber in Bahia.

Whichever way things might be arranged, it does seem that some money needs to move now in order to facilitate progress and it would be good to get things going again in the wake of this recent visit.

I hope the above is useful, do please give me a call if you want to discuss anything.

All the best,

ED.

***

May 2012:
The Frames

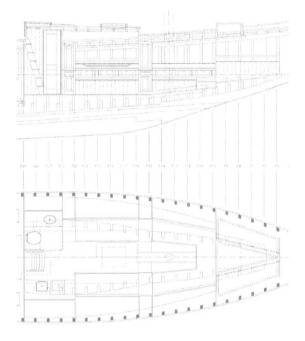

Kathini

A story of love, loss and a little boat building

Coming home to California was painful only because I had the memory of saying goodbye to Marco and we both shared the sinking sensation that he wasn't coming home any time soon. Email correspondence with the consulate in Rio was harrowing, as were the exchanges with the attorney. Most emails began with discouraging courtesy openings - "It is with regret that we inform you..." or, "Thank you for your continued correspondence, however we lament to inform you that...". It had been a year since Marco had been denied entry into the US, and, many thousands of dollars later, we had basically made no progress. My spirit was becoming more and more restless working a job that severely underutilized my skills. I knew I had been born for more than just closing mortgage files, or any other task confined within an office for that matter. I felt a need to metaphorically let go of the edge of the pool and swim, but my confidence was frayed and I lacked the fortitude. The recent events that had transpired, including unemployment, divorce and the immigration fiasco, had taken the wind out of my sails. Working part time on a project in which I had no experience or skills certainly didn't help the confidence part of things either.

Ed's email summarizing our trip and the next steps to take made it evident that more professional administration would be necessary in order to get our project off the ground. Our conversations revealed several points that needed attention - someone who understood the building process should be in Cajaíba regularly, to instill some rhythm and assuredness. Materials and provisions should be assessed ahead of time and deliveries planned accordingly. Both Ed and Charles seemed to be satisfied with my translating and initial organization of things, but we needed someone hands on who could usher the project along from the more practical side of things, making the process more seamless. Ed referred me to a few contacts and we brainstormed a few local options - after all, this was the boat building region of Bahia. Boat building was more advanced in several pockets of Bahia and there were many others that were comparable to any other boat building centers of the world right in southern Brazil.

I was working on sourcing materials as early as 5 am in California, just to be able to reach contacts in Brazil during regular business hours. Then I'd work on mortgage files from 9 - 5 before picking up the sourcing again at the end of day; leaving emails ready for sending the next morning and watching YouTube videos about wooden boat building. I'd look up boat building terminology in both languages into the wee hours all the while still trying to get my visa-banned son back into the US.

In April, I took Easter weekend to go back east and visit my brother, who was living in Annapolis, Maryland, with his wife Lidia and daughter Aida. I was in the eye of a personal whirlwind, moving rapidly around in its cylindrical funnel and feeling dragged down by life and all the inevitable chaos stirred up by the recent events. That weekend, by chance, we visited with a childhood friend whose wife was an image consultant in Washington D.C. As we were chatting, later on in the kitchen and over a glass of cold Chardonnay, she asked -

"So what do you do back in California?" As I filled my lungs to give my reply, I had the sudden impulse to answer her question with a question.

"What would you say I *look* like I do?" and then I amended. "I mean, if you don't mind my fishing around in your expertise, what would my image say about me?"

Without missing as much as a beat, she said, "well, surely something to do with fitness..." She held onto that thought as if mentally feeling into some invisible terrain.

"Or better... wellness," and then she added decidedly "...but something more alternative like yoga or meditation."

Bingo... The woman who had been introduced to me just minutes before nailed exactly who I was. My love and commitment to all things nurturing and of consciousness was oozing out of me but I was too busy playing business to see it. That night I vowed to go deeper into the practices I loved and be truer to myself. Stepping away from work for that weekend and being out of my usual surroundings had helped me see things from a fresher perspective.

***

Finding a project manager that might handle all the needs of the project at hand proved harder than expected. There was a local architect whose degree was actually obtained in naval engineering

- but she was busy with her projects and when I mentioned the possibility to Zezinho he was not remotely enthused.

"Isn't she a house builder?" he said, with subtle defiance.

"Well, she's an architect - you know, she designs houses but her degree is in naval engineering...."

"Right...so she doesn't actually *build* houses *or* boats really..." he concluded, without deigning to hear the rest of my sentence.

"Oh, no, I suppose not," came my rejoinder, "but..."

"No, ya, not a good fit- huh?" Zezinho offered. "Besides, we're not really used to women in our yard you know? I mean, not me, I'm fine - but most men here, you know..."

The men at the yard didn't take offense to the fact I was a woman because I had kind of come with the project - like a pit that comes with the fruit - but by golly they were not about to consent another woman come in to tell them what to do.

We made mention of a building crew Ed had worked with in Martha's Vineyard, back in his intern days that he highly recommended, but naturally their expertise came with a tab directly proportional to the experience they brought with them. Ed and I discussed the matter via email exhaustively - taking local builders into consideration, but Zezinho was equally opposed to having local supervision as well.

"Well..." Zezinho put his thoughts simply, "They were not the builders you chose, and, if you *had* chosen their yard, I wouldn't be going over there to supervise *their* work... because that wouldn't be right, so I wouldn't want them to come over here and supervise mine."

All the diplomacy within me couldn't talk him out of his personally ingrained truth. He was paralyzed in fear of building but wanted to hold the opportunity close to his chest - something about the project spoke to him and he knew this was his moment and his chance.

I scheduled a pow-wow with Charles. It was now well into April.

"Oh, yes. Hello Paula" Charles' courtesy was genuine. "How are the boys and how are things in sunny California?"

"Peachy thanks," came my upbeat reply.

"Have you managed to get our Marquinho home yet?" he asked fondly, using the diminutive for my son Marco, just as I was about to dive into my reason for calling.

"Oh, well no...but I've been working with an attorney back in D.C..."

"Goodness, that must be costing you a small fortune - well good luck, and let us know if you need help in any way" he chuckled.

My heart always shrunk at the mention of anything related to Marco, or his immigration process, but I mustered a cordial little chortle in return.

"So, ya, thanks for making time for our meeting" I said, getting back to the matter at hand. "Ed and I have been discussing options for project management, ever since we returned from the yard in the first week of March."

"Right...it's been six weeks no?" Charles acknowledged accordingly.

"Yes, and as you know, we have deemed that it would be of utmost benefit to have someone on site to keep the cadence of work going as well as to favor the accuracy of these hugely impactful stages of the building process."

"Yes, I see, and have you found any locals?"

We - uh... no..." I stuttered.

"I mean frankly, if I'm going to have to invest enough to equal the cost of building another small yacht to get these folks from Martha's Vineyard back there, I see no real sense in building locally."

"Yes, I see..." I said, feeling gutted and not knowing why his affirmation would have affected me in this way - but it had.

"Well, the issue at hand is - can he get this project off the ground - I mean, it's preposterous that he'd agree and then just sit there and do nothing but build that dreadful shed...and with our funds and then produce no boat!" Charles protested.

"You know, I've been speaking to Zezinho quite regularly and he says things are moving along...." I said appeasingly, understanding that Charles had been stirred into a state of reasonable frustration.

"Yes, well, has he completed the frames as per Ed's instructions?"

I could see Charles' case easily coming together.

"Not all of them, no...." my statement hung.

"Has he made progress on finding, cutting and stacking the planking timber?" he continued.

I took the time, between his questions and my negative responses, to wonder why I defended this project at all, but couldn't find a tangible reason. I was going to shift our topic to the fact that I had now successfully sourced all the fastenings to the specific alloy Mr. Burnett had requested, but on second thought realized that shelling out six thousand dollars for the initial order of premium fastenings, when there was nothing ready to fasten back at the yard, might jolt him into further frustration.

"Listen, Analida and I will be going down to Bahia for Analida's birthday next month and we are going to be visiting the yard and making a decision. You might want to convey that to Zezinho."

Much to my dismay, Ed's response to my email filling him on the progress, or lack of, so far, was not much friendlier. I had relayed my conversation to him via email, looking for advice on whether we should move forward with purchasing said fastenings and sending them down with the Graham's. My initial plan to DHL them down had failed miserably. I had found that due to the harmonized code under which the bolts fell - it would take months for our package to go through customs in Brazil, even if it took only a week to arrive in Brazil - the wait at customs was monumental. Ed's response to my email was succinct:

Maybe Zezinho should be acquainted with the fact that if he doesn't get on and start making some serious sawdust it is likely that the project will be terminated? That might just scare him into complete non-action, but I get the impression from Charles that we aren't far off being out of a job. As that means me as well as Zezinho, I wouldn't mind seeing evidence of some action!

All the best, ED.

***

Summer was just around the corner and I had a lot to tend to on my plate. I was a year into working on Marco's immigration case with the attorney in D.C. and struggling to stay on top of the payments. I was working full time processing loans and my heart was heavy with a sense of not putting my efforts into whatever it was my heart felt I should be doing. The idea of delving deeper into the world of yoga appealed to me as it would not only further my plan of dedicating myself to something I believed in, but also help balance out my emotions throughout what I could feel was a time of deep change. I fervently worked through my goals in the form of a daily to-do list:

1) look into courses for yoga teacher certification
2) procure 6-foot threaded bronze rods (keel bolts to be cut into lengths)
3) call attorney to make payment - sell jewelry?
4) negotiate raise...
5) Be graceful :)

I always wrote a cheeky little reminder to myself at the end to break the rigorous tone of my to-do list. That habit developed into another that kept me on track with maintaining some sanity which was to include self-care activities into my "to-dos'" (go for delicious walk, meditate for 10 minutes, bake chocolate chip cookies, etc.) and to treat them with the same value of importance as the rest. It was always rewarding to check those off with an equal sense of accomplishment. The list grew and grew with each task, breaking down into a series of follow ups and developments. One morning, after composing an email to Charles and Ed about what progress there had been at the yard the past few weeks - which was truly a re-worded description of the tasks we were still waiting to see completed, I decided to work on finding a place to work on my yoga certification. One call led to another but that day as I spoke to one receptionist, at a studio in Sherman Oaks, she up-sold her course by stating: "our teacher is extremely experienced and has a certificate from Loyola Marymount University..." a new revelation inspired my mind.

"Oh? There's a University that certifies yoga teachers?" I asked, now compelled to learn more. I finished our conversation and pulled the information up online. Loyola's curriculum seemed the perfect match for me ! The nerdy scholar in me reveled. The next course was starting in late August and going through to December - perfect. The price point made the next item on my to-do list a certain priority - US$3600. Once I picked myself up from this flooring cost realization, I put a call in to the course registrar.

"Yes, I'm interested in enrolling for the Yoga Teacher Training Course in August? I'm wondering, is there a payment plan available?" I inquired optimistically. Not only was I informed that there were no payment plans available but the course cost twice what other courses cost and was also near full to capacity. The registrar promptly urged me to enroll at my earliest convenience online. "I'll definitely do that - thank you for your help." I ended our conversation no less motivated but determined - "If I'm meant to be in that course - I'll be there." Within the disorienting fog of disempowerment, that little statement of affirmation bravely stepped forth without notice, instinctually. I turned my datebook a month ahead to late July and added - 'follow up with course at LMU" and crossed the first item off my list. Now, how can I increase my income? Extra hours and obtaining a raise came first to mind.

***

Analida and Charles had in fact gone to Brazil for Analida's birthday in mid-May. They had taken with them the initial lot of bolts: 500 3/8" carriage bolts; 600 nuts and washers to go with those; 240 1/2" carriage bolts; 300 nuts and washers to go with those; 2 large steel clamps and 12 long assorted drill bits. It seemed that their presence had whet Zezinho's appetite for the project a bit and he assembled what bits he had with chains as he had months earlier for Ed and I, to display to Charles. This averted the potential crisis of having the project cancelled, allowing us a little more time to organize our next trip. It was also quite fortuitous, as I had been asking Zezinho for pictures to no avail and with the ones Charles finally sent us - Ed was able to ascertain that the fore keel seemed to be over-planed at one end, along with the fact that the ends of the bolts on the frames were poking through one side to the other and had to be cut and blunted for safety. This knowledge was extremely useful and Charles was encouraged by the fact that the once called: 'House of Faith in God' was now being used as a store for our bronze bits and for the frame by frame stencils that Ed had thoughtfully left for referencing. Some interest was at last shining through the lackadaisical tempo of our boatbuilding village.

***

My follow up call to LMU regarding a payment plan for the course as well as inquiring about a student loan, were both met with negative replies. My request for a raise with my broker however, and my proposal to work more hours, had been accepted. I was now operating with a 30% increase in income, including the longer hours worked on the boat. It turned out to my advantage after all that Charles was averse to hiring an on-site manager for the boatyard, although it had also provoked intense bouts of anxiety and feelings of ineptness which frayed my self-confidence.

"Do you have time for a skype chat?" an email asked, coming in one early morning from Mr. Burnett.

"Yes, of course." I replied, as I made my way to the dining room hurriedly.

With my hair still coiffed in 'bedhead' mode, I sat a little dazed in front of my MacBook Air, skimpily clad in a lacey lime green Victoria's Secret nighty, unaware that my camera would pop open upon accepting his video chat request.

"Are you... in your pajamas?" Ed said, squinting at the screen flabbergasted by my informal attired attendance to our call.

"Oh! Crap, wait! Excuse me, I mean..." I jumped up to my feet so fast and clumsily, that the lightweight Ikea dining room table jumped up as well from the thump of my thighs hurrying out from under it, sending a spray of morning coffee all over the place and causing me to proffer expletives while racing to my room in bare feet for a robe.

A side effect of shifting jobs, the real estate crisis and our immigration debacle, was a plummeting credit score. I had closed most accounts after divorcing Marcelo, and was now tentatively building up new credit under my name alone and certain stores extended credit more easily than others. Victoria's Secret was one of these, so I had been dutifully nursing my credit score back to health one colorful piece of lingerie at a time.

I put on a robe and made my way back to sit before the active skype call as gracefully as I could muster after such shit show.

"Ok...crisis averted." I said grinning - making light of my embarrassment.

"Right..." Ed wore the expression of looking mindfully over imaginary papers and shuffling them, a lot like news anchors do on TV when they need to look busy.

"I hope I'm not interrupting?" he began, displaying a smirk that matched his wry English humor.

"Not interrupting... but you do realize it's an 8-hour difference between you and me so it's still 6 a.m. here? I was fresh out of bed" I explained slightly vexed.

"Ok, let me know if it's better to speak later?" he appended.

"Well, I have work all day today and unless you are willing to discuss bolts and screws at 2 a.m. your time, our window would be now." I said, having a go at some sarcasm.

"Right…. Well, it's quick. I saw your email about replenishing screws in a timely manner and as Zezinho uses them on the frames…."

Our conversation came to the conclusion that I was to put together a container and get its contents to Cajaíba by early 2013 - it was now August 2012. This task came to aid my plight of working more hours, but I had also just committed to working more hours at my mortgage job. The next few weeks leading up to our trip to Brazil consisted of harrowing hours and juggling of tasks. I was now dealing within the business hours of three time zones as I was sourcing most of our items from the east coast, confirming specifications with Mr. Burnett in UK time and then double-checking quotes locally in Brazil to see if the item was worth importing after freight and tariffs.

My to-do list grew daily and there came a time when paying the immigration attorney had to be dealt with. Dotty was the friendly office assistant who called to check in.

"Good morning Miss Carocci, it's Dotty from the Attorney's office…" I was still using Marcelo's last name at the time.

I'm referring to the office in generic terms so as not to toe over any legal lines that could be crossed by revealing the five partners' last names, but I assure you it was a posh and renowned office.

"Yes, Dotty, hi. How are you?" I said, heart now in mouth.

"Well, thank you, and thanks for asking." Dotty continued on in the same breath.

"Miss Carocci, I wanted to check in with you regarding the outstanding balance of $4,375 dollars - would you like to make a payment towards that balance today?"

All I could hear was that the number she suggested was abundantly more than what I had to live on in a month.

"Uh yes Dotty, as a matter of fact I would. You said I could make a payment *towards* that amount?"

"Yes ma'am." the voice confirmed

"Let's see..." I calculated, as I uttered the number slowly back to her - "four thousand... three hundred... and seventy-five..."

"Yes, ma'am..."

"Hmmm...I'll make a payment of $75 today thank you," I declared decidedly.

"You want to make a payment of 75 dollars today?"

"Yes, please." I confirmed.

"Towards your outstanding balance of four thousand three hundred seventy-five dollars - leaving a balance of 4,300 dollars?" She seemed to be under the impression I had not understood the number she delivered.

"Yes please, also, I'll be paying by credit card if that's ok."

Dotty took my information and sent me a receipt for the seventy-five dollars. Over the next few calls we became a little chattier and something told me Dotty's heart went out to mine and that she understood my plight.

***

Communication became better slowly but surely, as I became accustomed to incorporating tasks in the different time zones into my day. Early morning Skype sessions between Ed and I became more and more common as we grew tired of the flurry of emails crowding our inboxes. I have the feeling it was amusing for him to see me sleepy headed and dazed but trying my best to concentrate on whatever we were discussing that day. Some days we'd wrap up business quickly and chat a while about our day, or Susie (his black lab) or James (my Siamese cat) and this made the calls increasingly pleasurable.

As summer progressed, so did our project in the quaint Cajaíba. Ed's onsite presence earlier that year followed by Analida and Charles' visit in May seemed to coax things along. Communication between Ed, Zezinho and I had become more consistent and Ed grew accustomed to marking up pictures sent by Zezinho, to show the changes he wanted to see or suggest. Zezinho felt more supported and more closely guided, diminishing his fear of failure. He even displayed progress for a few weeks but his cadence began lagging again towards the end of summer. One day, catching up with Ed regarding his big Gloriana barge event via Skype, we decided that a new visit to our boat building site might go a long way toward getting the hull structure ready by the end of 2012.

"E-ed..." I said his name in two syllables, so as to add dramaticity to my tone, "you never told me how it was at the Queen's event?"

"I did indeed," he said in sprightly manner, maintaining an off-handed reply to end the discussion whilst remaining polite.

"But you didn't send pictures and tell me all the juicy details!" I countered, bouncing my right leg wildly, that was crossed over my left – furry slipper dangerously close to flying off my foot.

"Don't be silly...there was nothing juicy about it - we launched the boat - the Queen came on board - we rowed. The best part about it was the rowing actually." And then he added, "There was plenty of press there, google the photos..." he suggested, displaying a nonchalance of having been the boat designer of choice commissioned to design the Queen's barge for her 60th Jubilee - an event that most would have boasted over for months in advance and forever after.

"But E-ed... it's funner if I get the photos from you," I insisted as I twirled a perfect curl around the index finger of my left hand over and over.

"If by 'funner' you mean more fun, it's just the same... as a matter of fact, you'll have more photos and better quality online." He stood his ground kindly adding "...and for future reference, *fun* does not take the comparative form like a standard adjective." he instructed, making mirth of my American domain of English.

"*Whaaat*?" I teased back, knowing very well that he despised when I responded in my valley girl way and would correct me indirectly by responding with: 'excuse me?'

"Funner is not a word, but look, can we get back to discussing progress at the boatyard now please?" he pleaded, trying to regain focus on our current situation.

I giggled, as I threw my head back and taunted, "Funner is not a word? Even funner!"

Ed rolled his eyes with jestful intolerance. "Right.... so, Carol went to Bahia last week and reported no progress whatsoever?" He queried directly, pinpointing the true subject of our call.

Carol was Analida and Charles' right arm. She kept rigorous records of all expenses, reports, receipts, reservations, bookings and most everything else that kept the Graham family moving forward with their lives. There were six lives to look after and it was not uncommon for one of them to miss a flight, misplace keys to the house or forget a bank card in a cab somewhere on the globe, generating a chain of extra tasks for the diligent and regimented family manager. Carol had gone to Brazil to organize her own wedding which was to take place at the Graham villa in Barra Grande and as a courtesy had offered to check in on the project by paying a visit to Cajaíba. Unfortunately, her email in that regard had stirred our need to have an immediate Skype session to discuss our next steps. In it, she stated that she had intended to go Cajaíba but that Jorge had said the Lillibelle was inoperable so she had to call the visit off. When she phoned Zezinho to let him know, he had consoled her with the truth. 'Oh, don't worry, I haven't done anything in weeks!' he guaranteed proudly. The fact the Lillibelle was once more in mechanical disrepair topped by the fact nothing had been done at the boatyard for weeks had Charles composing a tempered email to us the night before, so here we were, figuring how best to deal with the situation at hand.

"Ok, so judging from Charles' email, he suggests we plan to be in Barra Grande in November - but it seems to me that that will overlap with what you Americans deem an important holiday...?" he left his thought trailing, providing me the opportunity to state my mind.

"What? Thanksgiving? Nah, I'm fine being in the boatyard sweating streams...I'll give thanks when this thing takes off. Or floats off as the case may be..." I said, referring to our beloved project.

"Well, if that's the case then let's see...let's plan to arrive on the 16th of November and come back the other weekend then... say the 23rd?

"Well, I kinda have to work that Friday..." I began tentatively..." just so I can feel okay about taking the whole next week off..."

"Of course, of course...sorry - of course. So arriving Sunday 18th then?"

"Ya, but you can travel ahead of me if you'd like," I suggested.

"No, no... we'll meet at the check-in area at Guarulhos on Sunday morning - let's start looking into tickets..." came his final delegation.

***

November 2012: The Hull

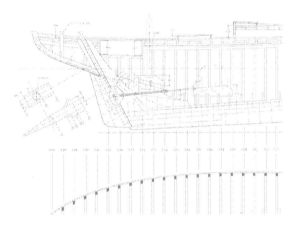

Kathini

A story of love, loss and a little boat building

Autumn temperatures in Southern California were in the high 70's to low 80's as one who paid 9.5% state sales tax at the time would expect. I called it a sun tax, because I truly felt privileged to live in California and to be back in the US where I was raised. My father had moved to Washington D.C. from Brazil early in 1970 to look for a more promising future for all of us. He landed a propitious job at the Inter-American Development Bank using his strongest attribute - personal networking. He had my mother sell our small home and come to join him later that year, once he was settled, ready to move us all to a 2-bedroom apartment in Silver Springs, Maryland. There were plenty of firsts associated with that move - first airplane ride, first time I saw snow, first time I left our border collie Sassy...It was a coming of age experience for a 5-year-old and I was soon to have my first school experience too - in a foreign language. Early on, I learned that the way to overcome my fears was by just moving forward afraid. It might well have been just that that was my most valuable skill learned for life so far - especially now when

I was finding my step again and experiencing growing pains as well as many *firsts*.

Getting a container together for overseas shipment and procuring a company to do it, called for navigating new seas for me. For starters, purchasing a plethora of items I had never even heard of, so my days were also filled with researching phone calls and trial and error. I found a wonderful little backyard manufacturing company in Amish country Pennsylvania to lathe some ½" bronze rods so that they could be cut on site into perfect floor-to-keel bolts - saving us thousands on buying larger bolts and shipping them down. Between several trips down - Analida, Lilly and myself, managed to get past customs smiley-faced whilst toting 6 or 7 of these 6-foot silicon bronze rods each - passing checkpoints upon arrival in Guarulhos and then finally delivered to Cajaíba.

Concomitantly, I decided it was time to become a United States citizen since the only reason I hadn't previously done so was the $800 bucks involved in fees. I figured as a US citizen I might have more pull in Marco's case and in bringing him home. A barrage of paperwork, a few vaccines and medical exams later, and I became a citizen of the beautiful America I had pledged allegiance to long ago in my first year of elementary school when I mouthed the words and didn't even know what they meant. I pressed on with filing my appeal for Marco.

At my mortgage work, I had become increasingly dissatisfied. I felt I was severely under employed and my spirit was knocking from the inside out. The money situation had me scrambling month to month. Regardless, I had made a pact with the universe that I would step out and commit to the ridiculous amount I had committed to paying for my yoga teacher training course at LMU (given my budget, not the value received for the course - I love you LMU...) and that in turn *it* (the universe) would provide for me. I had no idea how the funds would come, but it was no longer my problem - I was following my heart and there's a magical certainty that comes from fiercely believing in your heart's calling that resembles a graced madness. I can't even remember exactly what the circumstances were, but I received a bonus at my mortgage job which covered the first payment and the following payments just fell into place due to the longer hours involved in organizing the container.

***

The bright, airy, ocean-adjacent campus at Loyola Marymount was just what the doctor ordered for my tired 9 - 5 working soul. The 3 hours I'd put into the boat project before work quickly became 5 - 6 hours a day, which had me working well into the evenings aside from making dinner for the family. I found that the more I could stitch pleasantries into my day, the better I could get through them, so I blasted my jams on my car stereo and sang along. I stopped at Baskin & Robbins for a cone of mint chocolate chip ice cream without guilt and devoured it sat on the lawn at the park across the street. I found uplifting videos on YouTube that lulled me into a more peaceful sleep, drowning out the usual mind worry of how things were going to work themselves out. Before I knew it, I was finding a rhythm that made juggling sensitive issues a little more playful. I began making fun of myself along with Ed instead of getting defensive and our conversations became less of a battle ground and more therapeutic - at least they had for me.

***

November rolled around and as fore planned I spotted Mr. Burnett's tall build and expressive demeanor from a clear distance as I wheeled my cart in the direction of the coffee shop where he sat examining his notes next to the check-in area. He glanced up casually from his coffee and returned to being absorbed in his notes, not having registered who it was actually walking up to him. Upon second look, his head jerked up and his expression lit in lapsed recognition as he realized my silhouette approaching.

"You didn't text me when you landed..." he exclaimed, jumping eagerly to his feet.

I took my last two strides in his direction and added, "You were supposed to be at arrivals to greet *me* remember?" I said, alluding to a couple we'd seen kissing passionately at arrivals the last time we were at the airport which I had pointed to announcing to Mr. Burnett that next time I'd expect similar reception. I rolled my eyes and laughed, flinging my arms lazily around his broad shoulders that rose well above my own.

"Urgh...you're so useless..." I uttered teasingly.

He exhorted a suppressed laugh, carrying on the conversation with the usual arrival formalities - "How was your flight?" he asked.

"It was alright...you know - I don't mind traveling with my knees next to my ears at all..." I taunted " I kind of consider it a yoga pose now... *Coach asana*" I joked.

"Goodness, you made it in with all that?" he said, nodding towards my overloaded luggage cart.

"I did..." I said proudly. "I rested my hands on the cart handle and just smiled and pushed right past customs..."

"Let me help you with that..." He offered, taking over the cart and setting off ahead of me towards check in.

"Thanks". I replied in return. "I'll let you do that since you're the one having a good hair day."

I had learnt with Ed to complete my thoughts with random comments at times, knowing they had the unique effect of causing a slight annoyance along with some humoring power over my otherwise reserved interlocutor.

Our flight to Ilhéus was not direct and we had to deplane in Brasilia before continuing on. As we headed to our next gate I announced -

"I'm running to the girl's room k?"

"What? Can't you go once we're onboard?" he bemoaned, anxious about connecting flights as he could be.

"No, Ed, how am I gonna sneak past the bar for snacks if I wait to go on board?" I called back to him over my shoulder, as I half walked, half skipped away from him so as to squelch any ideation of him stopping me.

I came back to meet him at the front of the boarding line 10 minutes later.

"See? Plenty of time..." I said, as I chewed slightly open-mouthed on my warm *pão de queijo* - a delicious cheese bread that is loved and cherished everywhere in Brazil. He shifted his eyes and turned his face away in an avid attempt to conceal the amusement coming across his face.

We arrived to a lazy, golden-hued Camamú early that afternoon, where Jorge collected us in the Lillibelle and zoomed us off to the Graham compound for our stay.

***

The house was fully prepared for the Graham's arrival - furniture fully decked out in crisp white covers, the massive wooden tables adorned with candles and majestic tropical flower arrangements created with flora collected from the bountiful gardens. The magnificent wooden dining table made especially for the new house to seat 30 guests comfortably was set for a late lunch and Olivan informed us that the Graham's would be arriving soon to the local landing strip. Lunch would be served around 3 pm if we cared to enjoy the beach in the meantime, he offered.

Barra Grande didn't have a landing strip of its own, but there was a neighboring five-star resort down the beach, whose notables were whisked in and out by jet or light aircraft - and that's where the Graham's would fly in. Ed helped Olivan take the weighty, cumbersome bags, containing the numerous silicon bronze bolts, a few more 6 foot rods and a some tools and drill bits to the garage. Ed had thoughtfully brought a hand planer and a few special-order drill bits in our order to make Zezinho's work easier. I followed, carrying a few of the more manageable items, though acutely aware that the voluptuous, indigo blue ocean was summoning my spirit quite profoundly.

"Well, if that's all then, I'll be burying my tired toes in that beach over there..." I said, with the avid intent of enjoying the next two hours of peace and calm before the formalities of our business trip began.

Ed was concentrated, tallying all of our loot and making sure everything was up to par.

"Fuller make the best countersinks," he announced admiringly, displaying perfect domain of subject-verb agreeance. "These are going to make such a difference," he continued enthusiastically.

"Let's see......taper set.... micro dial...did you bring the drill stops?" he asked, surveying the materials zealously.

I shifted from one foot to the other, not actually recalling what drill stops looked like. I replied nonetheless with the confidence that I was well acquainted with my thrice-checked checklist.

"Of course ..." I said matter of factly - lightly shrugging my shoulders.

Ed's eyes lit up effusively. "Ah! Here they are... sweet nibblets!" I'd never seen him so excited about anything except maybe an unidentified jelly-like organism strewn on the sand at low tide - but I had to take my opportunity to taunt him.

"Sweet nibblets???" I said, mocking his accent. "You picked that interjection up while having tea with your great aunts did ya?" I added a mischievous chuckle.

He coddled the pieces in his large hands and took one last appreciative glance at all the bits and bobs adoringly, before putting them down hurriedly, standing up and exclaiming his usual, -

"Right...let's get on with it shall we?"

"Let's..." I was quick to agree. "...and if you no longer need me I'll just be..."

Ed interrupted my obvious intent to ditch him by interjecting his own wish.

"Yes, and shall we discuss our plan for the next few days at the boatyard?" He proposed with eager eyes.

"Hmmmm... shall we?" I projected, echoing his words slowly and giving myself ample time to think of a good reason not to. "Oh! Yes, we *could* discuss all that, as we walk the beach and inspect what the tide left behind no?" I grinned, hopeful he would approve the suggestion.

"Let's see..." he replied pausedly, using the same tactic as I to devise a reason *not* to mix any semblance of pleasure into our business. "Hmmm...I'm afraid it's too late for me and the sun is a bit too strong" he replied with a grimace - examining his watch as a means to reinforce the point that this unfortunate predicament was to no fault of his.

"That's what sunscreen is for Ed! Come on, let's get those pasty feet of yours out of captivity!" I protested heartily.

"No, no..." he declared, defending his plan. "But I suppose you can scuttle off and enjoy yourself... we'll discuss the sternpost assembly after lunch?" his latest plan now squelched my hopes of a leisurely nap on the hammock after our meal.

"Perfect!" I said, giving him an awkward and uncalled-for hug, delighted as I was to go off on my own. I felt an irresistible craving to stretch my eyes over that boundless ocean horizon. I wasn't aware yet how much healing I was experiencing with each trip.

I made my way up to the princess suite and settled in as quickly as I could. I chose a bikini and organized my curls under a wide brimmed hat before slipping on my flip flops and heading down the wooden stairs and across the lawn. The dogs ran excitedly to meet me, finding no elation on my part to take them for a walk. I patted them each on the head adding, "come at your own risk...I won't be coming back for any of you if you trail behind."

I continued determinedly across the lawn, toward the thatched-roof kiosk that faced the ocean when I heard a short, authoritative whistle call the dogs back - Olivan was always so thoughtful that way. I waved in gratitude.

***

Our routine developed efficiently over the next 7 days. I would allow sunrise to be my natural alarm in the mornings by keeping the shades that faced the bed in my suite opened. I'd be gently awakened by the golden-pink hue of sunrise reflecting off the ocean, gleaming straight past the crisp white voile mosquito net draping romantically over the four-post bed. I would slink out of bed and onto the lawn for my morning yoga practice and then venture off for a brisk walk on the beach. I sang as I walked at times, my spirit feeling free walking on a perfectly smooth stretch of sand untouched by footprints, still so early in the morn. I found a voice within myself that nurtured the parts of me that had been on autopilot for so long. Since leaving home at age 17, I had to fend for myself and it felt like I had to prove that I was perfectly capable of being 'out there" in the real world without a chaperone. I was still 'on the run' - I was beginning to realize - from failure, from vulnerability, from what I sensed were others' expectations of me.   I fought desperately to prove that I could - that I was equipped, that I was enough, but my toughest opponent was the fear inside myself.

My morning musings were followed by meeting Ed at the breakfast table, followed by Charles and sometimes Analida, if she wasn't entertained in impromptu meetings with the staff. After concluding the morning's ceremonious greetings, including inquiries regarding the quality of one's sleep and the like, Charles revisited the plans that had been discussed the night before over dinner.

"So we've told Jorge to meet us at the pier at 8:30 sharp?" Charles synchronized.

"We have." I replied definitively.

"And Zezinho knows we are arriving at 9:00 and is prepared to have workers onsite throughout the day so we can perform all the tasks as Ed planned?" he inquired further.

"He does." I affirmed.

"Do we have all the tools then as per Ed's request here? And have you instructed Olivan to pack those in the car?"

"We do, and I have" I assured Charles again, adding, "More importantly, we have snacks and water because let me tell you - it will be a long day," I said as forewarning, being no stranger to the effects of being hungry on Mr. Burnett's mood.

"Oh...right. Well, let's see how we go then. Perhaps we can work straight through and come home for a late lunch - we've got plenty of time since we'll be here all week no?" Charles' consideration mainly addressing Ed.

"Yes..." Ed replied absently, busily inspecting the unique and plentiful spread of fruits, and marmalades (appointed by HM herself) and other local delicacies such as tapioca, pão de queijo and fried plantains. "That's supposing that Jorge will be at the pier at 8:30 sharp...." he continued with a sniff.

"He will be..." I interjected rapidly, intercepting Ed's comment before Charles could perceive the snark behind it and immediately emitting a staged smile that expressed no concern whatsoever of our boatman's timeliness.

We finished our breakfast, triple checked our car load and were off to the pier to meet Jorge. We parked as close as we could and then began unloading to prepare for our walk down the sandy cobblestone road that led to the pier. Almost at once we heard a few men running towards us yelling.

"Carregador!!! Carregador moça??" they offered shouting in street market fashion. We were approached by several "carriers".

These are men and boys who help locals or tourists with carrying everything to or from the end of the pier, which was a sizeable 400 - 450 ft. walk. There was no coming near the pier without being approached by them or the men in orange or dark blue vests (there were two local companies competing for business) trying to sell day tours to the neighboring islands.

"Passeio nas Ilhas!" they shouted - offering up the boat ride to adjacent islands to whomever was within earshot of their yelp.

The little village was effervescent with people coming and going as there was a local religious holiday the next day. We employed the help of a carrier that wielded a nice ample wheel cart, fit to accommodate our tools and bolts and headed to the end of the pier where we could see the Lillibelle anchored and waiting nearby.

"Bom dia Jorge!" Charles called out, as he waved him over.

***

We loaded our goods and off we went to our first day at the yard together. We de-boarded 20 minutes later in Cajaíba and were unloading when a smiling Zezinho showed up with a wheel barrel and his son.

"Welcome!" he greeted us cheerfully. "This is my son Sid" he said, pointing to the muscular, lean 20 something young lad manning the wheel barrel. We began making our way down the pier and through town towards the boatyard, passing the bars which were especially noisy.

"Don't mind the banter," Zezinho offered. "It's a religious holiday and everyone is celebrating, " he explained.

"Oh?" I replied curiously - what saint?

"Dia do Cristo Rei... I think..." he said, unsure of the exact reason or day for the holiday himself.

I turned to share my newly acquired information with Ed and Charles to find them attentively awaiting my translation. I paraphrased:

"They're celebrating that Christ is King by boating in crates of beer for the people...." I declared, fully aware of the facetiousness that my translation evoked.

"Oh.... well Christ will surely be happy to hear that..." Charles stated on cue, with his typically humorous sarcasm.

Ed chimed in as well, "right on... Jolly chap he was..."

We continued past the makeshift bars that lined the main thoroughfare. The colorful houses were adorned with people at the window, gazing out on the crowd and trading greetings, causing us to go relatively unnoticed to our conspicuous zinc roofed yard. As we entered the boatyard, Ed seemed pleased to see the sternpost assembly and a few frames tentatively assembled with clamps and chains.

"Ah, very good..." Ed smiled gently, affording Zezinho some encouragement.

In the days leading up to our arrival, Zezinho had confided in me, letting me know that he was not sure he would have much to show us when we arrived. He said people in the village didn't really want to help him for two reasons: First they didn't think he was capable of building something as different as this boat; and secondly, they weren't willing to risk being associated with such a fiasco. Unfortunately, Zezinho's fear of erring at this point, would put him in a situation where he would fail nonetheless - as by freezing in his tracks and not trying, he would surely not succeed. Ed and I exchanged emails which revealed a very humane and compassionate being under the British veneer one usually experienced in transacting with Mr. Burnett. We both had a full understanding that this project was teetering on being scrapped, yet for some odd reason we all felt completely invested in it at a heart level - Zezinho, in opening his heart to us about his situation; Ed, who already possessed a letter of engagement which guaranteed his remuneration for design and could have easily moved on to the next thing; and me, who had nothing to add to this process but my tree-hugging spirit - we seemed *enlisted* to bring this project and story to life and that is what we were out to do on this journey.

"Let's have a look at the sternpost knee and then we'll head over to the pile of timber to see what piece he selected for the hog." Ed stated, keeping to his plan for the day.

As the day progressed so too did the heat, making it an incredibly intense job to translate every single word issued from either side of the conversation. The day took a huge toll on my brain so I was relieved when Charles came back from exploring and proposed we head back to Barra Grande within the hour after surveying the hog timber.

"Ya, it was a good first day and we want to respect the holiday - from the looks of it we're the only ones working today and we don't want to ruffle any feathers..." Ed agreed, much to my surprise.

Zezinho appeared grateful that we were calling it quits too, as he seemed to feel judged for violating the holiday as well.

On our way back to the pier, the same bars we had passed on our way to the boatyard were now packed with more clients - the ones we had passed on our way in, now a few pints of beer deeper into their state of intoxication.

"Cerveja?" Charles proposed, being lured to the little yellow bar at the foot of the pier by a group of women dancing to loud and inciting samba-rhythmed music.

Ed, who seemed much more at ease around Charles than when traveling solo with me, needed no coaxing. "Let's!" he exclaimed heartily, accepting the invitation to join Charles at a little metal fold out table, that was improvised under the shade of a ficus tree for the "gringos".

We sat enjoying our ice-cold beers as more and more women joined the circle, displaying their samba skills and twerking wildly for their new found and pale-skinned audience. One woman, who displayed a raunchy, almost Philistine-like semblance, was especially brazen in moving her hips and buttocks as a way to entice our designer, who was smiling courteously but obviously extremely uncomfortable with the erotic movements being directed specifically at him. Charles offered him more beer in an attempt to perhaps ease the discomfort, but when the beer bottle arrived, it was our exotic dancer who was quick to grab it, inserting the bottle neck into her mouth sideways and flipping the metal bottle cap off using the sides of her teeth, thus producing an open bottle in front of us as she spat the bottle top onto the cobblestone - eyeing our engineer provocatively all the while.

Ed shifted nervously in the folding chair next to me, prompting me to bring my head closer to his and say out of the corner of my mouth, "no translation needed there...."

"Ok, I'm terrified right now," he said, in what I believe was a moment of sheer frankness mixed with humor.

The crowd cheered and gauged Ed's reaction, to ascertain if he had taken any interest in the provocateur. With all eyes on him, he leaned towards me, about to say something, when Zezinho turned and made an extended motion with his head and eyes that suggested:

"Go get that…"

Not attracted to the rough looks of our entertainer in the least, Ed desperately proposed:

"God almighty, can't we just say I'm committed? I don't want to offend her."

I leaned in close to him and put my hand on his knee as if to indicate intimacy and whispered a snarky, "ok, but you owe me one…" in his ear.

I looked up and glared at the dancer, clearly indicating that the engineer was not up for grabs by simply changing my body language to one of lascivious interest. Confused at first, she finally got the message I was sending, as I grinned a fine line with my lips while reaching over and taking a big sip of his beer - all the while keeping my eyes on her.

The dancing and boisterous environment kept us enticed for another 30 minutes or so before we decided it was time to head back to the compound for the home prepared meal awaiting us. Charles and Ed wandered ahead down the pier as Charles assessed the engineer's impression of the day's work and Zezinho and I fell back into a more parochial pace, induced by the heat and beer.

"Miss Paula, I'm sorry about that. I didn't know you and the engineer… I mean, it wasn't clear to me that you two…" Zezinho was sifting for words, puzzled. A year into the project and he hadn't put Ed and I as an item but more as work companions. I had to laugh at his bewilderment.

"Oh! ya, we're not… I was just keeping him safe from ol' steel trap over there!" We then dove into a commiserate laughter in silent understanding of what I was referring to.

"Poor Ed, he was shuddering just thinking of the damage she could do to him," I added, the two of us now in hysterics. Zezinho and I continued our conspiring laugh, as we neared the end of the pier where Jorge was just whipping the rib boat round into position for boarding. As usual, he had slipped away minutes before our decision to depart for the day, professionally making his way to the boat unperceived in plenty of time before us.

Charles' and Ed's physiognomies were expressing interest in our amusement.

"We're imagining what terror golden jaws could have inflicted on you had you succumbed to her twerking capabilities..." I replied, supplying an unprompted answer.

Charles and Ed joined in on our banter, as I included Jorge in the conversation to see if I could have a glimpse of the color of his teeth through a smile. Jorge was cordial in his stringent demeanor and he was not a man of gratuitous humor, but even he graced us with a few good chuckles that shone his pearly whites and his mortal side.

***

The next few months saw us coming together in an effort to make sure work kept at a steady pace. Even if slower than desired, it became clear that we needed to establish a rhythm and a method, and that our presence greatly impacted that rhythm and enthusiasm at the yard. Zezinho began sending pictures of his work almost weekly and Ed would copiously comb through the images, scrutinizing every detail that might indicate any issue and then send alterations and encouraging comments where due.

"Could you please have him send a shot with a view looking aft with the hog and sternpost/ knee in position?" Ed asked.

I'd pass on the request and days later we'd have pictures. Sometimes a week later, but this was progress nonetheless and we were milking it for all it was worth.

***

By the end of the year, life was slowly stabilizing for me. Yoga teacher training was a wonderful reprieve from the two masculine universes I was navigating and the academic environment nourished me. It seemed I was finding some footage in the boat project and the idea of searching for an onsite manager kind of dwindled. I was gaining some headway in my mortgage career and actually feeling some confidence again so it was under that momentum that I started looking for offices, where I would be in a better position to increase my income. I came across an office in Los Feliz, a ritzy, newly gentrified area in East Los Angeles that had once been a place where old money lived and that was now booming with hipsters moving in to revitalize old real estate, with their neighborhood shops and artsy endeavors. I showed up for the interview absolutely open hearted which I soon learned gave me a confident demeanor. I was starting to get a sense that whatever happened was happening for a reason and just released. Not only did I land the job for the salary I asked, but I also came in with two huge requests for time off. One for the year end trip that was now on the books as a business trip, and one for my oldest son's wedding that was to be on January 24th of the coming year. I walked out to my car after the interview with a new spring in my step.

Marco's immigration process was still my weak point. Not only was the whole process coming out to be a small fortune, but the lack of progress and explanations as to why we had found ourselves in this predicament was riling, even to the most even keeled individual. My conversations with Marco were bittersweet. I loved catching up with him and chatting, but our chats would almost inevitably end up in pain. Whether we had a great empowering conversation, where we'd feel confident, exchanging reassuring comments, backing up our expectations with whys and wherefores of how our efforts would work, or whether we felt weak with hopelessness - hanging up the phone was always a reminder of our distance and the reality of the situation.

"Well, it looks like I'll be missing one more semester at college," Marco sighed, seeming especially defeated one day.

"Baby... and do you think it might be prudent to maybe begin a parallel course there? Just to keep busy and...."

"No!" Marco interrupted my thought point in haste. "NO!! Mom, what kind of an attitude is that? I'm coming home and when I'm home I'll get back to school - at this point why would I put myself through the whole selection process here just to study for a semester and go home?"

I couldn't argue that logic from the perspective that he'd be coming home soon, but the uncertainty of the truth behind that statement made me wonder how long he'd really be out of school.

"I know baby, but if we position ourselves to file another appeal..."

"Mom, we *are* going to file a second appeal, so it's *when* we file the appeal not *if*, and I just don't want to discuss going to school here ok?" his voice now frayed with the weight of his dilemma.

When Marco was denied his visa, it was much more than a visa on the line - it was the prospect of living with his family in California, going to a university which his good grades would surely afford him, and his first long term romantic relationship interrupted by this arbitrary decision.

"Have you talked to Kevin?" I searched for a less sensitive subject but failed miserably.

"Ya, we talk all the time. We FaceTime, we WhatsApp... but he's got his life to tend to you know...." his last word muffled under the pain in his heart.

I was now beginning to falter myself. "He'll be coming there soon, no?"

The silence on the other side of the phone gave me time to feel the hot tears springing in my own eyes.

"...ya..." I could tell he was trying his best to not burden me with his grief.

We breathed deeply and waited until one of us could wrap up the call.

"Ok Mom... don't worry, we'll figure it all out soon. I know this is all happening to make us stronger. It'll be okay. I'll talk to you later k ..."

"Ok baby, be well. I love you more than life..." I said, still curbing my pain before hanging up and caving into sobs.

Kevin and Marco had met when we lived in an apartment complex in Valencia and they had grown their relationship into a wonderful balance of you do you and I'll do me, keeping their own unique autonomies. They navigated the initial awkwardness in their relationship in such a natural, loving way between them that it was hard to think of the one without the other. They melded so naturally that no official beginning had to be announced - they became Kevin and Marco as naturally as there's day and night. Each distinct but so connected in their essence. Seeing them suffer the distance between them was heart wrenching after being so close every day, being neighbors and best friends that they were - they were inseparable.

***

January 2013:
The Planking

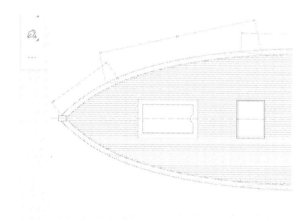

Kathini
A story of love, loss and a little boat building

*H*i! Thanks for those. Great to see some evidence of action. This is an exciting time as we suddenly start to see a three-dimensional boat appearing out of a pile of two dimensional bits - from here the impression of size will change at several key stages which is always interesting!

It's a bit hard to pick out detail with these relatively low-res pics, but the overall impression looks ok. The spacing between the frames doesn't look perfectly regular, and there are a few unfair steps from one frame to the next both of which I hope indicate that these frames are stood up temporarily at this stage and have yet to be located and aligned perfectly. To aid with all things, I would normally suggest a cross spall be fitted at a known height to each frame (near the top). This holds the frame heads at the right distance apart and gives a level that can be eyeballed from a distance relative to the other frames. Pic attached of another boat at this stage showing how *each frame has a cross brace at the same level. There are also some longitudinal battens ("ribbands") wrapped around the outside to keep things fair from one frame to the next. It's all about accuracy of setting up to ensure the frames are fair and that we end up with the boat being the shape we want it.*

Otherwise, I would quite like to see some close ups of the joints between the components of an example frame. We discussed how they should all fit together with Zezinho, and how they should be bolted. What I can see looks ok but it would be nice to see more.

Similarly, I wouldn't mind seeing some pics of how the backbone at the stern came out. Again, all discussed but I have yet to see anything that allows me to check they got it the right way up!

Otherwise, I should give you some advanced warning that I may be moving house AND office in April. That's about the time we had anticipated a trip to Cajaíba so anything we can do to pin some dates down would be handy. If it all goes pear shaped I may not want a return ticket....

Hope spirits are high at the yard and with you both.
All the best,

Ed.

The boat project was finally taking off. Our last visit in November had gone a long way towards getting Zezinho to simply move on with what he had, and working alongside him for days on end, as Ed did, truly instilled the confidence and rhythm he needed to carry on. Our improved communications also went a long way towards keeping the ball bouncing and we were soon looking at months of advanced planning, aware of the lag between the beginning of sourcing the items, purchasing them and effectively getting them onsite. All 40 frames were due to be assembled by the time we arrived in April, so we would now be moving on to matters of planking and deck structure. Our items for the container had, for the most part, already been sourced and purchased and then delivered back east to a warehouse. From there, the shipper would collect everything and prepare it into a container, which would be bound for the port of Santos in São Paulo and then shipped up to Bahia, likely by truck.

I now no longer had to juggle working different time zones as a sudden turn in events had found me at my new, wonderful mortgage office one winter day, when suddenly I looked down at the configuration of the papers on my desk and something clicked - just like that. I felt a sense of 'deja-vu' like I recognized that exact scene somehow and I was suddenly sure of my move to come. "My goodness, this is my last day here..." I remembered this exact moment - with a level of certainty that made that moment uncommonly powerful – and irreversible. I walked into the broker's office and let him know I was putting in my two-week notice. This man was such an angel he suggested "go home, take some time off and let me know in two weeks if you still feel the same. I think you might just be too tired." He said shocked at my sudden resolve after having put in weeks of dedicated and peaceful work. I had developed an efficient pace at this firm and was happy on the surface, but my spirit spoke loud within me - it's time to let go and move on, it said. I listened.

***

It was decided that we'd fly out to Brazil for Easter holiday. Zezinho had kept to his promise of sending pictures of progress periodically and though we weren't moving forward at the envisioned pace - we were moving forward and that was good. The container items that we envisioned for this first phase were now all purchased and delivered to a warehouse back on the east coast and ready to head to Brazil. Spools of rope from New England Ropes, Andersen winches, Schaefer blocks, Hayn rigging hardware, 8 large blue fenders, 2000 silicon bronze flat slotted wood screws for planking and deck, plus 1500 of all sizes for miscellaneous tasks, 2 Delta anchors, 300 ft of Peerless 7/16" chain, a PYI max prop classic 3 blade prop, a beautiful binnacle mount compass and our Jabsco Electric Quiet Flush head among an assortment of repair kits and spares. It seemed we had found our pace in the cycle of visiting the boatyard to see what had been achieved, then spending a day commenting and suggesting corrections, then a day or two working on those and then a day or two going over the next phase and leaving a hand-written task list with boxes for checking off the tasks. Anything that came off a printer, we had found, produced an overwhelm to our Brazilian builder, so we resorted to handwritten sketches, notes and task lists on paper early on.

We arrived late in March on Good Friday. We had agreed that we should respect Good Friday as that is a big deal in the local culture, work Saturday, spend Easter Sunday with Analida and Charles, who would be leaving the day after and then we'd pick up again that Monday and work through to the following Thursday.

"I checked out your website..." I noted, striking up conversation with Ed as we drove from Ilhéus to Camamú down the high speed two-way road.

"Oh? What'd you think?" Ed asked enthused, easily taking interest in work related topics.

"Pretty primitive actually..." I smirked, seemingly apologetic, though not at all.

He gasped at my sincerity. "Wha... Well, I don't very well source my clientele online..." he sparked.

"And let me just add that you're very well set up to keeping it that way..." I concluded, in my new-found snark.

"Well... "he fumbled for words "if you can do any better I'd be open to hearing suggestions." he queried defensively.

"I do have a suggestion actually..." I pondered. "Hire someone to build it for you." I stated point blank.

"I did, but..." he tried to explain, but I cut him short.

"I mean a professional, not a 12-year-old from your rowing club." I contended humorously. Ed was an avid rower as well as an active youth mentor at his local rowing club on the banks of the River Dart in Devon.

"Well, I brought my camera...it's not fancy or anything, but perhaps you could take some pictures...?" he said tentatively.

"Yes! Now you're talking Ed!" I expressed excitedly. If you actually hire a professional to build your website, you'll need some really good pictures, and I'm happy to take those for you free of charge." I taunted. "It's included in our friendship." I added with a grin and appended. "You do realize we're friends now right?" I pressed on.

He looked out his window and nodded, quietly taking in the lush scenery.

"Did you remember to tell the driver to stop at our *empada* place?" Ed inquired concerned. Neither of us did very well when we were hungry, we had found on recent trips.

We had acquired the habit of stopping at the *Casa da Empada* off the BA-001 for a quick freshen up, a Heineken and two empadas - a Brazilian-style pastry that can be filled with goodies savory or sweet. We usually ordered two savory each and then shared a sweet one or I'd take a few "brigadeiros" (delicious Brazilian fudge rolled into bite-sized balls) for the road.

"Yes Edwaaard...." I replied in a monotone, dragging out his name to convey the absurdity of his thinking I would travel two hours without food.

We arrived that evening to the house to find Charles having his customary power swim in the infinity pool at dusk.

"Bem vindos!" he ventured, in more of a Portuguese accent from Portugal, than Brazil. "Did you have a good trip?" He asked, seeming in excellent spirits.

"We did thanks..." Ed replied on our behalf. "We ran into some tropical showers and it looked like we were not going to be able to make our landing in Ilhéus, but it all worked out."

"Right... that landing strip in Ilhéus. One definitely worries about ending up in the ocean if the pilot doesn't stand on the brakes." Charles was very familiar with all the different treks into Barra Grande from São Paulo including via ferry and bus when one flew in from Salvador.

We convened on the oceanfront veranda of the original house and were served cocktails as we went over plans for the next few days. Each wing of the house was now referred to as new house and old house though both were equally aged but one acquired after the other.

***

The days after Analida and Charles left were productive. We kept to our schedule of having Jorge collect us from the Barra Grande Pier at 8:30 am arriving back at the house just around 6 pm, making it so we were almost always graced by an unforgettably beautiful and incandescent sunset on the way home. We worked nonstop at the yard with Zezinho, who was busy with the corrections he and Ed had identified and discussed the first day. Wilson was busily preparing timber for planking, which would be his job once the structure was ready to plank, and Raimundo, who was now busy preparing heftier bits like the horn timber and finishing the beveled hog. Zezinho's son Sid was 23 and quite keen on working alongside his father. He was bright and attentive and Ed appreciated the interest he took in the project. I shadowed Ed, translating whatever instructions or comments he made, and we worked through to the end of that trip leaving us with the feeling that we were now well on our way.

April 4, 2013:
Hello All,

Sorry about the delay with further reportage - I have come back to the usual pile of stuff begging for urgent attention and am struggling somewhat!

I hope the photos and earlier notes give you an idea of the current state of construction. To answer your question Charles, I am in general pleased with the quality of execution of the various parts. This is seen in the way all the different and seemingly obscure shapes come together to form a set of smooth curves (note the battens sprung around the frames in the photos). There are (an inevitable) few things that don't line up perfectly yet, but we discussed all of these, established where the error lay and agreed the procedure for setting things right. Zezinho and the boys will have to do a bit of patient and careful checking and adjusting before moving on and I think they understand this - problems with fairness (the smoothness and harmony of curves) ignored at this point have a habit of biting one in the backside later on so I was keen to encourage them to take the time needed to get it right now. Assuming they manage to regain momentum after this Easter break I would hope they could be ready to start planking by the end of this month.

As for onward planning, Zezinho seemed confident that planking would take a couple of weeks, but I view this as somewhat optimistic. Again, we spent a fair bit of time discussing various aspects of the planking process, and although agreeing with each of the principles that we discussed, I don't think Zezinho yet fully appreciates the time that the general increase in sophistication of the work will add to his estimate. Once they are up to speed, I would think they will do one plank per side per day. There will be about 18 planks per side, so that makes 36 days' work. Add a few more days for the process of getting up to speed, hope for five productive days a week and it's 8 weeks. We may live in hope of more rapid progress but experience suggests modesty of that particular hope is in order.

In terms of materials, there seems to be a good load of planking timber in stock, and we now have I think enough screws in Bahia for this stage of work. More will follow in the container for the deck. Having explored the local option, we are purchasing special drill bits in the US and Fed-Exing these to Zezinho's Camamú address. These drill bits make the right sized tapered hole and countersink for the screw in one go, the alternative being to change drill bits three times for each screw. Multiply the time saving (and quality / repeatability) by 3000 holes and you get the idea!

After planking there are some large internal timbers to be sprung in and following that construction of the deck frame can start. I would also like to get the ballast keel fitted around then. So, my next job is to do my final checks relating to weight and position of the ballast so we can get fabrication of that underway. This is one of two things in the boat that are really beyond Zezinho's experience. He knows a bit about ballast keels, but his comments (and suggestions) regarding this indicate that he does not appreciate the importance of various aspects as they relate to this boat. As such, we have pretty much agreed that we need to source, and deliver the keel to him, and I would like to be there to help bolt it on in the right place (slightly important...). Paula will be researching foundries in The São Paulo area (Z was going to suggest one) and I will send them the information they need direct.

So, looking at time scales, and subject to a bit of monitoring of progress, we might expect them to finish planking around the end of June. I hope it will be possible to have the keel on site by that time also, so we are perhaps looking at the next visit in July, or August (if it rains....). At that visit the aim will be to approve the planking, check the top edge of it (the sheer line) is fair - this being the single most important line in the boat from a visual point of view, help out a bit with the big internal longitudinals, discuss and confirm the way the deck frame is to be done, and bolt on the ballast keel.

Incidentally, the container will have in it the various fastenings that are required for progress beyond planking (including the keel bolts), so the target for that getting to Bahia is late June.

With most boat building projects, once that stage of work is reached we might speculate that the boat is half done. You may draw your own conclusions regarding possible schedule to completion based on that....

The other aim on this visit was to consider the logistics for the later stages of the project. Launching is going to be fun as there is barely enough tidal range to float the boat off the beach. However, the beach we need is pretty firm so moving the boat on it (in a cradle using rollers if I have anything to do with it) should be entirely practicable if time consuming. My current thinking is to complete the timber elements of the boat at the yard, launch and move her elsewhere for the technical fitting out (connecting up of electrics, plumbing and engine) and the rigging. We had a fun discussion with Zezinho about stepping masts, but again this one is taller and probably somewhat more fragile than he is used to and the method he was suggesting, although time proven, scares the willies out of me in this particular case. We did a recce into Camamú, where it was suggested that the bridge might be useful, but there are a couple of factors (including high voltage power cables) that make this less than ideal.

My general proffered option would be to move the boat from the yard to her eventual mooring off Campinho. Jorge indicated this to us, and although we might like to upgrade the gear a bit it's a nice spot. Once she is there, we will be looking to do the technical fit out and rigging. Zezinho and the boys can still be working on small stuff assuming it is not a big problem for them to come over from Cajaíba, although we want their work to be largely complete before launching as once any boat moves out of the shed productivity goes down the pan. In an ideal world, I would like to send a systems chap from here to do the plumbing and wiring and complete the engine installation. Good practice in these elements is fundamental to the safety and reliability of the various systems and will have more of a bearing in your use of the boat than most other aspects of the project. I have someone in mind for this work, and the plan would be for him, the Vetus chap (who we met at the boat show Charles) and I to plan the systems here and put together an order for Vetus in Brazil to deliver to the boat. Some of the things I know they can't supply (the toilet and a pump for example) are going into the container.

As I think we have known all along, the single most tricky bit of this project from the practical side of things is probably the spars. Zezinho I fear, has little conception of what these will be like - I simply had to ask him to believe me that he would understand when he saw them. If they are to be made in Bahia we will have to ship in the timber, and someone to make them. We would also have to ship in separately the various fittings that are attached to the spars. To me at least, far and away the most appealing option is to have them built and finished in the UK by the spar maker I would normally use: http://www.collars. co.uk and ship them out complete. I have discussed this project with Jeremy (at Collars) in the past and again today - they send spars larger than this all over the world so from his point of view it's not a problem. Based on preliminary information Jeremy is going to give an indicative figure for building and fitting out the spars. The fun starts when our precious 75-foot-long package arrives in Brazil. Jeremy and I are both in conversation with Peters and May, who are the shipping agents a lot of marine businesses (including us in the past) turn to for interesting jobs. They know the deal getting stuff into Brazil and are making enquiries. If they can get them as far as Salvador it may make sense to go up there by boat and get them - Zezinho being keen on this option, and to a certain extent me too as keeps us in closer control of their welfare! I will keep you informed as to the options and costs as they emerge, the aim being to put you in a position to evaluate and approve this whole approach within the next week or two. If it turns out not to be a runner we will find another way.

Once the spars get near to the boat (by whatever means), I think the best bet for stepping them is to use the big concrete piers at Campinho and a mobile crane that can be hired from Valença. We had a look at this and given a quiet day I think it's the safest option. Although government owned, we are assured we won't get into trouble if we drive a crane out there and spend a day stepping the masts. I suppose it's just playing with slightly larger fishing rods than are normally deployed from the same spot........ Again, I would like to send a rigger from here to make up the rigging (the materials and fittings are going into the container) so we can be confident it is safe.

Overall, my hope is that myself, Dave (systems chap) and Lee (rigger) can complete these last stages of the project and do trials in one trip. The tricky bit here will be ensuring that all the various elements (including us!) can be caused to arrive in the right place at the appropriate time, and that we will find an otherwise complete boat when we get there. This is all a little way off of course, but we need to map out a plan that allows sufficient slack for delay in launching (say) whilst still getting the boat to completion as quickly as possible. If you can approve this basic approach in principal, I can discuss in more detail with Dave and Lee so we can evaluate the time each will require to do their bit (and the costs) and work back to staged arrivals of components and us.

I think that's probably enough for this email, and I need to go and find some dinner too. If you want to discuss this all on Skype (or some other way) then please let me know.

All the best,
Ed.

***

My weekends were spent mostly outdoors, varied between days on the beach, in a canyon hiking, or on a paddle board on some stretch of water. Seldom did I want to stick around the apartment and dwell on anything I had dedicated my precious energy to during the week. I was learning to draw that vital line between my well-being and the affairs I was working on. I created a routine that ritualized my days according to what I was in need of achieving and then prepared myself to do it. If I was researching the lead keel we were now looking into fabricating for the boat - that's what I would do... second. I would always begin my day by strengthening myself and my confidence either by reading, meditating, or having coffee with my good friend Polet, who was a great believer in masterminding. We encouraged each other, sharing resources like talks and techniques and reading books about personal growth. I knew if I just dragged myself out of bed and attempted to face the day head on, chances were I would be at a loss and end up a muddled mess crying on my knees on the closet floor overwhelmed, succumbed under the weight of my stressors. Accepting this fact and exacting my own self-care, made my days easier to manage because I always knew where to start. I also had a new-found friend in David, a friend of Marco's. He was actually uncle to a high school friend of Marco's, and much closer in age to me, but Marco had always had close friends of all ages. David was uncle to Marco's friend very much like Brazilian uncles who are longtime friends of the family but are not blood related. He too was navigating life's occurrences and was in between homes for a few summers, so he'd come and summer in Marco's room while Marco was away - keeping me much needed company. We'd put on music and cook, sip on some wine and then head out to the balcony for a little smoke. I had long stopped smoking, but always enjoyed a ritual smoke with a close friend. My son Danny was fresh out of high school and attending a community college in town. As the middle child of a very young mother, (I was 23 when I had him) Danny and I had a lot of healing to do together as mother and son. Danny had always felt the effects of his younger brother (Marco) who had bonded very intimately with his older brother (Carlos) and mother, and that made him feel shut out. With Marco in Brazil we had much needed time to talk and just hang out a bit. He was never inclined to invite fellowship, but he was just being himself and getting through his semesters at school, and we had bonded in a deeper way by dealing with Marco's immigration ordeal and my financial stressors together. It was Danny who worked one whole summer to help me pay off a credit card after losing my job. Kleo was a close friend of our family through Kevin, who went to high school with her. She was a sweet teen with a huge heart that was surfing through life's waves that she navigated in her very own unique way. Her authenticity left one feeling awkward at times, but at the same time it was refreshing and inspiring. Kleo was the type of person who spoke openly of sex, masturbation, shortcomings and drama with an absolute unique naturality - such things that most of us are taught to conceal from a very young age. She became like family very quickly and not only did she have a key to our apartment but she also knew she could always find the door unlocked. Oftentimes I'd come home to find her napping on our sofa. She would sleepily ask how my day had been and listen to me with a heartfelt interest, though our worlds were so distinct.

"How was your trip to Brazil?" she'd asked one day over breakfast when I returned. My return flight had been overnight so I had arrived early that morning.

"Wonderful...." I replied and threw in a few curiosities for conversation.

"Did you fuck the engineer yet?" she asked, casually popping a piece of fruit in her mouth. We threw our heads back and roared in laughter. Life was lighter through her lens of irreverence and it suited me well those days when I was taking things way too seriously.

"Well?" She asked not allowing our uproar to distract her.

"Nooooo..." I said as an uncontrollable smirk etched its way across my lips.

"Ah ha!" our laughter once again filled the kitchen.

"Kleo...he's not interested..." I interjected "he's an uptight Brit...you know...." It was strange to even be airing such thoughts.

"I'm not asking if he's interested! Oh my God, you so want to fuck him!" she roared in laughter again "get it girl..." and then added "make his pulling you out of the water worthwhile!" She said thrusting her hips in lewd twerking movements in order to illustrate.

One of the most therapeutic things in life were the laugh attacks Kleo and I would have when we were together. She made it okay for me to be me and say whatever I felt like and that, I suppose opened the door to airing a few feelings I probably had going on under the current and that might have been peaked by the recent event at the beach. I thought back to that evening of quiet conversation and how at ease we were. I wrote it off as a part of the coming down from the adrenaline rush and the soft lull of the music that evening.

***

My sister Analida was always extremely generous and offering of help. Though I was acutely aware that I had to find my own way and not rely on anyone's beneficence alone, she always generously aided with whatever she could. I began feeling that there was no benefit in feeling bad, or sorry for myself for receiving help, but to simply be grateful and celebrate that I had people around me who cared and loved me, and who were in a position to express that care and love in practical ways. I began shifting my feeling towards gratitude rather than the weakening sense I had of receiving "help", because the latter made me feel vulnerable and unable and I was just beginning to become aware of the difference in the feeling tone between those emotions and how each of them made me feel. I decided that I would always take the opportunity to pay it forward in whatever currency was available to me - be it money, time or smiles. Having the support of my loved ones made me aspire to be a better person in that I was made keenly aware of how helpful and healing human connection could be.

It was within this mental attitude of gratitude that I began feeling the tide of events turning, and magically even, favoring me. I didn't so much need to "do" things as I needed to feel *inspired* to an action. As it was, I was spinning from all the pointless emails and billing statements that had achieved little to nothing regarding Marco's immigration case. I decided one day, after yet another pointless email exchange with the consulate in Rio de Janeiro, that's it, I thought - I'm done. I decided to dismiss our immigration attorney after months of depleting impasse and find out what would come-up next. I had this mental picture of being under a hot, slobbering monster that was pinning me down and grunting in my face in a terrorizing way when suddenly, in a moment of strength, I managed to get a leg up and roll myself on top of that thing and pin *it* down.

One day, after putting a call in to Dottie, the friendly office manager, I wrote a brief thank you email to our attorney for his services which I would no longer be needing and asked to be put on a payment plan so that I could take care of my remaining payments over the next few months - or years. I was open to facing whatever I needed to face and I was allowing myself to be guided in this way as the varying scenarios had gone frustratingly wrong when I did things my way. I had, like many of my fellow life-o-nauts, been reading up on all sorts of consciousness oriented literature to facilitate what I now began calling my *journey*. I read The Secret, The Power of Now, Power vs Force, I listened to TED talks, I studied Paramahansa Yogananda. I became a more consistent meditator and several aspects of my life began reflecting these changes.

One morning when I was in the bright sunny yoga room where our training was held at LMU, a professor came in with information that triggered a turning point in me. Loyola Marymount University was going to be offering America's very first Master of Arts program in Yoga Studies. Being constituted by yoga devotees of all walks of life, there was a chorus of "ahhs" in the room that followed the delivery of that bit of news - but I recall laying back on my mat and lifting my arms up above my head in bliss - this finally... *this* is what was waiting for me. This was my calling unfolding right before me and all I had to do was stay on path.

***

With the hull structure completed and planking now underway, we began extending our sights to the upcoming phases of our boat construction. Just when I had grasped what a horn timber and stern post assembly were, I was faced with new terms like spars, masts, rigging and the sizable task of procuring a 6,000 kg lead keel for our vessel in Brazil. The learning curve was huge and Ed and I intensified our communication out of necessity. We were quickly moving ahead towards our fourth solo trip to the boatyard - not counting the initial two reconnaissance trips that took place before construction actually began. Our first container had arrived in Brazil but it was held up in customs for months and cost a small fortune to release, but at this juncture the items were now on their way to Barra Grande. We kept boat items in a small storage room, adjacent to the garage where the utility vehicles of the house were kept.

Ed had proposed he'd try a different flight this time, one that flew via Lisbon, with the thoughtful intent of sparing the Graham's further expense. Placing his arrival later in the afternoon, he would arrive the night before into São Paulo and we would meet the next day at the domestic check in area at Guarulhos International. I also arrived the night before and took the opportunity to hang out with Marco and Carlos for the evening. I called Ed to check in on him.

"How's it going there?" I asked, hoping that he was in good spirits.

"Well, I'll have no trouble sleeping", he replied spiritedly... "...there's a pillow menu on my bed - so no complaints there. You really didn't have to get me such a nice place." Ed reasoned sensibly.

"It's the least I could do after you kindly offered to try the longer flight. You must be exhausted." It was not an expensive place but I appreciated his gratitude.

"Ya…" he agreed. "I'm pretty exhausted. 7:30 am tomorrow at check in?" he suggested.

"We'll have a 3 hour wait til boarding but ya, that sounds great." I knew Ed well enough to know that he was a nervous traveler. He did not like to cut his timing too close. "You sure you don't want to join us for dinner?" I double checked.

"Not tonight - thanks. It certainly doesn't help that you Brazilians dine at 9:00 pm but on next occasion I'll do my best to join ok? On the way back perhaps" he concluded.

"Of course, ya - that sounds great. K, well sleep well - see you tomorrow."

***

We met as agreed and began our trip by connecting in Brasilia. I ran to the girl's room to freshen up between flights and was moistening my curls with lotion, in an attempt to avert frizz, when a muffled voice came over the speaker system. The voice announced that our flight to Ilhéus was delayed.

I walked back to where I had left Ed and found him pacing.

"What took you so long?" he asked, approaching me and looking a bit flustered.

"Just taming the damn frizz …" and added "nothing you would understand with that Hugh-Granty hair of yours." I taunted.

Ed was having none of my humor today - "stay with me," he said, as he leapt more than strode ahead towards our gate.

I let him walk a few feet because it delighted me to see him rushing needlessly, and then sped my pace just enough to make earshot.

"But Ed...." he pressed on ahead of me hurriedly. "Edward!" I enunciated, "our flight is delayed." He was walking so fast that it took him two extra steps to actually register my statement of fact.

"Wha... for how long?" he exasperated. And then with immediate amendment. "Why?" he queried haltingly.

"Well, let's go talk to our airline and find out," I said, spinning on my heels to lead the way.

We arrived at the airline counter to find that our flight would leave at the scheduled time - the next day. Today's flight had been canceled. We knew that would set us back a full 24 hours if we just sat in Brasilia and waited around. We devised a plan that would get us to the house by nightfall. We took the next flight out of Brasilia to Salvador and then crossed the bay via ferry to catch a bus on the other side. This was easier said than done. We had quite a heavy load with screws and nuts and bolts, drill bits and other whatnots. Getting from the airport to the ferry, unloading our bags and crossing the throngs of people that were heading to the other side of the bay, and at rush hour, proved exhausting. When we finally squeezed on with the last batch of passengers, the gate lifted and the long blow horn announced that we were pulling away from land. The temperate breeze cooled and eased our bodies, now flushed from rushing and carrying the weight of our gear. We organized our bags and stood at the guard rail so as to enjoy the breeze and view. We exchanged acknowledged glances but we had no steam for conversation. We journeyed in this way until we were well into the bay and the land was invisible to us. A large cargo ship, carrying hundreds of containers, crossed in the distance. I snapped a selfie of us for lack of anything better to do.

We disembarked on the other shore and hired some help to carry our bags to the bus station a few hundred feet away. We got our tickets and while Ed went to the men's room I assessed the food situation.

"We should probably grab a bite here before starting our 4-hour journey with the chickens?" I suggested.

"We don't have time," came Ed's curt reply, shooting my plan down dryly.

"Ed, the damn bus arrives in 20 minutes and it'll take another 10 at least to load everything on it!" I explained, defending my hunger as he assessed the smorgasbord of little food stands that populated the outdoor bus station. "Come on…." I pleaded, "last thing I need is to travel hungry with an ill-tempered Brit for four hours!"

"Fine, let's grab a beer and a pastel - but let's be quick," he said. Caving under the influence of the inadequacy of the frugal snack we'd eaten on the airplane hours before.

We sat, each enjoying our beers and pastel. Ed was becoming familiar with all the roadside goodies to be had when traveling in Brazil. He made increasing efforts to order for himself and to say please and thank you in Portuguese to those serving us.

"Oh, I see…" I said, following an impetus that arose in me completely out of the blue. "You know how to be nice, you're just mean to me because you can be…" I looked at him while doing my best impression to express legitimate hurt.

"I'm not mean to…when was I mean to you?" Ed questioned, displaying that assorted mixture of shock and amusement that most men use when they're not sure where a woman is coming from.

"Always…" I said flatly, now legitimately feeling a little tinge from all the times he'd been short with me, or walked steps ahead, making me practically trot to keep up with him… "just always…" I reiterated my feeling of disdain.

Our beers arrived, interrupting our conversation, while our server poured our icy brews and then set the bottle back in its styrofoam sleeve.

"Cheers," Ed offered, adding, "if I didn't like you I wouldn't have risked my life to pull you out of the water," he claimed, trying on a little smirk as if to test my acceptance of such a statement.

"Only to pull me out so you could starve me at your will!" I blurted as we were now speaking in jest.

We finished our snack and made our way to the bus. It was hot and humid and within that languid atmosphere we quickly fell asleep. My head rolled onto his shoulder a few times until we both settled into the comfort of such intimacy. Though deeply enthralled in sleep, we were both acutely aware that we were crossing a tropical rainstorm, as the showers beat incessantly on the windshield of our bus, but we were both much too drained to care about impending death at this point. We woke up just outside of Camamú at dusk, as the heavy downpour had set us back a few hours. We arrived to the parochial little town that now smelled of fresh rain showers and was shrouded heavily in dramatic, blue-gray clouds, allowing just enough of the purple tint of the day's last rays to filter in and glisten off the graphite sheen of the cobblestone street that cut through town. We were both somewhat aware that we would likely have to sleep in Camamú this night, making our way to the boatyard straight from there in the morning, but we asked a local boater anyway.

"No..." our informant spoke in a way that sounded a lot like Zezinho. "The water is too murky from all the rain and the tide is not cooperating. We'll take you tomorrow morning if the weather allows," he confirmed matter of factly.

Ed and I surveyed the waterfront and spotted a small hostel facing the shore. The colors from previous pastel colored paint coatings, showed evident through the unkempt façade.

Ed removed a dress shirt from his bag and offered it to me, as the winds brought thick drops of rain upon us. I slipped it on over my flowery dress, just before it started pouring again. We jogged hastily through the rain, the last stretch into what was meant as a little reception area but was really just a simple sitting area that was composed of a common wooden work desk and swivel chair. Our luggage trailed in just behind us in a wheel cart. There was an image of Mother Mary and a small board with a scripture etched on it.

"Boa noite!" I said, greeting the innkeeper cheerfully.

"Ohp," he emitted, as the local one syllabled greeting goes, and then he completed with a: "boa noite," himself.

"Is it possible that you would have two rooms available sir?" I asked, entertained by the silliness of my question, being that it was a weekday and in such a small town, I was assured of a positive response.

"Yes, I have one room - but it will fit the both of you well," he said, looking down at whatever was distracting him since we'd arrived.

"Oh, right. But we need two rooms," I insisted.

The innkeeper now looked up and over his reading glasses. "Aren't you two traveling together?" he queried, looking surprised.

"Yes, but we're here for work and we're not - well...do you think I'd find another room in town?" I queried further.

Ed shuffled a bit in anticipation of an update - "Don't tell me they're sold out!" he mused, humored at such a possibility.

The three of us just stood there. Our cart wheeler cleared his throat and clarified, "it's a long and steep uphill into town - especially in this rain."

I turned to the innkeeper again. "So, you don't have two rooms?" I insisted.

"Why would you want two rooms if I have one to fit you both? You'll have to pay for two rooms you know."

"Oh!" I said relieved. "...but you have two rooms?"

"Well ya...," he said, adding, "but it's just one night and the second room is not really fit for you," he spoke at last.

"Ya... we'll take the two rooms if you have them," I reiterated.

The innkeeper set two registration cards and a pen to fill them out. He twisted his face as to express his perplexity.

We paid our rooms, tipped our carrier, took our keys and asked where we could get some dinner nearby.

"It's raining too hard for you to go anywhere," the innkeeper replied. "My cousin works at the pizza place up the hill - I can have him bring you pizza if you'd like."

We agreed on the 'house' pizza, which came highly recommended by our innkeeper's cousin and headed to our rooms for showering. When the pizza arrived, I tiptoed over to Ed's room and rapped lightly on the door.

"Ed! Dinner's ready!" I whispered, though it seemed apparent that there were no other guests residing in our modest hostelry.

"Should I come to yours then?" he asked, cracking his door open slightly and appearing freshly showered in his towel.

"Yes, we'll serve in my suite. I'm right over..." he cut me off.

"I know where you are silly - there are only two rooms in this place!" he chuckled. "I'll be right there," he said, closing his door again.

My room was really, almost technically, a closet. With a small bathroom that probably resembled a cell in a penitentiary, I was compelled to embellish the hovel with my flair. I pulled the musty bed covers off and put them in the bottom drawer of a small chest in the corner. Opening a small, louvered window allowed fresh air to aerate my little *pied a térre*. I sprayed some essential oils on the tired bed sheets, laying a fresh and colorful sarong I had packed along across it, improvising a table. There was no surface on which to eat so I figured we could sit on my twin bed, put our pizza in the middle and eat as elegantly as possible.

Ed gave the door two quick raps and pushed it open as I'd left it ajar.

"I'm sorry I didn't bring flowers or wine..." he smiled, his humor refreshing after a long and tiring day.

"All the better...," I smirked. "The monogrammed carafe is nowhere to be found."

We opened the box to find a huge 18" pizza that was thin as paper and appeared somewhat cold and moist from its commute through town under the rain. There gathered were the most random selection of toppings one could imagine. Peas, corn, and hard-boiled egg slices amongst them. We were quite famished and exhausted after a full day's travel so we settled ourselves each to an end of the bed. I sat Indian style facing him from the head and he sat at the foot of the bed - leg folded across - his right foot tucked under the left leg facing me. We chatted, eating with our hands and sharing a large chilled Guaraná - a fruity soft drink that is famously loved in Brazil.

We spoke of pizza, funny botched travel plans, and his childhood. I admired that he'd known what he wanted to do with his life since age four, particularly as I'd still not really known myself what my true purpose was, even up to this day. He told me that he had never once questioned that he wanted to build boats and that from an early age all he ever wanted to do was draw them. I inquired about his siblings, his mother and father and we spoke about the idiosyncrasies that each of our families possessed. We laughed at some and displayed annoyance at others and it was relaxing to not talk about work for a change.

"E-ed... now that we're in bed together...." I taunted, prefacing my next question.

He looked at me and rolled his eyes, knowing that I had learned his weak points as well as being completely aware that he had long learned mine, but he played along...

"We're not in bed together, we're using your bed as a table..." he elucidated my sly provocation.

"Sexier yet..." I grinned as I stuffed a fugitive black olive into my mouth.

"Well, you haven't told me much about your love life...." I pried, testing the territory and knowing well that this could end our talk pronto.

"What...? Oh come on!" He exclaimed, shifting uncomfortably before settling himself, again under my scrutiny. "What's there to know? There's nothing to know!" he exclaimed.

"Well, have you ever had a girlfriend?" I clarified, before amending, "I mean a romantic relationship with another being, be it a girl, a sheep or whatever..."

"Psh, of course!" but before he could proceed I cut in.

"And to clarify are we talking sheep or...?"

"Listen, I've had dates and I've had girlfriends and the lot, but it's just not on the top of my priority list right now." he said simply.

"Ya, fair enough... See? That didn't hurt too bad did it?" I made light, keeping my foot in the door nonetheless... "And when was your most recent relationship then?"

Ed crossed his hands and leaned forward a bit, as if he were about to explain Einstein's theory of relativity to me. "Well, it wasn't so much a relationship as it was a romantic interest..." he began.

"Ooooooo.... go on now..." I grabbed my pillow and hugged it as I leaned back on the headboard enthralled.

"Well, she's a sailor as well... and I know her from town."

Wanting this account to gain momentum, I hardly breathed so as not to disturb the telling, but my body language urged him on nevertheless.

"Her name is Lennie and she's an illustrator," Ed expounded freely.

"Oh!" I couldn't contain my elation - "An artist!" I exasperated.

"She has a daughter too but has no relationship with the father you see..." His account came off quite hesitant, as if he wanted to make sure he himself understood what he was explaining. My body language remained static as I took in his account.

"We've all gone sailing, her, her daughter, and I, in Turkey, about this same time last year..."

"Yes! I remember you went to Turkey, I just didn't know about all this... Ed, how cool..." I'd always been a sucker for a love story.

"Well, it hasn't really advanced in the way I intended and recently I found out she's moving across country. Chances are - we won't be seeing each other anymore..."

"What??? Ed, you can't let that happen!" I said, protesting his determinism to lose her.

"Don't be silly...." he looked down at his hands and up again, as if he might be prepared to hear my reasoning.

"I mean, I don't know how you feel about her, but if you love her - Ed, if you *love* her...you cannot just let love slip by like that. Every opportunity to love is precious."

"Well, I don't know if I can say I *love* her..." he confessed the latter in a way that revealed, at least to my imaginative and love tracked mind, that he did. "She's kind and very talented - you'd like her". I felt that I loved her already, just for the simple fact of making a man like Ed feel this way and say such things. His expression was tender and revealed a side of him I hadn't known.

We spoke of her and why things hadn't worked exactly as planned and I tried my best to indoctrinate him regarding matters of the heart - from my perspective anyway.

"Ed... you can't use your head to solve matters of the heart. It's not an equation, it's love and love is deliciously senseless. One cannot *think* their way through the fury of love - you need to *feel* your way through."

"Ya, well I'm not willing to go through the heartbreak aga..." he interrupted this thought, protesting - "Listen, some things are just not meant to happen and that's fine."

Our subject progressed to talk of crazy ex-lovers and stalkers. We cringed and even sang bits of Alanis Morrisette songs to illustrate the madness of past relationships. When Ed reverted to planning our next work day, I yawned - "Ooooh, that was a long day huh?" I said stretching my limbs as far as they would go.

"Ok," he said determinedly, springing to his feet. "See you tomorrow in the lobby for breakfast?" he asked, making his way to the door.

"Yes....9:00 a.m.?" I teased.

He twisted his lips to one side and said conclusively, "7:00 am it is." He turned quickly and ducked out the door.

***

The fact our flight had been canceled could have been taken as an omen. Almost every day we had an event to deal with. When it wasn't the torrential rains, it was a broken-down vehicle. We managed to go through every vehicle in the house and were now commuting in a quad bike. The Lillibelle was in disrepair as well so we tried taking the road to Cajaíba, proving a very bad idea under the heavy rains. Analida and Charles had just imported a British racing green Range Rover so we threw that into the rotation as well, but rains were so heavy one day, that the hood of the rover was completely submersed. Rains were nonstop day and night. Ed and Olivan improvised a piece of tarp so that we might come and go without getting soaked - but we still did under the torrential showers. It was 6 days of absolute downpour. Each day, Ed devised a different way to make it to the boatyard under the frenzied rainfall. We worked in drenched clothing all day, but the days were a little shorter as we had to heed whatever transportation we'd found, to make our way to and from work for the day. The rain had an interesting effect on us. I was quieter and more contemplative. Ed became increasingly stir crazy. He let out much of his energy preparing meals for us. He became accustomed to the kitchen in the old house and preferred the staff be dismissed earlier so he could take over the cooking. I had a lot of school work to do as I had just begun the semester in the Master's program at LMU. We'd get back to the house and shower and Ed would settle me in at one end of the long wooden table with a cold beer and some peanuts or chips. I would work diligently on my Sanskrit lessons while his cooking filled the air with deliciousness. The power went out almost every night due to the rains so we kept candles and matches on hand. Working internet was just a hope on most days, so he would accompany me into town for groceries and then we'd stop by the local internet cafe to check our emails. The owner of the cafe, Yolanda, was a local and exuberant smiling beauty, rolled up in her colorful sarong and matching tank top. She sold the most amazing chocolate truffles on the planet and if there was anything Ed and I shared, it was our addicted love of chocolate. I would lose myself in cheerful conversation with Yolanda, while Ed replied to his emails. We were seen together more and more in town and people began to become accustomed to us to the point that the yelling vendors near the pier no longer bothered to yell out as we passed. They knew we were not tourists but were working in Cajaíba. We were becoming locals.

One morning, the rains were so torrential we couldn't leave the house until close to noon, due to the extreme showers and unfavorable tides. I sat at the table dedicating myself to some physiology homework while Ed paced restlessly, already having revisited plans for that day's work multiple times. A loud splash made me glance up from my work to note that he had jumped into the pool despite the pouring rain and had begun swimming laps! He swam back and forth briskly until he emerged at one end and stood there glancing up at the sky as if to assess some situation. As he walked by the living room on the deck, he popped his head in and announced decidedly "we part in 30!".

At the yard, our days were productive despite being shorter and wetter. Planking was coming along fine, only a few hiccups in negotiating the twisting slope in the hull and closing the gap which appears when you plank in both directions concomitantly-from top to bottom and bottom to top. True, this was a slight oversight caused by offsite management, but somewhat simple to correct and Ed did not seem too worried as he seemed to have a plan for sorting that out. We marked the sheer line, which is the curvature of the top plank that gives the boat it's shape along the top plank that runs from bow to stern separating the side of the hull from the deck. Each day there was a new topic for me to learn - deck structure, beam shelf, fairing, plug cutting...it was all Greek to me, but Ed was good about filling me in before we went out. In this way, I could not only translate the language but also express the details in an elementary way, how I understood them, making it all much more palatable for Zezinho and crew. We had a local 'specialist' come out to bore what would become the prop shaft hole before all the planking was completed. It is easier done when you can see the hole through the sternpost behind it. We marked out the height of the bilge stringer in the boat and set out the position for the engine bearers and mast step. We now were not only sourcing a foundry for our lead keel, but also beginning to discuss system purchases, sails, caulking and painting. Our pace was picking up and we had several strands of work going simultaneously. We both flew home happy with the progress we'd made, but exhausted after a full day in São Paulo as we visited a marine supplier before our flights, in the hopes of sourcing a few components for the systems.

***

September 2013: The Deck

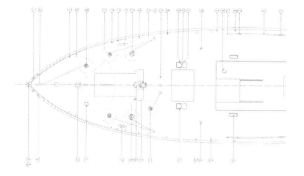

Kathini

A story of love, loss and a little boat building

W̶e both hit the floor running when we got to our respective homes. I had given Ed my iPhone 3 when we arrived in São Paulo since I had upgraded to the next version, and we now had one new dimension of communication between us - WhatsApp. The only downside to this decision was that I could no longer taunt Ed about his primitive little flip phone that had no internet connection - but I had to take one for the team. Managing the project had officially become my full-time job. I was still working my way up a steep learning curve regarding boat building, which is much more taxing than when one is already skilled at something. The masculine atmosphere was a bit perplexing as well, but we navigated between work items and lighter fare by sending each other funny animal pics and up-close pictures of our faces showing nostril hairs - anything that kept the momentum of the day running smoothly and interestingly.

We began discussing masts and spars needs and Ed was keen to use his trusted friend, and artisan Jeremy Freeland. Jeremy was an acclaimed maker of custom wooden masts, spars and oars in Dorchester on Thames, operating in the countryside of the UK. It was decided that Ed would travel to London in October to meet with Charles at his office on the posh Sloane Street where they would meet to discuss such crucial decisions, as well as other important details of the project.

One morning, upon speaking to Analida, the impending meeting in London came up in our conversation.

"Well Paula, I don't know how you do it," she said. "But it's amazing to me that this crazy boat idea is actually coming together. You're such a star..." Analida was always encouraging of me after we both married and had children. Before that, I was a brat to her and she bullied me into submission. The sort of things psychologists have written volumes about, that older siblings might do to their younger out of sibling rivalry.

"So, what are your dates for the meeting in October?" she inquired. "Let's schedule beauty treatments and have some quality sister time!" she asserted enthusiastically.

"Well, I'm not sure I'm needed there really. Not like they need translation or my pivotal remarks regarding mast fittings...." I said tentatively, not having even considered the possibility of attending before this instance.

"What? Paula, you are the project manager! You belong in that meeting as much as the two men and I intend to have you in that meeting room, discussing the matters at hand with them that day...in glorious attire of course..." she emitted a giggle from her own assertive outburst before continuing "...stop being such a nitwit!", she added for emphasis.

"Well, I suppose we do have logistics to discuss..." I began considering.

"Paula, you're coming to the meeting and we're squeezing in some fab sister time - that's that. I'm getting your tickets. Send me your dates as soon as we get off the phone, ok?" she decreed.

***

10/18/2013 12:04am
Good morning!

I spoke to Z and ironed out all the details we brought up regarding payment, deck timber, and the foundry info.

It seems you'll have the benefit of a personal update regarding all that later this week (see pic below). Do keep a secret for now as I have not told Charles and would love to retribute the surprise visit he paid me earlier this summer.

Bringing some sunshine in my pocket. Do advise if you are in need of anything chocolate covered and I'll be happy to oblige.

Paula :)

Ps: attached is a screenshot of my reservation and flight info in and out of London.

His response followed soon after:

Okey dokey,

Hope you have a comfortable flight and will see you next week. Happy to come a little earlier if we can get on with something productive before meeting with Charles and Analida.

Note that "shopping" is not classed as a productive activity, however drinking coffee is.

All the best,
Ed.

***

As it turned out, Analida kindly upgraded my ticket to Business class and I arrived in London fresh as a daisy that Monday. Analida and I had our quality sister time. We took long walks in the park, sipping on soy chai lattes from Caffé Nero. We attended the Frieze art fair with her son Alex. We got manis and pedis and had our hair done. We talked about the most diverse subjects from Marco's immigration case to my somewhat directionless love life. We enjoyed the unveiling of a new pipe organ that was donated to the Royal Academy of Music by Sir Elton John. It was a much-needed reprieve from the long days I'd spent in front of the computer and on the telephone, days that had succeeded the return from Brazil and it was lovely to hang with Analida, her youngest son Patrick and Charles. The others were away at school.

Thursday rolled around and Ed and I had decided that it wouldn't be worthwhile for me to come to Totnes on such a short turnaround time, so he came up to London earlier instead, so that we could meet ahead of the scheduled meeting with Charles. I was arriving just about 6 minutes past our appointed meeting time, to the café on the top floor of the Peter Jones department store at Sloane Square, when I received a text from Ed.

Have I missed you? I'm on the ground floor at main entrance.

Urgh! I rolled my eyes and began rushing down the escalators again. I was clad in a short, flair-skirted, brocade designer dress, black tights and a pair of black velveteen ankle boots. My hair was freshly highlighted and I wore a spritz of J'Adore, by Dior.

'I'm on top floor at café!' and then *'Coming down!'* I texted as I made my way hurriedly down the six flights of crisscrossed escalators again.

Just at that moment I received his reply … *'K! Coming up!'*

Urgh!! I looked to get off at the next floor to begin ascending again, when I saw an astonished Mr. Burnett glancing up at me from the landing I was just approaching.

"Hey stranger!" I galloped off the last steps of the escalator and launched my arms behind his neck as I came in close to give him a cuddle.

His eyes were glazed over, almost as if he wasn't sure it was me.

I giggled as I blurted "Oh right, I forget that you're not used to seeing me dressed!" and elucidated, after witnessing a by-passer's head turn, entertained at his bewilderment "I mean, dressed in city clothes!"

"Right... how was your trip?" he inquired, as we made our way back up to the café on the top floor.

"Great! I travelled like a true British classic yacht designer in biz class...." I grinned proudly.

"It's good to see you here," he composed, ignoring my jibe. "Did you come just for the meeting?" he asked.

"Eh, you know, Analida and I haven't really hung out in a long time. We've been doing girl stuff - which is why my nails are perfectly lacquered!" I vaunted, extending my hands to show off my nails, glazed in a luscious dark purple. "You should see my toes!" I suggested in fun, nudging his leg with the toe of my boot playfully.

We chose a table and decided to have soup and paninis, since we had a long meeting ahead. We chatted merrily about what a bummer it was that I couldn't come out to Totnes, and how there was a new cat café in town, where the cats mingled with the customers and soothed their state of mind.

"You'd love Totnes", he said enthusiastically "it's right up your alley with the crystals, the healers and the witches....".

"What? I'm a witch now?" I teased back.

We bantered in wit and I ate most of his soup which was miles better than the bland lentil soup I had chosen. When I asked about Lennie, his eyes darkened and he said bluntly, "I don't see how that concerns you..." and then under his breath, "I don't know why I ever mentioned that to you - now I'll never hear the end of it!" At this point, I had already learned to not take offense and just move forward with another subject when Ed was cross.

"I'll tell you what you'll never hear the end of...you should have told me the lentil soup here was crap!" I asserted reaching across to fill my spoon with his curry soup once more. Crisis averted.

We finished our meal and then headed to Charles' office for our assemblage.

We had a pleasant and productive meeting which lasted just over 3 hours. We had a long list of topics to address. Analida joined us at one point as we were taking the opportunity to discuss interior layout, finishes and fixtures, as well as galley and accessories.

It was decided that the mast and spars would be fashioned in British Columbian Pine, which grows in Canada and is known as Douglas Fir in the United States, where it also grows in the Pacific Northwestern part of the country. The masts hold the rigging and the spars and are the long bits of wood that support the sails, so these are definitely what are known as showcase pieces on a classic wooden yacht. Having been designed a 56' double ended ketch, there are two masts - a main measuring 70' and a mizzen measuring 52'. The logistics of getting these and all the hardware and fittings to the Brazilian port of Vitoria and then up the coast by truck, seemed daunting. Ed was unwavering in confidence and resolve. The masts were to be shipped partially "dressed", which, in layman's terms, meant with all their electronics and stainless-steel fittings in place. The fittings were to be manufactured by Hercules at Dartmouth, also hand chosen by Mr. Burnett, who was determined to cut no corners on this project. Everything was of the highest standard - each shackle and pin in the rigging of the utmost quality. It was surely a different experience than I had had so far, being under the zinc covering with the chickens and strays in Cajaíba. It was also decided that the main purpose of this vessel would be for short 'day sails,' with the family while on holiday in Bahia, so there would be no need for a shower in the head (which is what one calls the bathroom on a sailboat). The interior design was to be an open floor plan - meant for the family to convene for meals, or a quick nap, so no need for individual sleeping cabins - just stacked berths. A center table was to be an accent piece, with folding laterals for ease of movement, when meals were not being served. The galley was to be simple and functional, designed to serve mainly light fare like sandwiches, chilled wine and soft drinks for the day. Cabin and deck cushions were to be in breathable, mold and mildew resistant fabric and in classic colors like navy blue and white. A basic 12-volt system would power the instruments as there would be no appliances or heftier electrical needs. The fridge would be an icebox that could be loaded on and off as needed, containing the provisions for a day and nestled within a fine wooden cabinet with easy access from the top. Music could be played via marine grade Bluetooth speakers, onto which the youth could just plug-in their devices and push play. Everything was indeed customized to suit our family and lifestyle. I began drifting out of the conversation, my thoughts persisting on the huge responsibility of finishing this boat. The new wave of financial disbursements, now trumping the initial investment in timbers and fastenings by far, made my concerns even more considerable. Hard as I tried, the classic day yacht that sat in my imagination, did not match the rustic, ark-looking structure that was sitting back in our yard in Cajaíba.

We discussed the complex excel sheet that we had been adding to from the start and that Charles had now transformed into a shareable and amazingly functional worksheet. The work fronts were now various and divided into sections: hull, deck, systems, rigging, soft finishes, painting, varnishing, logistics and importation - the list went on and on. More and more suppliers, more and more items to purchase and deliver, we were in the thick of building a boat and it was as exciting as it was daunting. The days of bringing visitors to the yard and showing them a long piece of wood laying across the dusty chicken yard were over. We now had a boat to show for and the sense of responsibility and pride were growing along with the project. We decided a trip in November was in order and planned out the core work fronts to address over the next few weeks and who would be responsible for what. At this point, tasks were mainly marked with an E a P or a Z, indicating which of the three of us was responsible for completing the task. Charles' responsibility was to see to it that large amounts of money were made available for Carol to disburse as invoices came due, making him keen to question and then scrutinize every expense with a fine-tooth comb. Massive amounts of emails began to populate our inboxes and Ed and I worked as a tight team in making sure no task fell behind, or through the cracks. When mistakes were inevitably made, we covered each other's backs and worked together to solve the hiccups. The November trip rolled around in what seemed like days rather than the actual weeks that had passed, and we had a long list of tasks to go with it.

***

While I was working on juggling the multiple strands of work generated by our project, which had now assumed the dimensions of a classic yacht, I was maintaining my firmness of purpose by staying anchored and open to finding the next sure step towards a positive outcome in Marco's immigration case. Meanwhile, Marco had gone to meet Kevin and some friends at a resort on the Mexican Riviera and summer had come and gone. We talked often, always keeping each other motivated and milking what we could out of any positive details we could find during this surreal episode of our lives.

One afternoon, I had granted myself some time on the couch - which was rare in my life, as I was essentially a human *doing* rather than a human *being*. I had always had to have a plan, seeming control with something always brewing, but this particular afternoon, I had gone for a light hike in a local canyon and afterwards found myself sitting on the sofa having Cinnamon Toast Crunch cereal and staring at the TV which was off. The set sat off 98% of the time. I would not even have had a TV had it not been for watching the Olympic games, World Cup football matches and other such events that the boys enjoyed. Yet, there I sat, lost in this parallel universe that we dive into when we're quiet. As I glared absently at the screen, a suggestion arose - *talk to the best immigration attorney money can buy.... here in LA.* Maybe a Latino attorney, who knows the system from the inside out - but definitely someone who dominates this game. The other half of my mind was quick to answer, '*ha! with what money? Another attorney - the first one didn't work...I don't have time or money for another attorney to waste...*' My defiant spirit took the conversation back to the positive, '*you said you'd go with the flow and be open to guidance...here it is: get the best attorney money can buy*'. I pulled up my laptop and searched: "immigration attorney Beverly Hills" I tried several other searches and browsed to see if anything spoke to me. My mind spoke again, '*this is silly, even if we find an attorney, how are you going to pay for it? We still owe the last one*'. I pulled up my balance on my banking app...$280. Before my heart had the chance to sink, my eye caught an offer - *First Consultation $250*. Hmmmm... I picked up the phone with my mind still protesting, '*what are we going to do for food the rest of the month?*'

"Hello?" Before the bickering voices could come to an agreement within me, I had scheduled an appointment with an attorney on Wilshire Blvd in Beverly Hills in two days' time.

I showed up to the beautiful office building and found a shady parking spot on a side street. As I pushed the coins into the parking meter my mind wondered how it would all turn out, as butterflies fluttered around in my stomach. The building was luxurious and the elevators easily the size of my dining room. I pushed the button to the top floor and checked in with the receptionist, who escorted me into the stately office within minutes of my arrival.

"Hi, nice to meet you." I began, not certain where to start the conversation as I accommodated my nerves in the oversized tufted leather wing chair facing his desk.

"How can I help you?" came the attorney's direct reply. He was clearly not interested in niceties, getting straight to the heart of the matter.

I sat across from the type of man I was used to working with in the mortgage and real estate business – confident and well groomed; straight to the point, no coloring of a story – so I knew from experience to keep it down to about 3 minutes and answer questions from there rather than pour my emotional heart out.

After hearing my summary of the case behind a poker face he posed one question – "have they supplied you with a reason for denial since?"

"No, they say it's confidential but he was still 17 when I began requesting, so …."

"Ok, well, here's what I can do," he countered, unconcerned with my conclusion. "I can put a case together for you – I'm confident that we have one."

I listened intently. Hope had begun circulating my being, causing a gnawing soreness in the pit of my heart, like a muscle that had not been exercised often enough.

"I can have the case together in about 8 - 10 months."

"Like, *resolved* in 8 – 10 months?" I cut in, desperately thinking that he could not possibly mean just getting paperwork in order to file in that time.

"Just to get the case together to file," he continued, confirming my worst fear. Driving the point home he added "…and that, of course, if everything runs smoothly".

My heart sank. My mind was busy doing the math that added up quickly to stomaching at least another 18 - 20 months of this ordeal, being that the appeal could take about that same amount of time as well once filed.

"Right…." I bit my lip, feeling myself crumpling quickly on the inside.

"I can put the case together for you for $12,000, plus filing fees. The follow up will be charged hourly. We require a deposit of $5,000 for that once the case is filed."

I didn't understand if the $12,000 had to be paid up front and in full, or monthly, but I did understand that at this point, it didn't really matter. I stared out the window over his shoulder, onto the horizon and past Beverly Hills, as I tried to gain control of my emotions, but the heat induced from digesting the devastating words I had just heard was wreaking havoc on my insides, circling wildly throughout my imagination, falling heavily on the pit of my stomach, rushing straight up through my heart and flushing my face - only to find its way out cascading from my eyes in a torrent of scorching tears.

"I can't do that...." I broke down sobbing, "none of it...I can't wait another two years and I can't afford any of that...I can't any of this – Oh my God..." I covered my mouth with my hands to suppress the flow of hopeless words.

He handed me a tissue and clasped his hands together under his chin, taking in my general state.

"I'm sorry," I said frankly. "I'm a desperate mother." I tried to etch a smile through trembling lips.

"I understand," he said, sitting back in his elegant leather swivel.

We sat in silence for about 40 seconds while I composed myself and then my mouth uttered words I had not consented to or ever planned to speak.

"Do you have a strategy you'd advise me with if I were to take on this case myself?"

"Your only chance is to claim emotional hardship." After these words, he proceeded to pour out his vision, that, though little understood, I listened to with all my might.

I drove home in a trance-like state. Lost in my thoughts and in all that had led to this moment, somewhere along the journey home, every cell in my body came to an agreement - I was going to take over this case and win it and I believed it.

*****

My trip to London in October brought about a frenzy of quoting, purchasing and figuring out delivery logistics all at the same time. November, which was when we had decided we should visit Cajaíba once again, rolled around quite quickly and I couldn't write and reply to emails quickly enough. There is quite an acute cultural difference in quoting things in the US, in Brazil and in the UK. In the US, sales reps reply promptly, are quick to upsell, and make recommendations and state what they can and can't do and there are no exceptions to their policies. In the UK, everything is in black and white and even if you clearly order one part that will not fit in with the other - they will keep to themselves and allow you to order as you please as they would never overstep and assume that you don't know what you're ordering. Come to think of it, this explains why Ed was always so annoyed when our reps in America would get back to us with suggestions instead of a quote. In Brazil, most businesses depending on how far north or south they are on the map, (the closer to the tropics, the more susceptible to the island rhythm they are) ordering usually entails one introductory email and 5 - 15 follow up emails before you hear back with a quote. Even if I wrote requesting a quote for a sizeable order, the reply always came after three follow up emails and a couple of calls -

'Hi Ma'am, we received your order for a million screws... unfortunately we don't have those in stock and we're not sure when we'll be placing our next order. Want to try us back next month?' They will however bend over backwards for you and break every policy known to man - if they feel like it - to please you. I've seen people ask their cousins to put things on the bus on a Sunday afternoon for Zezinho to pick up at the bus station early Monday. They are slow to start, but once you build momentum, you're in business.

***

My bags would surely get me in trouble this time, I thought, knowing full well at this point that I had been extremely fortunate when it came to getting past check in with heavy, overloaded bags. The 6-foot threaded silicone bronze rods that were sitting in Cajaíba were evidence of that fact. Ed and I spoke daily - sometimes two to three times daily and for longer periods of time. While we worked through codes and specifications we had gotten to know each other a lot better. As a result, on several occasions he had to deal with my moodiness due to the irritation I felt at not being proficient in what we were doing together and that gave me a gnawing sense of insecurity. We both learned quickly that I did not perform well when I was insecure, nor when I was hungry for that matter. Ed, on the other hand, felt no insecurity whatsoever when it came to his trade. He was quickly triggered at the first hint that anyone would even consider that he didn't know exactly what he was looking for at all times, but take the conversation beyond business to that of personal or emotional realm and you had a deer staring straight into your headlights.

"Morning sunshine..." I greeted him cheerfully beginning our conversation one day.

"What can I do for you?" Ed replied abruptly, indicating by his tone that there would be absolutely no beating around the bush today.

"Dave from Jamestown has received our order and has put most of it together," I said, plunging straight in. "But he's wondering if we wouldn't prefer the Raymarine model attached, rather than the one we quoted him, as he says that's a newer model?"

"I am quite aware of the models that are available and have done my research thank you" came his curt reply. Let's ask Dave to keep to quoting and I'll keep to actually designing the systems?" he finalized, with a lilt of a question lacing his superior voice.

"K!" I replied quickly. Ending our interaction, as not to stir things up and considering his busy day.

In time, Ed would stick to the same courtesy when I was having one of my hot and bothered days and we navigated the days up to our trip within that synchronicity, but for the most part our interactions were riddled with pics of up-close cow noses, moist dog tongues and lose translations Ed would put together in google translate 'blessing' our efforts in a certain phase of the project such as "may the Baby Jesus help us to reconcile the planking gap" alluding to the strong religious vein of the Camamú bay.

***

Our arrival in Cajaíba had our makeshift boatyard looking pretty legit, with more workers, materials and threads of work on site. Ed and I would daily work in the company of Zezinho, Raimundo, and Sid (Zezinho's son). Most of the caulking was done in our absence as it's a fairly noisy process. In our case we combined caulking with tree fiber and finished the seams with a commercial goo called Sikaflex which made our finish close to impeccable. Bunging is plugging the countersunk holes where one has screwed or fastened the planks to the hull with wooden plugs so as to protect the screws from water damage and from creating rust stains as well as preventing water from seeping through those holes into the hull over time. Ed chose to bung each and every fastening for a more elegant and long-lasting finish. I did plenty of bunging myself, an activity that made my mind feel like it was off duty. I found it quite a meditative process but most of the bunging was done in our absence by Sid, who would usually stay in Cajaíba during our visits, even though he lived in an adjacent village most of the time. Sid was quiet with expressive eyes. One could tell he was a bright young man and he bore a mild and respectful demeanor. He had been living happily with a woman nearly 30 years his senior since just after the project began in 2011. Ed often remarked on how much potential Sid displayed and what a good job he was doing at following instruction and learning new techniques. Sid's progressive outlook was a clear expression of a new generational ideal emerging in these parts. He had gone beyond the previous generation's limited education, that ended around middle school in its majority, or of the generation before having been home-schooled or educated according to whatever their families' trade may be. Because the economic structure of these regions had yet to be heavily affected by a heavier presence of capitalism, they survived wonderfully by keeping the family nucleus and businesses tightly connected. This seemed to keep incidences of unemployment, homelessness and other by-products of capitalism to a bare minimum.

On this particular trip, Marco had joined us in São Paulo and flown up with us to Bahia. With the exception of just one day, when he deigned to venture to the boatyard with us, he'd stayed back at the beach compound, enjoying the house and solitude-filled days most of the time. Meanwhile, Ed and I invested long work days at the yard. We spent umpteen hours balancing ourselves on the cross beams, then down in what was to become the cabin, discussing the deck plan and organizing how to fasten the keel once it had been delivered. I had finally found a small boat maker in the south that had connections to a foundry who had agreed to handle the transaction for us for a 5% commission of its total value. Lorena, the owner's daughter who had taken over the boatyard from her father and grandfather, was an experienced and trustworthy businesswoman and she made what could have been a nightmare of a thing into a pretty straightforward process. Following and transmitting all of Ed's instructions, she was able to closely coordinate getting the six-ton keel cleared to travel the over 2,000 kilometers it would take to find its home. Once it made it through the tumult of precarious roads and up to Cajaíba, it would be attached to what semblance of a boat we had at the time. Due to the weight and nature of the load, Brazilian road authorities required special licenses be obtained, as well as requiring our haul to be escorted by a pilot vehicle on certain stretches of road. For this, all sorts of preparations had to be looked into. As we had plenty to do at the yard, we scheduled a full week for this particular trip, allowing us plenty of opportunity to mingle within the village and its people.

In Barra Grande, there was a British woman who was holding a luau at her beach-front property down the beach from us. It was a full moon and by some miracle, Ed had agreed to come along to the event with Marco and I. We had had an exceptionally long day at the yard so I wanted to make sure that I really enjoyed this particular night out. I took a long shower and braided my hair to one side for the occasion and donned it with a large white flower I had picked from the garden. I chose a slinky halter top to match my miniscule black mini-skirt and made my way to the veranda. My fresh flowery scent was wafting through the air as I sought out a sign of Ed and Marco's whereabouts to join up with. As I walked towards the oceanfront veranda, I saw the typically svelte figure of Mr. Burnett, rocking himself gently on one of the heavy wooden rockers, his head turning slightly as if picking up on my scent. As I walked around him from behind he rose on cue seemingly looking for clever words that had escaped him. Instead, the words "Y-you look stunning!" tumbled out of his mouth, clearly unauthorized and displaying the possibility that he'd caught sight of the feminine version of the genderless manager that had been working beside him, usually covered in a light layer of sweat and sawdust. He quickly reverted to his characteristic nonchalance adding a hasty refrain:

"We'd better be on our way already before the moon retreats," he stated absurdly.

"Don't be silly…" I replied softly, raising my arms to give him a gratuitous embrace for his words of adulation – unintentional as they might have been. "K…Let me see where Marco is…" I added soothingly, slinking away leaving a disconcerted engineer in the wake of my fragrance.

The people were jubilant and beautiful in the sultry evening air. It was an exhilarating night and everyone was freshly dressed, their sun kissed complexions displaying happy smiles. The musical number was a delicious raspy-voiced jazz singer who, by chance, was our hostess' daughter. The sexy tones of blues and bossa nova lulled the evening into a solid progression, as we nursed our cocktails and mingled with the others. Some of the guests were familiar faces, like the beautiful Yolanda from the internet café. There was Giovanna, the sprightly Italian red head married to the tall, dark and handsome Rodrigo with whom she had had her third child days earlier. It was such a treat to be out for some enjoyment, away from the worries back home and at the boatyard. For that evening we were just fellows enjoying a warm, magically moonlit evening.

Ed and I wandered to the edge of the property that overlooked the ocean. We watched the silver path that formed over the rippled ocean surface and we were awestruck. We stopped under the bounteous tropical foliage and for a moment our body language spoke of intimacy, through silhouettes etched against the pomegranate and lavender palette the horizon provided lavishly through its firmament. I became aware of the deeper breaths Edward was taking. His visage hovered unprecedentedly close to my shoulders which seemed to be reflecting a curious light that now appeared to tantalize the otherwise incurious man. A growing enticement began filling the space between us, as we released into the present moment, unheeding of any supervision the intellect might customarily impose. It was in the midst of this intoxicating magnetism that we were both suddenly startled back into reality.

"Oh! There you are!" Marco bolstered, his silhouette approaching in long-haul strides. His demeanor oblivious to the physical forces his innocent entrance had dissipated.

"Oh hi!" I blurted, snapping out of my reverie. Ed cleared his throat and rehearsed a short cough, taking a long draw from his now moderately warm beer, as he looked out and away towards the horizon.

"I was looking for you guys..." Marco continued, completely unaware of the moon induced aura under whose influence the engineer and I had fallen.

"I think I've about had as many cordial conversations as one can with strangers for the night..." Marco confessed, lifting his nose with an expression of suddenly catching a whiff of something unknown in the air.

"All good? I mean I'm happy to make my way home myself – I'll see you guys when you get there..." he offered generously, now sensing perhaps he'd interrupted an intimate moment.

"I'm ready too..." Ed was hurried to add. "We've got a long day at the yard tomorrow..."

"Wait, tomorrow is Sunday..." Marco interjected, reminding us we had made plans to cook octopus rice for lunch – and by we, he meant him and Ed as I'm somewhat repulsed by such delicacy but had offered to make side dishes for the feast at any rate.

"Yes, well, nonetheless..." Ed said under his breath, cutting through us to make his way back to the patio from where celebratory voices and music were still emanating.

Marco and I trailed behind making small talk. On the way home Ed seemed enmeshed in his own private universe. Upon arriving, he was quick to excuse himself, stating he was retreating for the night. Marco and I took the opportunity to enjoy a wonderful catch up session, as it had been a long while since. We were all up to date before finally bidding each other a peaceful good night.

***

Sunrise arrived mysteriously filtering through the layers of heavy rain clouds forming in the distance. Surveying the morning spectacle from my favorable position on the deck of the princess' suite, I rushed to get myself out on the beach before the rains rolled in. My steps were somewhat hurried as they passed what would normally be my routine morning yoga spot. Today, I felt a real sense of urgency in my need for a soothing beach walk and chant instead. I decided to veer right on the beach as opposed to my usual route to the left to better enjoy the golden/pink-hued rays the rising sun was bringing with it. Savoring the beauty through long breaths, I pondered the last weeks leading up to this trip and how intense everything had been. My sensitivity to everything had been so enhanced by the fact I had been putting Marco's case together in between calls, emails and research related to getting the keel molded, mediating Zezinho's pictures and Ed's instructions back to him regarding planking and caulking procedures, all the while getting the timber readied for laying the deck, as well as getting reports to Charles to keep the funds flowing. While it had been a relief to no longer deal with the attorney and his apparent fear of ruffling feathers at the Department of State, it felt like a huge responsibility to be handling Marco's case by myself. If I messed things up it would be fully on me. I took a deep breath and felt grateful I had filed the appeal before leaving L.A. I wasn't sure what soothed my spirit most, the feeling of accomplishment for having filed the case to my satisfaction, or having made this trip after ticking the numerous boxes on the prolific task spreadsheet that we had put together for this particular trip. In any case, this morning I was making sure to fill my lungs up all the way with each breath – and be present.

I took my time meandering across the lawn back to the veranda where breakfast was normally served at the old house. Upon stopping to rinse my feet before stepping up on the deck, I caught sight of Ed in what had become his usual spot on the wooden rocker that faced the ocean. He looked up with tender eyes – as if he had heard all my thoughts as I walked. I guess I must have worn the look of all the turbulence and musings on my face and he seemed to feel an uncharacteristic empathy for me that morning.

"Black with sugar as usual?" He said, as he promptly rose to his feet to serve me a cup.

"Ya..." I said absentmindedly, and then quickly correcting myself "I mean – yes...please – you are kind."

He attentively walked the impeccably white mug over to me while offering food. "I believe the help will come in later today if at all," he said. "Shall I make us some pancakes?"

I felt my features light up instantly. "You make *pancakes*?" I queried enthusiastically.

"Why...yes..." he stated, matter-of-factly, seemingly confused at my sudden alarm.

"From scratch???" I said, still slightly incredulous of his skill.

"Of course... how else would one..." but before he could continue, I interrupted his explanation popping excitedly to my feet and leading the way to the kitchen myself.

"I accept!" I said. Nothing could cheer me up like pancakes... and homemade ones! I was simply delighted.

I sat perched on one of the kitchen stools at the counter that separated the open plan kitchen from the large lounging room amused, as I watched Mr. Burnett hunt his ingredients down to prepare his homemade pancakes in the kitchen.

"Let's see... eggs, some flour... do you suppose they'd have a pinch of baking powder?" he pondered.

He wrangled everything together and began mixing us what I would have described as crepe batter back in America.

"Oh! You're making crepes!" I declared earnestly.

"Yes, *pancakes...*" he insisted, while explaining to me that I was to begin eating mine *immediately*, wanting me to enjoy his creation "warm and with lime and sugar on top" as he pushed the neat little plateful of indulgence in front of me. I needed no further convincing to begin without him and was happy to let him win the discussion of calling crepes pancakes – *'potayto – potahto'!*

We sat enjoying our breakfast together perched on the counter, each on his side, calmly conversing like we were rarely able since we were usually pushed by the need to get to the boatyard to start work on our task list. Today I felt a comfortable intimacy in opening my heart to Ed and sharing with him how much dealing with Marco's case had worn me out on an emotional level.

"You know...I'm not a hovering mother," I began defensively. "He can live wherever in the world he'd like, but just pulling him out of our home like a radish... that just broke my heart...you know?" My tone was swiftly becoming disconcerted and shaky. "He's welcome to live anywhere as long as it's not against his will.... and also, he's away from his first love." I added, topping my lamentation.

"Oh?" Ed replied, "he's got a girlfriend back home?"

"A boyfriend..." I clarified, feeling a sense of relief in mentioning that fact, in the event he himself might have felt uncomfortable in sharing his own ambivalent seeming sexuality with me. At this point, I wasn't decided completely on what Ed's inclinations were, and why he was so emotionally aloof. Was I repulsive? Was I too old? Was he in love with someone else? Was he gay? Was he a virgin? I was afraid to ask, but I knew the currents in his river ran deep, and I respected that.

"You know…" he began, returning to the previous topic. "Sometimes it's better to leave things to simply flow along for themselves, to take their own course." He pondered. "I told you I was in the same predicament in America back when I was 17, right?" Ed offered sensibly, scooping a ladleful of batter into the hot skillet for another "pancake."

Ed had shared his story with me while we were strolling the beach one day on a previous trip. One summer in his seventeenth year he had interned at a boatyard in Martha's Vineyard. He had become enamored with a local girl there that summer which made it much easier for him to accept an invitation from the yard owner who asked him to stay-on and work there for a few months longer. He went back home to the UK for a few weeks to tend to things I can't recall, ever excited to return back to the US in a few weeks' time. Upon his return however, when asked by the immigration officer at the checkpoint what his business was, he innocently answered that he would be working at a boatyard in Martha's Vineyard. Not possessing the proper work visa for America and coming in simply on a tourist visa, resulted in the officer promptly turning him around on his heels and sending him right back home to the UK. His tourist visa was then cancelled for infringement of status, as it is illegal for one entering the US on a tourist visa to work during their stay without the proper work visa.

"I was heartbroken too," Ed continued. "My dream of working at a boatyard in America was shattered and to make matters worse I wouldn't likely be seeing my summer love ever again…"

"Oh God…see?" I reiterated, commiserating. "It's inhumane…"

"Yes, and my mother just let it be. She told me to just follow my dream at home and you know, I don't know, my life might have been completely different had I not stayed home. I went to school and I am who I am today and it's alright." He seemed to have parallel thoughts running through his mind as he stated his conclusion to me.

"True... but I don't want Marco to be anywhere against his will. We shouldn't have to deal with these things in the 21st century Ed... it's so primitive." I protested, not withholding the frustration in my voice.

"Would you have another pancake?" He offered the pan in my direction.

"Well, now that you've upset me with this subject I'm gonna have to accept!" I declared in sarcasm.

"Listen..." Ed reasoned further, while sliding the golden warm treat onto my plate. "Just let Marco deal with his own things – he's a big boy..."

"He's my baby...." I taunted, with a streak of seriousness reverberating through my statement.

"You need to let him become a man...he'll be fine." Ed let his eyes rest on mine a while longer than usual to make his point.

I agreed cordially but deep down I was a mother protecting her cub and by golly I was gonna bring him home no matter what it took.

"Ok..." I said, lowering my eyes before exclaiming, "E-ed! These are going straight to my thighs!" as I continued digging into my tasty breakfast undeterred.

We had a delicious Sunday together, the three of us. Marco and Ed went to choose a fresh octopus in town while I worked on a research paper for school. We enjoyed lunch with chilled *vino verde* after which I indulged in a nap in a hammock. Ed took a picture of me trying to sleep with my hand out actively petting the dogs.

***

This specific trip was laden with work threads to check, correct and initiate. We discussed the keel fabrication tirelessly. We discussed fitting it and this particular day fitting it with something called a *deadwood*. This is the bit the ballast is actually fastened onto that takes the blow in the event the bottom hits or drags over rocks or whatnot. Its job is something similar to a bumper which would absorb the blow of the keel rather than the hull or the boat bottom itself. Ed was interested in a bit that would prove sturdy yet malleable, not too heavy and able to bear the load. He brought this up and it made Zezinho's eyes light up instantly with palatable enthusiasm.

"I know the perfect piece," he declared excitedly. "And I know exactly where it is in the woods too," he added, with an expression that said '*eureka, I got this covered*'.

"Can you ask him if he's got pictures?" Ed replied. I translated before Zezinho started with his body in the direction of the yard gate, stating,

"Better...I can take you there. It's right here..."

"Oh? Is it right here locally?" Ed questioned affirmingly, clearly delighted by the chance to be able to survey the bit personally.

"Well, no – we have to take the car..." it's out in the middle of the woods – it's a tall tree and it just fell," I replied, translating to adapt Zezinho's refrain in English, which was not always an easy task.

Ed furrowed his brow at my translation, "How far *is* it?" he asked, in a whining tone that came out staccato.

"Well, it's not here, it's just outside town in the woods," came Zezinho's rejoinder. "We can go there after lunch if he'd like," he added, his instruction still lacking any estimation of timetables or distance.

"Ok, well, if it won't take too long we can go have a look after lunch. Has he already ordered lunch for us? Or we can just skip that today?" Mr. Burnett was all business now, a condition that precluded his need for food and today - I wasn't having it.

"Oh, ya, he's already ordered that," I shot off at bullet-speed. Releasing my reply, without even seeking confirmation from Zezinho, lest his answer be one that might leave us lunch-less yet another day. We had recently started asking Zezinho's sister in law, who owned a dodgy little bed and breakfast down the road, to prepare lunch for us upon our arrival in the morning, so that she'd have lunch ready for us by 1:00 pm. It was nice to have a home cooked meal, even if it was simple and punctually, at least 30 minutes late every time.

"Ok, well then let's go have a look at how bunging is going and discuss paying the seams – then we'll break for a quick lunch and go see the bit." Ed asserted.

Our lunch was served at 1:40 pm. Rice, Beans, lettuce, tomato and onion salad, *farofa* – which is a cassava root based flour we Brazilians love, sautéed with onions and other goodies, and fresh caught fish. The rustic wooden tables that accommodated us faced out towards the bay, affording us a privileged view. With Ed, there was no beating around the bush after lunch like we Brazilians love to do over coffee. He was motivated to get as much work done as he could, within every precious hour of our time in Cajaíba.

We three packed into Zezinho's Fiat shortly after heading back to the yard, so that Ed could make sure to leave instructions for the afternoon workers.

"Ok, so this shouldn't take longer than an hour all in all?" Ed voiced, as we set up climbing the long dirt incline that led out of Cajaíba onto the road.

"Ya, no..." Zezinho replied, "it's just a ways away really."

We made some small talk about upcoming phases of work and no sooner had Zezinho and I began chatting did Edward cut in.

"Is it much further?" he exasperated.

"Ya, maybe 20 minutes if that..." Zezinho said with confidence. "It's just near the waterfall," he added, in his normal nonchalance.

Ed's eyes moved wildly. "Waterfall? Near the waterfall?"

"What are you fussing about?" I interjected. "How do you know which waterfall he's talking about?" I asked, sensing his obvious annoyance and perplexed myself.

"Take a look around you...does this topography say waterfall to you?" His question flew right over my curly head. Before I could answer he shot-out "This is great. We really couldn't afford a leisurely tour to the waterfall today of all days," he cried. "For Christ's sake he said it was local!" Ed added, curbing his irritation.

We arrived nearly an hour later to our destination. "Here we are!" Zezinho declared. "This will be worth every minute in the car – it's the perfect piece," he said, pleased with himself. We followed, myself intrigued and Mr. Burnett clearly annoyed. When we finally arrived at the designated spot where the fallen tree lay, Zezinho extended his arms as if indicating a kingdom and said, "What do you think?"

Ed let out a suppressed sigh as he surveyed the bit unenthusiastically. "I don't think this is the right bit really. It's got this knot here..." Ed pointed to a bump in the timber that typically indicates a place where fracture can occur. "Also, it seems after we clean it up and cut this curvature out it will be a bit shorter than what we need."

Zezinho might not have understood the exact words that Ed spoke but he definitely understood the gist of his remarks. In a flash, his features lit-up again. "Oh, no, this isn't it," he said running in and to the left a bit, "It's *this* one!" We journeyed a few steps further into the woods and sighted the bit we were meant to find, just as the sound of rushing water made it to our ears. Upon close inspection, it was obvious that this bit did indeed fill all our engineer's prerequisites and he turned away satisfied, assured at last, that we had found the perfect bit.

"E-ed..." I said, imploringly. "Since we're already here – can we just walk 50 steps further and have a peek at the waterfall?" and then I added a largely exaggerated: "pleeeeease?"

I climbed over rocks and through to the rushing fall of water. It was so exhilarating after the drive and having withstood all sorts of bites whilst inspecting the proposed timber.

He succumbed being himself somewhat downtrodden by the heat and frustration. I hurried off ahead of him towards the increasingly thundering sound.

"A rainbow!" I sparked delightedly, turning my head in search of Ed as I climbed onto rocks leading to the fall.

To my surprise he was snapping photos of me, ensconced with the rainbow. I posed, smiled and waved and sat myself down to further appreciate the thunderous flow of water that sprayed all about me with stimulating force. I saw that Ed had walked on, climbing to very top of the falls, making his way up the side and then disappearing into the precipice above. I followed behind him, taking a few candid photos of him enjoying the invigorating mist himself, unbeknownst to him. Zezinho stayed behind talking to what seemed an acquaintance that was searching for a bit as well. I left Ed to enjoy a brief moment of solitude while I myself sat to contemplate the scenery.

Soon, we were making our way back towards the Fiat and packed in the car, we made our way through the barren dirt road to the yard - in silence which turned out to be just what we needed facing such an intense week of work. We made it to the yard with just enough time to hash-out the next day's tasks and discuss materials we needed ready and on hand for the next morning. We took our usual sunset-kissed ride back to the pier in Barra Grande and then stopped for a bright green cocktail at our new-found friend's bar.

***

The final days of our trip flew by between finishing the planking, getting caulking, paying and bunging, spraying the hull with 10 layers of termite deterring oil, choosing deck timber and design - among the many other tasks and finally deciding against molding the keel locally and going with my girl in southern Brazil. This meant an infinitely higher cost but with no foreseeable mistakes or accidents in handling the 6,000 lbs. of molten lead locally. On the way back through to São Paulo, Ed and I were so exhausted we were sleeping with our mouths open, which made for good entertainment for Marco, taking snaps we have to this day on his iPhone.

Upon arriving to São Paulo, we decided to have our family dinner at a time when Mr. Burnett could join-in as well as Carlos,

Marco and I. We treated him to a lovely gourmet burger and beer and then we were off for an early night's sleep as we had an early meet for breakfast and then we'd be off to see our systems supplier in São Paulo, before Ed's British Airways flight departed at 2:30pm from Guarulhos International.

February 2014: The Sails

Kathini

A story of love, loss and a little boat building

Life seemed to be going by so quickly. Between getting the boat-project in full swing and finally having Marco's case filed and under my control, the days passed like hours.

Back in California, my days were spent between going to class at LMU, following up on the strands of work at the boat yard, ordering systems parts in the US and Brazil and keeping the communication flowing between Zezinho and Ed as smoothly as possible. Our associate at Kalmar boatyard – Lorena, was such a helpful partner, accomplishing what she said she would at the exact times as promised. Between the two of us, armed with Mr. Burnett's meticulous drawings, we got the ball rolling on the keel and things began rambling quickly toward what seemed like reaching a halfway mark on the project which deserved much celebration.

Ed had requested that I schedule the sailmaker to meet with us at his earliest convenience so we could discuss moving forward with establishing the sails. Life was quickly moving favorably toward our next work trip that we'd scheduled for February. Meanwhile, I was getting ready to travel to Brazil for

Christmas and New Year's, and to be with Marco and family. I was beginning to feel a little more comfortable with handling my life and the decisions I'd made. My daily rituals played an integral part in getting me through the various ups and downs of the life I was negotiating at that time. Handling and supporting the boys through their final years of school and Marco's immigration case were mainly the focus. Navigating the boat project, (with a little more confidence than I'd possessed at the start) and getting myself through a pretty challenging Master's program in yoga studies was the other half of it. It went without saying that I was still healing from the aftermath of two broken marriages combined with those precarious ups and downs life can afford us as well. A year earlier I had begun volunteering at two different nonprofits which was such a source of purpose for me. It was so interesting how I just put the intention out there and the universe brought the perfect matches for me. The first volunteer opportunity was an absolute coincidence. One day I was riding somewhere with Kevin in the car and while turning around to put my bag on his back seat, happened upon some brochure materials for The Trevor Project. It was a crisis outreach and lifeline nonprofit for LGBTQ youth, that Kevin had shot a campaign for earlier that week. It was love at first sight. I immediately took action and looked to begin their counselor training program days later. The second opportunity I came across, again, totally by 'chance', was when a friend was having difficulties with her son. He was in the hospital, recently diagnosed with schizophrenia. It was Christmas time and my friend was in a quandary because her son was agitated by her visits but she didn't want to leave him without familial company during the holidays nevertheless. She asked me to pop around, believing my presence might have a calming effect - so I did. My first visit to the psych ward at Kaiser Permanente Hospital in downtown Los Angeles was impactful to me to say the least but it was even more than that. It had ignited a quiet passion of mine for achieving mental health wellness and in sharing the tools and holistic modalities to accomplish that goal. So began my weekly offering of yoga and meditation classes at the step-down facility where my friend's son was released to upon completing his hospital stay. All of this brought me out of the mundane day to day of checking items from a to-do list, making my life appetizing again. I was finally building a life wherein I could organically include a few of my real passions and it was life-affirming and inspiring. Not only for myself but I could sense the enthusiasm in those around me and that made my efforts ever more desirable and worthwhile. I'd yet to discover why I was actually involved in building a boat, but I was trusting the universe and enjoying the ride at any rate especially appreciative of the fact that I was getting to know the mercurial, yet extraordinarily talented Mr. Burnett better. I had always had a heart for people who feel awkward or introverted. Having been a bit of a wallflower myself I knew very well how to communicate with such spirits and Ed came across as a person from this tribe, though never admittedly so. In any case, that he was an essential part of the project, made it much more palatable than the technical aspects - and *that* kept me going.

It was in this general interlude of boat trips, keeping up with my Yoga Studies and getting ready for my trip back down to Brazil for the year's end, that I was sitting at my dinner table working on a budget early one evening when an email slipped into my inbox - an arrival that changed my life forever.

***

Date: Tue, 17 Dec 2013
From: USCIS-CaseStatus@dhs.gov
Subject: Case Status > Application Type: I-601, Application for Waiver of Grounds of Inadmissibility

*** DO NOT RESPOND TO THIS EMAIL ***
Your Case Status: Post Decision Activity

On December 17, 2013, we mailed you a notice that we have approved this I-601 Application for Waiver of Grounds of Inadmissibility. Please follow any instructions on the notice. If you move before you receive the notice, call customer service at 1-800-375-5283.

I sat motionless trying to comprehend the words on the screen. I had read so many emails with excessively bureaucratic language that I was used to having to read carefully before jumping to any conclusions. My heart began to race as the realization pumped through every cell of my body - but no - I couldn't afford to misunderstand this message. I hit forward and typed in Kevin's email. As I sat there bewildered and coming to terms with the fact that my son might be coming home for Christmas, my cell phone startled me back to reality.

"Hi..." Kevin spoke plainly. We both momentarily hung still in silence.

"Hey..." my elocution returned reticent.

"Ummm...I'm re-reading it and I think it means" ... "Oh my God..." Kevin's voice undercut my own, now reflecting the same similar state of incredulity as mine.

"Kevin.... he's coming home...oh my *GOD*...." I screeched, with hysterical joy.

"We have approved your case..." he reiterated, echoing the words from the email before coming to the same conclusion. "He's coming home!!!" he thundered, like a footballer who scored the winning goal.

"Hold up - lemme see if I can conference him in," Kevin said excitedly. "... we said our goodnights an hour ago..." I waited with bated breath, still soaking in the news that had thrown me into a daze, the sort I had imagined a hostage might be in upon being released from captivity. It's a state of disbelief that topples one over in a tsunami of emotions and catapults one into a parallel dimension.

"He's not picking up..." Kevin said. Marco was hours ahead in Brazil and had obviously turned in for the night already.

We decided to forward the email and just have him wake up to the great news. Kevin and I began chatting each other back into reality as our biologies adjusted to the rush. Kevin had been dragged through this saga right along with us for what was now on the eve of approaching three years. He had been instrumental in getting Marco back home in a multitude of ways and the celebration was ours to share.

We slept with our cell phones by our side so that we'd be there immediately for Marco when he read the news and needed us to talk him back down to reality, but the tactic proved unnecessary. He had taken in the news so much quicker than we had and with such an air of unexpected equanimity, that we were all three basically just launched into celebratory mode at once, and straight into making plans for his return. Kevin was also going to join us in Brazil for the New Year's celebrations, so we'd all be united again at the family's annual bash at the Graham compound in Bahia. That year, I stayed up and waited for 2014 to arrive with its first sunrise. There was too much to be grateful for to have allowed the sun to come up unwitnessed and I had come so far and learned so much. It had been three years since our lives had been shaken to the core by the distance imposed by this immigration dilemma which to this day we were still unsure of what had brought it on. I imagined what life would be like without this daily battle in my heart and days. What levity! It felt a lot like the day Mr. Burnett had pulled me out of the water - the buzz was the same and it felt good.

***

Our trips began to come around more and more frequently. We would barely get back to our respective homes from Brazil when we'd be discussing preparations for the following trip. Ed, Zezinho and I had gotten it down to a science. We'd come in to look over what tasks had been left to complete, make any necessary corrections or adjustments to those tasks, and then moved forward with discussing the next batch of tasks associated to the next building phase. As such, the months began to fly by in a blur of undertakings, inspections and progress reports. Our sail designer had come out to meet us in the early part of 2014, working closely with Ed in discussing fabric density, shapes and sail and rigging plans. Much of this knowledge I had no previous notion of, but luckily our sail maker also spoke English, making it all somewhat easier to absorb. Over our numerous conversations the sailmaker had told me that he too was an avid yoga and meditation practitioner and he was particularly interested in the fact that I would be practicing my discipline early the next day before my walk. So it happened that he joined me, convening first on the lawn for yoga practice, followed by my normal walk on the beach as per habit. Upon our return to the house we were both surprised to find a visibly bothered Mr. Burnett, as we joined him at the breakfast table.

"That was a nice walk was it?" he queried, visibly annoyed. "Yes? Enjoyable?" he added, not pausing for any reply and offering our replies up himself.

"Oh yes!" I quickly interjected, with an elevated tone of enthusiasm. "It was delicious!!" I added for good measure. Before I could complete my vivid descriptions of the blobs I had uncovered on the beach, Ed cut me short.

"Yes, well," he sputtered, "we should leave within 30, if you two can be ready by then. It would behoove us in keeping with the schedule." He touted brusquely, before turning on his heels and walking with swift broad steps back to his room. He had recently turned it into a quasi-office, so that he could enjoy a table on which to work within the climate controlled comfort of his room.

Gi, who overheard all this while walking in to replenish the fruit on the table, looked at me with a raised brow and twisted grin, as if to say, 'oh boy...'.

I trailed behind her back to the kitchen. "What in the world did you put in *his* coffee?" I asked, with a taunting smirk on my face.

She met my inquiry with her typically mischievous facial expression, asserting, "Oh he's been pacing wildly since he woke up to find you gone with that other one..." and then she added, "he was not happy let me tell you...he chomped on what little food he had like a mad stallion."

I turned around in silence to rejoin our sailmaker, not quite sure how to respond to Gi's loaded remarks. I was greeted at once with his humble apology.

"Paula, I'm sorry if our outing caused any upset...I didn't realize you and Ed... anyway, please forgive me."

I nodded, retracing the implications through my mind before adding a barely audible, "ya...me neither...".

I wasn't too sure how to deal with Ed's reaction, since he had always kept our relationship strictly professional though friendly. We had often even made jokes about the fact that everyone at the house and in town thought we were an item. One morning, I had asked how he'd slept and he mentioned that he needed a taller pillow, if I might have a chance to procure one. I was already tucked safely in my princess bed and nearing midnight, when I was suddenly reminded of his request made earlier that day. I hopped out of bed, grabbing one of my own thicker pillows and made my way down the stairs to his room; my bare feet tapping lightly on the wooden steps as I went skipping down - aware of an occasional toad on the steps. As I rapped lightly on his door to deliver the pillow, there was no reply forthcoming, the man fast asleep. I slid the door open gingerly and left the pillow beside his bed in the event he awoke. As I turned to sneak out, sliding the door closed gently behind me, I caught sight of Olivan. He'd clocked me stealing away, as he returned from his nightly ritual of turning the kiosk lights off outside. Ed and I had since chuckled about this scenario on occasion, imagining the message that my revealing, laced nightie may have conveyed, as well as the brisk light steps I'd taken in stealth leaving his room in returning to my cozy bed, and what all combined must have led Olivan to believe. I went on to point out that his systematically dismissing the staff from their duties didn't help matters much and for them to come in the next morning and find the usual two bottles of wine we'd washed our dinner down with, coupled with the empty scotch glasses we'd leave after our nightcaps sitting on the oceanfront veranda, that those signs alone did probably lead to some spicy, misconstrued assumptions. I snapped quickly from this reverie and pushed on with our sail maker.

"Would you like two eggs?" I asked, diminishing the repercussions of his apology with offerings of my own. "We'll have a long day at the yard so make sure you eat well," I mothered.

We managed to finish our breakfast engaged in a conversation of light pleasantries. By the time we met up with Mr. Burnett for the day, any remnant from the previously tense episode had largely evanesced and the awkwardness lifted. Our sail maker left the very next morning to continue his journey, leaving us two back to our usual routine for another four nights and five days.

Zezinho and Ed worked closely on initial discussions regarding the rudder. Zezinho took us to see a couple of prospective pieces and then we'd get back to the yard for more discussions regarding the laying of the deck, while more work was going on putting in bulkheads and finishing the deck frame. Zezinho also called in a mate from a neighboring town who fabricated stainless steel fittings. Ed wanted to begin work on a few bits, among which were the chain plates which as I understood are stainless plates on the deck to which rigging is attached so as to distribute the load and not snap a piece of your deck off. When Sunday came around, we gave Zezinho and crew half the day off and went for a quick sail on a small vessel that Zezinho had offered Ed and I the day before. It was the end of the work day and my hope was that the pleasant jaunt might help to lighten Ed's mood.

"This is a great little boat," Ed sparkled. He was delighted with the small, hand-built wooden boat that donned the local soccer team's logo, blazoned across its sail. Zezinho had borrowed the little jewel from his cousin, especially for our outing. "Too bad Zezinho couldn't join," Ed lamented.

"Well, he said we should just unplug and enjoy our sail... to which I couldn't agree more, I must say." I offered sensibly, having considered the burden of needing to translate Ed and Zezinho's every utterance, had he accepted the invite.

"Well, we'll make the best of it..." Ed replied, turning to face the horizon and shrugging his shoulders, clearly not able to comprehend why any human would decline sailing on such a golden pink afternoon as the one that lay before us.

"What? You can't be alone with me in a small space now?" I teased. Seizing the moment to taunt him playfully, which I so enjoyed, I continued "You understand Edward, that if this affair is going to work, we're gonna have to be seen in public and even get intimate eventually you know?"

Ed fussed with the sails and furrowed his brow, as if tending to some complicated sailing technique would shut me and my nonsense out. I chose a temporary retreat but made a mental note to return to this annoyance later on in our sail, when we were further out at bay.

As we sailed, Ed taught me about wind direction and how sailing follows the same dynamic as flying. He explained how the 'lift' caused by the wind propels the boat forward. He drilled me on the positions within the boat, teaching me that the phrase, "no red port left in the bottle," would remind me that port was signaled by a red light on the left side of the forward-moving boat and that starboard was lit by a green one on the right side. As I was wrestling a piece of rope into a bowline knot, which Ed was patiently helping me with, I lunged us into dangerous terrain with an innocent and heartfelt question.

"So we're *not* having an affair?" I asked, adding a playful, "I'm hurt." Although teasing, his evasiveness had constantly aroused my curiosity so my taunting was tinged with a bit of truth to it.

He sighed, fumbling for the words that would express his discontent, then reached to correct the knot I was lost in.

"Listen, I would never..." he began, reconsidering before continuing. "Not that I *would* never as much as.."

I cut in "...*no, never*...heaven forbid..." I'd emphasized the 'never', just as I took the piece of rope back, undoing the knot again.

"What I mean is, I would never have an inappropriate relationship with a coworker..." He tried to elucidate further as I echoed his words again.

"I know... inappropriate... coworker ...got it" I wrestled the rope back into the semblance of a bowline knot.

"Listen, you're delightful and..."

"Of course, totally *not* repulsive or anything..." I stuffed his mouth with words while enjoying watching him wrestle to stay afloat.

A smile now took over Mr. Burnett's face, as it finally dawned on him exactly what I was up to - setting him up to tease him. He squinted, looking over the horizon as he enunciated his words calmly now.

"Look, we both know you're delightful and beautiful and all that, but I'm just saying I'd never betray Charles' trust like that – you're his family." He dropped his last words off quickly, as if to dispel any further explanations.

His expression was that of a schoolboy who had delivered the correct answer to his math teacher.

"Got it..." I conceded. "So, no love if a person has a family? That is, in the event there was any love to be had of course..." I amended.

"No!" An energetic Mr. Burnett protested. "Listen, Charles commissioned me for this project and *you* as the translator/ manager. He is paying us to deliver this boat to him and I couldn't possibly take advantage of that trust by shagging his sister in law in his beautiful beach home while we're meant to be here for business – I just couldn't do that". Ed's case stood strong, his words full of unwavering commitment. I allowed them to linger there eloquently floating in the breeze between us before bringing them down with expressive impact.

"And if we were to shag on the beach?" I grinned, expressing a display of hope.

I delightedly threw my head back in laughter, savoring the hard to repress, if still guarded laugh of Ed's own. Getting a guy like Mr. Burnett to share a laugh was indeed a hearty feat to enjoy. Not that he seemed a depressed type – but he was clearly raised in the shade of staunch and duty and there was to be no horsing around when it came to life, particularly the business side. Black was black, white was white and the dial was to fall nowhere in between. Ed came from a family of few siblings. He had a brother and a sister that he was raised with and a half-sister. He loved his nephews. I pictured his mother to be an iron - maiden type, her Dutch heritage leaving nothing to that of the British man she had married. Ed spoke fondly of his family, but I got the vibe that he was hurt because he felt judged for not having settled down with a family of his own. He mentioned feeling he was treated differently when it came to making plans for holidays, because he had no children. He also resented questions regarding his life that he himself could not find answers for. The reticent fact remained however, that at 40 he had never been married, had never had kids, and this seemed to be a bit of a sore spot in the family.

We finished our sail and headed towards the pier as the afternoon quickly cooled under the silver-mauve clouds. Lights were just coming on as we pointed towards our usual destination pier-side. A wave of goosebumps took place over my shoulders where the sunlight played in golden hues.

"Oh, wait a minute," Ed interrupted his wide strides, while arching over his back pack with furrowed brow searching for something. "Ah...here you go..." he said, as he pulled out a man's button-down dress shirt and offered it up to me.

"No Ed, I'm fine – isn't that your travel shirt?" I asked. "I don't want to leave it stinky!" I said, arm hairs standing up.

"Don't be silly - you're freezing, albeit it's 22 degrees." Ed noted, quoting the temperature in degrees Celsius, as he courteously draped the shirt over my shoulders.

"That's more like it," he beamed. Ed seemed contented, even proud to see my rather small frame lost inside his large blue oxford, as he loosened a few of my curls that were stuck tucked in the collar.

"I just want you to know that I care." He said sincerely, all playfulness momentarily banished from his features as he glanced minutely, yet deeply into my eyes. Turning briskly, he sounded his command.

"On we go now," he enjoined merrily.

I was strangely elated by our day as well. We topped off our evening with some ice cream, purchased at the pharmacy on our way home, then retired early, so as to begin our last day of work with an early start. Our last days at the yard were customarily comprised of elaborating a list of tasks with Zezinho and pin pointing each spot on the boat with our work-thread. We'd sit in the spot where the engine was to be mounted for example and discuss the details of how it was to be mounted. Ed would always welcome Zezinho's insights and come up with a plan that Zezinho fully understood, and, oftentimes, agreed and helped come up with. We would annotate all measurements and then make sure he had all the tools and materials to do what was being asked, estimate how long the task would take and then move on to the next task. And so our trip wrapped up and saw us all off toward our next stage of construction.

April 2014:
The Lead Keel

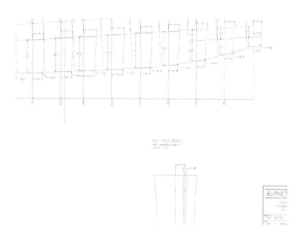

Kathini

A story of love, loss and a little boat building

On his end, Ed was diligently working on commissioning the masts from his friend Jeremy, at Collars, in Dorchester, UK. At the same time, he was designing the mast dressings with his partners at Hercules in Dartmouth. It became more and more important for all stages and threads of work to progress in unison and communication between all parties to be efficient and precise. Timing was of the essence and importation paperwork had to be flawless as any error could lead to crippling delays. We had hit our three-year mark and Charles was getting antsy to see a boat he could actually sail for the upcoming holiday with the family. As such, we moved forward swiftly, until we reached the trigger for our next on-site inspection in Brazil. Dave Robbins, a systems engineer from T. Nielsen, a renowned shipyard in Gloucester, who'd been a fellow associate of Ed's on the Gloriana Barge build, would come along with us to assess and possibly begin some systems work in our recently equipped engine room. After the bulkheads went in and joinery work began, we now had a better sense of compartments within the boat and work was ever more apparent. The deck had been 98% laid and work on the structures was underway. Our trip had been timed so that at its tail end we could enjoy Easter with the family. The months leading up to this trip had been a mix of events and scurried emotions for me. After finding out that Marco's case had been approved, we had been hanging, waiting with bated breath for his green card to be issued. Exhaustive communication with the consulate brought the reply that there was back office work to be done before issuing the visa. Meanwhile, I had received news that my eldest son Carlos and his wife were expecting my first grandson. I felt happy in general but could feel myself buckling at times due to emotions that shot between two extremes. There were moments when I felt like I'd just learned to ride a bike and was rambling down a hill at a way faster speed than I knew how to handle.

I scheduled my flight to arrive a day early to São Paulo so that I could visit my Mom and Dad and meet Ed at our usual spot at Guarulhos International the next day. I arrived in São Paulo and found Marco well, though still quite disheartened with the delay in hearing news from the consulate. The notice we received months earlier communicating his approval was issued by the Department of Homeland Security in the United States which in turn sent the notice to the consulate in Rio de Janeiro, but the consulate surely did not have our case as a top priority.

That evening, Marco and his cousin Patrick accompanied me to visit my parents who I had planned a quick Easter visit with.

"Hi!!!" we three echoed happily as we piled through the door of their apartment cheerfully. We made our way into the living room and settled into the lime green and aqua sofas that we had shopped for as a family in 1974.

"You look well..." my father began.

"Aw, thank you Dad," I spoke, incredulously, not being used to hearing positive remarks coming from him.

"...but you should try dressing your age. You're always dressing provocatively. Why can't you dress your age?" He said, grunting after my mother, who had gone to the kitchen for a tray of goodies to serve us. "Aida! Tell your daughter to be less provocative!" he called after her.

It was never an easy thing for me to visit with my parents. My spirit squirmed just being in their apartment, mainly due to always having to butt heads with my Dad on basically every front. Being the free-spirited hippie at heart that I was and having been raised by the conservative, overbearing military type he was, it was not surprising. Working within the behavioral health field had given me the awareness to understand and process a lot of what I had experienced at home when I was young. We had virtually been held hostage to my father's paranoia that we might be horribly harmed by an abuser and my mother's fear of confrontation - washing her hands of any control over the situation and drying them on her apron as she conciliated my father's excessive behavior within the boundaries of our childhood. In any case, we had our Easter visit. I took them flowers and a colorful chocolate egg and we were off.

***

I was introduced to a cheerful and eager looking Dave Robbins who, surely having been prepared by Ed previously as to what to expect, appeared more than ready for the task at hand, obviously keen to begin his first visit to Brazil. Dave, as the systems engineer for T. Nielsen & Co., one of the top and most reputable shipbuilding and restorative specialists in the UK, had already designed a blueprint for our engine systems with Ed in advance, their present plight was to discuss and fine-tune on site. *Systems* includes most everything that functions within the shell of the boat - the engine, electrical wiring, plumbing and all the instruments and electronics, so it was key that they settle on a design and come up with a shopping list so that we could place our order with Marine Office, our importer in São Paulo. It was a list Ed and I had long been discussing and preparing.

We arrived to Cajaíba and hit the ground running. Ed inspected the hull alongside me, marking imperfections with circles in plain white chalk. He discussed fairing boards - which are basically giant boards with sandpaper on them used to give the hull its "sexy shape," as Mr. Burnett often put it. He explained how *fairing* was to occur over the next months and how he expected finishing standards to be. Never before had I heard him use words like sexy and curvaceous as in when he was referring to the shape of the hull; his passion for his work came manifest from his very core. After going over the task list that Zezinho had been left with two months earlier on our last visit, Ed left us two to our corrections, dashing off happily to the engine room with Dave, where no verbal translations were necessary. Every day began with an inspection of what Zezinho and I had accomplished the day before and then we'd be given our next prompts. Jorge seemed to have found his bliss in helping Dave and Ed, even despite the language barrier, and I worked on the odd task with Zezinho and crew which afforded me more time to contemplate the yard in a way I hadn't before. I was suddenly aware of the burden of stress that the constant translating, coordinating, and oft times being the buffer between the two disparate universes had placed on my shoulders. This involved not only the exclusive worlds of Zezinho and Ed, but also Charles, who represented a completely different realm altogether - unknown to this campestral setting. On one of the days, when the workers had gone off to lunch and Ed and Dave were off at the shop fashioning a piece to wedge something in the engine room, I found myself alone in the yard. I climbed up on the deck and sat there quietly, taking in the sound of the birds and watching the lazy procession of townspeople going about their day. It made me think how alike life is everywhere around the world and yet how different. I absorbed how interconnected we all are although living in such different states of reality. People in cities are working madly so they can come spend a few days in paradise. The folks who live in paradise are so deeply enthralled in the present that it leaves us city folk curious as to their contentment. Their lives, seemingly unencumbered by mortgages, cell phone bills or car payments to pay, leave them time to ponder the simple things, like picking the perfect fruit with which to make fresh juice to serve with lunch, or sewing that perfect outfit for that special birthday celebration, their days are filled with simplicity and flavor.

That evening, while Dave was preparing himself for dinner, Ed and I were on the veranda alone, each on our laptops, working on our separate projects. I was working on an essay regarding the nuances of varying translations of the Bhagavad Gita, and Ed on his rowing club affairs.

"Can I bring you a glass of wine?" he asked, bringing his attention away from his screen and towards me. His voice brought me back from the musings between Krishna and Arjuna, but only barely so.

"That'd be lovely..., thank you," I replied absently, my words fluttering dreamily from my lips as if in a trance, still focused on my work, I was unable to look up from the page with any real commitment.

Edward returned with two generously filled glasses of red which he knew to be my preference and handed me a glass.

"Cheers," he said, extending his glass towards me with an open arm. "Here's to what is soon to be your new profile picture" he proclaimed gleefully, a smile etched across his face.

I returned a confused glance with a tilt of my head. Sensing my incomprehension, he elaborated, taking a sip of his wine before continuing.

"I posted a picture of you online that I took this afternoon," he boasted. "You should check it out - I think you'll be pleased" he completed proudly.

"You did...?" I stuttered vaguely. Not only was I still completely immersed in my confabulations regarding the Gita, but Ed's words made no clarifying sense to me. He was not particularly fond of social media, nor of randomly snapping photos for that matter.

Curious, in my feminine way, I left what I was doing to check out his post. It turned out that he had captured the special moment when I was sat atop the deck, considering life in all its profundity and posted it on his page.

"Aww Ed... that's so sweet..." I began.

"It's a good shot, no?" he queried boy-like, searching for my response. "I was just passing when I saw you there. You seemed lost in your thoughts and I felt it was a moment that just begged to be captured," he rationalized, before thoughtfully adding: "you should make it your profile pic."

I agreed, allowing my enthusiasm to open up and share my thoughts about all I had been contemplating on the deck that afternoon. Ed listened to my soliloquy regarding life and humanity intently, and all my philosophical meanderings, before topping them off with his own unique verdict.

"Well, I find it all boring and senseless," he pontificated bluntly. "I don't see what all the fuss is about and I'm utterly unimpressed by it all," he concluded, standing. "Well, I'm off to take a shower," he announced. And with this, our philosophical conversation came to its sullen end.

***

The Graham's arrived at the compound and with them came our brother, Frank, his wife Lidia and their daughter Aida, as well as a few other family members that were held dear. We saw Dave Robbins off and our momentum at the boatyard waned. The town of Cajaíba came to a complete stop for the Easter holidays which began on what was our Holy Friday. Between our families we had close to 20 people at the house and our days were spent by the pool. The youth lounged by the pool with their feet dangling off their loungers, keeping rhythm with whatever music their headphones boomed in their ears. Meals were loud and there were bursts of singing and dancing after dessert. Mr. Burnett was reserved as usual, but couldn't help but being somewhat engaged as the family now all knew him and included him in their romp. Come Easter Sunday, my two siblings and I took the time to call home and wish our parents a happy Easter. We found that they had unexpectedly turned back from Rio de Janeiro where they had gone to a festivity at the Air Force base where my Dad, now 90, and the other few World War II veterans still alive were to be honored. My mother said he didn't want to talk as he was feeling *'under the weather'* but it just didn't add up that they would have driven 500 km there, arrived and then turned back. My mother sounded scared so I made a mental note to call back later that day to check in on them again.

Analida broke out all sorts of paints and clean canvases after lunch, so that anybody interested could engage in painting and everyone settled in content to an afternoon activity. As I walked to my room, I walked past Mr. Burnett's and thought to pop in and see how he was doing.

"E-ed..." I whispered, enunciating his name in two syllables just loud enough for him to hear.

I saw him busying at his desk, likely trying to get some work done now that he was comfortably sheltered in his air-conditioned room.

"Come in," he said, waving me forward while turning back to whatever was enticing him on his screen.

"I just wanted to see how you're holding up with all the fanfare," I said, sliding the rattan panel open.

"Oh, right...I'm fine. I'm just giving the family some space to be."

"Aww Ed, you are kind, but you know you're quickly becoming part of the clan - and for that...I apologize..." I smirked. Ed continued gazing at his work. "You wanna go catch the sunset at the lighthouse later?" I proposed heartily.

"Hmmmm...ya, around 4:30 or 5?" he suggested.

"Ya... let's take the quad?" I proposed, knowing this option was sure to lure him.

"Ooooo...okay, that oughta be fun..." he said, squinting at his screen.

We rode up the steep hill to the lighthouse just before sunset. We were both laughing because I was having such a hard time holding onto him during the steep climb, particularly as he negotiated the huge puddles of water the recent rains had left behind. I had mud on my face and had hit his back hard with my teeth when he swerved suddenly in an attempt to avoid a ditch. It was a glorious sunset and it was one of the few times that we went a day without talking boatyard business. We talked about his friends and his life back in Totnes. I queried him regarding who was who, connecting faces to names as I had been interacting with several of his friends on Facebook. Not only from my own, previous posts, but from his latest post which had included me and had caused quite a bit of interest, considering he was such a reserved bloke. I spoke about the pressures I had been feeling and he encouraged me in the only way he knew how. He told me to stand up for myself and to not accept less than what I deserved. The air had chilled quickly after the sun went down and I was wearing a sheer flowery dress so I felt the cold pucker my skin. As I hopped on the back of the quad and we headed back down the hill, I sheltered myself close behind Ed to protect myself from the wind. We rode back to the house slowly, him deep in thought, my arms grasped securely around his torso, that was dressed in his usual white tee and uniformed khaki bermuda shorts. I felt he was more peaceful and comfortable than I'd ever seen him and I felt so grateful for our talk. As I pondered all this I tightened my arms around him and lay my head on his back the rest of the way home. We arrived back to the house in time for showers and dinner and headed off to bed early as the Graham's and all their guests would be flying back to São Paulo first thing the next morning. Ed and I would stay behind for an extra two days at the yard as there was much still to do.

***

Our last days at the yard were dedicated to going over the task list that would trigger our next trip down. We made some fairing boards and I worked along with a few of the guys on that project, while Ed and Zezinho worked on marking a piece for the rudder. At lunch on our last day, we walked down to the small posada where Zezinho's sister in law served us lunch. We were amused that a hen had nested inside the barbeque and laid her eggs where she was sitting with pride. We took a table and each ordered a beer, since we had worked a long morning, we thought to take a late lunch and then just head back to the house by 5 pm. As we awaited our food the TV blared the day's news:

"The co-pilot of the German Wings flight that crashed into the French Alps, named as Andreas Lubitz, appeared to want to destroy the plane." The female reporter lamented. *"Officials said the black box voice recorder transcript stated the co-pilot was alone in the cockpit. He intentionally began descent while the pilot was locked out."* She continued. *"It further said that there was "absolute silence in the cockpit" as the pilot fought to re-enter it. Air traffic controllers made repeated attempts to contact the aircraft, but to no avail. Passengers could be heard screaming just before the crash."*

"Wow...that is crazy..." I commented, as I paraphrased the news to Ed. "They're saying apparently he had suffered from bouts of depression but was on and off his treatment."

Ed listened, seemingly interested, but refrained from making any comment.

"The dude basically committed suicide, and took 144 lives with him!" I expressed passionately. "If that's not a matter that deserves our full attention as a society...we really need to cut out the crap and talk about these kinds of episodes." I continued, gaining momentum. "People need to be able to talk openly about what they're navigating and ask for the help they need." I was now firmly atop my soapbox, presenting my take on the behavioral health issues I had such a heart for.

"I guess..." Ed pondered plainly. "But if I wanted to take my life I wouldn't be going to anyone for help - I would just take it - it's not like talking to anyone would suddenly change my mind," he confessed.

"It might..." I insisted. "You know, no one wants to die...they want their suffering to end. We are stronger when we bond as humans and expose our vulnerabilities." I replied, speaking from lived experience. Ed shrugged as he set his eyes on the food that was arriving and the subject was quickly dropped.

***

Jorge dropped us off at the pier, where we each consumed two of the delicious lemongrass, "stress-relieving" cocktails we so enjoyed. We were ready to finalize our shopping list at Marine Office, now that Dave had finalized his on-site visit and inspection with Ed. We pulled the list out and had a huddle round what to source where, and what was portable enough that could be distributed into family suitcases over the next few months. I would put together a budget forecast and request funds from Carol, the Graham treasurer, organize those purchases and have them delivered each to the location where they would meet their conveyor and continue to their final destination, along the planned chain of logistics. Evening fell quickly and by the time we got back to the house, Olivan was not only waiting with cocktails, but had a delicious prawn stew prepared, the table all set and waiting for us.

"We had some fresh prawns left over from the holidays so I took the liberty of planning them for your dinner," he transmitted happily.

"Oh! That's wonderful!" Ed responded. He was delighted not having to cook as we had had an extremely long and tiring day, as most of our last days turned out to be at the yard.

It felt really special that we had a beautiful table set for us with wine, flowers and candles, so I made sure to come from my princess chambers dressed appropriately for the occasion. I had recently purchased a fresh, long white dress with romantic embroidered touches at the hem and Ed had been with me. As he sat patiently, just outside the door of the pier-adjacent shop, nursing a frosty beer, I had tried and modeled a succession of dresses in the makeshift 'dressing room' that consisted of a colorfully patterned sheet, hung pell-mell on a rod in the corner; the house cat slipping in and out at his leisure under the barricade.

To my surprise, as I came down to dinner, I found a smiley-faced Mr. Burnett, waiting for me at the bottom of the stairs, a chilled glass of rosé in his hand to greet me, as I moseyed down the steps fresh-faced and bright eyed to meet him.

"I hope you don't mind, but I thought this might suit our prawn stew better," he explained, considering my preference for red wine. We were both clearly elated over what was turning out, not only as a singular moment for us, but with a special dining experience to go along with it.

"This is perfect!" I said sunnily, readily accepting the chilled delight from his hand, as we made our way through to the veranda. The ocean veranda afforded a tremendous view and we glanced toward the horizon to see if the full moon had come up.

"Moonrise should be just in time for our nightcap tonight." Ed determined, with pronounced authority and glancing down at his mobile. By now, he had an app that predicted every meteorological phenomenon known to man on the iPhone I had given him and he seemed proud to be utilizing it.

I had decided to skip investing any time on school work this night, pushing it forward as a duty to be dealt with during the international leg home. So it seemed too that Mr. Burnett had rid himself of the impetus to pour over the day's progress, so we spoke on subjects not often touched upon. We were well involved in conversation regarding Marco's case and how my conversation with my mother had left me suspicious of what had propelled them on an early return home before Olivan chimed in.

"Dinner is served!" he announced. "Please, make your way over to the table while I fetch another bottle of rosé that I left chilling for dinner." He said disappearing back into the house.

Dinner progressed deliciously. Our conversation was as deep and rich as our creamy prawns, drenched as they were in a delicate and velvety involucre, served alongside thinly sliced potatoes au gratin. We both savored every bite as we allowed the conversation to take us into deeper subjects that we likely had not shared with many, if any of the people nearest to us. We laughed, I snorted. We wiped tears from our eyes after the long bouts of hard laughter. We even entertained the idea of opening a third bottle of rosé but elected instead to have port with our passion fruit mousse and then head over to the ocean veranda for moonrise. As I pushed my chair back from the table to start for the veranda, my head signaled that it was dangerously light. I now concentrated more intently just to put one foot in front of the other, so as to make my way across the deck. I excused myself to go to the ladies' room for a refresh, taking the opportunity to take a few deep breaths and look at my face in the mirror which was always sure to have a centering effect on me.

As I walked back, I found Ed quietly sitting in his place on the ocean-front rocker. A tray held the contents for our usual nightcap - two glasses, a bottle of Glenfiddich - Ed's favorite single malt, that I too had now learned to savor with new-found respect, along with a few pieces of dark, bittersweet chocolate. All the lights had been switched off, as the pitch-black backdrop favored stargazing from our unique vantage point. I sat across from Ed on one of the built-in couch perches that made the veranda so cozy and inviting. Ed muttered a barely audible 'all good?' checking in with me. "Ya..." I returned, in almost inaudible tone as well, both lost now in our oblivion.

We sat quietly in our daze for a while, until I reached for a piece of chocolate, in hopes it might help to reel me back in. I looked back on the day, the beers at lunch, the double-dose of the lemon grass, stress-relief concoction we'd ingested while conferring over the next phases at the bar, followed by Olivan's artisanal caipirinhas and beaucoup chilled rosé as well as the port with pudding. As I was thinking back, I lost track of what I was tallying and why. Ed considered my move for chocolate and shrugged as he stuffed a piece in his mouth as well, before reaching for the Glen. He glanced up at me as he twisted off the cap from the bottle, lifting it as if he were cheering an invisible glass. I meant to reply but I reached for one of the oversized pillows that lay on the veranda instead, to prop myself up for the ride. As I accepted the glass of neat single malt, I grabbed one more square of the chocolate and made myself comfortable.

We sipped as we gazed up at the constellations in silence. It seemed time had retreated for the night, tiptoeing out and leaving us to enjoy the evening undisturbed. A warp made it seem like each minute was an hour of considerations within my mind. It felt less and less awkward when mine crossed Mr. Burnett's eyes. He too now seemed un-bothered, allowing his gaze to land on my slender silhouette undeterred. He was not diverting his glance like in the past, when he'd lingered only briefly savoring one of my curves, staring at my tummy stealthily or admiring my thighs while I sat next to him in the Lillibelle traveling home after a day at the yard. I took a deep breath and closed my eyes, laying my head back against the wooden pillar that propped up my pillow. I was suddenly, completely aware of where I was, but even more cognizant of the fact that Ed had moved across the veranda closer to me. He was searching to see if the moon had shown any signs of its imminent arrival yet. I sat up, swinging my legs off the veranda to join in the interest. The moment seemed impossibly long and during the interim of haziness I forgot what we were looking for. Ed looked deeply into his glass of malt as if his fortune were to be read at the bottom of the glass. He placed it down on the table between us before walking around and joining me there on my cushion. I made no motion to move as he allowed his presence to settle into the space between us, as if our energies were being attuned before impact. As he drew his chest closer into my back, it seemed our breaths were rehearsing synchronicity. I could hear nothing at that moment but Adele, singing softly from the playlist I had left playing on repeat from the Bluetooth speaker in the adjacent room. Our hearts could be heard through the music, beating wildly to the point it seemed that at any moment they would reach utter insanity and hurl themselves out of our bodies onto the wooden deck; and there they would meet throbbingly. Time was moving so slowly it seemed to be conspiring with the universe that held us up in the moment - coddling us in its magic. Edward leaned in further towards my ear inquisitively, as if searching my aura for a lifeline, checking for a scent that would grant him permission to enter. I turned my face slightly, to feel his visage. His lips landed on the corner of my mouth, that was now curving upwards and into a sexy smile. As I leaned my head back and over my shoulder, the moon shone incandescent rays, viciously over the ocean, lighting an inebriating path towards our intercourse and igniting the passion with which his lips engulfed mine in repeated caress. I relaxed into the moment, feeling no part of me left unattended, until I awoke again, my head on the wooden pillar that propped-up my oversized pillow. Across from me Ed came in and out of focus. It seemed that he too was working hard at focusing on reality. We tried exchanging intelligible sentences with our mouths but all we could hear was love, disguised in an intense desire, dangling there between us. I at last gave in to a deep slumber as did too an exhausted Mr. Burnett.

**

The next day found us back on the Lillibelle, whizzing across Camamú Bay towards Camamú, where Marquinhos our driver was waiting to take us to Ilhéus. No mention of the night before was made and we recouped well from the frenzy of liquor we had pumped ourselves with by consuming plenty of fresh coconut water at breakfast. The day was bright and we enjoyed the lush greenery of our surroundings. I made small talk with Marquinho about the hazards of the road we were taking, which prompted him to mention that a couple from Barra Grande had been in a fatal head-on crash days before, coming home from their Easter holiday.

"Oh? My goodness, that's so sad..." I said, wondering who it was, considering that it would be unlikely someone we knew.

"Ya, I don't know if you've ever been to that internet cafe next to the pharmacy?" Our driver inquired, as I felt the butterflies in my stomach begin to stir with the onset of the realization to come. "It was the dive instructor and his fiancée Yolanda." He confirmed. "He survived, but she died instantly."

I was overcome with grief, as I translated the devastating news for Ed. "Our sweet, beautiful Yolanda...my goodness..." I lamented. "She was such a ray of light and happiness..."

"That's certainly a shame..." Ed replied solemnly. "Godspeed. I hope she didn't suffer much."

"Apparently, she died on impact..." I replied, still crushed at the thought.

"Ya... I would dare say the gravest part of dying might be the pain one might experience...." and then, with a heavy sigh, he continued "...though relief of it would surely come with death."

We continued our trip and arrived to Ilhéus airport in time to have a bite at the restaurant, in the upstairs lounge.

"I can't get over it..." I started, as we worked on eating the chicken filet we were sharing. "So much life inside of her...it just makes me more and more certain that we need to live today Ed - we need to live right *now* - not tomorrow, or next year - because they may never arrive." Expressing these heartfelt emotions caused a shift in my spirit. They seemed to reveal things within me undiscovered before and at that very moment I felt a vastness open widely within my heart.

As I was savoring this expanded place of bliss, Ed's own sentiments seemed to burst forth from what mine had stirred within him.

"I *do* live my life! I live my life very well thank you," he proclaimed. "I don't know why people think that I'm this repressed pile of bones. That I'm not living my life to its fullest, it's a crock of shit!"

My expression shone a look of complete disbelief, as my eyes widened, my mind racing to think of something to say that would avert this sudden outburst.

"I'm alone, yes, I'm alone! But that doesn't mean there's anything wrong with me. I'm perfectly happy with the life I'm living and not having a family does not make me handicapped... And I don't need anyone's pity!" he said, throwing his cutlery down on his plate.

I was gobsmacked yet tried to offer some solace. "Ed.... I..." His discontent would not permit any input.

"Fuck everyone! Fuck *you* if you think that for one minute...."

I was in sheer awe of the moment and at a loss for how to deal with it so it was a surprise when my reaction tumbled out of my mouth.

"Wait, did you just tell me to go *fuck* myself?" I blurted indignantly.

My desire to appease him vanished quickly. The rage was quickly interrupted by a desire to erupt into laughter due to the candor of my words. We both refrained from any more talk, lest the hole we were digging forged any deeper. Instead, we both looked down forcibly at the food on our plates. Ed excused himself and went off for a walk, surely to cool down. When he re-emerged, he limited himself to inquiring if there was anything further I desired, or if he could request the check.

***

The plan was to swing by my parents' to say hello and then fly back to the fervid schedule of end of semester work at LMU. The freshly updated yard task list, which begged for an updated budget so that we could move forward with the purchasing, was next on the agenda. The lead keel was near its finishing stages and the logistics of getting the 6,000 kg keel 2,600 km from the foundry to our yard urged my attention. I had also committed to joining my cohort for a summer program in Rishikesh, India, and had to jump through a few loops to get a visa stamped in my passport. The Indian consulate demanded you mail your passport into their office in San Francisco, promising to return it within two months but with the trips to Brazil being so close in between, I had to time that transaction quite carefully.

***

"Hi Dad..." I sat across from a completely different man than the one I had seen on my way through São Paulo just weeks earlier. "What's going on? What are you feeling?" I asked searching.

"I'm just tired." He said, his posture crumpled up within his pajamas backing-up the words he'd barely uttered.

"Ya?" I said tenderly. It was so rare to see my Dad with his head down, not commanding the conversation and shouting orders at my mother. "Do you feel sick at all? Any symptoms?" I queried, meaning to assess the situation.

"I just don't want to live anymore..." came the words from the man who had dominated my life with his force. This currently frail man had dictated my every move, bulldozed my every desire and shaped me into the woman I was by virtue of being the strengthening resistance that makes one overcome and flourish into what we're meant to be. He then set the truth out before me quite plainly - "I'm ready to die."

It was not the first time I had heard such a revelation from someone. I'd routinely taken shifts at a crisis lifeline, but still, there is an aftermath that triggers even the most climatized spirit when those words are uttered by one's own progenitor. I kept our conversation simple to keep the space between us uncluttered.

"Are you thinking of doing something specific?" I asked. The words seemed to have a physical impact on him as he cringed a bit under their impact.

"No...I couldn't do that to your mother...." he winced.

"Mhmmm..." I uttered, my spirit filled with compassion. "So that's why you've stopped eating...?" my question lingered halfheartedly, having already reached my conclusion with a sudden, deep-feeling upheaval of emotions that were both empathetic and merciful.

My mother had been distressed over the fact he simply stopped eating after they got back from Rio. She told me he had had a harrowing argument during their visit with my half-brother while they were there. She cringed at the cruelty of the words and violence with which my half-brother, who was in his 60's, had verbally assaulted his elderly father. I understood the girth of the story almost instantly, being an insider to the commotion my father's leaving of his first wife in the 1950's had caused. Divorce was not an easily digestible tidbit in those days and there had been a lot of hurt left in its wake.

Ten days went by tending to this impasse. No hospitals would have my father as he displayed no symptoms of physical disease. His malady was ethereal, of things born from the subtle realms of spirit and emotions that science has yet to venture into. My last conversation with my Dad contained very few words. He spoke less and less, his spirit lingering dangerously close to departure, our communication consisted of less verbiage.

"Dad, I'm sorry," I said that day, taking his hand. It was an utterance that contained volumes and volumes of significance for me and overflowed from my heart. On the surface I was referring to the fact that we had in fact finally checked him into a hospital because we didn't have the wherewithal to watch him succumb at home unassisted.

His eyelids squeezed out a fair bit of moisture that could be characterized as a tear or two, but he stood tall inside as he prepared for the journey home.

"And Marco?" My father's barely audible, two worded utterance carried monumental meaning, their true concern conveyed a palpable 'Have you heard back on his case, when is he going home, are you holding up okay?'.

"We should hear back any day now Dad..." I coaxed, my voice now trailing off as fiery tears welled in my own eyes and overwhelmed me. "Any day now..." I said, as he squeezed my hand with what little fortitude he still had left.

I received the news that my father had passed at 06:30 am the next morning while overhearing my eldest son Carlos who had taken the call from the hospital.

"I understand...yes...we'll look into the next steps...thank you," he replied.

I tiptoed back to my room and sat quietly, preparing mentally to deliver the news to my mother. She lay asleep in the bed beside me. Carlos quietly pushed the door open, having himself prepared to deliver the news to us.

Hours later, still dazed by the preparations spurred by the earlier news, I checked my email to find that I had gained an advocate in a parallel realm:

Immigration, Rio <ImmigrationRio@state.gov>
Tue 5/6/2014 9:05 AM
You; Marco Esposito

Dear Mr. Esposito,

Your visa has been issued and forwarded to your residence. Please await delivery.

Regards,

Immigrant Visa Unit

United States Consulate General Rio de Janeiro - RJ -Brazil

***

I flew home immediately after my father's funeral the day after his passing. Marco purchased a return ticket home and was scheduled to arrive the day after I did. My trip had been extended by nearly two weeks at this point and I was grateful to be going home. Upon opening the door to my apartment, I laid in my usual spot on the white carpet of our living room floor, which we playfully referred to as "the portal" because that was my meditation spot and all of us had the habit of laying there 'recharging'. It was so soothing to walk in and just lay there, regaining presence of mind. I began to center my thoughts, as all of life's latest events swam around my mind, taking turns at my attention. 'Wow, my father is no longer here on this planet.' 'Wow, Marco is coming home!' 'Wow, I have a shit-ton of work to catch up on for the boat project and for school'. A text message lit up my phone, distracting my tired and somewhat overwhelmed mind from its musings.

"Hey, are you in town?" it was my girlfriend Andrea.

My friends were used to my long stretches of overseas travel since the project had begun nearly 4 years earlier.

I reached for the phone, rolling on my back to reply but decided to call her rather than text. We'd been trying to connect for a few months now and our communication had been limited to a few short texts ever since I'd been engulfed by the project and my master's program. It had been eight months since she and I last had a beach day together in Zuma, where she had told me all about her new boyfriend Mark. Andrea was the fun girlfriend you'd comfortably talk to about anything and had been introduced to me a few years earlier by a mutual friend who thought we'd make a good friend match - her being half Brazilian - so I agreed to meet her on what we playfully called a 'blind date' for coffee and we'd been friends since.

"Hey..." I began when she answered.

"Hey! How's it going? Oh my God, it's been awhile - are you in town?" she queried excitedly.

"I literally just got off the plane, walked into my apartment and threw myself on the floor to recoup..." I declared, before we both began laughing, that mental picture being so available to us.

"Well listen, we have so much to catch up on, but I texted you because Mark is in town with his friend..." Highly allergic to being matched-up to strangers by friends, I vaguely remembered Andrea having invited me and my having refuted an invitation earlier that year, to go for a beer with her boyfriend and *the friend*. I anchored myself.

"Right...." I replied, lingering on thoughts that somewhat relieved my awkward hesitance; I had more excuses than a sunflower has seeds to decline her offer at that point.

"Ya, so I know you're tired, but do you want to go for drinks tonight?" she coaxed.

"Girl, I got so much to catch you up on, but for one - I just buried my Dad yesterday morning. Two, Marco arrives tomorrow at the crack of dawn and I want to be there waiting!" My tone went from the heaviness that one would use to announce the news of the death of a loved one, to the close to squealing tone one uses to say they have just won the lottery.

"Oh my God! That's amazing! You did it!" Andrea knew very well of the whole immigration debacle and of the havoc it had wreaked in my life. She had had to put up with me explaining the whole case the last time we were on the beach, when all she had wanted was to concentrate on telling me about her new-found love. "But I'm really sorry to hear about your Dad..." she sympathized - "you poor thing, you must be exhausted".

"I am...." I conceded, fulfilled, to have dodged the going out with the "friend" subject.

"Well listen, let's do it on Monday, because Tuesday they'll be heading to Vegas for a show. After everything you told me, you really need to come out and relax a little. It's just a drink - I'm not trying to set you up or anything," she pressed on.

I succumbed to her logic and agreed to touch base the coming Monday and carried on with my usual arrival routine; unpacking, doing laundry, taking an extra long shower - allowing time for an extended beauty-routine, then shuffling off to the market for fresh organics.

It wasn't long before Kleo and Kevin arrived, and Danny came home from school. We had so much to catch up on and celebrate. We laid in the portal and just talked until we decided what we wanted to eat. We'd all concluded that we'd organize a little welcoming committee with our closest friends, to go to the airport in the morning and that Kleo would paint a long, 'Welcome Home' banner we could all hold. Marco's cousin Lilly, (number three of the Graham children) flew-in from Chicago, where she was living while attending Northwestern University, to welcome her cousin with Justin, her boyfriend and a very close friend of Kevin's.

We all set out early in the morning to welcome Marco and then head to Il Fornaio, his favorite breakfast spot in Beverly Hills, where I had worked years earlier upon arriving in the US. It was Mother's Day and I couldn't have received a greater gift. It was a delicious family celebration and having Marco for Mother's Day brunch was surreal to say the least. I went to bed that night in a daze of elation and anxiety regarding how things were going to progress. I was certainly happy that there would be no more immigration emails to rob my peace. I felt like Erin Brockovich, having overcome this gargantuan institution that bears no concern for basic human ties.

***

Days were busy and laced with gratitude every time I remembered Marco was home. I had given in and joined Andrea and her boyfriend for a drink with the friend from out of town that Monday after a hectic day of budgeting and placing orders. It was a good idea after all and the friend - Mike, was a witty conversationalist. When I asked how his day had been - looking to make friendly conversation, he came back with:

"Oh, pretty good actually - I won the lotto..." he espoused nonchalantly, grinning from behind his crystal blue eyes.

As it turned out, Mike was from New Zealand and had been notified that he had won the immigration lotto that day and could begin the process for procuring a resident visa in the United States. I chuckled and congratulated him but made no mention of my recent immigration nightmare with Marco. I had no intention of waking the sleeping dogs within my soul. The following week Andrea invited me over for dinner.

"The boys are making vegan sushi and we thought you might like to join," her text read. This invited serious consideration as Kevin, Marco and I were laying in the portal, beyond the point of hunger and trying to figure out what we wanted for dinner.

"See ya suckers!" I taunted them, as I went off for sushi. I knew they needed no support from me for anything. They were in heaven every minute of the day just being back together again with no time constraints or distance between them.

After dinner, the four of us (Andrea, her boyfriend, Mike and I) went out for a long walk with the dog around the neighborhood, to enjoy the Santa Clarita evening with its warm, desert scents. Mike and I got to chat a bit as we got to know each other better.

He had been on the road with bands almost all of his life, working as a sound engineer, leaving very little time for cultivating much of a family life. He had been through three marriages each suffering from a different toll and he seemed to long for some care and settling. We finished our walk and I decided to take the opportunity to head home for an early night.

"Good night guys! Thanks for having me over! The sushi was delicious!" I chimed, as I beeped my car door open.

"Well listen, Andrea added, think about coming to Vegas with us for the show this weekend - we can leave Friday at lunch. It'll be so much fun!"

Mark and Mike were on the road with Rod Stewart who was doing his customary spring season in Vegas at the Caesar's Palace. The men took the opportunity to bring their motorbikes and get some riding time in, commuting across the desert every week from Santa Clarita to Vegas. Going in on the Thursday - and then back to Santa Clarita again on the Monday, this would be their final weekend on that schedule.

"Awn, I'd love to, but I'm so behind on work and school I couldn't possibly indulge in a weekend off...but next time k?" I drove off happy with the veracity of that statement.

Two nights later it was Thursday morning and when I woke up my inclination had shifted completely. My intellect knew of all the reasons why I should *not* go - but something inside of me whispered incessantly *to* go. I called Andrea and informed her of my change of heart which left her elated. The next evening, we both drove through the desert in her Lincoln Navigator, stopping to take in the night air and for a clandestine pee among the cacti. We caught up on our lives and before we knew it we were in the parking lot of the *Double Down*, a dingy little dive bar in Vegas.

We shot pool, had tequila shots and lots of laughs and then headed back to the hotel where Mark and Mike were staying. Mark suggested breakfast since it was just past 4 am. He made us eggs and toast in his and Andrea's apartment which was actually a one bedroom suite. They insisted that I take the couch in their lounge when the invite was first made, but for some reason, after breakfast, they were bidding Mike and I goodnight and shuffling us off to *his* room.

"I'm sorry..." I began, "I didn't mean to impose on you - I can just..."

"Don't be silly," Mike interrupted. These rooms are huge and no one would have to twist my arm to share a room with you..." he added charmingly.

We each showered and ended up staying awake and talking til daybreak. It was like we had always known each other and were just catching up on how our lives had been since we'd last met. The mixture of his respect for me, with just the right amount of admiration while I spoke, was so attractive and palatable to someone who was used to Mr. Burnett's fastidious company. We finally fell fast asleep, propped up on the bed amongst the numerous pillows. In the morning Mike awoke to use the bathroom. I followed in after, upon his return to bed. As I was in the bathroom freshening myself up from my very, very uncharacteristic night out in Vegas, I congratulated myself with a smile in the mirror for having been so spontaneous and having allowed the flow of life to change my plans. I thought back on the trail of times recently past, when I hadn't catered to my spontaneity and how much I admired and had a real passion for that trait. I'd forgotten how being spontaneous had kept me youthful, radiant and true to myself. I admired my image in the mirror and as I let my neon pink nightie slip onto the travertine floor I gave myself a little wink, granting myself permission to go back to bed utterly bare skinned, as a prize for my spontaneity and to Mike for his gentlemanly behavior.

***

Back at LMU, I had papers to write, midterms to make up and presentations to prepare. I was also dealing with a barrage of emails regarding the finishing touches being put on the keel and securing the logistics of getting it to Cajaíba. Our container had just been freed up at customs in Brazil and it contained the anchors, anchor chain, a quiet flush for the head, a few electronics and many, many screws and rigging bits. Finalizing the order for the sails and the systems was in order and my head was swimming with deadlines. Mine and Ed's next trip to Brazil was impending and I was keeping everything abreast by working organized shifts between school and boat and trying to keep my self-care routine strong, to keep the candle from burning at both ends. It was in this frenzy that I received a call early one morning. It was Analida, who had stayed in Brazil with my mother after my father's passing so that I could come back to work and school.

"Hi Paula - I hope I didn't startle you with the freakishly early call..." she began.

"Oh, no problem...for a minute I thought it was Dad..." I mustered a chuckle making an allusion to my Dad who after a certain age made it of no concern to respect the time difference between our countries and had been known to ring my cell phone at 3:30 am to let me know he had dropped a postcard in the mail for me and to keep an eye out for it.

"Ha-ha... ya...well listen, I'm afraid I've got a bit of concerning news for you..." I didn't even have the chance to refuse the news altogether - my emotional hard drive had no more room for any concerning news and so I would have gladly passed on whatever she was about to say.

"Mom got up to go to the bathroom last night and felt disoriented when she was coming back to bed..."

"Oh God...don't tell me..." I sensed the ominous tone of the news.

"Ya, she fell and cracked her femur - as a matter of fact, it might have been the other way round. The doctor says there's a possibility she fell because her femur snapped due to the advanced state of her osteoporosis, but either way she's going to have to go in for surgery."

At age 87 we weren't too confident about putting my mother under for surgery, but there was no other option. Her surgeon scheduled her at noon on World Cup Opening Ceremony day - a day when virtually all of Brazil completely stopped to savor the event, so we were surprised but grateful that he made this concession to fit her in so she wouldn't have to wait any longer. I traveled back to Brazil a day ahead of time and arrived in time to see her off to surgery at the hospital. She was happily sedated and clutching her bobblehead Neymar for luck when they wheeled her away. Neymar was the Brazilian national team's star player that year and the whole country put their faith in him - and my mother was no exception.

Surgery went well and she was serene in recovery three days later, when Ed arrived and we scuffled off to the boatyard. Needless to say all of Cajaíba had stopped now as well, all watching the World Cup, but we pressed on marking bulkheads, planning cabin storage and lighting nevertheless. We discussed how we'd go about drilling holes for the keel bolts and aligning those holes so that the bolts could pierce down from the cabin floor, down through all the layers of the keel into the lead. In the evenings, we lounged a bit over a cocktail and then Ed would cook while I did my school work. One night he was cooking and poured me a glass of wine, which he thoughtfully served with some olives in a small wooden bowl and some crisps. As I was savoring my hor-d'oeuvres and working on a presentation, a text from Mike came in.

"Hi sweetie. Can you chat a bit?" the words lit up my phone.

After our outing in Vegas Mike had told me he was very interested in getting to know me better and asked if that would be okay or if he should 'bugger off' if there was no interest on my part. His stark sincerity was extremely captivating to my free spirit. Since he was constantly on the road, I had agreed to come out and see him while he was working in Philadelphia on one occasion and in St. Louis on another. The romance was refreshing and each time I went to meet him I became more emotionally involved by the space he afforded me. This gave me the freedom to decide whether I wanted to go any further or not in the relationship without any real pressure.

"Sure. Let's *try* Skype?" I suggested, knowing full well that the connection in our region of Brazil was anything but stable.

A few minutes went by before the familiar Skype ring was dinging away on my computer speakers.

"Hi..." I smiled at the screen, as I sat back in my lounge chair, propping my feet up comfortably, glass of wine in hand.

We chatted for a while and it was not long until Ed headed out to the veranda to see if I needed a refill. He arrived just in time to hear us saying our goodbyes.

"Alright darling, sleep well. Have a productive day at the yard tomorrow, won't you?" Mike said sweetly, as a prince might, just before signing off.

"*Darling*?" Ed mocked. "Is there something you've failed to tell me?" he mused with a smirk.

"Noooo...I *deliberately* did not tell you because I'm just seeing him informally." I said, recanting a bit.

"Well you should tell him about the '*informally*' bit, because if he's calling you darling, I'm not sure he got that memo..." Ed replied snarkily.

"What, you're my Dad now?" I retorted.

"You can do whatsoever you want. The point at hand solely being, that his tone is not of someone who is thinking you are informally seeing each other..." Ed reasoned.

"I'm just living in the moment Edward," my smirk now gave me away. "You know, just keeping it family rated." I poked further.

We managed an extremely productive trip, even despite the distraction caused by the World Cup games, and even made time to catch a game ourselves at a local bar where we spent a lazy afternoon jeering at the TV like two soccer buffs. Ed had purchased a Brazil jersey and I had brought one along for myself so we had fun in painted faces, enjoying beer and just mingling with the locals. Planking at the yard was finished and one could already see the bodacious curves that the 56' Burnett Ketch was growing into. Her deck was laid and work on the rudder had begun. Things were looking pretty favorable at the yard, which had Zezinho wearing a snazzy fedora hat as he strutted us proudly to and from the pier every day. He had stuffed a proverbial sock into everyone's mouths at the village and the boat was now turning heads. We were also hitting all of our inspections out of the park, triggering payments that flowed into Zezinho's bank account, so he was riding high. We were moving forward at a fair speed and were now poised to come back within a month for our next trip to inspect the keel before having it trucked up.

***

My mother was staying at an assisted living facility and my sister was sharing the room with her so she would not be left alone, not even for a minute. When Ed and I were passing through town one day, we decided to swing by and take tea with them one afternoon.

"Lida..." I began, "I wanted to thank you for staying with Mom - but I realize you've got a life to get back to as well." I reasoned. "How about I go home and organize things so that I can come back late June and stay with Mama for the month of July? It's only fair - you've been here with her since May."

We agreed that would be fair. Our brother Frank and his wife Lidia had a school aged child and could only make it out on the weekends, which we understood fully. Of course, entering into that agreement meant I would have to withdraw from my summer classes and forego the trip to India. I was fortunate to have the most compassionate and understanding professors a pupil could ask for in that regard. They each made concessions so that I could still complete the credits necessary to graduate with the first cohort come May 2015 without joining them on the trip and attending my classes remotely.

The next five weeks were a unique growing experience of coming of age. Caring for my mother, in that setting, six months away from my 50th – it was definitely life changing and its effect reverberated in all the decisions I made thereafter pertaining to how I lived my life. I was the youngest person at the senior living facility by far. That season changed my perspective in so many ways about what it means to be 'old' and how important it is to live life in the present moment, because time catches up to us all, taking many cards off the table. I witnessed men who had been powerful businessmen, federal judges and other previously prominent figures, being spoon fed by nurses who baby-talked to them like they were 4 year olds.

My mother and I chatted all day. I helped her bathe and placed her in front of the dressing mirror with her make up bags within easy reach on a little table, patiently watching her 'put on her face' for about 30 minutes each morning. She always said that the day she didn't bother to put on makeup anymore, that I could just have her committed.

From the assisted living facility, I could still work a bit while my mother napped or watched TV. I could keep things moving at the yard to some extent as well as get some schoolwork done. I would have the eventual skype meeting with Ed as needed, but the person who would check in on me daily at the same time was Mike. The residents would walk by me on my laptop and come around to see who I was talking to and most of them would be amazed at how we could date over skype. More and more Mike had displayed a cool, calm and collected demeanor, with a very laid-back disposition. It was wonderful to talk to him for an hour at the end of the day, when all I needed was some encouragement and a chat to decompress.

Summer flew by and so did my weeks in Brazil. I got most of my schoolwork done and Lorena and I had successfully coordinated the keel be transported to Cajaíba on a semi-truck, with the aid of a motorcade, composed of two flagged safety cars. Off our keel went on its trip up the winding coastal roads from Itajaí, in the southern state of Santa Catarina up to our little Cajaíba in Bahia.

Mike was just wrapping-up his latest tour and popped in for a short visit with family in New Zealand before heading to California to welcome me home. Over the summer our conversations via skype had brought us close in a way that dating personally might have failed to do, with all the distractions that going out for romantic dinners, theater nights and having intense sex might have posed. I didn't notice it at first, but Mike had made his way deep into my heart, with his gentle, yet direct approach and I had opened my heart to him at a time in my life when expressing that vulnerability was all I had needed to feel secure. When he heard I'd be coming back to California he spared no effort to be there for me when I got back, even though he could only be in town for three days. Mike flew across the globe to be there for me.

***

"You're soooooo sweet..." I cooed, one very hot afternoon, having decided to have cocktails at the same bar where we'd gone with Andrea and Mark the first time we'd met. "It's so nice to be home and to have you here. Those poor old folks back at the home are missing our conversations as we speak..." I taunted him humorously.

"Yeah," he agreed with a snicker. "Well, you've been gone a long time and I wanted to make sure you settled back in properly," he added, in his delicious kiwi accent, of which I probably understood maybe 85% of what he was actually saying.

Mike was a provider. He was a trustworthy, respectful and generous man, with a huge heart. Which is why, when he was in the midst of explaining to me why he'd flown across the globe to see me and how he'd looked forward to all our talks and how it felt like we had known each other for lifetimes - it was easy to agree with his final summation.

"Which is why Paula..." he continued, leaning forward as he took my hands into his and looked unabashedly into my eyes as he announced: "I've come to ask you to be my wife..." and then he reiterated, in the aftermath of the dead silence that his statement had gaped wide open between us - "Paula, will you *be* my wife?" His words were confident and unrehearsed.

"Oh? Wait, what?" I giggled a bit at the absurdity of it all, lost in the moment and the ecstasy of the fun surprise that life had prepared, but before he could finish his sentence about my 'not having to reply immediately', I blurted out an enthusiastic affirmative.

"Yes! ... I would love to be your wife." It would have been a beautiful movie scene except he hadn't brought a ring. He began explaining how he'd come to the conclusion to propose but thought he wouldn't have the courage to actually ask me, but then, had suddenly found the courage to do so.

"You *accidentally* asked me to marry you?!?" I burst out laughing, absolutely understanding his conundrum but having fun with it nonetheless.

I excused myself and went to the girl's room to splash my face with water and call Kevin; who had made me promise to call him before I ever accepted another proposal again. I had just failed terribly in keeping that promise and on top of that had forgotten to bring my cellphone to the bathroom.

"I just got proposed to!" I announced to the hostess who was washing her hands in the sink next to me.

"Oh! Congratulations! What'd you say??"

"I said Yes!!" my face beamed.

***

Our next trip out to Brazil was a major one. We had built the boat from the ground up and had tied a few wooden rafters to the columns in the boatyard at strategic points to keep it standing without tipping over. Our keel was now only days away from arriving and we would have to lift the boat, which at this point weighed close to 14 tons, slip the 6-ton lead keel under it, screw that on and then let everything back down onto what would be its final launch position. If this sounds next to impossible with only raw manpower and 2 VW bus jacks to rely on - it was.

Ed and I met at Guarulhos airport and made our way to Barra Grande as usual. I hadn't told him I was engaged yet - for so many reasons - but the fact remained that I had planned to tell him, I was just waiting for the perfect opportunity to arise to share my happy news. Unfortunately, as it turned out, that *perfect* opportunity was not the one in which it finally ensued.

Olivan picked us up at the pier, punctually as usual. Jorge had dropped us off, after having collected us in Camamú, where we had driven to from the Ilhéus airport once we'd landed. Ed hopped in the front and I sat in the back of the Kawasaki mule, which was our favorite vehicle to buzz around in. We roved down the dirt road on our way through town - still saying our hellos and catching up with Olivan.

"Olivan, tell me the news...any news in town?" I inquired cheerfully.

There was always news of some life event having occurred in our absence and that we'd learn about upon arriving back in town. The 27-year-old gardener who was sadly electrocuted and perished. The girl who had committed the atrocity of taking ant poison to protest her lover's departure. The mother of three, who had left the husband for a female mistress. Life was intense here and available for everyone to witness, the community being so very small.

"No news this time!" Olivan announced in good spirits. "It hasn't been that long since you guys last came after all..." he noted rightly.

"What about you? What's the news?" he looked through the rearview mirror, smiling broadly.

"Hmmm..." I pondered. "No news really...well.... I'm getting married...but.." Olivan's knee jerk reaction was to pull his foot from the accelerator, causing our vehicle to jolt.

"Whaaaaat?" he blurted, overjoyed.

As Ed turned to inquire what I had just said that had been so groundbreaking, he was interrupted by Olivan's profuse good wishes.

"Congratulations! Yes! Bravo! Congratulations!" Olivan's smile overwhelmed his face, as he congratulated - Ed.

"I told him I'm getting married." I said flatly... I can't think of anything I've ever done that was as stupid and inconsiderate as it was to deliver the news in that manner to Ed, within that whirlwind frenzy.

"You're getting married?" The word married was enunciated several tones higher than in regular human speech.

Olivan was still celebrating and innocently congratulating us, so my initial priority was to set the situation straight with him.

"No, Olivan, not to Ed... You don't know the guy, but you'll meet him soon." A look of sheer perplexity came over Olivan's face, as it quickly dawned on him that Ed too might have just found out.

"You... are getting *married*?" he repeated. "What? to the guy who called you darling?" Ed asked bewildered.

My face flushed. I was at a loss for words to explain, as there were so many aspects that had led to my decision. I was completely caught off guard, although it had been my own, inadvertent stupidity, that had gotten me into this awkward mishap.

"Yes Ed, it's not a big deal," I said as casually as possible, trying to brush it off.

"It's not a big deal? It's not a big deal? Why didn't you tell me? You didn't think I might like to have known before? Christ, we just traveled four hours together and you didn't tell me?"

As he shot the questions out, I tried the best I could at that moment to defend myself, knowing full well that in fact I had certainly erred by my initial hesitancy to share such precious news and more so from my ill-timed disclosure of that news.

"It's not! No.... Ed, we slept most of the way..." I said gasping, and then, finally, "*I...didn't think you'd care alright*!!" I exclaimed, with such an uncanny amount of emotion and in such volume that it summoned a disturbing silence into the vehicle.

Ed looked out over the landscape cringing slightly whilst veining interest in the flora. Olivan clasped the wheel tightly. I fought back hot tears of embarrassment for not having told him in the first place and confused as to why I hadn't.

As evening fell, Ed came out of his room. He had retired there immediately upon our arrival to the compound, having stated that he wanted to shower, rest and work on some calculations until dinnertime. I too had gone to my room for much the same reason, so we were both fresher when we met out on the veranda for our typical cocktail.

"Listen, I'm sorry if I ..." Ed began.

"No..., *I'm the one who's sorry.*" I interrupted. "I don't know why I...."

"It's fine... listen, it's fine," he said kindly, saving me from coming up with any more pointless explanations for anything at all. "Congratulations..." he said, with perhaps the most tender expression I had ever seen on his face and then topping it with an encouraging: "you deserve a good man."

"Thank you..." I remarked, a timid smile etched across my face. I looked down, still quite embarrassed. I was puzzled at the amount of emotion the moment had brought up in us both.

"Right, come on then...I'm going to teach you how to make Yorkshire pudding tonight..."

He proceeded to lead the way into the kitchen somewhat enthusiastically, in his customary large and confident strides.

He pulled out the filet mignon that Olivan had left out thawing for us and began imparting his knowledge concerning the history of Yorkshire pudding upon me. Which I was soon to discover, was actually not a true pudding at all. He walked me through the recipe and heated up the oven at just the right temperature - pouring himself into teaching me the details and craft of the traditional British treat. He cubed the filet and prepared it with a Bourgogne-style sauce, which paired amazingly well with the perfectly cooked vegetables and *'pudding'* - which was actually a savory bread. While we delighted over our savory meal, our glasses filled with a sensible amount of wine, Ed's famous petit gateau, for which he'd especially brought a dark, bittersweet chocolate in his bag from the UK, was baking scrumptiously in the oven, filling the air with a marvelous scent. We listened to Daft Punk over the speakers and he pulled a few quirky dance moves, while asking me to excuse him if the lyrics were a bit racy. We revisited the news of my engagement over scotch on the veranda, this time in a settled and heart-filled way, and I told him that Mike might come to meet us this time around, for a day or two, as he was in South America on tour.

"Good... I want to see who this character is..." sipping his scotch he concluded "to make sure he's a worthy suitor..." he completed in the most British of tones downing the remaining contents of his glass in one gulp.

***

There was nothing rushed about this particular trip. We came out with the sole objective of fitting the keel and Ed was bent on having the process go seamlessly. Our first day at the yard was dedicated to inspecting the tasks that had been left to do the trip before, which were pertaining mainly to painting the bilges and bulkheads and correcting a few, final details on the deck, as well as issues with planking and fairing. The second day, Ed requested everyone who was to be involved in fitting the keel, be present for a general briefing. He marched in utterly focused but in good enough spirits to smile, say hi and risk a 'bom dia' here and there.

"Bom dia..." he began, signaling for me to translate the forthcoming.

Ed explained what the next days entailed in a nutshell and what our timeline looked like. We would have this briefing in the morning on this day, to clear up any questions we might have. In the afternoon, we would gather materials and discuss tomorrow's work, which would involve positioning the lead keel, parallel to its final place on the boatyard floor and then preparing for the lift. There was a lot of digging to be done, as space had to be created so that one could position himself to work at a feasible angle to the keel. The day after that, we would begin raising her up about 10 - 20 cm in the air at a time, to make space to slide the keel under her, and work from there. We would use a piece of timber on top of the lead ballast as a spacer to go between the hull and the lead. Using this to transfer the bolt hole positions from the lead to the hull, then drill up from underneath the lead, which is why the keel had to be lifted and straddled on beams leaving room for access. The spacer would then be moved under the boat to continue drilling the holes up through the hull, so as to not leave unwanted holes on the bottom of Mr. Graham's boat.

Ed brought a beautiful piece of white canvas in his luggage, to be stretched over the keel. It was to be soaked in layers of thick tar, in order to seal the spaces between the imperfections of each surface in its gooey goodness. The boat would be lowered onto the keel adhering it to the deadwood. Once the holes were aligned we would run the screws from the cabin floor down, and then tighten the nut and washer at the counter bores on the underside of the keel, which was sat on the parallel transversal beams, allowing just enough space for the motivated worker.

Our briefing had the men scratching their heads and raising eyebrows but the trust they placed in Ed's leadership was unwavering. They had watched this 'gringo' arrive with his pale face and velcro-strapped sandals, laptop bag slung across his chest, with cloth handkerchief in tote, single-handedly showing them a completely new way to approach something they had been learning going on five generations. Initially, when the workers saw the minimal dimensions on the bits of timber he requested, they thought surely the boat would collapse, as they possessed little to no concept of engineering the load. The local way of building was anchored to the concept that everything had to be hefty and robust to be sturdy and here Mr. white guy comes with planks as thin as 2.5 cm and not only gets this boat to stand, but is getting ready to latch on six tons of lead to the bottom of it. Zezinho would always try to sneak in extra width or height to make sure construction would be sturdy, but Ed became quite cross, when upon measuring for the frames he found the boat length was 14 cm longer than his initial design had called for. He explained to Zezinho that they had to stick to the exact measures or else the boat would be much heavier than anticipated, throwing off a number of crucial calculations. Things were very simple and hands on with the local boat building process - if one needed a waterline there was no calculating it - they'd put the boat in the water and mark the waterline wherever it fell naturally. There was virtually no calculation in their way of working. They had learned that in Ed's process, everything was calculated and fell perfectly into place magically and they knew the keel fixing process would be no different.

On the eve of day three, Mike arrived. The day was charged with apprehension over the actual beginnings of lifting the boat. A ditch had been dug from which one could work under the boat 'comfortably', sat on its edges, or somewhat safely - though with their feet in sea water, that emanated from the freshly dug hole - with access to the underside of the keel which sat on two hefty transversal beams. Hefty, but with the fourteen-ton hull about to have its weight increased by six tons, one had to be naïve to believe that they would withstand the weight in the event the structure slipped from its support on the rafters. Two hand-pumped, VW Kombi bottle jacks, and one driven engineer were the extent of the technology at hand for the process. As Zezinho and Ed pumped the jacks, in a somewhat synchronized fashion - 10 pumps at a time counting out loud, there were men at each of the six points, where the hull structure was braced by wedges, that then leveraged the support provided by the rafters that were tied to the beams and that held the very boatyard structure up to its trusses. As the hull structure was lifted, wedges were driven wherever space was created - keeping the structure locked into place, so as not to suffer any sudden movements that might quickly gain momentum, causing complete loss of control. The screeching and moaning of the heavily loaded wooden bits, shifting and giving way for the structure to rise, was beseechingly ominous of the risks at hand. Zezinho's brow was beaded in sweat, as he asked for further clarification on the height to which the structure needed to be lifted. Mike was instrumental in giving Ed feedback, circulating through the perilous points and calling back status. Being on the road with bands from an early age, Mike had plenty of experience setting up stages and flying hefty sound gear in the air. He was a strong ally, as he fundamentally understood Ed's plan, but he was taken aback by the rawness of it all nonetheless. The pauses in between each set of pumps were taken to surveil how the rafters were holding up.

"There's a lot of pressure on this one here!" the voice of a worker called out from starboard aft.

Ed requested the point across from that one be loosened a bit before proceeding. Ten more pumps. The timber groaned heavily, causing the workers to glance up at the structure and then at each other - the tinge of fear beginning to taint their eyes. As the next ten pumps were underway, there was a blood-curdling screech, followed by a thunderous snap that caused the crew to spill *en masse* - like cockroaches fleeing a room when the light switch is flipped on. Zezinho looked over to me in a clear motion of, 'what the fuck...' wiping his brow with his forearm.

"Everything under control? Do we need to check..." My peremptory effort to check in with Ed, was met by a shortened temper.

"Let's just focus here! Can everyone just stay put at their stations please - we're almost there!" He bellowed.

Mike walked past me and winked, as if to say, 'don't worry, he knows what he's doing...'

"We're almost there! Let's stay focused!" I translated, encouraging the men on site.

Everyone settled down, regaining composure - drying their hands and nodding one to the other affirmatively, readying themselves.

"Ok...go!" Ed ordained the next set of ten pumps.

This time, before the third pump, one of the back rafters snapped into mid-air under the pressure, sending its two halves and dozens of splintered bits flying across the yard, causing the men to scatter once again.

Zezinho jumped up from his place visibly enraged, as he spoke in a low threatening tone. "This is not good...." he grumbled, walking decidedly away and towards the work table. He had stood as if to collect something but that *something* was not as much a tangible thing as it was some needed courage.

"Paula, we should rethink this." he said, every bit of lightheartedness now gone away from him. "Someone, if not many of us, could die if this structure budges - the whole yard will come barreling down on us." Zezinho seemed to be earnestly pleading now, either for us to stop, or to simply reaffirm him of the feasibility of carrying on.

Ed sat still under the hull, assessing the points within his view with what seemed like hawk eye precision. When he turned around, ready to speak, there was not a cell in his body that conveyed doubt, as he mandated loudly: "Let's press on! Ten more centimeters," he instructed encouragingly.

A general discomfort made everyone shift and start up a bit. Glances crossed, as if a sudden whiff of insanity had just been perceived.

One of the workers called to another - "Dude..." he said, pointing his station out for the other to take over, as he proceeded to walk off the site and towards perceived safety.

Feet shifted and before any more awkwardness could lift, it was met with Ed's next command "Ok! Let's go..." he shouted.

Zezinho walked over to the jack he was manning with stunted gaits of mistrust.

Ed called out for the last round of pumping to begin. "Ready! One...two..."

Upon the first crack, Zezinho stood up decidedly and then stepped back from the structure with a look of annoyance on his face that was closely linked to fear. I searched wildly for some affirmation from Ed, but his eyes became stormy and inaccessible, as he continued pumping the structure up on his own. His navy-blue tee was now plastered to his back by the sweat of his frustration. Everyone had now stepped back from their posts, knowing full well that at any minute the whole yard could topple over our heads. We all stood back and watched in silent awe, as Ed fiercely finished pumping-up his jack, and then walked over the other jack, to continue his singularly minded efforts. All the while the structure was emitting sounds of suffering from the immense pressure it was made to endure. There was an eerie silence and in those 30 - 40 seconds that seemed to have lasted an eternity, everyone held one eye on him in suspended disbelief, while the other eye was searching for the nearest exit route in the event any more wildly threatening cracks were heard. Ed finished his last pumps, and sat there in silence for a minute before getting up to his feet decidedly and walking toward the yard gate. He nodded an assertive head towards the crew, as a tight grimace etched across his face. As the intense sunlight met him on the other side, he squinted, walking towards the waterline in his usual gaping strides whilst wiping his hands on his khaki bermuda shorts.

Zezinho looked at me and the others and started a sentence he dared not utter. He shook his head as he motioned for everyone to take a break.

***

At Collars in Dorchester, Jeremy was busy putting together the final touches on our order of masts and spars. The mast dressings, which consist of lights, bars, loops, fittings, spreaders and all sorts of bits that will comprise rigging once the masts are stepped, were also being prepared. They were being shipped partially pre-installed on the masts and also loose within the crate, but safely packed in foam. We were using an importation agent in southern Brazil, having learned our lesson the hard way last time round, in dealing with all the paperwork ourselves, not to mention the horrid delays and fines that went along with it. Our agent was asking for all sorts of details, including itemized descriptions, photographs and weights, for every single bee-bob in the 25 meter crate. The crate was actually custom made for us and carefully marked with instructions in English *and* Portuguese. Ed was going crazy having to bother poor Jeremy with such frivolities of paperwork but was easily persuaded back to the cause when I would remind him of the ins and outs of our last container fiasco. Luckily Collars were using a freight agent by the name of Gerald Price who did a formidable job, also in coordinating transportation from Dorchester to the Port of Tilbury, with a chap named Crispin. There were documents that the Graham's needed to obtain as importers, documents to be filled out by the exporting parties, many pertaining to just getting everything through customs and into the country, full stop. We were even asked to provide customs with a certificate stating that the timber the crate was made from was termite free. Excel sheets flew back and forth in such quantity and rapidity that it made me get over myself very quickly - at least in my fear of sharing and contributing to the work of other peoples' sheets. Charles was excel sheet master of the universe having used them in his trade since the very first version came out in 1985. And Ed... well, Ed was an engineer who designed 80' yachts that actually floated and I ... well I was a cheerful yogini who hugged trees and knew how to use coconut oil in 101 ways.

One day, I was flustered to tears, overwhelmed as I orchestrated deliveries, purchases and progress. I was trying to enter data into one of Charles' fancy multilevel spreadsheets, complete with currency/exchange formulas and if/then scenarios and then it all simply went to hell in a handbasket. I messed up on the spreadsheet and the formulas all went off. I was too busy to have a major meltdown so I called on our secret weapon - Marchesan. Mike Marchesan was Marco's high school friend who had always been the 13 going on 30 type of kid and renaissance man. He had many talents and one of them happened to be excel sheets. Ten minutes after he arrived, the crisis was averted and I proudly moved on and back to exchanging cute animal pics with Ed. If there was a surefire way into Mr. Burnett's heart - it was animals and a tightly knit excel sheet. Our work was punctuated with funny animal pics and a profuse exchange of pictures of his black lab Susie - who we fondly called Snoozie as she aged, and my Siamese cat James; sleeping in every position and surface known to man.

Our next trip was immediately upon us, as was the next and then holiday season arrived. Ed completely lost his business protocol during the weeks just before boarding our masts on the ship. He called me at wee hours of the morning, concerned that we needed to double check logistics, or that we needed more slotted wood screws. He texted wanting to know if our importer certification had been issued yet, just hours after having asked that very question. I was irritated that he was polluting my quiet time with his worries, because I had plenty of my own to contend with, but being in meditation mode first thing in the morning I pacified myself. 'you're going to miss this one day Paula'. I could not actually imagine such a scenario, but went with the intent of it nonetheless.

It all came together one fine day; the Graham's importation certificate was issued, every 't' was crossed on the bill of lading, every 'i' dotted on the excel sheet, entitled: *Itemized Shipment Values and Codes* - and all the duties and levies were paid. Our crate was shipped and Mike and I traveled for what would be our wedding trip to Brazil. We were married on the palm tree-laden lawn at the Graham compound at 4:44 am of January 1st, 2015, following a traditional Brazilian all night New Year's Eve bash - complete with all guests elegantly clad in white and a DJ who kept the dance floor pumping. It was all beautiful and unforgettable but the honeymoon was short-lived as four days later Mr. Burnett who refused to attend earlier was arriving to join me for boatyard duty.

March 2015:
The Systems

Kathini

A story of love, loss and a little boat building

There was much to do at the yard and so much more as the systems container was about to arrive through our representative in São Paulo - Marine Office. There was finalizing the details of the sails, which were thankfully being fabricated by North Sails, our reliable supplier in Southern Brazil, who were English speaking. I cordially laid all that out on Mr. Burnett's lap, for him to deal with. Ed had recently purchased a stone home in the small merchant town of Totnes, in Devon, where he lived and he was busy refurbishing floors and windows, cabinets and closets himself. Pictures of his progress on the renovations were soon mixed into the ones we exchanged of James and Susie, as well as the first flower that blossomed in his garden early that spring. Sadly, Susie was unwell, making Ed cringe at the thought of having to leave her behind for his upcoming trip to Brazil. Dave Robbins was traveling with us on this particular journey and all airline tickets had already been secured, so off we all went despite the preoccupation with ol Snoozie dog.

I was under quite a bit of stress myself. Stuck in my final semester at LMU, I had beaucoup school work to get done if I wanted to graduate with my cohort in May. Just off the top of the list, was a 100-page thesis that was due in four weeks' time and that I had barely had the chance to outline. I was also planning our US wedding in Pasadena, as the one in Brazil had been for family exclusively, and more so for my mother to attend, as she was unable to endure an international flight to America. The 'big one', was scheduled for April 18th, days after I returned from our trip, so I had to make sure everything was tip top and on the ready. The container, with all the system components, had arrived and been successfully released from port. I didn't have to deal with the logistics of getting it to our yard in Cajaíba, because I had used Marine Office's trusted transportation company...or at least I was led to believe they were trustworthy.

Early on the day that I was leaving for Brazil, I was packing my suitcases when my wedding dress arrived via courier. I was so elated that I tore the package open enthusiastically and tried on the dress right then and there. I had custom ordered it online with glee, only to discover that it was about three sizes too big! I quickly stuffed the dress back in its package and thought: *I can't - not right now.* I kept packing and going through my mental list - did I pack the drill bits, the counter sinks, the finishing plates that Ed had requested? As I was packing colorful bikinis and sarongs I thought to call to make sure our systems order had arrived in Cajaíba. It was meant to have arrived that morning.

"Hi Zezinho!" I was excited that he had picked up the phone, as he often did not, and I was also oh-so-ready to check another item off my list. "Has our truck arrived yet?" I asked, anticipating.

"Nooooo...Miss Paula, I talked to the driver last night to see if he wanted me to meet him at the main road and bring him here, because it's a little tricky, but he stopped replying to my texts..."

"Hmmm...but he said he was nearby?" I queried, pressing further.

"Nah, he said he'd be here today but didn't tell me where he was specifically."

"Right..." I mentally devised a multi-step plan on the spot, to make sure the worst case scenario didn't happen. Here I had two handsomely paid Brits, comfortably sat in their business class seats on their way to install five figures worth of equipment on our boat, and the truck with the equipment was missing. The fact my wedding dress hadn't fit properly quickly paled within the context of that scenario.

I called Marine Office. I called the transportation company. I called the driver. Long story extremely shortened, (I will graciously leave out the fact that my angel, mantra-chanting mouth, actually called one of the parties a cunt) I discovered that our shipment had not even been loaded onto a truck yet. The promise now was that it would leave that day and drive non-stop on a dedicated truck, straight to our yard, and that it would be there by the time we all arrived, *maybe* sooner. I settled into my airplane seat and doused myself in essential oils, in a concerted effort to appease the stress, stop clenching my teeth and to calm the angry scenarios that were creating havoc in my mind. I then distracted myself further, by gainfully working on my thesis a bit, before the cheap wine came around on the trolley.

We all *rendez-vous*-ed at the usual cafe by the check in area at Guarulhos International airport. Dave and Ed were chipper, and I looked like Lurch, the butler from the Addams family. I could not wait to land and call the transportation company to make sure the truck was on its way. I was coming unglued with anxiety when the human on the other end of the line said plainly: "you know, I don't see that truck on our roster..." and took a sip of his coffee. By now, I wasn't sure if I should even be boarding. I was tempted to go over to the company and scream until all the glass in their office shattered.

"What?!?" Ed was as infuriated as I was. You need to call Marcelo at Marine Office and get on his back for this. It's the company he recommended to us!"

The fact was, that Marcelo had already received all his payments in a timely manner and could not find the wherewithal to summon any fucks to be given at this point - and he made that point crystal clear to me when I called a week earlier. We boarded our flight and decided to deal with the whole thing when we got there. I'll kill all the suspense right here to say, that the lying, cheating transportation company not only did not do what they said they would do, but that our load arrived 5 days after we did. That situation cost me a crack in my molar from clenching my teeth in anger. Ed, surprisingly carried some pretty impressive painkillers, so I curbed the intense pain with those, until I could be seen by a dentist in Barra Grande. The fiasco turned out okay in the end, because Ed and Dave worked on the bits that each of us had hand carried into the country. It might not have been perfect, but in the end, it all worked out, pangs of anxiety and all. Ed left me to plane the rudder with a rattly electric hand planer to keep me busy, and to keep the ornery energy moving out of me. Zezinho and his son worked on further aligning and boring the propeller shaft hole which our local 'expert' who had previously gone out to do the task, had bored about 1.5 centimeters off from where Ed had marked it.

We all kept busy and when the load finally arrived early on Sunday, we celebrated with chilled coconuts. We tended to lifting the 255 kg engine up onto the deck with an A-frame that Zezinho's crew had built, and then eased it down into the engine room and into perfect alignment with the propeller shaft hole without further ado.

Our ten days in Cajaíba flew by. It was an extremely busy and productive trip, so Ed and I relaxed on the flight back to São Paulo, playing dominoes that we'd cut out from the kid's kit that they give out to the children who come on board. As I was grazing my pile for the giraffe to match the one he had just set out in front of me, I pouted:

"E-ed...I can't believe you're not coming to my wedding in LA. You could have just flown back with me..." I protested because he had also missed the wedding in Bahia.

His face was kind and thoughtful as he offered: "It's going to be beautiful nonetheless, whether I'm there or not."

"But you have a gabillion miles racked up by now and could fly first class if you wanted..." I whined on - insisting.

"Yes, but Snoozie would have to go a longer time away from home and it makes her so cross..." he pleaded in his defense, knowing I could grasp that scenario fully and with empathy.

"Now own up - you don't have a giraffe do you?" he asserted, and then facetiously added "I don't pity you one bit miss" as a sly grin came across his face.

I conceded, ceasing my entreaty because I also understood that he was going home to begin some serious packing, and that he would be moving into a new home in just a few weeks' time.

"I sent you an LP as a gift on iTunes by the way..." he said randomly, surprising me again with the proficiency he had gained on his smartphone. The one he had initially been so reluctant to try.

"I hope it worked," he continued. "It's the music by the chap you liked that I put on the other night." he clarified.

"Awn Ed..." I really appreciated that side of Ed that showed how much he cared by paying attention to the subtlest details.

"I love you..." I said, from the bottom of my heart as I leaned my head on the shoulder of his neatly pressed travel oxford.

He winced, emitting a barely audible utterance that sounded like a reciprocal response.

The LP he sent me was a young musician by the name of Ben Howard, from whom Ed had recently purchased his new home in Totnes. I played it on repeat for quite some time as the lyrics were sweet and the music resonated deeply. Ed had particularly put on a song for me that spoke of keeping a strong heart and holding one's head high and I felt that this is why he thought of me when he first heard it. Whether he realized it or not - he was rooting me on in my journey in a deep-seated way - hoping that everything I believed in - all the good I saw in the world was true - at least for me.

***

I landed at Los Angeles International three days before Mike and I's wedding. I took the first day to unpack, do laundry and decompress. The second day began with what quickly became my top priority - the dress. I didn't have time to fuss with the online supplier that had botched my order, so I decided I would give myself a day in Beverly Hills and see what I could find there. As it turns out I found a store that had a beautiful selection of Boho dresses, which suited my personality to a tee. So with a skip in my step, I took myself dress shopping on Beverly Drive. Having worked up an appetite, I indulged in a delicious lunch. I treated myself to a mani/pedi and sipped on iced chamomile tea - and it was all a gift from me to me - I was happy for myself. I felt for the other brides in the shop, who had friends hovering around them hooting and offering an inadequate amount of advice to the bride; making her all the more confused. I was grateful that I just walked in, chose the dress that had lit me up, tried it on and was out of the ritzy little shop within 40 minutes.

The days rolled by as guests arrived from Brazil and New Zealand. Andrea, who had introduced Mike and I, was my bridesmaid, and Mark, her boyfriend, was Mike's best man. My oldest son walked me down the aisle and the setting was incredibly romantic at the Los Angeles Arboretum, where we had chosen to have an outdoor ceremony under a Brazilian pepper tree. It was spring and peacocks grazed the property screeching excitedly, opening their colorful tails to the guests' delight. The reception was infused with a tasteful, Mexican flair and the dance floor was assembled on one of the decks surrounding a beautiful treehouse-like structure where we arranged high top tables and a white sofa lounge with candles stringing down from the branches. Everything went as planned and I was elated but felt a little stir in my heart when I thought of Ed's absence. We cut our cake and went back to The Langham Hotel, where our wedding party was staying and continued our celebration at the garden front bar. It was all a dreamy interlude in the midst of so much change in my life. It was the fairy tale wedding I had never had and Mike was my prince.

***

Our next trip back to Brazil was quickly approaching. I was working hard between school and keeping things going with mast delivery. They had finally arrived in Brazil and releasing the crate from customs went somewhat seamlessly, after all the initial preparations that were made before shipping it out. The logistics of getting it down to Cajaíba went flawlessly as well, with the highlight going to the 22 men who hand lifted the crate and walked it down about 100 m to the boat house by the water's edge where it would remain until our next trip in. Masts delivered, I began concentrating more on school, until graduation day came around May 11th - marking a year since Marco's return home. It was such a happy day for me. I could barely remember that it had ever been an issue enrolling for my teacher training, or finding the means to pay for my program once I was accepted. It was an interesting blur of happy that came just after a time of such intense stress.

It was in this blur that one afternoon I received a text from Ed, who had moved to his new home just days earlier. He had suffered the loss of ol' Snoozie, who had passed away from kidney failure, but who Ed had excused from a reason to die.

"It was just her time..." he said, almost in an effort to save *me* the pain.

We had been speaking several times a day, either via WhatsApp, or Skype, or email, depending on the subject. That afternoon I was preparing a grilled cheese sandwich and tomato soup lunch, a little later than usual, as I had been swept away by the day's work when his text popped in via WhatsApp:

"Well, it's done...." he captioned a panoramic photo of the living space of his home.

It was a cozy little chalet style house with a loft overlooking the living room. There was a little ladder-like stair up to the loft and exposed wooden ceiling beams towered over the A-frame structure. Something about the photo irked me, but I couldn't put my finger on it. I wasn't too sure how to reply to him, which was uncanny. Time suddenly became blurry and seemed to progress slowly, as in when one watches a car rolling over, or remembers the exact place where they were when they received shocking news. The moment was vividly being etched in my mind and there was no shaking the feeling off.

"Happy times ahead..." I wrote after a few moments of looking at my phone in silence. A blue heart emoji punctuated my affirmation. I waited for a response but it didn't come. As it was just past 10 pm his time, I went on to have my lunch but was still bothered by something in my spirit that I couldn't recognize.

The next morning, I woke up disturbed. I wasn't sure if it was the impending trip to Brazil or what, but my first order of the day was to touch base with Ed:

"Skype at 8:00?" I wrote, sending off the message as I stepped out of bed to begin my routine. Mike was in the kitchen preparing breakfast, so I took the time to have my yoga practice and meditate, but was unable to focus, and ended up heading to the kitchen for breakfast instead, where I shared my heart with Mike.

"I'm a little concerned..." I said, after explaining to him exactly what had transpired over the last 18 hours. He didn't think much of it but supported me nonetheless.

"Honey, if you're worried, just give him a call..." he offered.

I didn't want to call. I had already texted him and my heart felt something was off - like he was in danger. He hadn't gone on WhatsApp all day. I checked Facebook, understanding that he was a frugal user of that social platform as well. His text had arrived on Wednesday and it was now Friday. No communication had arrived from his end. Not a reply to my WhatsApp, nor a reply to the email that I had sent, wherein I had forged an obvious need for help in a situation, because I knew if he read it, he'd reply to my urgent-sounding request. Nothing returned.

My stomach churned when I opened my eyes to Saturday. I could no longer stand experiencing the symptoms of my angst, whatever the cause was. I hadn't realized how we had gradually become such an integral part of each other's lives over the past years and how intricately I knew *him* but not really *about* him. I thought to reach out to his family but knew how cross he'd be if I alarmed them in the event he had just gone for a sail. I had barely finished that thought when my phone lit up with a message from Jordan - one of the kids at the rowing club who was quite close to Ed.

"Hey Paula, sorry to bug you, but have you and Ed gone off to Brazil for work?"

My heart dropped. I knew that Ed would never miss a commitment at the rowing club and if Jordan was asking, there was a good chance that he had.

"Jordan, I haven't spoken to Ed since Wednesday. If you haven't either, then I believe something is wrong and you should contact the police." I spilled over my concerns, as surreal as they were, bringing such relief to my soul. I felt my spirit had been begging me to take such a stance, but my mind interfered with thoughts of how silly Ed would say I had been to worry.

I picked up the phone and called Jordan almost simultaneously to sending off my message. Hearing my concerns, he confirmed: "he hasn't gone out for a sail or a row - I checked the log we keep at the club." My heart began wildly searching for a story that would make sense on the one hand, and calmly accepting something I could not put into words on the other. I was strangely numbed by the lethargy caused by it all. Jordan found words to calm me somewhat and promised to keep me posted. Within hours he texted me back:

"Hi...police say they won't break in until Monday as it's a bank holiday here and he might have traveled to see family unannounced, he explained. Also, we're scared of breaking down his brand-new door and having to deal with his temper if he comes home to it after a long trip, ha-ha," he added, in an attempt to keep things light.

The aura I inhabited, from the minute Ed's message arrived that Wednesday, suspended me in time, warping my senses to what felt like extreme connection. Something was stirring an unfamiliar discomfort in me but I just had to go with the flow of things at that moment to stay grounded. That Monday, I laid in bed, eyes shut before waking up fully, though so fully aware and present in the moment and then I saw Ed's face looking down at me from directly above, as if through a porthole on a boat. He was looking inquisitively at me as if asking: "why are you so worried?" I was shaken immediately into sitting up in bed and checking my phone for any updates from Jordan.

"Any updates?" I sent off a message to Jordan.

"We're at the station now - will keep you posted," came Jordan's prompt reply. He was with a few other close acquaintances from the rowing club.

I got up and showered and tried to do whatever it is we do when we wake up. Everything was beginning to fall out of focus. I was quiet. My spirit was keen in expectancy. I went about attempting to get anything done that morning. It was just when

Mike, Danny and I arrived to have lunch at our usual Thai place that the message arrived.

"Hi Paula. We've arrived to Ed's house to find that his body's been here a few days. I don't know what to say, I'm so sorry."

The force of the realization knocked the wind right out of my lungs. I began breathing in a short pant, followed by two exhales. I was too shocked to cry immediately but gave in when my son Danny turned to me and said solemnly: "Mom...I'm so sorry....".

Another text further elucidated the scenario in which he was found immediately following the first:

"There was a note and in it he apologized to whomever had to arrive at the scene and find him this way. He was hanging."

***

I spent all afternoon in our darkened room in bed, as if struck-down by a physical lashing that provoked not only pain, but insult. I was pulled out of this dimension and into another realm that had me lurking between life and death. I remained there in that oddly comforting state for as long as I could. Quietly swaying myself back and forth sitting in bed hugging my knees, between bouts of crying and sheer silence, I became lost in the immensity of a spot of sunlight on my bedroom wall. Mike gave me all the space I needed and only came back to check in on me just past 7 pm - when he cracked the door to the dark room asking softly: "Sweetie, I've made some soup. Can I bring you some?" Surely, I would have thrown up the soup had I accepted it. Nothing was digestible within me and yet I felt Ed so comfortingly close to me. I had brief flashbacks to little conversations we'd had about things unrelated, like our mutual love of lighthouses and storms and the lighthouse photography that shows the gigantic waves towering over them, like Plisson, the French photographer takes. I felt intimate with death now, having someone I loved and trusted on the other side. I felt empowered by the fact that if and when I died I'd have him to welcome me there - and that actually made the prospect seem appealing. It crossed my mind how offensive it was that he had left me to deal with this sorrow and what if I had left him to deal with the pain of my own act, had I the courage to do so? Indiscriminate thoughts towered tall over any censorship I could ever possibly impose on myself. I even pondered the seemingly frivolous favor of how lucky I was to have the recipe to his petit gateau and to know how to make his signature 'pancakes'. I thought how unfortunate it was that I hadn't jotted down his Yorkshire pudding recipe, but upon further thought, imagined that if I tried it on my own, that soon enough it would come back to me. There was extreme sadness and there was a profound understanding and this - this is what I carried in my heart for all the days leading up to the memorial service his family held in Totnes weeks later; such thoughts and feelings as these.

***

Over the next few weeks, life took a 180-degree turn from what it had been in recent months past. For one, all work at the yard came to a screeching halt. Not only was the crew broken-hearted at the news, but I obviously didn't have the knowledge to lead work on my own. I half-heartedly saw to it that what we had begun be finished and kept in order until we started the project back up again at some point. As far as my income was concerned, it had trickled down to near zero by this point, in relation to the number of hours I had been working the previous months when work at the boatyard was steaming at full force. This state of affairs brought to fore a lot of the stressful issues I had dealt with in the past, destabilizing me all the more. The situation was mitigated somewhat however, because I was now only responsible for half of the household expenses that I had been in the past. It had become so much easier to keep myself afloat after marrying. Mike was a generous man, never expecting me to split the costs of anything with him. There was an unspoken agreement between us that I picked up bills that summed up to roughly half of our expenses and he'd cover the other half. This arrangement kept me validated and in control of my life.

My arrival to Heathrow Airport brought back the bittersweet memory of my last visit to London with Ed. Our pre-meeting escapade at Peter Jones department store with the lame soup at the cafe. I found myself seeing the simplest of everyday scenarios in a new light; experiencing things with a newfound awe, like: 'Wow...I never thought it would be Edward's memorial service that would bring me to Totnes for the first time.' Already sat on the train, I recalled anecdotes Ed had told me about his own commutes, to and from London. I looked out the window at the variety of landscape that rushed past and thought how if one poises their eyes straight out the window, they can see the bushes and the variety of things for what they actually are, or simply see a slur of colors and shapes flying by if one looks forward or back. I correlated this concept to life: in the present moment, we see things for what they are and in the busyness of it, we can become lost in between what was or will be and it can all just become a blur.

Upon arriving in Totnes, I was naturally overwhelmed with emotion. This was Ed's stomping ground. The 'kids' from the rowing club - who were in reality mostly in their late teens to early twenties, so not really kids at all - had invited me to join them at the greasy spoon where they'd had breakfast with Ed countless times before. We traded our stories and reminiscences of Ed amongst us, which brought about a refreshing amount of cheer. The Ed we knew and loved was pieced together in fuller perspective as we traded anecdotes. Like the time he filmed himself pouring a bucket of ice cold water over his head in the spirit of raising awareness for the ALS campaign that went viral. He ceremoniously dipped a thermometer into the bucket to show that the water was at zero degrees before carrying out the feat. I felt privileged to be among the people around whom it seemed he felt most comfortable - the youth at the rowing club. I had chosen to stay in a stone home just outside of town that dated back to the 1500's and Jordan kindly offered to drive me there, so I could drop my things off, freshen up and then head back into town where he would show me around a bit. I chose it especially because it had a magical labyrinth in the yard and the bonus was that the innkeeper was a seasoned spiritualist - the type that had led Ed to say many times that I'd fit right into Totnes if I ever moved there. The home was quite a way out of town, set amidst fields that one could only dream of amongst the cobblestone roads and the whole scenario appeared to be directing one's soul to unknown places. He took me past Ed's house and to the rowing club and then to the marina, where Ed kept and worked on Colin - his own beautiful little wooden sailboat, that he had worked on with some diligence, when he was in need of a therapeutic outlet. I felt sort of like a character in a novel mingling amongst the townspeople. In coming face to face with me their countenances would light up and they'd say: "Oh! *you're* Paula!". One woman even mused: "I would've sooner recognized your bare feet as I've seen those quite a bit!" she smiled, referring to a photo I had posted of mine and Ed's boatyard-grimy feet, dangling over the pier one afternoon, as we sat waiting for Jorge. I too was getting to put faces and personalities together, connecting faces to names in stories that Ed had shared with me on so many occasions. Later that day Jordan and I journeyed out into a field where we could see a castle in the distance that the locals believed to be haunted. We watched the sun as it reverently set on this surreal day.

***

Analida and Charles had arrived that morning on an early train. Analida had planned to join me later at the bed and breakfast for a couple days following the memorial service, as she too wished to celebrate Ed by getting to know his little town of Totnes better. I arrived early to the rowing club with Jordan, who had kindly offered to collect me again from my B&B. Ed's family opted for having a memorial that Ed himself would have organized. An informal gathering of friends, topped by a pig roast and overlooking the Dart from the terrace at the Dart-Totnes Rowing Club where he had so often enjoyed spending his days. There were no fancy flowers but we were all instructed to bring hedge flowers that we cut ourselves. We walked into the clubhouse where the memorial was to be held about 30 minutes early.

"We saved this seat for you," Jordan motioned to a seat in the front row with a neatly folded program on it. "And those two can be for Analida and Charles when they arrive," he added, pointing to the seats next to me.

I thanked him and asked if he would kindly lead me over to Ed's parents. Ed's father was outside on the terrace that led out from the main room overlooking the river. His mother was quietly in conversation with someone who seemed to be helping her with planning. As Jordan and I walked over, I wondered if I should open the heartfelt smile I had been keeping inside for the day I met her. I was meaning to convey to her all of my love - just for her being Ed's mother, but on second thought figured she might be distraught and misinterpret my intention. I did my best to show gladness in my eyes alone, reverencing my tone as I greeted her.

"Hi. It's so nice to finally meet you - I'm ...."

She cut me off as if she couldn't bear to hear the rest of my sentence. "I know just who you are dear. Please..." she waved her hand towards the assemblage: "take a seat" she instructed.

'Oh...right.... okay," I replied with difficulty. Her curt reaction confounded me and now *I* was the one who was feeling distraught. Being a mother myself, I had expected an instant bond to emerge between us, seeing as I had been so close to her son over the past few years. I consoled myself with the understanding that Ed had really only shared with me so many details regarding his mother as a direct response to my insistent inquiries about her. They had not been forthcoming from his own initiative. With that in mind, he might not have mentioned much about me at all to her. "Oh God, if I told my mother about you I wouldn't hear the end of it," he'd explained once, on a day we were combing the beach after low tide, seeking-out interesting treasures. I wasn't sure what he had meant exactly by that statement, but we were distracted by a purple-blue blob on the sand, which took great precedence over the whole matter at any rate.

Jordan made no comment as he walked me out to the patio to meet the Dad.

Ed's father rose to his feet and greeted me with kind eyes. He thanked me sincerely for having traveled so far for the memorial. He offered me tea and asked questions about the boat and the yard. I instantly took a liking to him. As guests arrived, we made our way into the salon and I was introduced to Bill (Ed's brother) and his lovely wife, before quietly taking my seat. I was bewildered. I felt at that very moment as if I had just entered a rocket ship bound for Mars. Life had saved a seat for me on this perilous journey that was absolutely so new to me as to be completely unfathomable. It bothered me knowing Ed's remains were still refrigerated somewhere in a precinct while the police 'investigated'. I did not like that situation one bit and it physically hurt me that we were already 40 days into this and meanwhile my dear Ed was still in a box somewhere, waiting. I realized 'he' himself was not boxed - he was clearly out and about; curious soul that he was. As a matter of fact he seemed ever so close. At times, I could swear I'd heard him whispering for me to stop being silly, as I sobbed at some memory. I missed our texts. I craved just one more funny animal pic. I would even have delighted in one of his after hour calls to check-in on the status of our importation certificate, but here I was, inconsolable and missing moments that I used to dread. I listened intently as first the brother, and then the father walked to the podium. Followed by the college professor and finally the royal who had commissioned the Gloriana barge.

Tears jumped to their fate from my eyes, like people caught in a fiery building. I could hardly bear to listen to such heartfelt renditions of this man whom I so dearly loved without it breaking my heart over again. Analida and I sobbed quietly and discreetly as we could and at times we would lean on each other for some comfort. She too was a huge fan of Ed and his spirit. Now and again I would raise an eye at the mother who stood boldly off to the side of the podium with no evidence of a tear shed likely numbed by her sorrow.

Rain fell lazily from morning to afternoon, seemingly mourning our loss with us. After the service, I walked around drying up every puddle the rain had left behind with the hem of my skirt. It was dramatically long with its icy gray colored silk layers and it swooned along with me as I went about hugging people I had never met - greeting them as if I were a character from a novel. I instantly loved Lennie from Ed's narrative at the hotel in Camamú. She was riddled with grief and fear, poor thing, but it was meaningful to know her and hug her tight. People came to me and threw their arms around me as they exclaimed: "Paula!" and then proceeded to explain in what context they knew me. It was all bittersweet and by the end I hadn't had the courage to stuff one bit of pork in that social-butterfly mouth of mine. I found my way outside to relax a bit, drink beer from a bottle and chat with the rowers.

At night, Jordan invited me to join a few of Ed's friends at the pub where they customarily enjoyed a burger and a brew together. Once again, I felt privileged to be included amongst his closest friends, in celebrating him by eating and sharing anecdotes about the person who had brought our lives together. I scheduled tea with the ex-girlfriend that he had told me about, and even with the 'stalker'. I met up with each one as there was a mutual curiosity in getting to know about our unique interfaces with Ed.

Analida and I explored Totnes in the morning and then tried to break into Ed's house in the afternoon. I say that jokingly (and not), because we were looking for Ed's spare key amongst the vases at his doorstep when a neighbor approached us and asked if he could help.

"Oh no...." we giggled nervously, like it was silly of anyone not to be checking underneath every vase at a random house. "We need no help thank you."

The stranger then imparted the news to us that the resident had sadly passed away. We both did our best to act like it was absolutely new information we were hearing and walk off the front doorstep as naturally as possible. I'm not sure exactly why we wanted to go into his house. Maybe it was just to sit on his couch, just like one might do in trying to bring the home some cheer from a loved one...I don't know. It's the silly things we do when our hearts are broken and looking for some comfort, some sort of contrived outlet to try to make sense from the madness of it all I suspect. I had called the police precinct in Torquay - which I suppose is where the governing authorities are seated for the town of Totnes - weekly since Ed's passing. Making inquiries as to any progress being made in the investigation and wanting to have access to the note he left behind, they spoke to me only from the kindness of their hearts. As was the protocol in these affairs, they'd advised me early on that I should seek news directly from the family. In a desperate attempt to procure news of my own accord, I even told an attendant, who had stated point blank that she would give me no information unless I was family, that I was the fiancée of the deceased and estranged from the family. Again, I plead temporary insanity in that particular instance.

***

From Totnes, I rode a train to Gloucester to visit the fine folks at T. Nielsen & Co. to discuss the possibility of their taking over our project through to its completion. T. Nielsen was a reputable yard, known for building, restoring and rigging ships. They enjoyed a stream of steady clientele from all across Europe and Nordic countries, flaunting a considerable waitlist, and consequently, were not extending a hat towards our project with any particular enthusiasm. I met with Dave Robbins, who showed me all around the yard and introduced me to the boatyard dogs (names?). I met with Sarah White, who ran the administrative aspects of the yard and quoted for potential projects. She was precise in manning the estimates with the amount of labor needed and managing timelines so that projects could be taken to completion within the times and budgets given. Tommi Nielsen, an avid sailor, yacht master and seasoned shipwright, which is like a boat builder but encompasses knowledge of a larger scope of the process that overlaps into designing. Tommi was a Danish man with an interesting character. He possessed a clear love of his trade, wanting absolutely nothing to do with Sarah's administrations whatsoever, which is why I dealt specifically with Sarah on the day I visited in regard to numbers and the finer points of business, but interacted much more intensely with Tommi throughout the remainder of the process, which involved his strengths and skills. I sat across from Sarah who was pleasantly informal but clearly meaning nothing but business. Immediately under her ministrations, our lovely little project became doused in business jargon, as she evaluated it strictly under the lens of tasks, costs, budget and work breakdown structures. Although we had worked with ernest investment before, we had allowed for curating and allowing the folksy, more intercultural aspects of the job to flavor it; considering our building location and the natives who were involved intrinsically in our working progress. Sarah quickly browsed what we had achieved in the past years and in evaluating the tropical locus in which the project was being completed, did not flinch when I said "Charles would like the project completed within six months". An experienced businesswoman, Sarah held her own and left no gap in her plan of action to being blustered by any client, no matter how much the yard stood to gain. She unapologetically stated: "We will not commit to a timeline without going on site and even so, judging from the time your own management has taken to complete the tasks to date, we will refrain from any commitment towards Mr. Graham's expectations. We will schedule to assess on site and develop a work plan, budget and timeline from there." She declared emphatically bringing our discussions to an end. What I heard on my end was: 'No, *no dear, you don't tell us how long this is going to take - we tell* you *how long it will take* us *to do it.*' Which, in looking from the business point of view, made absolute sense. I felt a little bit like a mother who sees her daughter going out in makeup and heels for the first time - our little downhome project was now a transaction on the books of a professional yard.

***

The following weeks were spent recuperating from the warp Ed's passing had immersed me in. I exchanged a few emails with Ed's brother, who, sympathetic as he seemed to want to be, could not understand how his brother could have done this to them. I requested access to a few files and drawings I knew were in Ed's laptop and his brother uploaded them to a dropbox for me. On one occasion, he shared details about how Ed had taken his life with me, and how he had gone about it in his usual orderly and systematic manner. I had graduated from the offensive feeling of having been left behind, to full-on compassion and respect of Ed's choice. The transformative effect of my new outlook on the manner of his passing may have brought me considerable relief from the pain of being left, but I still missed him dearly. I could hear his response to almost every thought I had in my head, as if he were still interfacing with me day and night. Jordan kept me in the loop as well, letting me know that the family had sold Colin, his personal sailboat/project shortly after his passing, and that they were also preparing his house up for sale. All of it was very bothersome and completely surreal, yet I enjoyed bonding with Jordan as I had heard Ed make endearing mention of him frequently during our time together and it seemed he was my ally of sorts throughout the whole ordeal, which was extremely comforting. Things Ed had shared with me in the course of our friendship came back to me in a new light and I could feel his personal pain now profoundly, untethered from my own.

September 2015:
The Masts

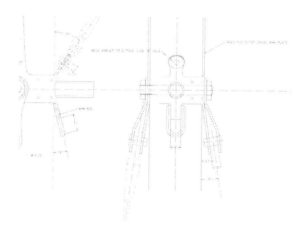

Kathini

A story of love, loss and a little boat building

T Nielsen presented us with an offer to fly out in order to perform an assessment and come back with a plan and costs to completion. Going back and forth with T. Nielsen regarding the plan they proposed and the details required in organizing our trip, slowly filled my days again. We decided to spend September 18th through to the 30th in Cajaíba so that a full effort could be put in place towards assessing the project and getting the ball rolling again at the yard. It would be only Dave, Tommi and myself in the initial lot and further labor would be added as and when needed.

Our travel date came around quickly. Going through the familiar motions of packing boat items and getting on the plane for Brazil without the perspective of meeting a smiley, or ornery Mr. Burnett to greet me on the other end seared my heart. My breath fluttered in doubt that such grief could even be withstood. My lungs could barely expand to receive fresh air, seeming in fact to collapse a little with each exhale causing an agonizing shortness of breath that reverted me to the short, gasped breaths, followed by two short exhales, that I had experienced shortly after receiving the fateful news. I pushed on trying desperately to control my breath but as we touched ground at GRU in a gray mist that morning, hot tears sprung to their fate protesting my attempt to hold back the memories of arriving - taunting Ed about having to be at arrivals to greet me passionately, or how my waiting for the last minute before boarding to go to the restroom and get snacks would stir his brown locks bringing a storm into his eyes. Being familiar with the drill, Dave Robbins sat with Tommi as I arrived that day, not too sunshiny on the inside, yet mindful to irradiate some cheer on the outside. This time we hopped on a flight to Salvador and took a light plane to Barra Grande as time was of the essence and there was much to do. We all shared the common interest of seeing this project afloat; aside from the fact that every minute was being billed dearly. I allowed Dave and Tommi to sit together and took a seat up front by a window where I could press my head up to it and allow the pain to flow through my breaths. As I attempted to center myself, my thoughts drifted to recall the time months earlier, when Ed and I took turns putting down our animal dominoes, riling each other up on the way home. Through all the responsibility and stress of our agenda he still checked in on me to make sure I wasn't in pain due to my cracked tooth. "Are you okay?" he'd ask caringly inspecting my semblance and send me up to my room for rest as soon as we'd return from the boatyard. As episodes of that trip carouselled in my mind, each memory would strangle my breath anew. We flew from Salvador into the small airfield that was about a 10-minute drive from the house. I was able to manage niceties and general conversation along the way, but upon arriving to the house and having to greet Olivan and Gi, I succumbed to my despair, collapsing into

Gi's arms sobbing, completely overwhelmed with the rush of memories. Pulling a brave face, I promptly excused myself, and headed towards my suite. My heart crumpled a bit in my chest as I walked past Ed's room swiftly, being cautious not to focus the sight of the empty room in my peripheral vision - unprepared as I was for this. Olivan said he would bring my bags up promptly as he took in the sight of me. Through my own tears, I could see that he was clearly heartbroken as well.

I rejoined the men for dinner to discuss what our steps would be for the upcoming days and review a few questions regarding the status of certain threads of work before bidding them an early good night. We'd reassemble bright and early the next day for our trip to the yard. I arose at dawn and invested in a short yoga practice before taking my matinal walk along the beach. I stopped along the way to write a message in the sand for Ed. I knew he would read it from wherever he was - *'I miss you Edward'* I etched into the sand. I utilized a sea bean pod that we had commonly found on our walks together amidst the sea drift that looked and felt a lot like a fountain pen to write the sentiment. I could have never conceived ever having to say those words to Ed, much less writing them in the sand for him to read in his absence. I walked back to the house, rinsed the sand from my feet and tip-toed past his former room before succumbing to peering in through the rattan screen.

"Edward?" I called softly as if not to disturb. I slid the door open whispering: *'excuse me'* and walked past his bed to his closet to fetch the plastic box where he kept a few of his personal belongings. I pulled the plastic lid up to find a British Airlines business class necessaire kit, with a few essentials inside - including a few of the painkillers he had kept on hand since his knee surgery. There was a folder with boat drawings, the Brazil jersey he had worn to the world cup game a year earlier, a penny, a few screws and a washer, two pairs of Havaianas flip flops, that I had bullied him into buying lest I would continue to make fun of him in his corny velcro-strapped sandals. One of the pairs were Minion-themed as we both loved the Despicable Me movie and the characters in it. I had often encouraged Ed to adopt a little girl (or two or three) like Gru in that story and just get his own family going between a little girl who would adore him and Snoozie, his dog.

"Love is the answer Ed..." I would say - to which he would flash a quick sneer.

I finished looking through the items and slipped out of the room, sliding the door closed quietly behind me. I showed up to breakfast as fresh-faced as I could muster, ready now for the day at the yard with my new partners.

***

The bay was absolutely still that morning. On most days, waters ran fairly choppy due to the interface with the ocean and the windy passage that blew through the landscape on the horizon. Today we glided over a glassy lake with ease. I had never before seen the water so placid and clear and for a moment it seemed that I was in a dream, such was the beauty of the moment. Tommi and Dave corroborated the experience, snapping pictures and conceding that in fact this truly was an amazing sight. We all became silent. Jorge seemed transported comfortably to his own parallel universe as he looked out onto the horizon. A quiet chill took over me and a profound stillness settled within - commanding peace to my heart. As we approached the sight of Cajaíba from the Lillibelle, my heart shuddered a bit. I braced myself in the knowledge and presence that seemed suspended all around me and stayed strong as we sped up to the pier where Ed and I had de-boarded countless times before. The same pier we'd both hung our feet from relaxing after a busy day at the yard. I was reminded of the love we both shared of having become sooted during our work day. Dirty, like children leaving the schoolyard at the end of the day, wearing our work on our visages like badges of honor. A sheer layer of sawdust coated our forearms and splats of tar punctuated our clothes. The last time we were together on this spot, we had dangled our dirty feet over the edge of the pier and I'd photographed them. I'd taken an up-close shot of Ed's grimy feet and said to him: "now there's *your* next profile pic..." and then added a snarky: "you're welcome". Indeed, that shot has been his profile picture ever since.

Tommi and Dave de-boarded and I fell-in behind them, lost as I was in my memories. They both respected my need for contemplation and gained distance ahead of me. I brought my head up from the very spot where my mind's eye could see our shapes interacting that afternoon, the sun seemed molten like a fireball rising in the horizon. As my eyes met the waterline, I turned to face the long walk down the pier alone. Upon waking from the film my mind replayed, my breathing became uneasy and my spirit stirred in an unfamiliar way. As I walked, unrushed by the task of keeping up with Mr. Burnett, my lungs seemed stitched tightly from the inside, keeping them from expanding to take in a full breath. Hot tears began streaming from my face as my lips sealed together and I pronounced a long sounding 'Mmmmmm'. Like a child who wants to say mother but is not equipped to enunciate the word in its entirety. The scalding tears cascaded in such rapid succession that they were blinding. I could barely see where I was going, but I knew instinctively that the path was straight. I finally released into my anguish and allowed myself to melt into that moment of overpowering grief. I was riddled in sorrow and rightly so goddammit. As I stopped fighting my impulses I became more present. I began noticing subtleties like the familiar scent that the bay breeze, enmeshed with the woodsy odor of sawdust and village life gave out. My senses seemed heightened and I felt the warm, somewhat sticky breeze graze my skin. The sudden realization that a black bird had been cawing frenetically alongside me while I was walking finally sunk in. His wings were lightly crested with a golden-yellow and his face expressive cackling and cawing as loud as he could and doing flips on the handrail as if desperately trying to get my attention. I tried to focus in better, squeezing my eyelids and wiping the tears with the sleeve of my t- shirt. My face was swollen and my nose was messy, as I concentrated on the expression on the bird's face. It donned a beseeching look, like he was begging me not to suffer pleading: "Come on...please don't do this...". I snorted a little laugh at the complexity of the expression on the bird's face. I half cried half chuckled a few times as I began composing myself again. Walking down the cobblestone thoroughfare I became lighter and the feeling of aloneness left me. I began nodding to acknowledge the townspeople who were looking on in pity as I passed by, unaccompanied. I was slightly amused that, in that moment of reminisce, I even missed keeping up with Mr. Burnett's long and purpose-driven strides.

(As I write this a bird just flew straight into the veranda where I'm seated and flew about two feet over my shoulder cawing full blast...hahaha. I'm just writing this for your benefit

dear friend and reader - it's the universe winking at me or Mr. Burnett rolling his eyes at all my drama...)

We used our days up to the last twinge of light. Working hard we were able to tally what was where and take stock of the storeroom that Ed had set up in one of the garages at the house where the electronics and more valuable rigging bits were kept. Tools and fastenings were kept at the boatyard in Cajaíba, while bulkier items like the anchor chain, head (i.e. the toilet), galley sink and others, were kept at the boat house in Campinho, where Lillibelle was housed when she was off water. Dave worked intensely putting together a list of tasks that were completed and one to complete. Tommi tinkered a little everywhere - putting in his two cents about what needed to be corrected and how - which was in fact usually Ed's first priority as well. Once Zezinho was occupied with working on the *what* needed to be corrected and how list, Tommi settled into planing the rudder and making fairing boards with the crew while teaching them the art of shaping the hull into the impeccable curves that Mr. Burnett had conceived. Tommi's passion for his trade was clear to see. I put together an informal update of how we found things at the yard during our flight back to GRU.

Hi both!

Just a quick summary of our trip as performed from Sept 18 - 30. We arrived and found everything well - our journey in was made swift by arriving through SSA and taking the light plane to Kiaroa.

Task One:

Our first task was to open Ed's little storeroom up - pull out every last screw and piece of electronic and complete somewhat of an inventory. We removed all the vehicles from the garage, swept out all contents and pulled in a few tables and began separating and laying each piece in its due category. Sadly, we dislodged a tarantula measuring about 10" in diameter from her current dwelling in the process, but we are happy to report that she is alive and well elsewhere on the property.

I photographed each rigging piece and sent to Lee for assessment - I have been in communication with Lee and his assistant and extremely pregnant wife - Gemma.

First conclusion after task one: approximately 98% of everything purchased has made it to the beach. We have very few items outstanding that await their journey in my bag next time and an outstanding genoa sail to be delivered in the near future to Carlos' house in SP.

Task Two:

We assessed not only the current state of progress but especially, the quality of the tasks left behind to be completed following our last visit in April. This is a long and intricate topic that will surely be the kernel of your forthcoming meeting with T. Nielsen so I will be brief in my personal assessment. Combining my lay perspective with inference taken from the comments of my colleagues on this trip I'd say the overall grade to be received would be an 82% - with some items nearing perfection and others causing raised eyebrow. Pressed to give examples I would state the rudder as a high scoring item and the toe rail finishing as a low. Both required and received many hours of precise manual labor to be brought to standard but the details are many and prolific and should be left to the experts.

Task Three:

After our initial appraisal of inventory and general state of completion we set out to establish a comprehensive task-list comprised of everything from tightening a bolt behind the keelson 3 times to the left to bringing the whole of the deck finish to the standard demonstrated by the T. Nielsen team. The task-list was extensive and included numerous items from previous task-lists that had not been brought to full completion or suffered an accident such as having a tool dropped on it or from having its fine finish performed by a chainsaw, leaving machine marks that surely have poor Ed cringing - wherever he may be - may there be plenty of single malt to help him cope with that sight. In general however, the lay eye is quite accommodated and the expert eye is quite pleasantly surprised with the whole given the surrounding environment.

Task Four:

We now rolled up our sleeves and just plain began working next to them daily - wielding finishing tools and supervising work. The main issue here was a catch-22 situation caused by few workers on site vs the risk of having too many unsupervised workers wreaking havoc with their chainsaws and power sanders. We literally had to ban such devices from coming anywhere near the project in the end though they are in fact needed in finishing a few more expansive surfaces. It was all very harmoniously done and the general spirit of the team is of cooperation and best-effort.

Task Five:

Tasks assessed, we summoned Olivan to bring a truck load of equipment to be measured and dry-fitted and at the end of those days performed the same task in the opposite direction so as to preserve all electronics and systems panels and components in safe storage at the house in BG. This effort was extremely fruitful and when we next arrive all surfaces should be finished, varnished, painted or oiled to specification leaving only actual installation to be easily performed.

Task Six:

Concomitantly to the measuring and dry-fitting of all deck components, the matter of where to source stainless fittings for the rudder and deck in general was surveyed and addressed. We met with Didi who is capable of fabricating stainless fittings locally and assigned the simplest fabrication tasks to him as the quality of his work was greatly appreciated by Dave and Tommi, and I was assigned the task of finding a more sophisticated shop in SP equipped with a laser cutter equipped to precision cut all pieces straight from the AutoCAD drawings. There are several options being considered on this front which I will leave you to discuss with the team upon meeting.

To sum up:

The finishing portion of the project seems quite extensive in number of fronts and requirements. Launching was profusely discussed and assessed throughout our stay and the tides carefully measured and considered; aspects *such as mooring, on-going maintenance, deck cushions and awnings, cabin furnishings and cabinetry logistics, boarding ladder, yard insurance, and style-line - which is the boat designer's signature piece or the owner's family crest or monogram or something to that effect etched in the bow. I have also pushed forward with registration and am working with both Zezinhos (Camamú and Cajaíba) to have paperwork in order for sailing by the time it hits the water. Much is to be discussed regarding yard insurance and again, the T. Nielsen team have vast experience on this front and valuable input to offer. All this leads to the recommendation that these matters be addressed and realistically put into a timeline as soon as the opportunity is available. All these factors are fresh at hand and clarity and precision shall be of essence in completing the project in an efficacious way.*

I'm forwarding a few select pictures for your enjoyment. :)

Lots of love,
Paula

May 2016:
The Launch

Kathini
A story of love, loss and a little boat building

Our following trips to Brazil saw us with completed project plan and timeline expressed in a multipage spreadsheet that contained roughly 300 line items that needed to be addressed. Dave was plugging away at systems while Tommi did his best to keep the woodwork he was managing with Zezinho's crew, to the least of his high standards. I was working on getting all the materials to the yard for the impending paint job, which had all of us a bit on the antsy side. The conditions at the yard were far from optimal for a proper paint job to occur, with the free range of debris flying around the yard - so we opted for the very best (which in this case meant most forgiving) paint we could find on the market. Another concern was the infamous *teredo worm* which bores into wooden boats in warm waters devouring the wood as termites would on land, posing a huge threat to our vessel once she was afloat, so we discussed anti-fouling coats which protect the part of the hull that remains submerged year-round from marine growth and other harmful organisms.

We began discussing launching more intensely and decided on pushing the boat out of the yard on a cradle that would slip over very hefty timber beams that were positioned in front of the yard, leading all the way into the muddy edges of the bay during low tide. It favored our plan that that particular stretch in front of the yard hides a solid rock foundation under the mud, so we could actually slip the boat out as far as we could using man, woman and children power and then have a tractor pull it out as far as possible into the bay at low tide. After that, we'd simply wait for the tide to lift her up into floating. In Cajaíba, launch day is regarded as a huge festivity - more so than even a wedding ceremony, and as such everyone is invited to push. The launch *party* in particular was the only thing people around the yard were actually planning however. How many crates of beer will it take to push this thing out to bay? How many kilos of meat should we barbeque and should we have sausages as well was what was forefront in their minds. They had done this dozens of times before and found it interesting that the gringos were doing so much math and calculations. I noticed it was all making Zezinho a bit squeamish.

It was only in May 2016 that we headed out with a crew to finally set her afloat with the help of the spring tide, which is when the tide was deep enough to collaborate with our plan. We needed over 2 meters for the boat to float and the tides in Cajaíba seldom hit that depth averaging 1.93m - but they did during the spring tide. The spring tide has nothing to do with the actual season of the year, but occurs when the Earth, sun and moon align, causing the pull and bulge of the tide to be a little more intense than usual thus causing a greater tidal range. In our case, we needed 2.10m in order for our boat to float so it was to be this tide, or the tide that came in September. William, the second in the order of the

Graham children, came out during his college break to participate in the launch. The night before the launch the boat sat proudly in her cradle, ready to be pushed out to sea in the morning when we wrapped up our day. Launching had been exhaustively discussed by the team and I noticed Zezinho was withdrawn when we said our goodbyes.

"Is everything ok?" I asked him, as he was walking us to the pier at the end of our work day.

He grinned a sly grin and returned "This is the part of the project I'm most confident about - don't you worry 'bout a thing." he assured me.

"Ok, I just wanted to make sure you're not losing sleep over it or anything." I replied, keeping it light.

"Ya, no, I'm definitely not sleeping tonight," he confided, "but it's not because I'm worried" he added assuredly. We left it at that and whizzed off across the bay with the promise of returning the next morning for launch.

The next morning, upon approaching Cajaíba in our craft, Jorge slowed down suddenly and looked back at me as if he was trying to tell me something with his eyes - but it flew straight over my head. He looked in the direction of the waterline again and signaled with his head.

Dave Robbins turned around in disbelief before exclaiming: 'they've moved the boat!"

Our surprise was bittersweet but Zezinho had begun the launch party without us. As a matter of fact, the party was over. The boat was now way out in the bay, perfectly positioned, even better than we had imagined and poised waiting for the 3 pm high tide.

It was difficult not to notice the offensive tinge that clouded the air when we arrived. Zezinho and dozens of other people, stood around now celebrating, with loud music blaring, a sizzling barbeque – and we just kind of stood around like lemons, having missed the whole damn thing. It was a relief of course to see her beautifully sat awaiting her time - but the nerve of them! An undercurrent that had formed since Ed's passing became evident. Zezinho and his crew respected Ed because he came in with a humble approach, allowing a mutual exchange to occur, as he questioned them on how they would go about a certain task and respected local traditions and knowledge. T. Nielsen, on the other hand, were not here on a cultural expedition - at all. They meant business and they had come to finish a boat - full stop. There had since been some malaise in the air, when snide comments were made or loud laughter tipped the local crew off to the fact that the Brits were having a laugh at their expense and at the pace at which things were done around here. There was never again quite a harmonious work environment as when Ed was leading the team. The Brazilian crew had had their egos stepped on and in turn were now making jokes and poking fun back at the Brits. There was not a lot of translating needed at this point and in fact quite a bit of damage control was dispensed in an effort to keep a potential fist fight from erupting at times. I can understand now in hindsight, that Zezinho must have thought to himself: 'fuck that...' when he saw the Brits doing their calculating, measuring, diagramming and predicting taking away from their launching ritual and decided to take matters into his own hands rather than spend another miserable day taking orders.

***

Everyone was atop the deck waiting for the tide to rise when we felt her budge slightly. Ever so gently, she went afloat, lifted by the tide from her cradle and we all erupted into cheering. Zezinho's brother positioned his boat and powered the engines to pull her away from her cradle so that we too could start her engine. It was an exciting moment and we motored her back and forth along the Cajaíba waterline with Zezinho proudly displaying his work along with his son. It was such a beautiful moment and such a testament to everyone's commitment and hard work. As the sun set gloriously on the horizon we arrived to her chosen mooring spot in Campinho where work would proceed, and lifted a toast to Ed for having conceived her and leading us with his commendable valor. The sunset shone golden as I'd never before seen it with rays of glory crowning its splendor, radiating brilliant light in every direction. Charles poured champagne over my head, baptizing me for having received my 'sea legs' and again proposed a toast. "To Ed!" Charles commanded and we all cheered and celebrated. Within my heart I carried joy and exhilaration for our Mr. Burnett.

***

Our trips would no longer require going out to Cajaíba as the boat - still nameless at this point - was being moored in Campinho. We had discussed names previously however, Ed was adamant that she should not be named until she was afloat, as naming her on land was considered by many an omen. Ed had liked the prospect of naming it after our mother "Aida', whom he'd met when visiting for tea with me a year earlier, but Analida quickly stepped in with the suggestion it be named after the Graham matriarch - Charles' mother Kathini - which I've been told means 'little one' in Swahili.

The next steps required careful planning as they involved first lifting the masts and then dangling them one at a time over the boat before threading them in through the holes on the deck, onto their step below deck, one at a time, all while floating the boat dangerously next to a raw concrete platform. Ed had favored a rigger by the name of Lee Rogers. Lee was known for his classical style of rigging so we moved forward with using him as we had with honoring all of Ed's previous plans, including where we should 'step the masts'. The platform had been left behind in Campinho as a reminiscence of an effort to build a port from which the abundant local resources could be distributed. Because the access road would need to cut through a part of protected Atlantic forest however, the initiative never came to fruition. Ed had eyed the site and thought that among other options proposed by the locals, this one had been more suitable, being that it was a fairly quiet stretch of water. He realized we needed calm waters to be able to perform such a delicate task. He had shown us how the process was to be performed by dangling a pencil from his fingers over a bit of wood that was playing the part of the boat, simulating the bit of wood bobbing madly from underneath. This illustrated how actually dropping the mast and missing the hole would destroy the boat by breaking her into a few pieces so we would all be well aware of the risks involved.

It was late June when we arrived along with Lee the rigger carrying his vintage leather doctor's bag that transported all his bee-bobs. The masts had been delivered earlier that year and had been laying in a box beside the boat house for months. It was now time to open the box and organize all the pieces so that the masts could be *'dressed'*. If there's one thing I've learned working around men these years it's that they love destroying things as much as they love building them - so they loved opening the box using crowbars - much like firefighters use if you've ever seen them breaking down a door - and ripping the box open. The savage ripping was done with some care but there was an interesting dimension of pleasure in that act for the men. Once the box was opened we all had fun pulling out the lime green expandable spray foam that held everything tightly in its place. This was an entirely new concept around here and I saw quite a few bits of the lime green novelty being stored in people's pockets to take home and show to friends. All this 'fun' was had in the most organized way, being mindful to not lose any bits on the ground around it. The time came for the masts to be removed from their box and Campinho did not fall behind Cajaíba in wrangling up a few strong men - some of them as raw and brute as you'd ever seen on the tail end of those illustrations that show the seven stages of mankind - these guys were strong. I had received the video with the men unloading the box from the big rig that drove them up from the port down south and the most amazing thing is the hooting, hollering and cussing that goes along with dispending such strength. It was no different on this occasion. After the masts were dressed they would have to be carried perhaps 400m to the edge of the concrete platform where they would be stepped - this time with wires and most of its rigging bits in place so heavier as well as cumbersome. The masts and spars - which in this case were the booms, were set out over logs that served as a rigging table for Lee and he spent his days comfortably working inside the boat house knotting, braiding, splicing, and doing a lot of intricate work at a table we had especially made for him. Dave and the others were busy in the engine room and needed no translation so I just went between visiting each workstation seeing to it that they had what they needed. I spent a lot of time watching Lee work and it brought to mind how much watching someone lost in their talent and in the zone is grounding. Dave was melting away in the engine room while Nigel, one of the blokes on the T. Nielsen team was installing a beautiful skylight and hatch he had fashioned by hand in Burma Teak and brought in their luggage. I took a deep breath of fresh air and lowered myself down into the engine room to check on Dave.

"How's it going doctor?" I humored.

"Looks like she's gonna make it after all..." he played along. "Whose bright idea was it to build a boat out in this oven? I want to have a word with them!" he carried on in jest.

We began talking about how Charles and petit comité had come across Cajaíba one sunny afternoon in an unpretentious venture through the bay on board the Lillibelle during the holiday season of 2010/2011 when the family united for the year-end holiday. I told him how we were told that the trade was struggling as youth would depart Cajaíba towards Camamú and neighboring towns looking for jobs rather than stay and learn the skills that their forefathers had dutifully passed down for four generations before this one. It no longer made sense to learn boat building in Cajaíba as there was no longer a market for these oversized wooden vessels. Telling the whole tale to Dave kept him from suffering in the hot engine room and it gave me the opportunity to revisit the past six years which I hadn't really stopped to do. Dave listened intently and seemed to ask just the questions that I needed to answer for myself. We spoke of the cultural challenges and of how my relationship with Ed had developed. We spoke of how life brings the experiences we need to grow and it all wrapped back around to the fact we were likely a trip or two away from completing this boat.

"Ya, all that...." I concluded. "I leapt out of my previous career searching for something I could sink my heart into and the universe brought this project along...just like that... the boat actually became a by-product of all that we lived together."

"You know that could be a book...." Dave added convincingly.

"It could huh?" I fell in love with the idea more every time the subject came up in conversation with someone. "It's not so much an amazing story, but it's such a delicious little slice of life" I marveled.

"Yes!" Dave echoed "*all* that *and* you built a boat..." he considered and then added gingerly "Well there's your book title right there!" he said proudly and amended "I'll expect an honorable mention for coming up with it too!".

***

The day came around when masts were ready and they were hand carried to the concrete platform by a long line of cheerful jeering men. Large tractor tires were strung over the edge to keep Kathini from being scuffed up against the concrete, but the waters were still as one could hope for that day. We had hired a crane to lift the masts and there were some questions raised around if the small bridge connecting the platform to the land could withstand the weight of the full-sized crane driving over it, but now came the big day and we were all about to find out. The masts were laid out onto cross beams so as to keep them from being scratched and surfaces were protected as to prevent any sort of 'whoopsies' from happening. Nigel had mentioned something about how it is customary to lay a coin on the step where the mast will stand for good fortune. It reminded me that I had 'sika flexed' a note to Ed in one of the seams of the boat one day when we were bonding the stainless-steel finish at the stem. I asked Dave if I could bring an item for the stepping ceremony and he said absolutely, adding that usually it'd be a coin with the crown on it. I brought a sterling I borrowed from Lee, the penny I had found in Ed's belongings and a Real which is the Brazilian currency along with a little note to Ed. *"You'll sail in our hearts forever..."* it read. I laid the items at the foot of the mast before the mast fell down thunderously onto its step.

***

September 2016 found us coming out for what would likely be our last trip as a building crew. This time we finished rigging, hoisted the sails, tested all the electronics and planned her first sail. The eight of us, myself - Dave, Nigel, Tommi, Jorge, Zezinho, Sid, Lee and Lucimaria (Zezinho's step daughter who I had grown especially close to and fond of as she was a balancing ray of light and feminine energy) - boarded excitedly and were heading north motoring happily and carefully along. After 30 minutes of motoring, the question of how far we'd go came up. Being in their familiar territory, Zezinho and Jorge agreed that heading to Ilha do Sapinho might be a nice first venture, but Tommi and Dave did not want to risk going out that far. I was fully aware that this was a celebratory moment for us all as it was our first time taking her out and we wanted to do something memorable. Tommi and Dave had their eyes keenly glued to the instruments, while Jorge and Zezinho were all eyes on the horizon they had been familiar with since birth. Zezinho had ordered lunch at the little lunch shack at Sapinho towards where we were headed so all of us could celebrate our last day working together. Tommi and Dave suggested going back to Campinho to start packing up as we would leave next morning. Tensions began rising as this episode was a culmination that illustrated the cultural differences and tension that this project had straddled all along - two distinct ways of going about the same life that didn't see eye to eye but were each grounded in their experience of how things should be led. Zezinho was irritated to the point that he jumped into the dinghy and rowed himself all the way to Sapinho for the celebration he had envisioned and he did not look back as we turned around and headed back to Campinho in our vessel. Silence hung heavily over all of us and we ended our trip each enthralled in our own thoughts. This was surely not how each of us had imagined our first trip out, but there it was in all its glory - thought provoking as it was.

December 2016: Sailing

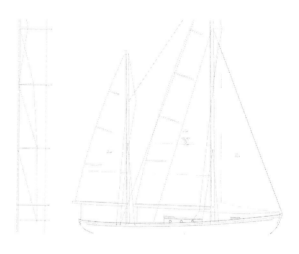

Kathini

A story of love, loss and a little boat building

That year it became clear to me that it was time to move forward with whatever it was that was looking to emerge within me. Dave strongly agreed it was time to find someone to skipper the boat and this was my next challenge as year-end rushed into our realities.

Charles was finally going to get to sail his boat proudly over the Christmas and New Year holiday with the family and I set out looking for someone who could handle our girl and the waters of the Camamú Bay confidently. We found a couple from New Zealand who were experienced sailors to come out and spend a month at the house performing sails with the family and helping us fine-tune the finishing touches that would take Kathini from the final stages of construction to becoming the family day-sailer which Charles had envisioned all along.

We had an exhilarating maiden sail and ventured into ocean waters with the family and there were beautiful pictures to go with it. A successful holiday gave way to further items on my ongoing to-do list for what was nearly another year. Charles had envisioned participating in a regatta from the northern capital of Recife to the island of Fernando de Noronha nearly 300 nautical miles off that coast and planning that entailed finding a captain. I had been speaking to a captain in Rio Grande do Sul southern Brazil where there is a strong sailing community and was excited to hand over the baton to him so that I could move forward with whatever the next chapters were in my life, but his father passed away and he had to withdraw from working away from home to care for his mother as she reorganized her life after her loss. It wasn't long before our trusted sail provider from Ilhabela in the southern state of São Paulo provided us with a candidate. They all agreed there was a need to install a roller furler for the genoa sail and that was done when the first full maintenance trip was performed in September of that year.

In November we set sail from Recife to Fernando de Noronha participating in the REFENO regatta that occurs annually in northern Brazil. Sailing at open sea revealed an extremely powerful connection to the ocean within me and I was in a meditative state for the majority of the 36 hours in which it took to place second in our category. I laid on a dry patch of deck near the cockpit and reveled in how unforgettable this moment was as I recalled the scenes during which I thought this day would never arrive. In a moment of extreme clarity and oneness – I felt this was truly a dream come true.

***

Coming home to California now held different perspectives for me. I had left my second marriage behind and was happily building a life with Mike. The harrowing episode with Marco's immigration case had left me expanded and with a newfound sense of interior strength gained. The nerve wrecking career change was behind me now and it felt like I was on a path of self-development that gave me much to look forward to. I had gone from having never lost a dear one to now having three allies on the other side as in November of that same year my mother passed away in a journey that took me to the depths of my understanding of the urgency that there is in living life - *now* - just the way it is. I had pushed forward into finding fields that activated my gifts within volunteering. I had pushed forward with obtaining a Master's degree in a field of study where my heart dwelled and cemented a vital self-regulatory routine in my life without which I'm not sure how I would have navigated many of the episodes life's tides had laid out ahead of me. It all brought me to the realization that sometimes life is happening while we're thinking we've got everything planned, but that there are powerful gifts contained in the unknown and unplanned. I realized that while we might think we're serving others, we're actually reaping bountiful healing for ourselves. While we're fighting a circumstance, there's another one, way more profound unfolding in our existence – teaching us humility, resilience and overcoming, and especially that while we're searching for our way - if we're able to keep loving the days as they progress, that we'll experience all that *and* we'll build a boat.

THE END

In Loving memory of Ed Burnett and his faithful friend Susie

First efforts...

Mr Burnett working happily from his makeshift office.

The boatyard.

Coming together.

First meeting at the Graham complex.

A little boat building, a little World Cup 2014.

Captured by the proud photographer Ed Burnett - Project
manager in contemplative moment.

Cajaíba waterfront.

Keeping measurements standardized.

The boardroom.

Ed, myself and Zezinho during lunch break one day.

Jorge and I now relaxed after boat launch during visit in 2019.

First family sail circa January 2017.

Sailing Kathini.

Made in the USA
Columbia, SC
05 August 2024

40056110R00224